PRAISE FOR ISLAND 731

"Robinson (Secondworld) ... hael Crichton territory with this terrifyi... f Dr. Moreau. Action and scientific expl... oned, making this one of the best Jurassi...

... arred Review

"Take a traditional haunted-house tale and throw in a little Island of Dr. Moreau and a touch of Clash of the Titans, and you wind up with this scary and grotesque novel. Robinson, a skilled blender of the thriller and horror genres, has another winner on his hands."

— Booklist

"[Island 731's] premise is reminiscent of H.G. Wells' The Island of Dr. Moreau, but the author adds a World War II back story...vivisection, genetic engineering, Black Ops, animal husbandry and mayhem. This is the stuff that comic books, video games and successful genre franchises are made of."

— Kirkus Reviews

"A book full of adventure and suspense that shows 'science' in a whole new horrific light. This is one creepy tale that will keep you up all night! And it is so well written you will think twice before taking a vacation to any so-called 'Island Paradise!'"

— Suspense Magazine

PRAISE FOR SECONDWORLD

"A brisk thriller with neatly timed action sequences, snappy dialogue and the ultimate sympathetic figure in a badly burned little girl with a fighting spirit... The Nazis are determined to have the last gruesome laugh in this efficient doomsday thriller."

— Kirkus Reviews

"Relentless pacing and numerous plot twists drive this compelling stand-alone from Robinson... Thriller fans and apocalyptic fiction aficionados alike will find this audaciously plotted novel enormously satisfying."

— Publisher's Weekly

"A harrowing, edge of your seat thriller told by a master storyteller, Jeremy Robinson's Secondworld is an amazing, globetrotting tale that will truly leave you breathless."

— Richard Doestch, bestselling author of THE THIEVES OF LEGEND

"Robinson blends myth, science and terminal velocity action like no one else."

— Scott Sigler, NY Times Bestselling author of PANDEMIC

"Just when you think that 21st-century authors have come up with every possible way of destroying the world, along comes Jeremy Robinson."

— New Hampshire Magazine

PRAISE FOR THE JACK SIGLER THRILLERS

THRESHOLD

"Threshold elevates Robinson to the highest tier of over-the-top action authors and it delivers beyond the expectations even of his fans. The next Chess Team adventure cannot come fast enough."

— Booklist - Starred Review

"Jeremy Robinson's Threshold is one hell of a thriller, wildly imaginative and diabolical, which combines ancient legends and modern science into a non-stop action ride that will keep you turning the pages until the wee hours."

— Douglas Preston, NY Times bestselling author of THE KRAKEN PROJECT

"With Threshold Jeremy Robinson goes pedal to the metal into very dark territory. Fast-paced, action-packed and wonderfully creepy! Highly recommended!"

— Jonathan Maberry, NY Times bestselling author of CODE ZERO

"With his new entry in the Jack Sigler series, Jeremy Robinson plants his feet firmly on territory blazed by David Morrell and James Rollins. The perfect blend of mysticism and monsters, both human and otherwise, make Threshold as groundbreaking as it is riveting."

— Jon Land, NY Times bestselling author of THE TENTH CIRCLE

"Jeremy Robinson is the next James Rollins."

— Chris Kuzneski, NY Times bestselling author of THE FORBIDDEN TOMB

"Jeremy Robinson's Threshold sets a blistering pace from the very first page and never lets up. For readers seeking a fun rip-roaring adventure, look no further."

— Boyd Morrison, bestselling author of THE LOCH NESS LEGACY

INSTINCT

"If you like thrillers original, unpredictable and chock-full of action, you are going to love Jeremy Robinson's Chess Team. INSTINCT riveted me to my chair."
— Stephen Coonts, NY Times bestselling author of PIRATE ALLEY

"Robinson's slam-bang second Chess Team thriller [is a] a wildly inventive yarn that reads as well on the page as it would play on a computer screen."
— Publisher's Weekly

"Intense and full of riveting plot twists, it is Robinson's best book yet, and it should secure a place for the Chess Team on the A-list of thriller fans who like the over-the-top style of James Rollins and Matthew Reilly."
— Booklist

"Jeremy Robinson is a fresh new face in adventure writing and will make a mark in suspense for years to come."
— David Lynn Golemon, NY Times bestselling author of OVERLORD

PULSE

"Rocket-boosted action, brilliant speculation, and the recreation of a horror out of the mythologic past, all seamlessly blend into a rollercoaster ride of suspense and adventure."
— James Rollins, NY Times bestselling author of THE SIXTH EXTINCTION

"Jeremy Robinson has one wild imagination, slicing and stitching his tale together with the deft hand of a surgeon. Robinson's impressive talent is on full display in this one."
— Steve Berry, NY Times bestselling author of THE LINCOLN MYTH

"There's nothing timid about Robinson as he drops his readers off the cliff without a parachute and somehow manages to catch us an inch or two from doom."
—Jeff Long, New York Times bestselling author of DEEPER

"An elite task force must stop a genetic force of nature in the form of the legendary Hydra in this latest Jeremy Robinson thriller. Yet another page-turner!"
— Steve Alten, NY Times bestselling author of THE OMEGA PROJECT

ALSO BY JEREMY ROBINSON

The Jack Sigler Novels

Prime
Pulse
Instinct
Threshold
Ragnarok
Omega
Savage

The Chesspocalypse Novellas

Callsign: King – Book 1
Callsign: Queen – Book 1
Callsign: Rook – Book 1
Callsign: King – Book 2
Callsign: Bishop – Book 1
Callsign: Knight – Book 1
Callsign: Deep Blue – Book 1
Callsign: King – Book 3

Standalone Novels

The Didymus Contingency
Raising The Past
Beneath
Antarktos Rising
Kronos
Xom-B

The Jack Sigler Continuum Series

Guardian

Secondworld Novels

SecondWorld
I Am Cowboy

The Antarktos Saga

The Last Hunter – Descent
The Last Hunter – Pursuit
The Last Hunter – Ascent
The Last Hunter – Lament
The Last Hunter – Onslaught
The Last Hunter – Collected Edition

Nemesis Novels

Island 731
Project Nemesis
Project Maigo

Horror (Writing as Jeremy Bishop)

Torment
The Sentinel
The Raven
Refuge

ALSO BY SEAN ELLIS

Jack Sigler/Chess Team

Callsign: King - Book 1
Callsign: King - Book 2 –
  Underworld
Callsign: King - Book 3 –
  Blackout
Callsign: King –
  The Brainstorm Trilogy
Prime
Savage

The Nick Kismet Adventures

The Shroud of Heaven
Into the Black
The Devil You Know
Fortune Favors

The Adventures of Dodge Dalton

In the Shadow of Falcon's
Wings
At the Outpost of Fate
On the High Road to Oblivion

Novels

Ascendant
Magic Mirror
Wargod (with Steven Savile)
Hell Ship (with David Wood)

Secret Agent X

The Sea Wraiths
The Scar
Masterpiece of Vengeance

SAVAGE

A Jack Sigler Thriller

JEREMY ROBINSON

WITH SEAN ELLIS

For H. Rider Haggard and Edgar Rice Burroughs.

SAVAGE

"Oh, reader, had you been at my side on this day in Ujiji, how eloquently could be told the nature of this man's work! Had you been there but to see and hear! His lips gave me the details; lips that never lie. I cannot repeat what he said..."

~Henry Morton Stanley, 1872

"Barbarism is the natural state of mankind. Civilization is unnatural. It is a whim of circumstance. And barbarism must always ultimately triumph."

~Robert E. Howard, 1935

"The darkest thing about Africa has always been our ignorance of it."

~George Kimble, 1951

PROLOGUE

Brussels, Belgium, 1878

Henry Morton Stanley stopped speaking for a moment, studying the hungry faces gathered around him. He sensed that everything—his bold plan, his reputation, his career, perhaps even, in an indirect way, his life—might hang on his next words. He cleared his throat and spoke.

"So I took off my hat, and said, 'Dr. Livingstone, I presume.'"

There was a moment of silence, and then the room erupted in laughter.

Stanley hid his relief behind a wry smile. He had been worried that something would be lost in the translation from English to Flemish Dutch, but it was an oft told tale, both by Stanley himself and in countless newspaper articles, which many of the assembled guests had no doubt already read. Now, nearly a decade after the fact, those words remained the perfect climax. Any further elaboration would only dull the impact of his clever punch line.

It was all rubbish, of course. He'd started it merely as a joke, a humorous way to avoid telling the truth, which he had not shared with anyone, but it had taken on a life of its own. The story was now part and parcel of the legend he had created for himself. He had been nurturing and cultivating this image—Stanley, the intrepid explorer, the man who found Livingstone—for a long time now, and soon he hoped to reap the fruits of that long labor. He would capitalize on his notoriety by finding an investor willing to fund his next great expedition.

Soon turned out to be much sooner than he could have hoped. A hand clapped down on his shoulder, and he turned to meet the regal gathering's host, His Royal Majesty, the King of Belgium, Leopold II.

"An excellent story," the king said, drawing him aside. "I would hear more of it."

Stanley had only dared hope for such an audience. "Certainly, Your Majesty."

"I have followed your exploits with great interest." The king spoke English, which surprised Stanley. It was unseemly for a king to make an accommodation like that to a visitor in his own house. Leopold, however, did not seem at all put off by it. "Africa fascinates me. A savage, dangerous land, but also, I believe, a place where bold men may accomplish great things."

"I could not agree more."

"The *Dark Continent* is a magnificent jewel, and yet, like any precious gem, it must first be cut and polished, using the utmost skill, for its true worth to be known."

Stanley was not surprised that the conversation had not yet come around to the topic of his exploits. Leopold, like most men of power and prestige, was not so much interested in listening to what others had to say as he was in having an audience. So Stanley merely nodded.

"I have a vision for Africa, a bold vision, but also one that requires the skill of an expert gem cutter, as it were. The wealth of Africa is tremendous. You, perhaps better than any other man living, know this to be true. And you know, better than any man, why it cannot so easily be taken. It is not enough to simply tramp back and forth across the continent, taking out only what can be carried. I want to *own* Africa!"

"You mean to claim it for Belgium."

"Belgium has no need of territories. No, you mistake my intent. I mean to own the land for myself. As much as I am able. I want to create a free state in Africa—a commercial enterprise, not a political one. But to do so, Africa must be subdued first; her savages introduced to the ways of civilized behavior and Christianity, so that they may provide the labor we need to reap the bounty of this land."

"A bold vision indeed," Stanley agreed. "But I warn you, Africa is not so small a place as it appears on our maps. And I do not speak merely of the distances, though they are considerable. A journey of just a few miles, what we might travel by horse in a single afternoon or by train in just an hour's time, might take days...days of hacking through impenetrable jungle, all the while plagued by flies and disease, foul water, every manner of deadly beast and of course, there are the African natives themselves to consider. I was three years charting the Congo. It is no place for the faint of heart."

"I am quite familiar with your search for Livingstone, and the Congo expedition as well. In truth, your familiarity with the place is the very reason I have sought you out."

Stanley took a deep breath. This was the moment for which he had been waiting. He chose his next words carefully. "I did not reveal everything in the published account. You have said that Africa is a place where bold men may accomplish great things. You are more right than you know. If you will permit me, Your Majesty, I would like to share with you what really happened on the day that I found David Livingstone..."

As he concluded his story, Stanley searched the king's face for some hint of excitement, but there was none. The king did not smile, nor was there the expected glimmer of anticipation or avarice in his eyes. Instead, there was something much darker. "On your oath, this is the truth?"

"I know not whether the story is true," replied Stanley, trying not to sound defensive. "Livingstone was recovering from a fever when I found him. I cannot know if he really saw what he claims to have. But I will swear by anything you name, that this is, word-for-word, what he told me."

"Word for word? It was eight years ago."

"I wrote it down in my diary, even as he spoke." Stanley felt his heart pounding with trepidation. He had, on more than one occasion and usually by miserly investors, been accused of exaggerating the potential riches of the unexplored land to fund his expeditions. Did the king think him some kind of confidence artist, teasing him with fabrications, like some gypsy with a treasure map? "I believe it to be true, Your Majesty. I would not trifle with you."

"Trifle?" The king shook his head. "I'm afraid you're not fully understanding. This is no mere trifle. Do you grasp the significance of what you have just told me?"

For the first time in almost nine years, Stanley was not certain that he did.

The king made a chopping gesture with his hand. "I do not want to explore Africa, Stanley. I want to *own* it. This..." He struggled to find the right word. "This story of yours, if true, would undermine everything that I want to accomplish."

"Your Majesty, I'm not sure I understand how."

"If the savages knew of this..." The king paused, and then shook his head as if even speaking the words aloud was too dangerous. He gripped Stanley's shoulder firmly, peered intently into his eyes. "Greatness is set before us, Stanley. I want you to go to the Congo. Establish this new state, so that we may possess all the riches Africa has to offer. I wish to make you my agent. Survey these lands and acquire them for me, so that together we may launch this enterprise. Does this interest you?"

"Of course."

"Then you must do something for me. Tear those pages out of your diary, and never speak of this again. Will you do that for me?"

The request was like a knife through Stanley's heart. For years he had dreamed of learning the truth behind Livingstone's story, and now, instead of finding a patron who would help him accomplish that, he was being told to sacrifice it all.

And yet, what was he really being asked to give up? An uncertain reward that might amount to nothing more than a fever dream, in exchange for real wealth, real glory? Perhaps it wasn't such a sacrifice after all.

He sealed his pact with a single word.

"Yes."

Republic of the Congo (formerly Belgian Congo), 1964

The young man shifted into reverse and applied steady pressure to the accelerator pedal. The engine revved and the wheels began to spin, throwing up a shower of mud in front of the Land Rover, but the vehicle did not move. The driver shifted back into first gear and tried again with no more success. He pounded his fists against the steering wheel in frustration.

"What about the winch?" the youth in the passenger seat asked.

"There's no time," another young man said from the back. "They're right behind us. We must leave the truck, David."

David, the front seat passenger, shook his head, but the gesture was more an indication of his frustration than an outright refusal. "Keep trying, Ki," he told the driver. "Turn the wheels back and forth."

Ki did as instructed, but while the engine roared and mud flew, the Land Rover refused to budge.

"We have to leave it," a boy named Christophe urged, from the backseat. "We can take our chances in the jungle."

The idea sent a chill through David. Although he had grown up on the edge of the dark, Congo rain forest, he had never felt safe leaving the well-traveled roads that sliced through its dark depths. Out here, deep in the Kivu region, his mild aversion bordered on outright terror. Still, better to brave the uncertain risks of the jungle than face the guns of the mercenaries who pursued them.

It took him a moment to recognize that the others were waiting for him to make the decision, and that scared him even more.

How did I become the leader?

David would have been hard pressed to explain how he had become part of this rebellion in the first place. He'd been caught along in a wave of passion, seduced by the message that it was time to throw off foreign oppression. He didn't know much about politics or Communism. He had no idea who this Mao fellow was, and he couldn't find China on a map, but the oppression was real enough. He'd watched his father, all his friends and their families ground under the heels of the Belgians and their lackeys all his life. Yet, while he sympathized with the rebels and their position, he hadn't been given much of a choice. The rebels controlled the region and all young men were expected to fight for them.

At the beginning, it had felt a little like a game, playing at being a soldier, which wasn't surprising, since he had been just fourteen. War, it seemed, had a way of quickly aging a person.

He still wasn't sure exactly how it had all led to this, though. There had been persistent rumors that things were not going well, but new recruits like David were likely to be beaten or shot if they asked too many questions. So when the mortar rounds rained down on their camp, no one knew whether it was merely a skirmish or the beginning of the end. When the rebel leaders—none of them locals— had slipped away in the dark of night, the answer seemed plain enough.

The compound exploding around them, David and six others had fled on foot, unaware that pro-government forces had the camp surrounded. Two of David's companions had died, and another had been badly wounded, as they ran the blind gauntlet to freedom. But somehow the rest had slipped through the net and reached an abandoned plantation, where they'd commandeered an old Land Rover and headed west.

That had been six hours ago.

The rain, which had turned the road into a quagmire, pounded against the roof of the Land Rover. Although it was midday, the sky was so dark that it felt like dusk. David didn't know if the enemy soldiers were indeed right behind them, but to stop moving was foolish.

"We must be close to the border," Christophe said. "We have to go on foot, through the jungle. It's the only way."

"Songa can't walk," argued a different voice.

David craned his head around to look at the other passengers. Songa was the name of the young man who had been wounded in the escape. He was sprawled out on the floor, between the inward-facing safari bench seats. The only indication that he still lived was the faint tremor of his fevered shivering. The bullet had struck him in the abdomen, and David knew that the boy would not last must longer.

"We have to leave him," Christophe said.

David shook his head. "I won't leave anyone behind. We have to try the winch."

He didn't wait for Christophe's inevitable reply. He threw open the door, exposing himself to the downpour. What he saw nearly caused him to pull it shut again. The Rover wasn't merely stuck, it was mired in a veritable sea of mud that rose nearly as high as the running boards. David felt his resolve crumble, but he couldn't give up now. He kicked off his sandals, then braved the driving rain, swinging onto the vehicle's hood and crawling forward.

The mud was nearly up to the front bumper, and the winch mounted there was half-submerged. Tentatively, he lowered himself into the murk, cringing a little as it oozed between his toes. He pulled out several feet of cable from the winch, and hook in hand, he trudged forward. He had to fight for every step, wrestling his bare feet out of the deep, sucking mud only to plunge them in again, but he fought against the wet earth and reached a section of the road that was still firm. There were small trees alongside the road, but they would not serve as an anchor for the winch cable. In the rain loosened soil, they would simply be pulled out by their roots. He kept going, searching for anything that might work.

Suddenly, the world was filled with blinding white light, followed almost immediately by a thunderclap so close and powerful that it drove David to his knees. Yet, even more frightening than the close proximity of the flash was what the lightning revealed. On the road behind them, less than a half a mile away, was a convoy of dark green military vehicles, moving slowly but relentlessly forward.

Another burst of noise shook him. This time it wasn't thunder. David felt the heat of stray bullets streaking through the air around him. Most of the rounds found their target. The Land Rover shuddered under the impact of machine gun fire.

Unbelievably, two figures tumbled out into the mud—Christophe and another, whose name David did not know. He shouted and waved to them, but they paid him no heed. Instead, they slogged through the mud, desperate to find cover in the trees. When another volley of gunfire hammered into the Rover, David hastened after them.

His feet sank into the saturated ground with every step, and the low growing vegetation wrapped around him like the tentacles of some nightmare monster; the jungle was trying to swallow him whole. He struggled forward, ripping through the ferns and vines that clung to his clothes and skin, wrestling free of roots tripping him up. He found himself wishing for a long *panga* knife with which to hack out a path to freedom. Only then did he realize that he was completely unarmed. He had left his rifle in the Rover. As if to underscore the gravity of this error, the foliage overhead exploded into a blur of green fiber, as it was raked by a barrage of gunfire.

David threw himself flat, but did not stop moving. He soon discovered that crawling on his belly like a snake was easier than trying to walk upright, and after just a few minutes of squirming, the tangle of undergrowth opened up, disgorging him into the emptiness beneath the canopy of the deep forest. Hardly anything grew down here, where the sun did not reach. Even the torrential rains had trouble penetrating the network of branches, leaves and liana vines. A strange mist shrouded the forest floor, and the ground smelled of decay, but after just a few moments, David began to sense how overpoweringly alive the jungle was.

It was alive and dangerous.

Christophe and his companion broke out of the bush nearby. Both young men had held onto their rifles, but the weapons hung from their slings, forgotten. "They are coming," Christophe yelled. "Run!"

This time, David did not hesitate. He fell into step behind the others, and together they plunged deeper into the foggy void between the branches. Time passed differently under the jungle canopy. It seemed to David that hours went by, and yet his body said otherwise. If indeed he had been running for hours, he would have collapsed from thirst or exhaustion. The jungle was a strange, alien environment, where nothing was familiar and everything looked identical. They might have been traveling in circles or venturing deep into a part of the world where no man had ever trod. David didn't know which prospect was more terrifying.

Soon, the sound of running water filtered through the ambient noise of jungle birds and colobus monkeys. They were nearing a river. Not the Congo—they were too far east for that—but certainly one of its tributaries. If they followed the river, they would eventually find an outpost.

The others quickened their pace, searching for the elusive stream that would guide them back to civilization. The rushing noise grew louder and then abruptly became deafening, as they emerged from the woods on the edge of a pool that lay at the base of an enormous waterfall.

David had seen the falls at Kisangani and Ubundu—short drops that spanned the broad width of the Congo—but this was much different. This waterfall was high, perhaps a hundred feet or more, but half as wide. The water fell in a thin veil, which did not so much crash into the pool below as simply pour, like the flow from a well pump's spigot. The pool was similarly small, draining away in a small stream only a few feet across. The water above the fall was almost certainly the result of the rain. The fall, the pool and the stream might not even exist in dry weather, and that meant there was no guarantee that following the stream would take them anywhere.

Christophe pointed toward the fall. "There! Do you see it?"

David saw nothing but a translucent wall of water and darkness beyond.

"We can hide there. Behind it."

David still didn't see what Christophe saw, nor was he altogether certain that hiding was even necessary. Were the government forces still following them? He couldn't imagine that they would go to so much trouble to hunt down a handful of rebel conscripts. Christophe didn't wait for him to answer, but hurried to the edge of the pool and skirted it until he was nearly under the falls. The other young rebel remained with David, watching as their comrade cautiously parted the curtain of spray and vanished from sight.

A moment later, Christophe appeared again. His face was alight with wonder. "Come! You won't believe this."

David stared into the darkness behind the falls. His earlier trepidation returned. The darkness behind the waterfall was like the jungle, a place where human beings did not belong. The other young man evidently felt no such hesitancy. He struck out toward the waterfall and whatever lay beyond, leaving David alone with his fears.

For a long time, David stood there, watching the water pour down. Christophe and the other boy did not emerge, and David was starting to worry about them. There had been no sign of their pursuers. Perhaps the mercenaries were as lost as they now were, or perhaps they were wise enough not to venture into the uncharted jungle. Regardless, there was no reason for them to hide. They would be better off getting their bearings, settling on a destination and moving out before night fell and the jungle predators began to hunt.

He edged toward the fall. "Christophe! Are you there? Come out!"

There was no reply, but of course how could they hear him? The cascading water drowned out his voice.

He moved closer, along the edge of the pool. The water looked like quicksilver, a rippled mirror reflecting a turbulent sky. He called out again. When there was no reply, he ventured close enough to the fall that the spray showered him like raindrops. A narrow lip of rock protruded out from behind the fall, slick with moisture and moss, just wide enough to stand on.

"Christophe!"

He reached out a tentative hand, touching the water the way he might pet an unfamiliar dog. Despite the height from which it fell, the water felt soft against his fingertips. Emboldened, he took a great step forward and felt the water pass over him like a baptism.

It was dark on the other side, but enough light filtered through the fall for him to immediately see that this was no mere cave. He stood there, incredulous, unable to believe that a place such as this could really exist.

His amazement caused him to forget for a moment why he had feared to enter, but a shriek from somewhere in the shadowy depths of the hidden world brought him back to the moment. He opened his mouth to call out again, but before he could, a figure broke free from the darkness. It was the other young rebel. He was covered in something dark and wet, and even from a distance, David could see the pure terror in the rebel's eyes as he ran. A second figure moved into view behind the fleeing youth.

Not Christophe.

David spun away, plunging through the veil of water. He fell face down in the pool. It was far deeper than he would have believed, and for a moment he was held down by the weight of the falling water. Panic seized him and he clawed for the surface, desperate to put as much distance between himself and the waterfall as he could. A few seconds later, he splashed up onto the shore of the pool and got his feet under him.

He looked back just once, wondering if the horror he had beheld would emerge from that wondrous hidden place. There was no sign of it, but that was of little comfort to David. He turned away and ran back into the woods. He ran until he collapsed from exhaustion.

When his strength returned, he ran more.

ONE

Suez, Egypt, 2014

It was a day like any other in the Arbaeen district of the canal port city of Suez. Cars moved about on the streets, in a hurry to get wherever they were going. Pedestrians ambled about less purposefully on the roadside, or when necessity dictated, risked a mad dash through traffic to reach the other side. People idled in coffee shops, purchased kebabs from street vendors, and perused the wares of merchants. Only a few of those meandering about were locals. At the canal's end, the population of Suez fluctuated daily with tourists, sailors and passengers debarking for a day ashore, while they waited for their vessels to make the long passage through to the Mediterranean Sea or to meet a ship heading south, toward the Red Sea.

The locals barely even noticed the appearance of five more strangers.

They did not arrive together, nor did they appear to even be aware of each other. There was the young couple. European tourists. He spoke halting English with lapses into German, and she spoke halting English with lapses into French. Most of the Arab merchants spoke a smattering of English, so communication was not that difficult. The man, who was broad and tall, had close-cropped blond hair with a long goatee, and he wore dark Oakley sunglasses. He looked like he might belong to an American motorcycle gang. The woman was quite a bit shorter, and very shapely. It was difficult to tell if she was beautiful, because she was mostly covered up by a *hijab* and sunglasses that matched her boyfriend's. It was a bit unusual for a Western tourist to wear the ceremonial head scarf, but not enough so to make the locals take note. The pair bought some food and bottles of Orangina at a shop. At another, the man bought his girlfriend an Egyptian cartouche pendant.

Then there was the Chinese photographer, or at least everyone assumed he was a photographer, because he was lugging around a huge camera case. He also spoke halting English, and asked everyone he met whether they knew a good place to take photographs of ships entering and leaving the canal. When the question was answered, he would stare back, uncomprehending, through his dark sunglasses. Then he would wander off in the wrong direction, leaving the locals to scratch their beards in amusement.

The last two strangers appeared to be Arabs. They had swarthy complexions, thick dark hair and beards, and spoke perfect, if slightly old-fashioned, Arabic. The smaller of the pair did most of the talking. Smaller, in this case was a relative term, because at just over six feet in height, he was taller than most of the locals. Nevertheless, he was dwarfed by the other man, who was a good head taller and built as solidly as the pyramids. The two men did not attempt to question the locals or strike up conversation, but merely sipped their coffee in the shadow of an awning. From time to time, the smaller man would check his wristwatch—a closer look would have revealed a vintage 1967 Omega Speedmaster Professional—while the larger man mostly looked straight ahead, almost statue still. Like most Egyptian men, they eschewed traditional Arab attire for modern trousers and cotton shirts. The big man's muscles strained the fabric of his. Curiously, both were wearing dark sunglasses just like the others.

The sunglasses connected the five visitors in more than just a symbolic way. In addition to concealing their eyes, each pair of Oakley Half-Jacket 2.0 sport frames also hid a miniature Bluetooth wireless device that was linked to a next-generation quantum smartphone. The superior processing and data transfer speed of the quantum computers, which were an order of magnitude faster than anything commercially available, meant that each member of this group of visitors could send and receive real-time audio and video instantaneously. Because the processor used quantum entanglement, any lag of signal transmission was too minute to be measured. Nor was there any need for encryption. The transmission was not broadcast using radio waves, so there was no way for anyone to intercept it.

Images were recorded by a high-def camera in the nose-piece of each pair of glasses. They were viewed using a virtual, retinal-display projection system that beamed the video feed directly into the wearer's eyes. From his perch on the roof of a three story building near the port, the man the locals had dismissed as the 'Chinese photographer' was able to see everything that the others could, and in turn, he was able to share his unique perspective with them. That, however, was only the beginning of what was possible with the technology in the glasses.

Even a cursory look around was enough to transmit a wealth of data into the shared network. The information was also transmitted instantaneously to a mainframe on the other side of the planet. A sophisticated facial recognition program compared every single face that passed in front of the cameras against a dozen different databases, including several international terrorist watch lists. The information could be displayed visually if so desired, but at present it was enough to simply overlay the results of the facial recognition scan. Each person that entered into the virtual environment had a tiny icon right above their head: a green dot if a positive identification was made and the person was free of suspicion, a yellow dot if no identification was possible and a red dot if a person was of special interest.

"I think I've been out in the sun too long. All I can see is a lot of yellow spots."

The man on the roof smiled. He heard the voice as clearly as if the speaker were standing next to him, right down to the trace of a New England accent on some of the vowels. But if someone had been standing right next to him, they would have heard nothing at all. The sound was not played through ordinary electronic speakers, but instead utilized a technology called 'bone conduction' to transmit sound waves from tiny metal probes in the ear pieces of the glasses, directly into the skull of the person wearing them.

The statement wasn't completely accurate however. While there was a sea of yellow dots, all marking people whose identities remained unknown, there were four tags that were neither yellow nor dots. The icons marked the four other visitors, and if it were possible for the man on the roof to see himself, he would have found a fifth icon floating above his own head—virtually speaking at least. These markers were a bright royal blue, but each one was different. Each one was the likeness of a chess piece.

"Seriously," the same voice continued. The speaker was Stan Tremblay, but when he was working—as he was right now, albeit disguised as the German tourist—he was simply: Rook. "What good is facial recognition technology if it doesn't recognize any faces?"

The man on the roof nodded in silent agreement. His name was Shin Dae-jung—his *nom de guerre* was Knight—and he was not Chinese. Ethnically, he was Korean, but he had been born in the United States and considered himself, first and foremost, an American. Nor was he a photographer. His camera case contained a disassembled Chey Tac Intervention .408 sniper rifle. It was the tool of his trade, and he had been practicing his trade a long time, without any help from quantum computers and high-tech sunglasses.

"He's right, Blue," another voice said. "If the FRS is just going to show us a lot of yellow dots, then we'd be better off without it."

Knight was surprised to hear King supporting the wise-cracking and generally rebellious Rook. King, also known as Jack Sigler, was the field leader of the group, and he was usually the calm voice of reason. He was the shorter man presently disguised as an Arab, sipping coffee at the outdoor café. He wasn't an Arab, but his thick black hair, strong features and skin bronzed by years—a lot of years—in the sun, along with his uncanny mastery of the Arabic language, enabled him to easily pull off the deception.

Eight years ago, King had been an officer in the US Army Special Forces Operational Detachment D, better known as Delta or simply 'the Unit.' Circumstances, in the form of a crisis that threatened the safety of the entire planet, had brought the five of them together from different military special operations backgrounds, to form what King had called the 'Delta of Delta'—the elite of the elite, a new team answerable only to the president. The Chess Team. Since then, they had faced threats beyond comprehension—dangers that were the stuff of science fiction—and King had always guided them with a steady hand, no matter what the world threw at them. Except that after their last mission, where they finally, once and for all, dealt with rogue geneticist Richard Ridley, King just didn't quite seem like himself anymore.

"Egypt doesn't have a centralized picture ID database," a new voice explained. The speaker was not one of the five—in fact, he was in a command center on the other side of the world—but he was nevertheless an essential member of Chess Team. His callsign was Deep Blue—a nod to the marvelous chess-playing computer that had performed the impossible, by beating the then-reigning world chess champion, Garry Kasparov, in 1997. Deep Blue's real name was Tom Duncan, and he had once been the President of the United States. In his role as chief executive, he had created Chess Team, and he'd personally overseen their missions, anonymously at first, until necessity had forced him to sacrifice his presidency to save the nation he had sworn to serve. Giving up the Oval Office had enabled Deep Blue to devote himself full time to leading the team. The organization that had begun with the team was now a separate entity from the military, operating from their new headquarters in the White Mountains of New Hampshire.

"But we know what the target looks like," Deep Blue continued, "so just ignore the yellow dots and keep your eyes peeled for a red one."

The other members of the team—Queen and Bishop, respectively—did not add their input.

Queen was Zelda Baker, and while she pretended to be a tourist, there was no pretense to her relationship with Rook. Knight had known her before they were both recruited to Chess Team. She wasn't just the toughest woman he'd ever met, but she was also one of the toughest human beings on the planet. Pain and suffering were like fuel in her engine. She had joined the Army to burn away the memories of her traumatic childhood, and by surviving the two-month long trial-by-fire that was US Army Ranger school—the first woman to ever do so—she had succeeded. She had emerged stronger and harder than seemed humanly possible. It had only been in the last year or so that her old emotional scars had begun to fade, and that owed in no small part to her burgeoning relationship with Rook.

The other quiet member of the team, Bishop—also known as Erik Somers—was the enormous man sitting across the café table from King. Bishop was Iranian by birth, but he had been raised from infancy in the United States by adoptive parents. That he spoke some Arabic, as well as Farsi, Dari and a smattering of other tongues common to the Middle East, was only because of hours of immersive language instruction—American English was his first language.

Like Queen, Bishop carried a lot of emotional baggage. The only thing stronger than the simmering anger that had boiled in his heart from his earliest memories, was his extraordinary self-control, but the cost for that control was a stony, silent demeanor that repelled other people like a force-field. His size and his ability to unleash that fury made him a very effective member of the team. But it left him as isolated as a monk, when it came to personal relationships.

The delicate balancing act between rage and self-control had nearly reached critical mass a few years earlier, when Manifold Genetics had injected Bishop with an experimental regenerative serum that had made him effectively invincible. An unfortunate side effect of the serum was that its regenerative properties stimulated a primal fury, which had turned most test subjects into rabid beasts. Bishop's lifelong struggle to keep his anger in check had enabled him to do the impossible—to heal from even mortal wounds, without losing his sanity. The serum had eventually been purged from his body, evidently removing the good effects along with the bad, but the damage to his already compromised psyche would not be so easily taken away.

They had all changed a lot over the last eight years. Some of the changes had been good, like Queen's and Rook's deeper relationship, but they had all made sacrifices. There was really no such thing as an ordinary life when you were tasked with saving the world from things that even the US military couldn't handle.

The present crisis was almost run-of-the-mill by comparison to their typical day at the office. A Yemeni terrorist named Hadir al-Shahri had acquired a Russian-made RA-115 tactical nuclear weapon—a one kiloton yield 'backpack nuke.' Hadir was a known cell leader for Al-Qa'ida in the Arabian Peninsula (AQAP), and he had personally been involved in some of the most noteworthy international terror incidents, post-9/11. AQAP was playing the long game. They were not content to merely terrorize, but rather they had their sights set on destabilizing the existing political structure of the Middle East, removing the influence of Western nations and multinational corporations and ushering in a new Islamic age. It was almost a certainty that, if Hadir had indeed purchased a nuke, he would use it. The only unanswered question was the matter of target.

Chess Team was involved in this matter for the sole reason that the information had come directly to them from a source inside the Russian government. The sale of the nuke had been bait in an operation designed to flush out terrorists in Chechnya, and unfortunately, the mouse had gotten away with the cheese. The Russians were scrambling to cover their asses, and so far they had kept the whole affair quiet, which meant that Chess Team's informant risked exposure—fatal exposure—if the information was passed on to the international intelligence community.

Hadir had made only one mistake: he'd made a phone call to electronically transfer funds to the Russians, and then he had promptly replaced his disposable cell phone with another 'burner' phone. From that one call, Deep Blue had been able to pinpoint his position, and even though that phone stopped transmitting, Blue was soon able to pick up a new signal—the replacement phone. He had tracked Hadir and his purchase through the Caucasus, along the borders of Iran and Iraq, across Syria and ultimately here to the southern end of the Suez Canal.

The good news was that they knew his last location to within a square mile of the city. The bad news was that his phone had stopped transmitting, and they didn't know if he'd already left, or where he was headed next. Was the terrorist planning to put the bomb on a ship bound for a European or American port, or would he take it in the other direction, across the Indian Ocean? Or was the Canal a feint, a bluff to hide his real intent to use the bomb against Israel or simply disappear into the Arabian desert with his prize?

"Knight, anything on the sniffers?" King asked.

On the roof, Knight had just finished deploying a bank of portable detectors capable of 'sniffing out' slight variations in the background level of ionizing radiation. Such variations might indicate the presence of an unshielded radio isotope, of the kind that might be used in a dirty bomb. Unfortunately, if the RA-115 was handled correctly, its small plutonium core would emit about as much radiation as a smoke alarm.

Knight checked the sniffers for any abnormally high returns, but all the readouts were consistent with the normal amount of background radiation. He zeroed them all and set them to alarm if there were any changes, before making his report. "Nega—"

Before he could get the word out, one of the sniffers began beeping softly, registering a sudden gamma spike. "Hang on. Got something in Zone Three."

Knight did a quick visual sweep of the area. About a hundred yards away, a city block away from the main street where the team was focusing their search, someone had just opened a door. Knight squinted and the glasses responded by zooming in on the doorway. A face appeared there, someone Knight would have recognized even if a red dot had not suddenly blossomed into view above the man's head.

It was Hadir.

A moment later, the sniffer registered another spike as the terrorist stepped out onto the street, burdened down by an enormous olive drab backpack. He headed straight for a parked car, one of the ubiquitous white Toyota Corollas that had become a fixture in the nations of the Middle East. Four more figures stepped from the doorway right behind him, and one by one, a red dot appeared above each of the men. Another icon started flashing in the display, a prompt to open and read the data file for each of the men, but Knight knew enough already. These guys were all known terrorists, they had a small nuclear device and they were on the move.

He breathed a curse as he realized his rifle was still stowed in its case. He knew he could have it put together inside of thirty seconds, but his gut told him that in thirty seconds, the bomb would be driving off.

"Targets in the open," Knight said. "They're getting in a vehicle, preparing to move."

"Roger," King replied. "Bug out."

On the street below, the other four immediately stopped what they were doing and headed to their designated rally points—cars parked at different ends of the street that would allow them to move quickly, in just such an event. Knight swept the sniffers into his backpack, hefted the camera case and bolted from the roof.

He could still see the red icons in his display, their last known location marked and remembered by the computer, but the image was only useful now in helping them reacquire their quarry. He knew that Deep Blue was probably looking for local CCTV networks, or even real-time satellite imagery to provide them with constant updates, but those resources weren't as readily available in a developing nation like Egypt.

Knight swung easily off a second story balcony and dropped into a back alley, two blocks away from where Hadir and the bomb had last been spotted, and three blocks from his assigned rally point, which lay in the opposite direction.

Decisions, decisions.

As he was the only member of the team to actually get eyes on Hadir, he decided the wisest course was to reestablish visual contact before the car got lost in traffic. He sprinted from the alley, forced his way through the milling pedestrians and crossed the street. The virtual display flashed, warning of an imminent collision, even as the sound of shrieking brakes and tires skidding on the pavement filled his ears, but Knight never slowed. He vaulted over a vendor's cart and slipped through the crowd like a bead of quicksilver. He ducked into another alley, and a few seconds later he emerged a stone's throw from the door through which Hadir had exited.

The red dot winked out. The car was gone.

He scanned the street in both directions and caught a glimpse of white moving away, perhaps two blocks to the north. And then another further down the same street.

Knight shook his head in frustration. "Lost them. Look for a white Corolla. My best guess is that they're going north."

"Blue?" King's voice echoed through his head. "Give me something."

"Northeast would put him on the main road, about half a mile away," Deep Blue replied. "That's the most probable route. Once there he can either go northwest, toward Cairo, or southeast, which is a short ride to the port. I've got the plate number of the vehicle. If you see it again, the software will recognize it faster than you can."

"Northeast then. Rook, Queen, you take the portside. Bish and I will head toward Cairo. Knight, acquire transport and follow as you're able."

Knight frowned in irritation.

Cut loose without even a thank you. Oh well, it's not like I do this for the glory.

He skidded to a stop and began scanning the street for an unsecured set of wheels—not a car, though. No way he could boost a car without getting noticed, caught and drawn and quartered. *A motorcycle?* That would have been nice, and a lot easier to steal, but there were none to be seen. *A bicycle? A camel?*

The answer screeched to a halt beside him. He turned slowly and saw a black and white Fiat sedan with a large metal frame mounted to its roof. The driver had stepped out from behind the wheel and was making an inviting gesture.

"Blue," he muttered. "How do you say: 'Yes, thank you, I would like a taxi,' in Arabic?"

TWO

"I'll drive!" Rook didn't wait for Queen to protest, but dashed for the left-side door of the rented sedan, intent on taking the driver's seat. She was fast, but he easily outpaced her, seizing the door handle like it was the brass ring on a merry-go-round.

Queen didn't say a word. Rook thought that was a little odd since he'd been hoping for some spirited competition. She simply ran to the right-hand door, opened it and slid inside. Shaking his head, he opened his own door and dropped into the seat, one hand reaching for the keys and the other for the steering wheel. The engine roared to life and the car rabbited away from its parking slot, but Rook's hands were still empty. Queen, seated behind the right-side steering wheel of the sedan, blew him a kiss.

"Damnit!" He punched a mostly playful fist into the dashboard. "Who puts a steering wheel on the right side?"

"You drove it here," Queen retorted with a triumphant smile. "Blame your failing memory, not the car."

Rook's mouth worked as he groped for a suitable retort, but nothing came. Queen had that effect on him. She was as beautiful as she was tough, and not even the scar in the center of her forehead could diminish that. The star with a death's head—the mark of the brutal Vietnamese People's Liberation Army's Death Volunteers—had been burned into her skin by a particularly sadistic Death Volunteer officer, during a mission to save the world from a pandemic virus. He had tortured her brutally before branding her, but in the end she had survived and he had not. She now wore the scar proudly, as a sign of her triumph. Rook found that strangely beautiful, too.

"Rook, if you keep your eyes on the road," Deep Blue admonished, "instead of on Queen, you'll double our chances of spotting the target vehicle."

Rook straightened in his seat. "I really hate technology."

"Now you sound like King," Queen teased.

King's voice immediately echoed through Rook's head. "I heard that."

Rook wisely kept his mouth shut and focused his attention on the mission. He understood the operational reasons for having a completely unrestricted flow of information between the team members and Deep Blue, but it would have been nice to exchange a little playful banter with his best-girl without being on public display. He couldn't even look at her appreciatively without the others knowing. His thoughts were still safe, but it was probably only a matter! of time before Deep Blue and the team's resident techno-geek, Lewis Aleman, figured out how to wire the q-phones directly into their brains, and then nothing would be off limits.

Queen raced down the lightly-trafficked street, slowing only as they reached the intersection with the much busier *23 July Boulevard,* named for the date in 1952 of the revolution that had ushered in Egyptian independence from Britain. She rode the brakes as the front end of the sedan poked out into the thoroughfare, but then she cranked the wheel to the right and punched the gas. They shot into traffic amid a squeal of tires and horn blasts.

There were faint flashes of light in the virtual environment, as their cameras scanned every single license plate on the road ahead of them. Rook squinted to get a zoom-view of the road, even though he wasn't really sure what to look for. Knight had said it was a white Corolla, but that was about as helpful as saying water was wet. Every other car in the Middle East—including the rental he and Queen were now riding in—was a white Toyota Corolla.

"Technology," he grumbled again. "It's no substitute for—"

There was a flash in the display and a red icon appeared above a barely discernible white speck, far ahead of them and traveling in the same direction. Next to it was a readout of the distance to the target—0.56 miles, an exact GPS coordinate that kept changing and a compass azimuth of SE 148 degrees.

"Gotcha!" Queen said.

"Like I was saying," Rook continued, barely missing a beat, "we're becoming too reliant on these gizmos. We'll lose our edge."

Queen ignored him and poured on the speed, weaving through the mostly unregulated traffic and generally giving no indication that her edge had in any way been dulled.

"Roger," King said. "We're turning around, en route to your location. Don't press too hard. If he gets an itchy trigger finger, we're all toast."

The red icon veered right, following the road, and was abruptly lost from view, but Queen's assertive driving brought them quickly to the same bend where they were able to reacquire the target, before it could perceptibly deviate from the computer's prediction. Hadir appeared to be headed for Port Taufiq, at the mouth of the canal, presumably to put the bomb on a ship.

The distance-to-target indicator showed less than five hundred yards, and the numbers ticked off steadily at about five yards per second. Rook did some mental math—they were going about twelve miles per hour faster than Hadir's car. They'd catch up in less than two minutes. "Might want to back off a bit," he suggested. "We've got him."

Suddenly the numbers became a blur... 450...375...225. "He's stopped," Rook said, unnecessarily. Queen was seeing the same thing he was.

"No. He's turning."

After just a second, the numbers started going the other way, as Hadir's car sped off in a new direction—almost due east.

"Where the hell is he going?"

Rook meant it rhetorically, but Deep Blue provided an answer nonetheless. "This road runs parallel to the canal for nearly its entire length. There are only a few turn-offs, and all the main arteries lead back to Cairo. But further north there are bridges, tunnels and ferry crossings, and on the other side he could get on the road that goes all the way to Gaza."

"Israel, then."

"I don't think my taxi driver will take me that far," Knight mumbled, clearly trying to keep from being overheard.

"That makes no sense," King said. "If he was planning to hit Israel, he wouldn't have bothered coming all the way to Egypt."

"He may have planned to double back all along," Deep Blue countered. "This trip to Suez might be his way of leaving a false trail."

"That bomb is a hot potato. Every minute he holds onto it, he risks being caught, and he knows it. We're missing something."

Queen reached the left turn Hadir had taken and followed without slowing. The car slid a little, but she accelerated out of the skid and shot through the oncoming traffic, accompanied by a veritable symphony of irate honks.

"They must love Jesus," Rook remarked, and when Queen shot him a disparaging glance, he pointed forward. "Eyes on the road, dear. Hands at ten and two o'clock."

Hadir's car was now just 500 yards ahead and easy to pick out, because traffic on the northward bound lane was relatively light. There were just four cars separating them now. Queen eased off the gas until the range meter stabilized at 450.

"We've turned around and are heading your way," King said. "Maintain visual contact. We might need to intercept on the move."

"I'll need a pick up," Knight said.

"Negative." King's voice was flat and final. "We don't have time to stop. You'll have to sit this one out, Knight."

There was a long silence, and Rook knew that everyone else was thinking the same thing he was.

What. The. Fuck?

Stopping for the thirty seconds it might take to pick up Knight was hardly going to make a difference, while sidelining their designated 'long distance operator'—the one member of the team they were most likely to need if they were going to take Hadir out and not get vaporized in the process—was patently foolish. King had to know that.

What is he thinking?

The fact that no one said anything, not even Deep Blue, felt like a confirmation of Rook's suspicions.

King *was* different.

THREE

Bishop kept his eyes on the road ahead, despite the urge to glance at King. Off in the distance, he could see the chess piece icons that

marked Rook's and Queen's location, about three miles away, along
with the red dot that was their ultimate target. He unconsciously
squeezed the steering wheel in his powerful hands and pressed
down a little harder on the accelerator pedal.

It would have surprised Rook to know that Bishop completely
supported King's decision to leave Knight behind. There was a
time and place for caution, and this was not it.

King spoke again. "Hadir has a plan, and I don't think it's anything
we've considered yet. Why would he come here?"

An uncomfortable silence followed, as if the other parties to the
conversation were having trouble switching gears. Then King spoke
again. "He's going to take out the canal. It's the single most important
link for international shipping in the hemisphere. If he takes it out,
he disrupts the flow of oil to all of Europe and America. Shipping it
around Africa or across the Pacific would send gas prices soaring."

"A move like that would hurt the Arab states just as much as
the West," Deep Blue said. "If they can't get their oil to market, they
lose their most important source of revenue."

"That might be exactly what Hadir wants. Cut the strings that tie the
Saudis and other OPEC nations to the West, and those governments
won't last long. The Arab Spring will sweep the oil emirs out of power,
and open the way for a Muslim theocracy."

"If he uses the bomb in Egypt, he'll be killing Arabs," Queen
pointed out. "Not a great way to start a revolution."

"Can a little backpack nuke even do that much damage?" Rook
asked.

"King might be on to something," Deep Blue said. "The
section of the canal between Suez and Timsah Lake is less than
a half a mile wide. The RA-115 has a one kiloton yield. That's
certainly big enough to trigger a slide, which would block the
canal. The radiation would make repairs impossible in the near
term. The area is lightly populated, so civilian casualties would
be kept to a minimum. Hadir might consider that an acceptable
trade-off."

"That's what he's going to do," King said with that same note of certainty. "And he's doing it right now. Step on it, Bish."

Bishop didn't need the admonition. He was deftly threading their rental car through traffic and was nearing the turn that would send them onto the road paralleling the canal.

"I can catch him," Queen said. "Force him off the road."

"Negative," King answered, sharply. "Wait for us to catch up to you."

That did surprise Bishop. Queen and Rook were in the best position to stop Hadir. Sure it was risky, but the risk would be the same when he and King got there. Had he misread King's decisiveness in deciding to leave Knight behind?

He pushed the thoughts from his mind as he took the turn. In all their years of serving together, he had never had cause to question King's judgment. He wasn't about to start now.

The target was now slightly less than two miles ahead, but if they were going to catch up to it in the next few minutes, it would mean pushing the rented sedan like it was a Formula One race car. He applied steady pressure to the gas pedal, watching as both the speedometer and the tachometer needles started moving into rarely visited points on their respective dials. After only about a minute of running at over five thousand RPMs, the engine temperature needle also started rising, but one important meter was running in the opposite direction—they were rapidly closing the distance to Queen and Rook, and more importantly, Hadir and his bomb.

"Shit," Rook said. "He's turning...pulling off."

"Blue, overlay the sat photo," King snapped. A semi-transparent image, like the heads-up display of a fighter jet, appeared in Bishop's vision. It showed a satellite map of the area through which they were driving, with the icons now shown as points in two-dimensional space. The red dots indicating Hadir's car had left the road, crossed traffic and pulled into an open sandy area on the west side of the highway, across the road from the canal. Further west, three hundred yards away, the beige desert was transformed into green fields and orchards—evidence of the close proximity of human habitation.

"What is that? A dune?"

Bishop wasn't sure what King was talking about, but with the car hurtling forward at nearly 120 miles per hour, weaving back and forth to pass slower cars and avoid being hit by oncoming traffic, he didn't really have time to study the display more carefully. He considered taking the glasses off to have an unrestricted view, but that would mean taking one of his hands off the steering wheel, and that didn't seem like such a good idea.

"It's a berm, formed of material dredged from the canal," Deep Blue explained.

"The perfect place to plant that bomb if he wants to collapse the canal."

"He's heading for it," Queen said. "I'm going after him now. I can use his dust cloud for cover."

"No. Wait for us. That's an order."

Bishop was too focused on the drive now to even question King's abrupt and uncharacteristically authoritarian shift. On the map display, the little red dots moved away from the Queen and Rook icons, and stopped at the base of a low hill that was too perfectly straight to be anything but manmade. Abruptly, it split into five separate dots—the terrorists now tracking as individual signatures—all of whom began moving up the side of the hill on foot. Their motion barely registered now, and in the time it took for them to crest the hill, Bishop reached the spot where Queen and Rook had pulled off the road just ahead of them.

Rook had the hood of the rental car open and was pretending to tinker with the engine but was in reality covertly watching Hadir's progress. Queen was rooting around in the car's trunk, as if searching for tools, but the tools in this instance were a case of Uzi submachine guns. In addition to the noise and flash suppressors, each gun was equipped with a holographic sight that was wirelessly synched to the user's q-phone and glasses. When active, targeting crosshairs would show exactly where the bullet would go, so the weapon could be fired from almost any position, even around a blind corner. The system also automatically adjusted for the ballistic trajectory of the bullet over distances, which was particularly useful for long-ranged weapons like Knight's Intervention, but not so much for the Uzi, which had an effective range of 200 yards.

Bishop and King retrieved their own Uzis from the trunk of their car, and hustled to rendezvous with Queen and Rook. The latter glanced back. "Honey, the auto club guys are here."

Queen left the trunk open and came up to join them. Rook took one of the Uzis from her and wrinkled his nose in irritation. "A pea shooter to save the world from nuclear fire," he said, with all the gravity of a Shakespearian soliloquy. "Blue, why is it you can give us all these fancy gizmos, but can't come up with a way to sneak the girls past the TSA?"

'The girls' were a pair of Desert Eagle Mark XIX Magnum semi-automatic pistols, Rook's pride and joy. When the mission called for a covert insertion, such as a Zodiac launched from a submarine or a HALO jump, the pistols were always holstered at his hips. Lately however, the team was increasingly more reliant on commercial airlines to get them wherever they needed to go. So when it came to weapons, they were all forced to make do with whatever Deep Blue could procure for them on the local black market.

The Israeli designed sub-guns wouldn't have been Bishop's first choice for the mission either. He liked something a little bigger, like the venerable Browning M-2 .50 caliber machine gun on a portable tripod, but Uzis were easy to acquire in this part of the world. They were anonymous enough that, in the event that something went horribly wrong and they were captured or killed, there would be nothing to directly tie them to the US military. Although, given their current status, that was far less of a concern than it had once been. The Chess Team had almost completely cut its ties to the military, and Bishop wasn't entirely sure if that was a good thing or not. Autonomy had come at a price: no logistical support and no safety net. Despite the vast resources that Deep Blue had placed at their disposal, if they wanted to go somewhere, they had to get there on their own, and if things went FUBAR— military lingo for 'fucked up beyond all recognition'—well, then they were out of luck.

"What's the plan?" Queen asked.

Bishop squinted toward the rise. The map disappeared, and instead he saw a close-up view of the hillside. All of the red dots were still visible, but the terrorists to which they belonged were eclipsed from view. "No lookout," he murmured.

"We'll go in on foot," King said. "Rook, take the right flank. Bishop, go left. Establish visual contact and positive real-time targeting. We'll designate priority targets once in position, and then on my signal, we will take them out."

Queen cleared her throat. "Ah, forgetting someone?"

King shook his head. "Queen, you'll be the reserve element."

"*Excuse me?*"

Bishop winced a little at the acid in her tone, but he was even more surprised by King's decision. It was one thing to leave Knight behind because they were in a hurry, but leaving Queen in the rear with the gear made absolutely no sense.

King, however, just nodded in her direction. "Cover our approach. If anyone pops their head up, take them out. Once we secure the bomb, bring your car up to the base of the berm, so we can get it out of here ASAP. Okay, let's do this."

He didn't wait for an answer, but simply made an overhand gesture—the hand signal for 'move out'—and broke into a trot, leaving the rest to stare at each other in disbelief. Queen finally broke the awkward silence. "Better get moving."

Bishop turned away immediately and set off after King, veering to the left as he had been directed. He kept his gaze fixed on the slope ahead. King had already reached the base of the rise and was starting up the steep slope, following the distinctive trail left by the terrorists. Bishop wondered whether King would wait for Rook and him to catch up, or if perhaps it had been King's plan all along to leave them behind and take the objective single-handedly. It bothered Bishop that he couldn't easily dismiss that speculation.

He was halfway to his goal when he heard the helicopter.

For a moment, the sound of turbines and rotors didn't quite reach his conscious mind. Helicopters weren't uncommon around cities, and particularly since he'd been in the military, he found that he often tuned them out. It wasn't until he heard Queen comment that he actually started paying attention.

"Helo incoming."

Bishop swung his head around and quickly found the approaching aircraft. Queen had already tagged it, and Deep Blue had supplied ancillary data to identify it as a Bell Industries 206 JetRanger. By itself, that meant very little—with over seven thousand produced in its nearly fifty-year production run, not including numerous military and civilian variants, the JetRanger was arguably the most commonly used helicopter in the world. Bishop himself was certified to fly one. Far more revealing was the fact that it was painted a flat desert beige, with nothing at all to indicate who owned or operated the craft, not even identifying numbers on its tail rotor boom.

The helicopter was still a mile out, coming out of the south, but there seemed little question that it was heading their way.

"I don't like this," Queen said. "Bringing the car up now."

"Negative. Stay put."

"Sorry, King. Did not read your last. Queen out!"

A grim smile touched Bishop's lips. It was a small act of defiance, but one that had been sorely missing. King might have been acting squirrelly, but Queen was her old self. Nevertheless, the situation remained unchanged. Hadir still had the bomb, and they had no idea whether the crew of the helicopter was friend or foe.

A cloud of dust marked Queen's location and movement as effectively as the icon in the glasses' display. She was making a beeline straight for Bishop, who was closest to the approaching aircraft.

King spared Bishop the dilemma of having to decide whether to join Queen in her little mutiny. "All right. I don't like this either. Queen, if you've fixed your commo issue—" The exasperation in his tone came through loud and clear. "—pick up Bishop and Rook and get clear. Draw that helo off, if you can. I'm going to continue to the objective."

Bishop shook his head, but didn't comment. The helicopter was close enough that he could zoom in on it and make out the silhouettes of its occupants. The side door was open, revealing one of the passengers, a man wearing what looked like desert camouflage fatigues, his face swathed in a *kefiyah*-style scarf. The man was turned sideways in his seat so that his body faced out, and Bishop had no trouble distinguishing the rifle he cradled in his arms.

Bishop broke his long silence. "I think these guys might be military."

"Ours?" Rook asked.

"Not sure. Probably not. Could be Russians trying to roll up their missing nuke."

Through some trick of the Doppler effect, the helicopter seemed to pick up speed as it approached, and then it was past Bishop's location and continuing toward the hillside. An instant later, the report of a gun was heard, then another, and still more. Five shots rang out, all in the space of about three seconds, after which the helicopter began to descend, dropping behind the berm like a satellite over the horizon.

Bishop stared at the empty space where the aircraft had been. The rotor noise was muted, echoing weirdly off the atmosphere. There was a crunch of tires on sand as Queen pulled the car up alongside him, but before he could make a move toward it, there was a change in the pitch of the sound, and the helicopter rose into view once more. It smoothly banked away from them and headed west, quickly disappearing into the distance.

Bishop didn't get in the car. Instead, he sprinted forward and scrambled up the hill of loose sand. He was faintly aware that Rook and Queen were doing the same, and thirty seconds later, they had joined King at the top of the berm, staring down at the carnage beyond.

Hadir al-Shahri and his accomplices lay in a tight circle, motionless, awash in a small sea of blood. There had only been five shots from the shooters in the helicopter, one bullet for each of the terrorists, but the bodies were practically shredded, as if they'd been hit by close range shotgun blasts.

There was no sign of the bomb.

"What the...?"

Rook's voice trailed off, so King finished for him.

"Fuck."

FOUR

London

The heavily armored, black SUV, with three men inside, cruised south along the eastern boundary of Hyde Park. All three occupants gazed out the windows at the passing cars, people and scenery. Two of the men scanned for potential threats—cars moving up too fast, places where snipers might be concealed— while the third was simply enjoying the ride. His head bobbed back and forth as he admired locations he had previously viewed only in photographs or as names on maps.

Not only was this his first time in London, it was his first trip more than four degrees north of the equator. His travels, up to this point, had been limited to the nations surrounding the country of his birth. That country that had changed names several times during his lifetime: the Belgian Congo, Zaire and since the late 1990s, the Democratic Republic of the Congo. It was his dream that it might see yet another name change.

The man's name was Joseph Mulamba. The son of a Luba farmer, Mulamba had lived much of his life on the banks of the Congo River in the city of Kisangani. It had been called Stanleyville when his parents had moved there almost fifty years earlier, named for the famed British journalist and explorer Henry Morton Stanley, who had founded a trading post there, marking the navigable terminus of Africa's second longest river. It was an intense interest in Stanley that had brought Mulamba to London, though not for the reason that most people would have suspected.

As was the case for many of the native Africans living in the vast Congo basin, Mulamba's opinion of Stanley was complicated. Stanley was a white man, and a foreigner. In a quest for wealth and glory, he had arrogantly claimed a huge portion of Africa for foreign nations. Like Christopher Columbus, who by virtue of being the first European explorer to 'discover' a land that had already been inhabited for thousands of years, Stanley's claims rested solely upon a racial conceit: he was the first because he was the first white. And like Columbus, historians saw him as a divisive figure, responsible for the exploitation of a land that already belonged to someone else, and for the enslavement of the native inhabitants. His critics pointed to widely reported incidents of brutality directed at the porters in his expeditions. His contemporary, Sir Richard Francis Burton, opined that 'Stanley shoots Negroes as if they were monkeys.' Yet, despite these accusations, many Africans in the region credited Stanley with bringing civilization to the Congo and opening it up to the modern world, in a way that would not have been otherwise possible.

Mulamba however wasn't interested in Stanley's reputation.

The SUV turned right and headed down Kensington Avenue, along the southern edge of the park. Ahead and to the left the curving dome of Royal Albert Hall was visible, like a moon rising from the midst of the city. But Mulamba's goal lay closer, among the long row of elegant brick residences, many of them with historic pedigrees.

The vehicle pulled to a stop at the corner of Kensington Gore and Exhibition Road, in front of a house known as Lowther Lodge. Built in the latter quarter of the 19th century, the stately brick edifice had, for more than eighty years, been the headquarters of the prestigious Royal Geographical Society. The Society, which had been in existence for nearly two centuries, had counted Charles Darwin among its many members, as well as famed polar explorers Ernest Shackleton and the ill-fated Robert Falcon Scott, as well as the legendary Mount Everest conqueror, Sir Edmund Hillary. Scottish missionary David Livingstone and journalist Henry Morton Stanley were also part of the Royal Geographical Society's proud history.

Mulamba's fellow passenger—a former Royal Marine sergeant named Ian Woodhouse—got out first, firmly closing his door. He scanned up and down the street for a moment before rapping on the front window. The driver—another British military veteran named Bryan Clarke—turned off the engine and got out, likewise closing the door and checking his side of the vehicle before returning the signal. Only then was Mulamba allowed to get out. He thanked the two members of his security detail and then took a position between them for the short traverse to the public entrance to Lowther Lodge.

As Mulamba entered the lobby, Clarke fell back, taking up a position at the front of the building, where he could keep an eye on the SUV. Mulamba and Woodhouse continued inside and approached the reception desk.

The receptionist, a young man with an earnest and pinched scholarly expression, glanced first at the imposing figure of Woodhouse, and then at Mulamba. "May I help you?"

"Thank you," Mulamba replied. He spoke fluent French, along with Swahili, Tshiluba and Lingala, but he was less confident with English. "I am Joseph Mulamba. I am here for Henry Morton Stanley."

The receptionist gave a polite, if somewhat patronizing smile. "I'm afraid you've just missed him...by a hundred and ten years, actually."

Mulamba smiled as well—a polite smile that hid his irritation. "I understand. I want to read about Mr. Stanley. In your...*bibliotheque*."

"You mean our library, sir? I'm afraid our reading room is reserved for members of the Society." The young man paused, as if recognizing that he had made a potentially embarrassing assumption. "Are you...er, do you have your membership credentials?"

"I am not a member of the Society," Mulamba confessed.

The receptionist offered a sympathetic frown.

"May I join?"

"Certainly, sir. We have a variety of membership options. You can learn about them all at our website."

Mulamba was having more difficulty now managing his frustration. "Please, I do not have a great amount of time. May I join today?"

"What, right now? Well, I suppose we could do that. Let me just print you off an application. May I presume that you'll be selecting our ordinary membership?"

Woodhouse leaned over the desk, and fixed the receptionist in his laser-like stare. "Here, now, mate? Have you got a supervisor we could talk to? Someone who can get things done?"

The young man shrank in his chair, but tried his best not appear intimidated. "Sir, I assure you—"

"You know who this is?" pushed Woodhouse, jerking a thumb at his charge. "The bleedin' President of the Congo, that's who."

Mulamba put a restraining hand on Woodhouse's arm. "Please, Ian. I do not wish to..."

He was groping for the right word, when a paunchy but well-dressed middle-aged man seemed to materialize beside the reception desk. "Did I hear correctly? Are you Mr. Joseph Mulamba?" The man did not wait for a reply, but reached out and began vigorously pumping Mulamba's hand. "Jonathan Grigsby, sir. Assistant Director of the RGS. This is a rare and unexpected honor, sir. I wish that you would have phoned ahead so that we could arrange a more fitting reception."

"Mr. Woodhouse advised me not to publish my itinerary."

"Mr. Wood—ah, your bodyguard, of course. Well, it's no matter." He made a shooing gesture to the receptionist, who quickly surrendered his desk. "The full resources of the Society are at your disposal, sir."

"Thank you, Mr. Grigsby. I wish to see the papers of Henry Morton Stanley."

"Of course," beamed Grigsby. "We have a full collection of all his published writings in our digital archive. You are welcome to use one of the computers in the reading room, or if you like, I will arrange for you to have full access to the archive off-site so that you can peruse the information at you leisure."

"Forgive me, Mr. Grigsby, but I am not speaking of the published works. I would like to see Stanley's original diaries."

Grigsby's enthusiasm slipped a notch. "Ah, well let me see what we have. You do know that most of Sir Henry's journals are housed at the Belgian Royal Museum for Central Africa?"

"I was not aware of that." Mulamba frowned. "The portion I wish to read relates to the search for Dr. David Livingstone. Would that be in your collection?"

"The original?" A crease appeared in Grigsby's forehead. He seated himself at the terminal and began tapping on the keyboard. Minutes passed in an uncomfortable silence, and at one point, Woodhouse caught Mulamba's eye and tapped his watch meaningfully. *We've been here too long.*

Woodhouse was not merely being paranoid. While the newly elected president of the Democratic Republic of the Congo was popular with most of his countrymen, his bold vision for the future of his nation—and for all of Central Africa—was not embraced by all. He had enemies, a small but highly motivated minority of his countrymen, who feared that his promised reforms would somehow undermine their wealth and power.

Ironically, he felt much safer here, abroad with just two personal protection agents, than he did in the *Palais de la Nation*, his office in Kinshasa, where he would be surrounded by soldiers and bodyguards, any one of whom might secretly be plotting his assassination.

"Ah," announced Grigsby. "The original diaries containing his record of the search for Livingstone are in the collection in Belgium, but we do have scans of the document in our archives."

"What about the missing pages?"

"I beg your pardon?"

"Stanley removed several pages from his diary," Mulamba explained. "Including the entries where he described the actual meeting with Livingstone. Do you have those pages?"

"Well, no. As you've said, those are...well...rather missing."

Mulamba sagged in defeat. "I had hoped that perhaps those pages would have found their way into your collection."

"Sadly, no. If they still exist, they might be in the museum in Belgium. They aren't on record, but perhaps they were catalogued incorrectly."

"*Oui.* Yes, that is a possibility worth exploring. Thank you, Mr. Grigsby." Mulamba extended a hand, which Grigsby shook, and then Woodhouse was guiding the president back toward the exit. The bodyguard ducked his head out to check with his counterpart, and then held the door open for Mulamba.

The two bodyguards bracketed him for the short walk back to the SUV. Even though the vehicle had not been out of his sight the entire time, Clarke did a quick walk around the exterior, checking to verify that no one had tampered with it. When he finally gave the all clear, Woodhouse opened the rear door and gestured for Mulamba to get in.

"Thank you, Ian. I apologize for wasting your time."

The bodyguard smiled. "As long as your checks cash, my time is yours to—"

Woodhouse's head suddenly split open like a ripe melon, splattering blood, bone chips and brain matter all over the interior of the SUV.

Mulamba was too stunned to even move. He was no stranger to violence of this sort. He had witnessed countless atrocities during his childhood. Yet this was different. This wasn't a border village or a back alley in Kisangani. It was London. This was the civilized world. Things like this weren't supposed to happen here.

Woodhouse fell onto the floorboard and then slid back onto the sidewalk, as if his bones had turned to liquid. From the corner of his eye, Mulamba saw Clarke drop, similarly stricken. It occurred to Mulamba that he ought to pull the door shut and engage the locks. That would be enough. He would be safe inside the armored vehicle, safe from whoever had killed his bodyguard, but before he could move, a figure in a red hooded sweatshirt thrust his head and shoulders into the vehicle and brandished a pistol.

"Don't move," the hooded man warned. "Just be cool and you'll live."

Mulamba managed a weak nod. The man got in and pulled the door shut. Another similarly attired man opened the front door and slid into the driver's seat, and without saying a word started the engine.

As the SUV pulled away, continuing down Kensington Gore, Mulamba barely noticed the scenery passing by.

FIVE

The George Bush Center for Intelligence, Langley, Virginia

Domenick Boucher sat back in his chair and let his gaze sweep around his office. The room had a comfortable familiarity to it.

Even though much of his working day was spent on the move—visiting various directorate heads and their personnel, leading briefings in the conference rooms and the crisis center, shuttling back and forth between the White House, the Capitol, the Pentagon and other destinations throughout Washington—this space was his. It was, in every sense save the literal, home.

Boucher had occupied this office, and held the title of Director of the Central Intelligence Agency, for nine years, which meant he had been leading the organization longer than anyone in its sixty-six years of operation. That was longer even than the legendary Allan Dulles, who had overseen some of the most dramatic and controversial intelligence operations in the nation's history, culminating in the disastrous Bay of Pigs incident. Boucher would not have quite such a notorious legacy.

He had been thinking a lot about his legacy lately, ever since announcing his plans to retire.

Although he would not formally leave his post until the end of the month, most of the day-to-day operations were already being overseen by his interim successor, Danielle Rudin, the woman who would hold the job of acting D/CIA until the Senate approved President Chambers's pick for the job. Given the way Washington was functioning lately, that might be a long process. But politics were no longer Boucher's concern. He was merely a figurehead now, a placeholder.

It was a rare thing indeed for someone to hold an appointed post for so many years. Most agency directors lasted a year or two at most. Some were brought down by scandal. A few had chosen to fall on their swords—figuratively speaking—taking the blame for bad decisions made higher up the food chain. Most, however, came and went as administrations changed. Boucher had been appointed by Tom Duncan shortly after his election. When Duncan had been forced to resign from office late in his second term, Boucher had been one of the few appointees from the previous administration to keep his job, owing in no small part to his perceived role as the whistle-blower who had brought Duncan down.

No one knew, no one could ever know, that the president's fall from grace had been carefully orchestrated by Duncan himself, along with Boucher's help, to save the country, and indeed the entire planet, from a much greater threat.

When the scandal had finally slipped from the headlines, Boucher had been prepared to leave office as well, but the newly sworn President Chambers had implored him to stay, at least through the next election cycle. Oddly enough, it had not been Chambers's pleas that had prompted Boucher to stay, but rather the debt he owed Tom Duncan. For although Duncan had resigned from office in disgrace and slipped out of the public eye, he had not for one second forsaken his oath to protect and defend America from all enemies. Duncan needed a friend in the administration, and Boucher was that man.

Now, more than two years into Chambers's first full term in office, Boucher felt the time was right to shuffle off the stage, but it was going to be a big change. It was as if there was a countdown clock running in the corner of his vision wherever he looked, ticking down the time remaining before he wouldn't ride in the elevator, sit in his chair or visit with his secretary. He felt like a bright orange leaf on a tree branch in autumn, afraid to let go, but eager to see where the wind would take him.

The hum of an incoming phone call stirred him out of his musings. A picture of the person calling was displayed on the screen of his smart phone. It was a very familiar picture, as it was identical to the framed portrait hanging on the office wall. Boucher answered before it could ring a second time.

"Good morning, Mr. President."

"Domenick, hope I didn't catch you at a bad time." Chambers's voice sounded weary, but that was a chronic condition for men who sat behind the Resolute Desk.

"Mr. President, for the rest of the month, there are no bad times for you to call me. Next month? Well now, that's a different story." Boucher tried to keep his tone light, though in fact the call had him worried. The president wasn't the sort of person to call out of the blue and shoot the breeze. If he was calling the Director of the CIA, then it was because he needed something from the agency—needed it urgently. Also, Chambers knew that Boucher had handed over most of his duties to Rudin. That meant the president wanted something that the designated interim director could not provide.

"Glad to hear it." It wasn't a platitude. The president actually sounded reassured by the promise. "Do you think you could come by the office? Say, in an hour?"

It wasn't really a question. "I'll be there, sir."

The president had left instructions with Stewart Hulce, his Chief of Staff, to have Boucher brought to his informal office in the study adjoining the Oval Office. Because he controlled access to the president, the White House Chief of Staff was one of the most powerful positions in the government, and Hulce took both his responsibilities and his privileges as gatekeeper very seriously. His expression indicated that he wasn't at all pleased by this unscheduled meeting between his boss and the outgoing head of the CIA. He was even unhappier when Chambers asked him to leave them alone, but he slunk from the room without protest.

The president sank into his chair, gesturing for Boucher to sit as well. Then he skipped the customary exchange of pleasantries and got right to the point. "Have you been following this business in Africa?"

Despite having voluntarily side-lined himself, Boucher had not completely disengaged from day-to-day operations. He read and annotated the daily intelligence brief before it was forwarded to the White House, so he knew exactly what the president meant.

Approximately twenty-one hours earlier, Joseph Mulamba, the newly elected president of the Democratic Republic of the Congo—not to be confused, Boucher had pointed out in the margins of the paper, with the neighboring Republic of Congo—had been abducted off a London street while on a state visit. The police had no leads and no knowledge of whether Mulamba was even still alive. Within a few hours of the incident, General Patrice Velle, the chief of the Congolese Army, had marshaled his troops in the eastern city of Kisangani and declared himself the acting president. The cities of the DRC were on a knife's edge and poised to slip into chaos. This was actually a better state of affairs than what was happening in the eastern provinces, where the smoldering coals of ancient tribal feuds were being fanned into a fresh wave of ethnic violence. Further complicating matters, several of the stateless guerilla armies that roamed the Congo rain forest—really nothing more than well-armed criminal gangs made up of legions of indoctrinated child soldiers—were swarming out of the jungle, attacking rural villages and outposts.

Boucher let out a soft sigh. This was the kind of stuff he wouldn't miss at all. "I am, sir. I believe I added a footnote or two to the brief."

"Is there anything we can do about it?"

The question caught Boucher off guard. "Sir?"

Chambers drew in a breath. "You were there, at CIA, during the Clinton administration, weren't you Domenick?"

"Yes sir." Back then, he'd been a senior operations officer. It was hard to believe he'd come so far in such a short time.

"Do you know what Clinton said was the biggest regret of his presidency? I'll give you a hint: it wasn't that business with the intern and the cigar."

Even if he hadn't known the answer, Boucher would have been able to guess from the context. "Rwanda."

"We sat on our hands and kicked our heels, and a million people were slaughtered."

Boucher didn't respond. He understood, better than most, the sort of horrors that were loose in the world. He also understood how political realities could get in the way of the most honorable intentions.

Just six months before the events in Rwanda, an attempt by the US government to intervene in a similar humanitarian crisis in Somalia had led to a two-day long battle, in which two Blackhawk helicopters were shot down, eighteen American soldiers were killed and one was taken prisoner. The bodies of the slain were desecrated and dragged through the streets of Mogadishu. The images of these atrocities were dutifully recorded and broadcast by the news media, and many Americans began to publicly question why their sons were getting killed trying to save a bunch of ungrateful savages. With the bitter taste of that disaster still in its mouth, the administration had all but ignored the unfolding genocide in Rwanda, and innocent people had died.

Unfortunately, twenty years and two wars later, the attitude of the American public remained largely the same, especially with respect to Africa. Their antipathy was understandable. Despite numerous humanitarian missions and billions of dollars in foreign aid packages, nothing ever seemed to change.

Chambers regarded Boucher from across the desk for several long seconds. Finally, it was he that broke the uncomfortable silence. "You know something, Domenick? You're the first person I've talked to who didn't have a ready excuse for our failure."

Boucher spread his hands. "I'm sure you've already heard all the reasons why we didn't do more, and why we probably shouldn't get involved the next time it happens. From a pragmatic viewpoint, they are perfectly correct reasons."

"Pragmatically speaking," said the president. "It always comes back to that. My opponents in Congress say that until we can put our own house in order, we've got no business trying to help the Third World."

Boucher winced at the dated term. 'Third World' was a holdover of the Cold War era, when nations were divided into 'worlds' based on how they fit into the global chess game between the superpowers. The Western nations were the First World, the Communist powers were the Second and the developing nations of Asia, Africa and

Central America, who were pawns in the struggle, were the Third World. Despite the largely political definitions, 'Third World' had become synonymous with poverty, squalor and corruption.

"Pragmatism is cold comfort when millions of lives are in the balance," conceded Boucher. "It's a little like saying, 'Sorry, I can't rescue you from drowning until I finish waxing my car.'"

The president chuckled softly at the apt metaphor. "I'll have to remember that one."

"It's easy for me to say it. I've already packed my office. You have to worry about a re-election campaign."

"And if I lose that campaign, I'll lose whatever ability I have to make a difference in the world."

Boucher almost laughed aloud at that. Chambers's predecessor was proof positive that you didn't have to be president to save the world.

"Not very many people know what I'm about to tell you," the president went on. "And for now, it's best to keep it that way. You know that Joseph Mulamba was kidnapped in London. What you might not know is the underlying reason for his state visit."

"I just assumed he was looking for foreign aid."

"In a manner of speaking." The president drummed his fingers on the table for a moment, as if trying to decide how to reveal his secret. "What do you know about the African Union?"

"It's sort of like the United Nations. A treaty organization designed to promote peace and security among the African nations. They've done a lot to advance human rights and combat the spread of AIDS, but they're sort of a paper tiger, if you'll forgive the pun."

"What if I were to tell you that Joseph Mulamba wants to give it some real teeth?"

Boucher narrowed his gaze. "Just what exactly is that supposed to mean?"

"President Mulamba intends to transform the African Union into a legitimate federal authority."

Boucher leaned forward in his chair. "Let me make sure I understand what you're saying. He wants to create an African federation?"

"The United States of Africa," the president said, almost reverently.

Boucher shook his head. "It won't work. It will never work."

"I believe differently. Mulamba was in London to meet with the Prime Minister to get the Brits on board. His next stop was to be here, and I was going to pledge the support of the United States of America."

"Sir, with respect, the nations of Africa would never agree to this. There are so many reasons why this would never work."

"Mulamba presented a very persuasive argument to suggest otherwise. Look, I didn't ask you here to debate this or to explain myself."

"Then respectfully sir, why did you ask me here?"

"Because I want this to succeed." Chambers took another deep breath. "With Mulamba missing and probably dead, the odds of this happening are shrinking with each passing second. His legal successor, Gerard Okoa supports the plan, but the army is divided. If this General Velle takes power, that will be the end of it. I've drafted a resolution asking Congress to send American forces to supplement UN peacekeepers in the Congo. Unfortunately, I'm going to have to fight to make it happen, and that will take some time, which is something we don't have."

"You *are* the Commander in Chief. You don't need Congress—"

"If I act unilaterally... Well, I might be out of a job a lot sooner than the next election."

"Go public with it. Tell the American people what you've told me. Tell them how we'll be saving millions of lives."

The president shook his head sadly. "That's a nice idea. I suggested it to Stewart. Do you know what he said to me? He said, 'Mr. President, it's Africa. No one cares about Africa.'"

"The American people just might surprise you, sir. Let them decide."

"You might be right. God knows, I hope you are. But I can't wait for that to happen. So, I ask you again, is there anything we can do about it? Do you have any assets we can send in, something off the books, just to hold things together long enough to give this a chance?"

Boucher was impressed by Chambers's sincerity. He had never really thought of the president in any terms except as Tom Duncan's replacement, and Duncan was a hard act to follow. Even in defeat, Duncan was formidable and Chambers had none of Duncan's real world experience or savvy. Now Boucher found himself wondering whether there was more to Chambers, something that most politicians sacrificed along their journey to the top: compassion.

But the answer was still going to be 'no.'

No matter how much he wanted to help, the Agency simply didn't have anything to offer. As the Chief of Staff had so aptly pointed out, no one cared about Africa, or at least not sub-Saharan Africa, far removed from the influence of Islamic extremists, who were the latest hot-button national security issue. Even if he had assets in place—and he didn't—he would still have to answer to Congress about how the people were used and the money spent. Not even a pension and a gold watch would immunize him against that. There was, quite simply, nothing he could do.

That was why it came as such a surprise when he heard himself say: "I'll see what I can do."

SIX

Kisangani, Democratic Republic of the Congo

Monique Favreau was in love.

It took every ounce of her self-control to keep her hands in her lap during the flight. She wanted so badly to touch...to fondle the object of her infatuation. If not for the presence of her traveling companions, she almost certainly would have done so. But she was their leader, and it wouldn't do for her subordinates to see her behaving in such a way.

Her men didn't seem to share her fascination with the prize. Perhaps they were overawed by the presence of so much destructive power, terrified at being so close to instantaneous death. Favreau wasn't the least bit fearful. The possibility of getting turned to ash was something to which they should have been accustomed. They routinely carried blocks of plastic explosives in their backpacks for use in breaching doors or for improvising claymore mines. An accidental explosion that might kill them, along with anyone else in a hundred yard radius, was not outside the realm of possibility, yet they didn't seem to dwell on that outcome. This was no different. It was merely a question of scope. As Favreau saw it, the weapon she now possessed didn't really kill faster or leave a person any deader than mishandling a block of C-4, so why be afraid of it? She didn't fear it at all. So much power, and it was hers to use as she pleased.

When the Gulfstream V private jet finally landed at the not quite charmingly rustic airport in Kisangani and slowed to a halt near the terminal building, she immediately hefted her new prize onto her back, and exited the short flight of stairs to the tarmac. The thing was tremendously heavy, and although she was in excellent physical shape, she felt the strain in her thighs and knees, and in the soles of her feet. But she did not for a moment consider asking someone else to carry it. The ordeal was, in its own way, as exhilarating as it was exhausting.

With a bearing that was as erect and as confident as she could muster, she strode to the second of three waiting Russian-made VPK-3927 Volk armored infantry vehicles that were lined up at the edge of the runway. The vehicles would transport Favreau and her team to the nearby military camp, where Lieutenant General Patrice Velle had promoted himself from Chief of Staff of the

Armed Forces of the Democratic Republic of the Congo—to President of the country.

Although it was the third largest city in the country, boasting a population of nearly a million people, Kisangani occupied only about ten square miles on the northern bank of the Congo River. It was a short journey from the airport to the military camp, barely enough time for Favreau to make the necessary modifications to her prize, which mostly involved rigging a connection to the Volk's electrical system. A constant supply of power was essential to her prize's operation. Part of the prodigious weight of the device was its battery backup, which allowed it to be unplugged for transport, but like all batteries, it was only good for a few hours. She left the device in the Volk, with the engine running to ensure that the battery received a full charge, and she entered the headquarters building from which General Velle now presided over the eastern half of his country.

In her fifteen years of working abroad, first as an agent for the DGSE—the *Direction Générale de la Sécurité Extérieure*, France's premiere foreign intelligence service—and subsequently in her current position, as the director of operations for the private security agency Executive Solutions International, she had dealt with more than her share of tin-pot military dictators. Velle was no exception to the norm. He was a big man, a natural alpha, but his outward appearance was so cliché it seemed like self-parody. He wore camouflage fatigues decorated like a dress uniform, with shoulder braids and a full rack of medals and ribbons, which were far more impressive than his actual military career. His command center looked more like a throne room, and he was surrounded by toadying sycophants he called his 'advisors,' but who only advised him to do whatever he pleased.

When he saw her, a hungry, predatory smile split his fleshy face. "Miss Monique," he said. "You've come back to us! We have so missed your delightful presence."

Velle made no effort to mask the sarcasm in his voice, and Favreau was not naïve enough to think that he was merely being flirtatious. Even in her combat uniform, she was stunningly beautiful, at least by Western standards. She was tall and lithe, with long straight black hair and full lips, but that counted for little with Velle. Like many powerful men, he was instinctively wary of women, especially attractive women, whom he feared might use their sexuality to bewitch and enslave him. Favreau however, did not need to rely on her feminine wiles to control Velle.

"General Velle. It has been brought to my attention that you have not yet dealt with the situation in the northern Kivu region. We had an agreement. The scientific expedition is trying to find a way to recover the natural gas deposits at the bottom of Lake Kivu. If they do that, then the people of the Democratic Republic of the Congo will have no use for the services my client so generously offers them. Nor will they have much use for you as their leader. You must deal with them, immediately."

Velle made a dismissive gesture. "Killing a few scientists in Nord-Kivu won't put me in Kinshasa."

Favreau fixed him with a Medusa stare. "Ignoring the requests of the people who are making your little coup possible, will most certainly not put you in Kinshasa."

"What have you done for me that I could not have done myself?" he scoffed.

"I assume you mean aside from removing Joseph Mulamba from power?"

Velle snorted. "So you claim, but how do I know for sure? I have only your word. The news reports say that he has been abducted. He's not even dead. Bring me his head, and then we will talk about Kivu."

"As the democratically elected leader of your country, he is far too valuable alive." She kept her gaze focused on him so that there would be no confusion about what she meant. "Especially if other arrangements do not work out as planned."

"Your *employers*—" He stressed the word as if to remind her that she was merely a lackey, running errands. "—put me in charge for a reason. They need me to run this place, so don't waste your breath on empty threats."

Velle did not look as though he felt very threatened. A firmer hand was called for. Favreau shrugged. "A monkey could run this place, and probably better than you."

The room went utterly silent.

Favreau's carefully chosen slur had the desired effect. Velle abruptly changed from arrogant, strutting peacock, to an enraged bull.

Now she had his attention.

"Shoot this bitch!" Velle shouted. "No, give me a gun. I will shoot her."

Before anyone could show the slightest inclination to comply, Favreau held up a hand, displaying a small black plastic object that looked a little like a mobile phone or the remote control for a television set.

Velle froze but his rage did not abate. "What is that? A bomb? You bring a bomb into my headquarters? You are dead already."

"No General, I didn't bring the bomb in. It's waiting for me out in my car. But it is a very large bomb—a one kiloton yield tactical nuclear device, if it matters." She waggled the plastic device. "And in case you haven't figured it out already, this is a remote trigger with a dead-man switch. You do know how that works, right? Shoot me, I let go, and this entire camp gets vaporized.

"I'm going to leave now," she continued. "But I won't go far. See that you take care of the situation in the Kivu, and then we'll talk about how to get you to Kinshasa."

SEVEN

Pinckney, New Hampshire

Asya Machtchenko stepped out onto the porch of the Pinckney General Store and cracked the seal on the can of Java Monster Mean Bean she'd just purchased. She was still adjusting to her new life in the United States, and the list of things she disliked about it was nearly as long as those she liked, but Mean Bean was one guilty pleasure that heavily weighted the balance on the positive side.

Pinckney wasn't so bad. It reminded her of Peredelkino, the *dacha* village southwest of Moscow, where she had spent several summers during her childhood. The locals, who depended on the variable tourist economy, seemed to harbor no suspicions about this mysterious woman with the exotic accent, who had taken up residence in their midst. Yet, despite its quaint charms, sometimes Pinckney seemed as remote as a Siberian gulag.

Her eyes were drawn to a black Lexus crunching into the gravel parking lot. Her gaze lingered on the Virginia license plates as the vehicle eased up against the curb, just beyond the porch rail. The driver, a late middle-aged man with short, steel gray hair and a face that was still handsome despite a deeply-etched map of worry lines, lowered his window without turning off the engine.

"Pardon me," he said, "but I think I might be lost."

"If you think you are lost," Asya replied with a smile, "then it's probably true. Where are you wanting to be?"

"I'm supposed to meet a friend at the Bible Campground."

"Ah, you are true believer. You are not as lost as you think. Is close. I happen to be going that way."

The weary face cracked with a grin. "My lucky day. Hop in."

She descended the steps and found the passenger door of the Lexus open and waiting. She climbed in and slipped the Monster can into the center console cup holder before closing the door. "I think I am supposed to say something about not accepting rides from strange men," she said.

"I've been called a lot of things in my time, but never 'strange.'" He gazed at her sidelong. "You look just like him."

She knew exactly to whom the man was referring; with her dark hair and lean features, Asya bore more than a passing resemblance to her brother—her much older brother—Jack Sigler. "Thomas thought you would say that. Is why he sent me to meet you."

The man, Domenick Boucher, Director of the Central Intelligence Agency, put the car in reverse and backed out of the parking spot. "So how is your brother?"

"I don't really know him as well as I..." She realized how ridiculous the statement was and didn't finish. "Older and wiser, I think you would say. Turn right and follow this road."

Boucher drove in silence, clearly preoccupied with whatever matter had brought him so far from the nation's capital, and Asya was content to let him do so. They drove into the wooded outskirts of the small town and through the open gate of the Pinckney Bible Conference Grounds. Although a fully functional campground for religious retreats, its funding anonymously came from the headquarters of a very secret security organization known as Endgame, which was partially located under the grounds. Although the campground gate was never closed, it was by no means unsecure. Asya knew that their every move was being followed, and that at the first hint of danger, an armed security force would materialize out of one of the rustic cabins they were driving past, and descend on them like the proverbial ton of bricks. The park was technically open, but mid-week the place was deserted of campers.

The Lexus cruised past the small welcome center, turned right and passed the 'Snack Shack.' The road became dirt as they drove into the woods, past the campground's trailer park and onto a narrow path that wended into the forested foothills of an imposing block of granite called Fletcher Mountain. The trail ended at an overgrown trailhead parking area. Asya directed Boucher to stop there. They got out, and she led him to a small wooden outhouse near the trail signpost.

Boucher wrinkled his nose in disgust. "Actually, I don't really have to go that bad."

Asya grinned. The smell was overpowering, but the knowledge that it was just a mix of tert-butyl mercaptan and other odor-causing chemicals, and not actually raw sewage stewing in the New England sun, made it a little more tolerable. "This way, Mr. CIA."

The door to the outhouse was barricaded with two-by-fours and a sign proclaiming 'Closed,' but like the aroma, the look was merely for cosmetic effect. The door swung open revealing a spotless room, tastefully decorated in muted hues of green, and *sans* all plumbing fixtures, primitive or otherwise. A strong smell, like coffee mixed with cinnamon, filled the space, overpowering the offensive odor outside. When Boucher stood beside her, Asya pulled the door shut. There was a hiss and then a feeling of lightness as the floor began to descend.

"Ah, the old secret elevator in the outhouse trick," Boucher said. "It's like something from a James Bond movie."

"Who is James Bond?" Asya said, in her thickest possible Slavic accent. She laughed as he struggled to come up with an answer. "Relax, Mr. CIA, everyone in Russia knows who James Bond is. When I was young, he was symbol of Western decadence. When I was older...come to think of it, he is still symbol of Western decadence."

A faint tremor marked the end of the descent, and another door slid open to reveal a luxurious room that might have been the lobby of a high-rent office building or a four-star hotel. There was only one person in the room, a fit man who looked to be in his late forties, with extremely short salt and pepper hair. It was starting to recede from a forehead that was, like Boucher's, creased with the deep wrinkles that come with years and experience. He was the man Asya had called 'Thomas' but her brother and his friends always referred to him as 'Deep Blue.'

Boucher had a different name for him.

"Mr. President," he said. "Love what you've done with the place."

"You had better start calling me 'Tom.'"

"Tom and Dom. Sounds like a bad comedy routine, but your house, your rules."

Deep Blue turned to Asya. "He give you any trouble?"

She grinned mischievously. "No. I am a little disappointed."

"I'm glad you could come, Dom," Deep Blue said. "I'd love to give you the nickel tour, but we're kind of on a crisis footing at the moment, so if you don't mind, I'd like to do business before pleasure."

"Ah...sure. Fire away."

"We've got a loose ball on the field." Deep Blue briefly related the details of Chess Team's failed mission in Suez.

When he finished, Boucher's eyes narrowed in irritation. "I wish you'd read me in on this, Tom."

"There were reasons why I couldn't do that." Deep Blue glanced at Asya, but he didn't explain. "I couldn't come to you until we had positive independent verification that there really was a bomb in play. We were thirty seconds from securing it when that chopper showed up. We did verify the radiation signature at least."

"So who was it?"

"We don't have a clue. My source in Moscow assures me that it wasn't a Russian Spetsnaz unit. Honestly, I was hoping that it might be your people."

"You were right to turn this over to me. I'll make sure word gets to the right people."

Asya got the impression that Boucher wasn't nearly concerned enough about a missing tactical nuclear device in the hands of an unknown rogue element. Evidently, Deep Blue felt the same way. "Dom, is there something you're not telling me?"

Boucher looked away, nervous or possibly embarrassed. "Tom, is there somewhere we can talk?"

"We're in a top secret, underground facility that less than a hundred people in the world know about. I'd say you can talk anywhere you like."

Boucher's gaze flicked to Asya. Sensing his apprehension, she cleared her throat. "I will let you two catch up."

Surprisingly, it was Boucher that forestalled her. "No. Wait. Actually this is probably going to involve you as well."

"Me?"

"You. Your brother. The whole team. You should all hear what I've got to say."

EIGHT

Boucher felt their eyes on him, but he could only guess at the thoughts swirling behind those stares.

More than twelve hours had passed since the debacle on the edge of the Suez Canal, a period of time in which they had had very little to do aside from sitting idle in a safe house outside Cairo, second-guessing everything they had done. The Chess Team looked thoroughly beat, as they sat around the table in the briefing room. The story he'd told them had not improved their collective mood.

They were not really present in the room with him. Boucher knew that, and yet his eyes told him otherwise. No matter which way he turned his head, he could see them, rendered in three-dimensions with perfect clarity. He lifted his glasses momentarily, and the group of special operators blinked out of existence. But when he lowered the glasses back into place, they were all right where they had been. It was telepresence on steroids.

They had listened without comment as he related the facts of the situation developing in the Congo and of the as-yet-unresolved abduction of Joseph Mulamba. This clearly had not been what they were expecting.

Finally, Tom Duncan—Deep Blue—broke the silence. "What exactly is it that you want us to accomplish?"

That was a question that had troubled Boucher from the moment President Chambers had made his desperate plea. Before he could frame his answer, another voice chimed in—Zelda Baker, the one called 'Queen.'

"What about the bomb? Shouldn't that be our priority right now?"

"We can handle that," replied Boucher. "What we can't handle... what no official US government agency can touch right now, is the situation in the Congo. And if someone doesn't act now, the powder keg will blow up and a lot of people will die."

Rook, whom Boucher had first met years ago, when Chess Team was just getting established, shifted in his chair. "You want the five of us to stop a revolution?"

"You just have to buy the President enough time to marshal support for a peace-keeping operation. Mulamba had a plan, and President Chambers wants to make sure that plan has a chance to work. That means keeping the presidential successor, Gerard Okoa, in power, if at all possible. Mulamba was also working on some kind of renewable energy project at a place called Lake Kivu, at the eastern border of the country. Currently, rebel forces are threatening the team that's working there, so protecting them is critical to the long term success of the plan. Or failing that, rescuing them before they're overrun.

"Don't underestimate the impact a few individuals can have in a situation like this," he continued. "The abduction of just one man, President Mulamba, set this all in motion. There are a lot of people in his country who want his vision to succeed. They just need some help." He studied each member of the virtual audience. "You've all been through the Robin Sage exercise?"

Robin Sage was the fifth and final phase of the US Army Special Forces training course, conducted in rural North Carolina. It was a simulated exercise in which Special Forces candidates infiltrated the fictional country of Pineland, to train and lead a force of guerilla insurgents to overthrow an oppressive government. Despite the public perception that Special Forces operators were all unstoppable commandos who dropped behind enemy lines to destroy enemy missile sites and take out terrorist leaders, their primary mission was to act as a force multiplier.

While it was true that certain groups within the Spec War community—SEAL Team Six and Delta in particular—did train for high profile missions like hostage rescue and antiterrorism, every single shooter started with the basics of unconventional warfare. In terms of war strategy, they were called 'force multipliers' because a small unit of SF operators could embed with a local group of freedom fighters and turn them into an army.

Deep Blue shook his head. "You don't need to explain unconventional war to any of us, Dom. We've all lived it. The situation in Africa... It's like trying to hold back the wind. These countries are always about two steps away from a bloody revolution or tribal genocide, and nothing anyone has been able to do has changed that. I was in Somalia; I know."

Boucher had felt much the same way during his meeting with the president. Chambers had asked for something that no one—not armies, diplomats, or well-funded humanitarian organizations—had been able to accomplish, and now Boucher was asking these five weary souls to give it a try. "You're right," he said, defeated. "It's impossible. But I had to ask."

He was about to strip off the glasses and end the ordeal, when a voice that had been quiet throughout was heard.

"I'll do it," King said.

NINE

Near Cairo, Egypt

Queen tore off her glasses and made a gesture for the others to do the same. King was the last to remove his, and he did so with a detached expression, as if he didn't quite understand why she wanted him to do so.

"What the hell?" she said.

He stared back at her. "I said *I* would do it. The rest of you can Charlie Mike." Charlie Mike—CM—meant *continue the mission*, or in this case, find the bomb.

"Oh, I heard what you said. That's exactly what I'm talking about. We're a team. We work *together*. Remember?"

"You heard what Blue said. It's an impossible job."

"Oh, right," Rook said. "We can't do *impossible*." He made air-quotes to emphasize the last word.

Queen waved him off. "King, if you've got a reason why we should do this, I'd like to hear it. We all would. You owe us that."

"There's no reason. It's plainly a fool's errand."

"Bullshit. If you thought that, you wouldn't have volunteered yourself. What I want to know is why you're treating us like we're your children instead of your teammates."

She saw Knight and Rook nod and Bishop's gaze became a little more focused. They all felt it. King however, seemed genuinely surprised by the accusation. "What's that supposed to mean?"

"Ever since...since Tunisia, since you came back, you've been acting like you're afraid to put us in the fight."

"Have I?" The faintest hint of a smile touched at the corner of his mouth. "I guess maybe my teamwork skills have gotten a little rusty."

"Damn straight," Rook said. "Now, as much as I'd love to leave a tender moment alone, can you please explain why you just volunteered to single-handedly save Africa from its latest self-destruct?"

King took a deep breath and leaned back in his chair. "You know that old saying about history repeating itself? You can see it coming from a mile away and you just want to grab someone and shake them, but it's like nothing you do makes any difference."

"I think the rest of that old saying talks about learning from history. You can't make people do that. They have to figure it out for themselves."

"Believe me, I know. But that's the funny thing about history. How can you really learn anything? It's all just dry facts and statistics. A million dead here or there...life goes on. It's not real to you unless you watch it happen. I did, over and over again, knowing that it was going to happen, knowing that, even when I got involved, there was nothing I could do to change the outcome. But now...the future hasn't been written yet."

Queen could sense the others holding back from commenting, and she knew why. Despite the things they had all seen in their military careers—and some of those things had been pretty terrible—there was no comparison to what King had experienced.

It still boggled Queen's mind. Eight months earlier—eight months for her at least—during a mission to rescue King's parents from renegade geneticist Richard Ridley's Omega facility in Tunisia, King had been blown up in a mysterious explosion...or so they had thought at the time. A few hours later, King had shown up just in time to save them all from one of Ridley's creations run amok. When the dust had finally settled, King had told them how he had survived. It was a whopper of a tale, but the short version was that King had been blown back in time—all the way back to 800 BC—with no way to get home.

It sounded impossible, but as Rook had so eloquently pointed out, impossible was a fluid concept for the Chess Team.

King had been dosed with a regenerative serum, similar to the one Bishop had received but without the negative side effects.

Although after returning to the present he had voluntarily given it up, his physiology returning to normal, the serum had made it possible for him to survive the millennia and show up to save the day. To the rest of them, only a few hours had passed, but King had lived every minute of nearly three thousand years of human history, fifty lifetimes worth of war and unimaginable brutality. Worst of all, he'd been unable to alter the course of events. Everything happened just the way it had always happened, and he had been forced to witness it all. He fought in wars. Led armies. Staged coups. Defeated evil. He'd lived lives as vagrant nobodies, as revered heroes and demigods, as quiet farmers and famous warriors, in every part of the world. Whenever he could, he did what was right, but since the history he learned in school was the history he had already taken part in, he often knew how things worked out in the end. Wars, natural disasters and madmen claimed untold millions of lives throughout his 2800 years of life, and try as he might, he couldn't prevent the world from going to hell over and over again.

No wonder King is taking this personally.

"I know there's not a lot I can do," he said finally. "But it's like what happens when you see that your neighbor's house is on fire. You can't just stand by and let it burn. You've got to try and save him."

"*De Oppresso Liber,*" Bishop murmured. "That's what we do isn't it?"

Queen immediately recognized the Latin phrase. It was the motto of the US Army Special Forces. *Free the oppressed.* It was a message that definitely resonated with Bishop, and with her as well.

"I agree," Knight said, then shrugged. "You know, for whatever that's worth."

Queen gave them both a grateful smile, and then turned back to King. "Look, we're all with you. If you say you want to do this, then you don't even have to make a case for it...not to us anyway.

All I ask is that you get back with the team. I know we all kind of got scattered to the four winds for a while there...and you... Well, you really got scattered. But we're a team. That's how we win."

King looked at each one of them in turn, then he simply nodded.

"Great," Rook said. "I can't wait to tell dad. But a couple things first: A, what do we do about the missing Russian backpack nuke; and B, how in the hell are the five of us supposed to keep an entire country from going down the ⌐⌐ ?"

"You heard Bo⌐⌐⌐⌐ , Queen said. "He's going to take care of the bomb."

⌐⌐g rubbed his unshaven chin. "The five of us," he echoed, thoughtfully. "No. Not just us."

"You mean Deep Blue?"

"Him, Pawn and everyone else at Endgame." Pawn was the designated callsign for anyone temporarily attached to the team for special operations. It had once been given to Sara Fogg, King's fiancée, but more recently it had been permanently assigned to Asya Machtchenko, King's sister. "We won't be able to do anything meaningful without their help, and that means before we commit to anything, we need to know that everyone is on board. That," he concluded, holding up his glasses, "is what being part of the team means. So let's have a team meeting and figure out how we're going to turn this thing around. Like you said, that's how we win."

TEN

Dartford, England

Rook curled his fingers around the steering wheel, his foot tense on the brake pedal, eager to slide over and punch the accelerator.

"Relax," Queen said, from the passenger seat beside him.

He shot her a scowl. "Easy for you to say. You're not driving"

She laughed. "Since when do you complain about drivin"

He struggled to come up with a scathing retort, but the light changed and a taxi behind them laid on the horn. He shook his head and accelerated through the intersection. "When we took this 'Save Africa' gig, I thought we'd be...you know, saving in Africa."

"You've got a problem coming to a country where they have hot showers and flush toilets?"

"I've got a problem coming to a country where they drive on the wrong side of the road."

She patted his arm. "Once we find our missing African president, we'll be on the first flight back to the land of malaria."

"You always know just what to say to cheer me up, babe."

He and Queen had drawn the short straw—at least that was how Rook saw it—and been given the job of tracking down Joseph Mulamba and rescuing him from his abductors, while King, Bishop and Knight waited for transport to the Congo.

Despite his grumblings, Rook knew that this task was critical to the mission's success. Restoring Mulamba to power was probably the only way to prevent total chaos in Central Africa. The president was popular, and had received an overwhelming majority of the vote in the election that had put him in power. His return might not end the coup launched by General Velle, but it would erode the rebel power base to the point where further violence would be limited in scope. If Mulamba was already dead, there might be no stopping what had begun, but if his enemies had wanted him dead, they would have simply assassinated him and left his body behind with the two murdered bodyguards. Finding Mulamba was the most important part of Chess Team's new mission. Nevertheless, Rook felt as if he'd been taken out of the game.

Deep Blue, using the almost unlimited computing power at his disposal, had done what the combined resources of London law enforcement could not: he'd found Mulamba. Well, probably found him.

Mulamba's kidnappers had abandoned the SUV in an alley, hidden from the view of the closed circuit television cameras that lined most London streets. The police had checked the footage from cameras in the area, but had been unable to identify the kidnappers' waiting getaway vehicle. Deep Blue had taken the additional step of collecting all the camera feeds going back to the site of the abduction, near Hyde Park, and cobbled them together into a virtual recreation of the crime. There were several gaps in the record, but it was easy enough to connect the dots. When the full picture resolved, he found a significant time gap. The SUV had stopped for almost a full minute in one of the CCTV blind spots. Deep Blue believed that the kidnappers had used this break to transfer Mulamba to another car, and then continued on to the alley several miles away where the driver ultimately dumped the vehicle and escaped on foot.

Figuring that out had been the easy part. What he did next would have been nearly impossible without the quantum computer.

Deep Blue had used the footage from multiple cameras to track every single car that moved away from the suspected transfer point, and through a process of elimination, identified the getaway car. He then tracked the vehicle to a rural area near Dartford, about twenty miles southeast of London. By the time Queen and Rook deplaned at Heathrow, Mulamba's location had been pinpointed.

After picking up their rental car, Queen and Rook had made just one stop, at the main branch of the Royal & General Bank to collect the contents of a safe deposit box, which included two SIG Pro pistols with spare magazines, two SOG Ops M40TK-CP combat knives and several bundles of £20 and £50 banknotes.

Rook cruised past the driveway entrance to the farmhouse, letting Queen handle the visual surveillance, and continued down the road for another half a mile before pulling off and parking on the shoulder. "So, dumb tourists?"

"I'm thinking feminine wiles might work better. I'll distract them while you try to sneak in the back door."

Rook managed an enthusiastic grin to hide the fact that he wasn't entirely happy with the thought of her going up the long drive alone. He couldn't help feeling protective, especially now that they were together, but he knew better than to voice these concerns. She would knock him senseless for even thinking it.

Good thing she's not a mind reader, he thought, then glanced at her to make sure.

While Queen sauntered down the road, making a show out of enjoying the scenic vistas and fresh air, Rook looked over the hedgerow bordering the nearby field, watching for trouble. With his glasses on maximum zoom, he could just make out two figures near the farmhouse—one milling near the front entrance, and one standing on a gabled second-floor balcony. He couldn't see any weapons and at this distance the facial recognition software was useless, but the men didn't look like farmers to him.

He chose a circuitous path that afforded the best level of concealment behind trees and hedges. At a fast jog, he was able to cover most of the distance in the time it took for Queen to reach the driveway. When she strolled toward the house, waving like a bikini-clad model at a boat show, he darted from the fence line to a barn right behind the two-story house.

Although none of the men were now directly in his view, there were yellow dots floating before his eyes, marking the location of the men he had spotted earlier, along with two more that had come out to greet Queen.

"Hey guys," he heard her say. "Is this the house where Shakespeare wrote *A Midsummer Night's Dream*? Am I in the right place?"

"Should have gone with *Much Ado About Nothing*," Rook muttered, knowing that only she could hear.

"My boyfriend told me it was," she continued, a hint of flirtation in her voice, "but he's kind of a tool, if you know what I mean."

"You've got the wrong place. You need to leave. Now." Rook heard the tone of menace in the voice. The man wasn't buying the dumb blonde routine, and the only thing aroused by Queen's good looks were his suspicions.

Rook snuck to the corner of the house, crouching under the windows, as he made his way to the back door. The knob turned smoothly in his hand, and he eased the door inward a few inches, and then a few more. It wasn't until he had opened it enough to slip through that he realized someone was in the room beyond. Fortunately, the man's attention was turned toward the front of the house and Queen's performance.

One of the yellow dots abruptly went red as the facial recognition program identified a man outside. Rook ignored the information scrolling in front of his eyes, focusing on the room—a dining room, with a scattering of paper plates and plastic cups on the cheap table—and on all the places where another hostile might be lurking. Seeing no one else, he slipped inside and crept up behind the man.

More yellow dots changed to red, and Rook had to fight the urge to rip the glasses off. He was about to kill a man, and he didn't need any distractions.

He slipped the SOG knife from its sheath and struck like a viper. In one fluid motion, he wrapped his left arm around the man's head, covering nose and mouth with the crook of his elbow, and rammed the blade into the base of the man's skull, instantly severing the spinal cord between the Atlas and Axis vertebrae. There wasn't much blood, but the wound was instantly fatal, and the man went limp, like his bones had turned to jelly. Rook didn't let him fall, but instead dragged the lifeless body back across the room to the dining table and eased him into one of the chairs. As he did, the quantum computer recognized the dead man.

His name was Michael Caruthers, a former Royal Marine. Caruthers's military record was an open book, but there was scant information since his discharge four years earlier. Rook had a pretty good idea what that meant. Caruthers was a mercenary.

Emphasis on 'was,' Rook thought.

He didn't feel the least bit of remorse at taking the man's life. He had more regard for the terrorists and fanatics that he'd fought than he did for this man, who had once pledged to give his life for Queen and country, but now was willing to kill for a buck...or whatever they called it here.

He patted down the corpse and found a Skorpion vz. 68 machine pistol in a shoulder holster. The compact weapon, produced in mass quantities by Czechoslovakia during the Cold War, was cheap, and if you knew the right people, it was easy to come by, even somewhere like the United Kingdom, where access to firearms was strictly regulated. Except for the curved twenty-round magazine positioned forward of the handgrip, the Skorpion didn't look much different than a regular semi-auto, but it was lighter and smaller than one of Rook's Desert Eagles, especially with its wire stock folded forward over the barrel. Rook decided to leave it behind. It would just get in the way.

Caruthers had been standing at an arched entryway to a sitting room with a clear view of the front door. Rook could see another of the men—red-tagged as another former military man turned hired gun—standing in the doorway, facing Queen. There was no one else in the room, but there was a staircase leading up. Rook figured his chances of making it up the stairs unnoticed weren't great, but they wouldn't get any better by waiting.

"Take it up a notch," he whispered, "and then get ready to break contact."

"Actually," Queen said, in a voice loud enough that he would have heard even without the glasses, "you remind me a lot of my boyfriend. Big and dumb."

Rook rolled his eyes, then made his move, crossing swiftly to the stairs. The banister spindles wouldn't provide much cover, but he ducked low and ascended the carpeted steps slowly, on all fours, like a stalking cat.

"Last warning," the man at the door growled. "Get lost."

"Fine," Queen said. "I'm going. But I'm gonna tell my boyfriend what an asshole you are, and he'll be pissed. He might even come here himself and kick your ass."

"You tell 'em, babe," Rook said, under his breath. He reached the landing and checked both ways before continuing. There was a yellow icon floating to his left, beyond a closed door, marking the man on the balcony he had seen from afar. Rook's instincts told him that this man was more than just a lookout. Mulamba was probably in that room, too.

He crept down the hall, checking each door along the way—a bathroom and two bedrooms, all unoccupied—and came to the door at the end, behind which the unidentified gunman waited.

"Activate X-ray vision mode," he whispered, and smiled.

Deep Blue's voice immediately sounded in his head. "Sorry. There's no app for that. Yet."

"Useless." Rook knocked softly on the door.

"Yeah?"

A couple more muffled inquiries followed and Rook could hear the sound of someone moving through the room. When the doorknob started to turn, Rook threw his weight against the door, slamming it into the man on the other side, knocking him backward. Rook let his momentum carry him into the room. He pounced on the still uncomprehending mercenary and drove the knife blade down into the man's sternum, covering the body with his own and clamping a hand over the mortally wounded man's mouth to silence any outcry.

"What the—?"

Rook felt a cold surge of panic shoot through his veins. *Two guys! Crap!*

He looked up, saw another man standing near the French doors that opened onto the balcony. There was one more person in the room as well, a man that Rook recognized instantly as the president of the Democratic Republic of the Congo. Joseph Mulamba was tied to a chair and had a strip of silver tape over his mouth, but his eyes were alive with emotion—fear and maybe something like hope. Rook was only peripherally aware of Mulamba. His attention was fixed on the other captor, the man who was struggling to unholster his Skorpion.

Rook didn't bother trying to wrench the SOG knife free of the corpse, but launched himself at the still living threat. He cleared the distance in a single leap and drove the man back, through the open doors and onto the balcony where they crashed together in a heap. Rook succeeded in trapping the man's right arm across his abdomen, but he hadn't been fast enough to keep his foe from drawing the machine pistol. The gunman's finger tightened on the trigger and the pistol sandwiched between their bodies erupted in a burst of noise and lead.

A searing blast of heat scorched Rook's chest where it was pressed against the gun. The pain was sudden and intense enough that he thought he'd been shot, but he didn't let the injury slow him down. As the mercenary fought to get his weapon free, Rook delivered a knife-hand blow to the man's throat that ended all resistance. Rook rolled off the stricken mercenary, but it wasn't until he heard more shooting that he realized that stealth was no longer an option.

"Two down," he heard Queen say. "I'm coming in. Don't shoot me."

"Wait." Rook was still feeling a little disoriented after the unexpected struggle with the mercenary. He looked around and met the eyes of the bound hostage, the man they were here to rescue. "I think we're clear. Stay put. I'll be right down."

"Roger."

He moved over to Mulamba and plucked off the tape covering the man's mouth. Mulamba winced as the adhesive took a layer of skin, but he immediately broke into a smile. "Thank you, my friend."

"Call me Rook. And don't thank me until we're out of here." He saw that the mercenaries had used half-inch wide wire-reinforced zip-ties to secure Mulamba's arms and legs in place. He reached for his knife then remembered where he'd left it, buried in the chest of the mercenary near the entrance to the room. He'd driven it deep, and as he struggled to wrench it free, he felt like an unworthy knight trying to draw Excalibur from the stone.

"Uh, oh," Queen said.

Rook didn't like the sound of that.

A shout drifted in through the open balcony doors—definitely not Queen's voice—and a moment later, he heard two more sharp reports.

He definitely didn't like the sound of that.

He began wiggling the blade back and forth until it finally came free. Ignoring the blood that now dripped down onto his hand, he hastened back to the prisoner and slipped the blade underneath the zip-ties.

Queen spat a curse. "Alamo time. I'm coming in."

"Where'd they come from?" He gave the blade a twist and the plastic restraint parted, but not before pulling taut against Mulamba's wrist. "Sorry," he muttered.

"This is not a time to be gentle, Rook." The man spoke with an almost musical accent. "Do what you must. No worries."

Rook laughed in spite of the urgency of the moment. "No worries. *Hakuna matata*, right?"

Mulamba's smile broadened. "You speak Swahili?"

"Not exactly." He moved the blade to the second tie.

"I'm coming up," Queen shouted. "They've got both exits covered. Hope you've got an alternate exit up there."

"Damn. Where did these guys come from?" Rook caught Mulamba's blank look and added, "Sorry, Mr. President, got my girlfriend on the other line."

"Call me Joe."

Rook nodded.

"Not sure," Queen said. "Might have been in the barn."

"The barn? Damn." There had been five men in the house, and now a force of unknown size was swarming out of the barn.

Somebody had gone to great lengths to make sure that Mulamba didn't get away.

He cut the remaining bonds and then scooped up a discarded Skorpion. "Know how to use one of these, Joe?"

The African president eyed the weapon with distaste, as if the thought of firing it brought back bad memories, but then he nodded and took it. He unfolded the collapsible stock and snugged it to his shoulder. "I do."

"Coming in!" Queen shouted. She appeared at the doorway a moment later and dropped into a crouch beside the opening. She risked a quick glance in Rook's direction, and then said simply: "They're coming."

ELEVEN

Near Lake Kivu, Democratic Republic of the Congo

Felice Carter awoke to the sound of gunfire.

She rolled from her cot, still bleary-eyed, uncertain whether the noise was something from a dream or something real. Then there was another report, the chattering sound of a machine gun, and she knew it wasn't her imagination.

The war had found them.

The tent flap flew back and she jerked in alarm, but it was only Sam.

"Felice! The rebels are attacking. We have to leave!"

She scooted her backpack out from beneath her cot and slung it over one shoulder. They had known that this was a possibility and had prepared accordingly. As much as she had wanted to believe that the storm would pass, leaving them untouched, she had not let herself give in to the seductive lethargy of denial. She had packed her go-bag and slept in her clothes...

Just in case this happened.

The noise of machine gun fire was almost constant, and close enough that the sound itself was an assault on the senses. Sam urged her on with an impatient wave, then turned and ducked through the flap. She was only a few steps behind him when he suddenly jerked as if he'd stepped on a live wire. He pitched backward. A series of red splotches dotted his torso, gushing dark blood.

Felice skidded to a halt, throwing herself flat beside him. Over the staccato reports, she heard a different sound, like someone beating on the heavy canvas walls of her shelter, and a line of holes appeared in the fabric, allowing the early morning sunlight to stream in along with the sulfur smell of burnt gunpowder.

She crawled away from Sam's body, retreating to the back of the tent. Leaving through the front wasn't an option but she had to get out and reach the rest of the team.

She slipped her Gerber folding multi-tool from its sheath on her belt and opened the knife blade. More rounds pierced the tent above her head, but she focused on what she had to do. She stabbed the knife point through the heavy canvas and worked it back and forth, sawing open a hole big enough to crawl through. Through the cut doorway, she could see the dark brown and green of the rain forest, just twenty yards away, looking as foreboding as the first time she had glimpsed it. The jungle wasn't where she wanted to be, but it would get her away from the gunmen.

She edged out, just far enough to make sure the coast was clear, and then launched herself through the opening. In her peripheral vision, she could see the other tents lined up beside hers with almost military precision, twenty of them in all. Ten of them were for the science team, herself and her colleagues, and five more were for their locally hired support team, the latter sleeping four to a tent. Thirty people in all, twenty-nine now that Sam was dead. She wondered how many of the others were still alive.

She reached the edge of the clearing and crouched behind the nearest tree. The tents blocked her view of the attack, but she could see a low pall of smoke hanging over the camp. Above the din of weapons fire, she could hear shouting—the gunmen bellowing orders mixed with cries of terror from the victims.

Keeping to the tree line, she ran toward the south end of the camp. When they had learned of the political upheaval in distant Kinshasa, they had made a contingency plan to evacuate at the first sign of trouble, but this attack had come without warning. She wondered if anyone had made it to the trucks parked at the center of the camp, and if they had already left without her. All of the local men carried rifles, and she knew that at least some of the shooting was probably defensive fire. Perhaps they were holding off the attackers long enough for the scientists to make their escape. It was something to hope for, but she didn't think it very likely.

Staying low, she darted from the cover of the trees and made for the corner of the last tent in the row. It was, she recalled, where they kept supplies and food stores. It seemed likely that the contents of the tent were what the attackers might want most, but the situation had escalated beyond the point where the expedition could buy their safety by surrendering their stores. The attackers clearly intended to kill everyone and take whatever they pleased.

She crawled along the side of the tent and peeked around the front facing corner. She allowed herself only a quick glimpse, just long enough to take a mental snapshot of the camp, before pulling back and processing what she had just seen. It was enough to lift her out of despair.

One of the trucks was idling. She hadn't been able to identify the driver, but there were three figures huddled in the bed of the vehicle. Two more were crouched behind the front end, taking careful shots with their rifles in the direction of the attacking force.

She had seen the enemy as well, at least a few of them, arrayed at the far end of the camp, crouching behind trees, content to pin their victims down until they lost the will or the ability to resist.

The space in between was littered with unmoving forms. People she knew. People she had lived with, worked with, shared meals with, joked with, gossiped with and sometimes fought with. Her friends. Dead.

She felt something stir in her gut—a primal creature too long subdued, with the scent of blood in its nostrils.

"No."

The plea was a whimper, inaudible to anyone who might have been close enough to hear. *I shouldn't have come here*, she thought. *Shouldn't have taken the risk.* The beast—the ghost of a distant primitive creature that had become bound to her like a shadow during an expedition in Ethiopia two years earlier—responded to her rising fear. When it had first possessed her, the beast had nearly destroyed her mind, and in the resulting fugue state, had responded to external threats by destroying the minds of her attackers. She had mastered it, learned to control her emotions, but fear was like a fire that, once ignited, burned out of control. If the beast awoke, the world would burn. She squeezed her eyes shut, trying to erase the image of horror from her mind.

"Felice!" The shout snapped her back into the moment, the bestial presence momentarily subdued. She opened her eyes and saw Derrick, hunkered down in the bed of the truck but waving to her, urging her to join them.

Yes. Escape. But how will they get past—

There was a deafening boom, and in the instant that followed, she saw something streak out of the forest beyond the camp entrance and strike the front end of the truck. Then a wave of darkness crashed over her.

Her awareness returned in a blaze of green and blue. She was on her back, staring up at the sky. The noise of the battle was gone. All she could hear now was a low tone, like microphone feedback. She felt strangely tranquil, and for a moment, she dared to believe that the attack had been a nightmare from which she was just now truly waking. Then she tried to breathe, and when her lungs refused to draw so much as a gasp, the terror returned with a vengeance.

Sensations bombarded her: smothering heat, something stinging her eyes like a chemical burn, pain shooting through every nerve of her body. The ringing in her ears started to diminish, replaced by the crackle and roar of a fire. Her breath finally caught, but instead of fresh air, she drew in a choking miasma of burning metal and plastic, the sulfur of gunpowder and high explosives, and ghastlier still, the odor of cooking meat.

Where the truck had been, there was only a blackened shell, dominated by flames and a pillar of dark smoke. The vehicle, however, was not the only thing burning. The tent behind which she had been hiding—or rather what remained of the flattened, shredded canopy—was also ablaze.

The darkness surged through her, not just in her gut but electrifying every fiber of her being. She told herself to run, to escape back into the woods where the killers would not find her, and where she might, just might, be able to quiet the beast before it tore through her defenses and laid waste to everything, but her body betrayed her. She could do little more than turn her head to witness the holocaust that had devoured her friends and would soon burn her as well...and when she burned, the world would burn.

A shape emerged from the smoke, a man, tall and thin almost to the point of looking emaciated. He wore no uniform—just tattered jeans and a t-shirt—but the rifle he carried marked him as one of their attackers. He pointed the weapon at her, but there was not a hint of wariness in the way he moved. The battle was over, and he was about to claim the spoils due the victor.

Felice struggled to move, willing herself to get to her feet...to run...but it didn't happen. She lay there, unable to move, and as the man drew closer...twenty feet...ten...she knew that there would be no escape.

"Kill me," she rasped, and in his eyes, she saw that he would, but only after he was done with her.

Suddenly, the man pitched back as if slapped by an invisible hand. A red mist settled over his unmoving form. Two more men had come into the camp behind him, and they were instantly on their guard, ducking for cover behind the flaming wreckage, shouting in confusion and alarm.

One of them went down, his head practically dissolving in a spray of crimson.

The remaining man screamed an unintelligible curse and broke from his place of concealment. He only got a few steps before the same unseen force struck out like divine vengeance and dropped him in his tracks.

Was someone still alive? One of their local guides perhaps?

There was more shouting and sporadic gunfire from the forest, but it seemed distant now, unthreatening. With the immediate threat removed, Felice felt her self-control returning, and as the beast retreated back into quiescence, she was able to move again. She rolled onto her side, away from the burning tent, and then managed to sit up.

An ominous quiet fell over the jungle; the shouts and shooting had stopped.

Suddenly, she realized she wasn't alone. A figure stepped into view, as if materializing out of the smoke. Her first thought was that he looked like one of the tree people from *The Lord of the Rings*—*Ents*, she remembered, *they're called Ents*—brown and green, covered with what looked like leaves and moss, and as big as a walking tree trunk. It was camouflage, she knew. There was a man underneath it all, a man carrying an enormous machine gun. His face became clearer, peeking out from beneath a tree colored hat that was covered with leaves and twigs. His face was streaked with green and gray paint, and his eyes hid behind a pair of dark sunglasses, but she could tell by his features that he wasn't African.

"Are you all right?"

The voice sounded faint, distant, as if a much greater space separated them, as if he was speaking from another plane of reality. He repeated the question again as he finished crossing the distance and knelt beside her.

"I don't know," she croaked, and she discovered that she couldn't hear her own voice very well either.

With surprising gentleness for someone so big, the man put his hands on her shoulders and peered into her face. "I'm a friend. You're safe now, Miss Carter."

TWELVE

"**How do you** know my name?"

Bishop winced a little. Felice Carter was shouting and didn't even realize it. *Hearing damage from the explosion,* he decided. *Nothing permanent.*

"I was sent to get you out," he said. It was a lie, though more an omission than an outright falsehood, and given the circumstances, a full explanation wouldn't have made much difference. "I'm sorry we didn't get here sooner."

He had not been sent to get her specifically. He hadn't even known the names of the people he'd been sent to rescue. Domenick Boucher hadn't provided much more than a general location for what he described as 'a science expedition researching some kind of renewable energy project.' As they had flown over the area aboard *Crescent II*—Chess Team's dedicated supersonic stealth transport plane—they'd spied the attack already underway. At that point, more information about the individuals under fire wouldn't have made much difference to the outcome. He and Knight had HALO jumped from 25,000 feet—high enough that no one on the ground had even heard the plane passing overhead—but the only clear drop zone had been the shallows of Lake Kivu, which necessitated a damp hike through very unfamiliar terrain to reach the camp.

Bishop had assumed they would be Congolese nationals, but Felice Carter was an American. He had been able to make the almost instantaneous identification thanks to the facial recognition software in his glasses. There hadn't been time for him to fully process all the accompanying information, but two words had jumped out at him.

Geneticist.

Manifold.

Felice Carter had once worked for Richard Ridley, the man who had injected Bishop with the regen serum, sending him on a hellish journey to the edge of madness and back.

He shut this information away in a distant corner of his mind. Her association with Manifold did not automatically make her a villain. Anna Beck, Knight's girlfriend and currently chief of operations for the Endgame organization, had also once worked for Ridley. Moreover, there was enough additional information about Felice—something involving King and the Brainstorm crisis—for him to recognize that her work for Ridley was only a small sliver of her life story.

Doesn't matter, he thought. *My mission is to save her, not judge her.*

"We?" she asked after a moment. "You're not alone?"

"I brought a friend. Can you walk? We need to get out of here. The rebels will be back."

She tried to rise, reaching out to use Bishop for leverage. He remained there, kneeling to provide support, until she succeeded. He stayed there a moment longer, looking up at her, checking her for any signs of injury.

Where her coffee-colored skin was exposed—her forearms and face—there were raw abrasions too numerous to count, but all appeared superficial. Felice was tall, not quite six-foot he guessed, and she was lean and fit beneath her slightly scorched khakis and work shirt. She was attractive, too, though for Bishop this was nothing more than one more observation to be filed away. Appearances could be deceiving, and this was especially true of beautiful appearances—Queen was living proof of that.

He finally rose to his feet, towering over her once more, and turned away to let his gaze roam over the wreckage of the camp. His eyes were immediately drawn to the bodies, more than a dozen sprawled out in the open area near the burning truck. There was no sign of movement and he didn't hold out much hope that there were other survivors, but he had to make sure.

"Stay right here," he told her.

She nodded, but then tilted her head as if remembering something. "There's some data in the lab tent that I should bring."

Several of the tents had been knocked flat, and some were burning. Even those that still stood, furthest out from where the truck had exploded, were shot full of holes. "Which one?"

She pointed down the row, and then started moving in that direction, as if he had given her permission. Bishop frowned. He had been hoping to spare her the sight of her dead colleagues, but there was no turning her back now. Fortunately, she seemed to have developed a kind of tunnel vision, which Bishop knew often happened to people in a crisis. She passed so close to one corpse that she almost stepped on a hand, but she didn't seem to notice. The tent she sought had partially collapsed, but she threw back the flap and went inside as if nothing at all was wrong. Bishop just shook his head and turned back to surveying the camp.

"Deep Blue, this is Bishop." He didn't actually need to identify himself. The q-phones rendered traditional radio protocols completely obsolete, but old habits died hard. "We're going to need extraction here, ASAP."

"Understood," Deep Blue replied. He didn't ask about whether or not they had succeeded in rescuing the science team. Deep Blue was able to see everything and already knew the situation. "How secure is that location?"

"Not very. We got five of them." Knight had taken out the three in the camp with his Intervention sniper rifle. Bishop had found two more hanging back at the edge of the camp and dispatched them without a shot. "But there were several more that retreated. My guess is, they'll be back with more friends."

"*Crescent* is dropping off King and Pawn in Kinshasa right now. It can be back at your location in one hour."

Bishop thought that estimate was a bit optimistic. Kinshasa was more than 900 miles away, but *Crescent* could manage Mach Two if the pilots didn't care about burning up all the fuel, so it was possible. "Roger. We'll try to establish a secure LZ. Bishop, out."

The sign-off was another ingrained and totally unnecessary response. Deep Blue would continue to monitor everything he and Knight said and did, and would respond to them as easily as if he was standing there with them.

Felice emerged from the tent a moment later, now carrying a black backpack. "Got it."

She stopped in her tracks, as if being in the lab tent had magically transported her away from everything that had happened, and coming out had snapped her back into the moment. Bishop interposed himself between her and the carnage, drawing her gaze to his face. In an attempt to look a little more human, he removed his boonie hat with its adornment of fern stalks and other jungle flora, and gave her a reassuring nod. "Our ride will be here soon. Let's find a nice safe place to settle down and wait."

She nodded and made no effort to look around him, as he guided her back to the south end of the camp, where she had hidden earlier. He found a folding camp chair that had somehow come through the attack unscathed, and gestured for her to sit. "Now, one more time. Stay put, okay?"

Another nod.

Bishop straightened and did another 360 degree sweep of the camp. He had to do a double-take when he saw a chess piece icon floating above what looked like a pile of leaves, just ten yards away. Knight had entered the camp without making a sound, and his ghillie suit—an over-garment made from strips of camouflage netting and burlap—rendered him virtually invisible, even when standing right next to him.

"Sneaky," Bishop remarked.

Knight grinned up at him. "You make it sound like a bad thing."

"I'm just jealous." Bishop gestured to the camp. "We'd better do a sweep and then dig in. Could be a while before our ride shows up."

"I heard." Knight rose from his prone firing position and slung his perfectly camouflaged rifle across his back. He surveyed the wreckage and in a grim voice, added, "I don't think there's much left to sweep."

Bishop had no reply to that, but before he could simply turn away, a loud pop sounded from somewhere out in the jungle. Another sound like it followed almost immediately.

Bishop spun on his heel and threw himself at an uncomprehending Felice, tackling her to the ground and covering her with his own body. Knight dove down by his side. With no way of knowing where the rounds would fall, there were only two practical courses of action in response to incoming mortar fire:

Get down, and pray.

Bishop listened for the distinctive shriek that would herald the arrival of the explosive ordnance. The longer the noise lasted, the more likely the shell would fall well off the mark. If they were lucky, the whistling noise would last several seconds. The shells would hit a hundred yards or more from their location, putting them well outside the radius of a lethal shrapnel storm. That would give them plenty of time to pick up and run before gun crews could adjust fire and drop two more shells into their tubes.

They weren't lucky.

THIRTEEN

Kinshasa, Democratic Republic of the Congo

King crouched on the end of the ramp poised to hop down as soon as the ground was close enough. Hot jet exhaust, caught between the tarmac—which was still a good ten yards away—and *Crescent II*'s enormous turbofan thrusters, swirled around him and into the open cargo bay of the stealth transport. The exhaust was alternately trying to blast him back and suck him out. He glanced over at his sister and flashed her a grin.

Asya clung to the hydraulic cylinder on the opposite corner of the ramp, but she managed to loosen her death grip just long enough to flip him the bird.

Must be Rook's influence, King mused.

Crescent II dipped low with a stomach shaking lurch, followed by a strong jolt as the deployed landing gear bounced on the pavement. The pilots weren't going to land completely. There wasn't time for that if they were to have a chance of getting back to the Kivu region to pick up Bishop and Knight. This was as close to the ground as they were going to get.

"Go!" King shouted, and then he leaped down from the ramp.

Asya dropped beside him, flexing her knees to absorb the impact with the ground and putting out one hand to steady herself. She made it look easy. King didn't know Asya nearly as well as a brother should know a sister, but he felt a flash of familial pride. She reminded him a lot of Julie, the older sister he had grown up with and who had inspired him to join the Army in the first place. Over the years, his memories of Julie had faded and the sting of her tragic death in a military training accident had diminished to the point where he sometimes had trouble remembering that his two sisters were not the same person.

There was a loud roar as *Crescent*'s pilot cranked up the turbos and pushed the jet back up into the sky. King and Asya stayed crouched down to avoid being knocked over by the rush of air and waited until the storm abated. In a matter of seconds, the stealth plane appeared to shrink, and then the thrusters swiveled to cruising configuration. It took off like a rocket.

Only now did King take a moment to survey the landing zone, a large open area of tarmac adjacent to the runway of the N'Djili International Airport. The east terminal building lay off to their left, the gates currently occupied by three passenger jets. A line of green military vehicles, each with a crew of soldiers, separated them from the terminal. One of the trucks started forward, and King did not fail to note that the gunner in the center-mounted turret had his machine gun trained on Asya and himself.

"Easy does it," King said. The admonition was directed at Asya, but he hoped the soldiers approaching them heeded it as well.

The vehicle stopped a few yards away and three men, all dressed in woodland camouflage fatigues and wearing red berets, got out. One of them, the only one not brandishing an AKS-74 semi-automatic carbine, strode forward. He had a broad smile, which was at odds with everything else in the picture, but King returned a grin and raised a hand in salute.

"*Bon jour,*" the man said, greeting King like an old friend. He gave an answering salute before continuing in French. "I am Brigadier General Jean-Claude Mabuki, commander of the Republican Guard. We've been expecting you."

King had no trouble understanding the man, and probably could have carried on a conversation in a few of the languages commonly used in the African nation. During the course of his long journey through time, he had learned dozens of languages, and not just as a matter of survival. He had intentionally sought out opportunities to learn tongues that he knew were still widely used in the twenty-first century. French was a piece of cake.

King introduced them using only their callsigns. If Mabuki found this strange, he gave no indication. He looked them over and his smile slipped a notch. "Only two? I had hoped your country would be able to provide a larger force."

"Officially, my country isn't providing anything. We're here unofficially."

"Yes, I understand. Still, I'm not certain what you will be able to do to help us."

"I'm not really certain either," King admitted. "But if you can brief us on the situation, I'll have a better idea."

"Of course. Please, come with me. I will take you to meet with President Okoa." He gestured to the vehicle. The soldiers accompanying him opened doors on either side, and once King, Asya and the general were seated, they closed the doors and climbed up onto the roof of the vehicle.

As they drove around the terminal building, Mabuki briefly summarized the state of his country. The events were mostly the same as what Boucher had reported, but Mabuki provided insights that the official report could not.

"General Velle has the Army on his side," he explained. "They have been waiting for just such an opportunity to make their move."

"Why did President Mulamba not remove him from power?" Asya asked in heavily accented, but nonetheless passable French.

Mabuki gave a patient smile. "Africa is a complicated place, my friends. The simple answer is that many of the senior officers are loyal to Velle. The only way to prevent Velle from leading a coup was to keep him in his position. Velle is strong, but his control of the Army is not absolute. And he does not control the Republican Guard. We are loyal to the President. But there are many other players in this game. Arms dealers, mercenaries, rebels. They are loyal to no one, and they support whomever will make them wealthy. And the people will support whomever can keep them safe."

Mabuki elaborated further on the various factions that were contributing to the unrest as they made their way through the capital city, but King was only half-listening. It was a familiar story, and one that he had witnessed too many times to count. In the streets, he saw the signs of a populace gripped by fear of the unknowable future. There were soldiers everywhere, and military and police checkpoints every few blocks. Civilians carried on their daily activities, but there was a tension in their movements, as if one and all were prepared to bolt for cover at the first sign of trouble. It was a powder keg, and there was no way of knowing if the spark that would set it off had already been struck.

They arrived at the *Palais de la Nation*, the seat of power in the country, in name at least. The three story building was a sprawling structure that might have looked more like a college stadium than a government office, if not for the hundreds of soldiers milling about in the foreground. The walls were a flat and featureless white on what appeared to be concrete slab construction. A domed roof rose up from the middle of the structure. From the street it reminded King of the *Legion of Doom* headquarters from Saturday morning cartoons. Mabuki escorted them through a blue and yellow painted gate that separated the street from the brick walkway leading into the palace.

As they entered the palace grounds, King heard Deep Blue's voice. "King, I have bad news. There's no way to sugar coat this. I've lost contact with Bishop and Knight."

The words hit King like a plunge into an icy lake. He heard Asya give a little gasp, but like him, she kept moving, putting one foot in front of the next. "Lost contact?" King asked through clenched teeth. "What's that mean? Are they dead?"

"It means their q-phones aren't working anymore. They were alive when I lost the signal, but the rebels were firing mortars on their position. We built those phones to take a beating. The fact that we lost both signals at the same time..." Deep Blue didn't finish the sentence. He didn't need to. "It gets worse. Queen and Rook found Mulamba in a farmhouse outside London. He's alive, but they're pinned down. I thought you should know."

"Understood. Keep me posted. King, out."

Damn it!

FOURTEEN

The shit had hit the fan, and there wasn't a thing King could do to help any of them. The instantaneous connectivity afforded by the q-phones made him feel all the more helpless. The Chess Team were the best soldiers on Earth. If anyone could get out of a tough scrape, he knew they could, but that didn't make dealing with it any easier.

He flashed back to the conference call just a few hours earlier. It had not been as difficult to convince Deep Blue to commit to the operation as King had initially feared. Like the others, the former president felt the same compulsion to defend the innocent and the helpless—the ones who would almost certainly die first if the situation in the Congo continued to deteriorate. Because he was no longer constrained by political realities, the former president was actually eager to do something, anything, even if it seemed like a desperate long shot. His restraint stemmed, not from an ambivalence toward the plight of the Congo's people, but from a very real concern about putting his people in harm's way for a goal that was, at best, unclear.

King understood that kind of thinking better than Tom Duncan ever could. He had spent nearly three thousand years focused on one objective—saving his friends and family. It had become a sort of mania, almost impossible to let go of. Like an overprotective parent, he had become so used to the idea of saving them that now he couldn't bear to see them at risk. But risk was what they did. They were, one and all, willing to sacrifice anything, their lives if necessary, for a greater good, just as he was.

Easy to say, but a lot harder to accept, especially after centuries focused on the single goal of keeping them alive.

And for what? So they could die senseless deaths just a year later?

He choked down his helplessness and anger, and he followed Mabuki into the presidential palace. The general led them to a large conference room where several people were already gathered around a table. Given the awkward silence that followed their arrival, King guessed they had probably been arguing.

As he moved his gaze about the room, his glasses began supplying him with biographical data. The photosensitive lenses were now barely tinted, and would hopefully be passed off as ordinary spectacles. None of those present could see the information being beamed onto King's and Asya's retinas—the names of Congolese assemblymen and military officers, tribal leaders and of course, acting President Gerard Okoa. Not everyone in the room was African, however. A group of Caucasians sat near the president, two men with the sort of muscular physiques that could be achieved only through the use of illegal chemical substances—King dubbed them 'the steroid twins'—and another older man with doughy features and slicked back hair. King's attention, however, was drawn to the fourth person in their group, a stunningly beautiful woman with dark hair, who focused her laser-like stare in their direction.

Asya narrowed her eyes and stared back. "We don't like her," she muttered in Russia.

King knew his sister wasn't merely being catty. There was something dangerous about this woman, and she made no effort to hide it.

A name appeared before his eyes, seemingly superimposed over the woman's face. *Monique Favreau. Former officer of the DGSE. Presently field director of Executive Solutions International.*

King knew that name very well. ESI was a notorious private security company. Not just mercenaries, but an army of mercenaries. Only the wealthiest corporations could afford ESI—the diamond cartel and petroleum multinationals—and certainly not a poor developing nation in Africa. If ESI was involved, it meant that someone with a lot of money and power had taken an interest in the Congo situation.

Mabuki introduced King and Asya simply as 'advisors from the United States' and no one questioned it. King got the sense that there was a lot of advising going on. As they took seats, the acting president addressed them.

"More Americans." Okoa was a blunt man in both word and appearance. He was not exactly overweight, but thick, like an unfinished clay statue. "Why are you here?"

King studied him, wondering how much he could say about what they hoped to accomplish, and whether he could promise the man anything at all. Okoa claimed to be a strong supporter of Joseph Mulamba, but politicians could rarely be trusted to say anything that wasn't self-serving, and now that Okoa had a taste of power, King wondered if he would he still be faithful to Mulamba's vision of a unified Africa.

There seemed no point in lying to the man. "If I may speak frankly, Mr. President, my country is reluctant when it comes to interfering in the politics of a sovereign nation." Someone laughed aloud, a staccato sound, like the crack of a whip. It was the woman, Monique Favreau. King didn't stop. "But some of us are not willing to stand by and allow another genocide to take place."

Genocide was a powerful word. Even those who openly advocated the extermination of their hated enemies shied away from it.

Okoa was unmoved, though. "And since we have oil and natural gas, our genocide is much more interesting to you."

The not-so-thinly veiled accusation shocked King. "I don't know anything about that, sir."

"Is that so?" Okoa glanced toward Favreau and the other men. King did, too, and as he did, he heard Deep Blue mutter a rare curse.

An instant later, the facial recognition software displayed the name of the older Caucasian man. *Lance Marrs, United States Senator, Utah.*

Two years earlier, Marrs had taken advantage of an unfolding global crisis to target his number one political enemy, President Tom Duncan—Deep Blue. While Duncan and Domenick Boucher had ultimately turned Marrs's attack to their advantage, it had come at great expense. Duncan had been forced to resign from office in disgrace, providing endless fodder for late-night talk show comedians, and his accomplishments, the public ones at least, had been relegated to a footnote in history.

King realized that Marrs was staring back at him. "I'm not sure who you are, fella," the Senator said, oozing contempt. "I can only assume that President Chambers sent you here without the approval of the United States Congress."

"You can assume whatever you like," King said. "That's your standard operating procedure, isn't it?"

Marrs bristled, but King kept talking. "Speaking of assumptions, am I to assume that *you* have the approval of Congress?"

"I am on a fact-finding mission." Marrs enunciated each word as if that would somehow lend gravity to his statement. "This region may have strategic importance to the energy policy of the United States of America, so naturally my colleagues and I are concerned with maintaining stability."

King suddenly understood what Okoa had meant with his accusation. He didn't know exactly what kind of resources the Congo had to offer, but the evident collusion between Marrs and Executive Solutions International hinted at a well-funded agenda.

An agenda that would have been seriously threatened by Joseph Mulamba's plan to create a unified African federation.

Favreau spoke up. "Mr. President, we can end this crisis right now, right here in this room, without any meddling from foreign governments."

Okoa seemed to deflate a little. "And all it will cost me is the wealth of my nation."

"Sir, my employers do not want to take away the resources of your nation. They want a mutually beneficial partnership, that will help you and your citizens reap the benefits of those resources. What do you want to give your people? Jobs? Security? A future?" She cast a glance at King. "Or genocide?"

King subvocalized a message to Deep Blue. "Who is this bitch working for?"

Marrs was quick to add his input. "I am in complete agreement, sir. We do not, I can't stress that enough, do *not* want to meddle in your affairs. We want to help you help yourselves."

"ESI's client list is heavily safeguarded," Deep Blue said, "but the record of Marrs's campaign donors isn't. His super-PAC receives support from three different petroleum multinationals. Consolidated Energy tops that list. It's probably not a coincidence that Methods Logistics—the second largest oil field support company in the world—is headquartered in Salt Lake City."

King suddenly felt like he was in over his head. He was a soldier, a warrior, accustomed to dealing with threats head on. This was an entirely different kind of battlefield.

Deep Blue must have sensed his growing frustration. "Disengage," he advised. "You won't beat Marrs here. We need to find out more."

King scanned the faces in the room once more. Several of the politicians were nodding in evident support of Favreau's statement, and Okoa, too, seemed to be wavering.

King stood up and addressed the man at the head of the table. "Sir, it's not my place to advise you on matters of internal policy. I'm here to give you whatever support I can...until President Mulamba is restored to office."

The words had the desired effect. A stir of confusion arose among the government officials. Marrs looked bewildered. Favreau's gaze sharpened to its earlier intensity. She leaned back and whispered something to one of her steroid-infused goons.

She knows.

King drove the point deeper. "Maybe you haven't heard, but President Mulamba has been found. He's alive and well, and on his way back right now." *Please let it be true.* He turned to Asya. "Let's go."

No one stopped them from leaving the room, but as soon as they were in the hall outside, General Mabuki caught up to them. "Is this true? The President is alive?"

"He is." King didn't like deceiving the man with a half-truth, but revealing his uncertainty about Mulamba's fate would undermine what little advantage he had gained. "If you are as loyal to him as you claim, then let me help you hold this country together until he returns."

The general gave a pensive nod. "There is only so much that I can do, but I will try. I will speak to you again when the meeting is over."

When he was gone, Asya said, "Well that was fun. Are all your assignments like this?"

No, he almost said. *Usually there are monsters.*

Before he could utter the comment, a group of soldiers rushed toward them. At first, King thought they might be Mabuki's men, come to escort them to a place where they could await the general's return, but two things made him quickly realize this was not the case.

Unlike the Republican Guards he had seen thus far, these men were not wearing red berets. Rather, they wore soft patrol caps that matched their uniforms.

The second indicator was much more explicit.

The soldiers were all aiming their Kalashnikov carbines at him.

FIFTEEN

Dartford, England

Queen held her SIG out in a two-handed grip, the muzzle trained on the door. Behind her, Joseph Mulamba raised his weapon as well, but Rook placed a hand on the muzzle and gently pushed Mulamba behind him.

"Just stay back, sir," Rook said.

"Let him fight," Queen said, "When they come through that door, we're going to need all the firepower we can get."

Rook gave a nod. "I agree. So let's keep them on the other side of that door."

He advanced, his pistol at the ready, and knelt down. When he was as close to the opening as he dared get, he took his glasses off, set them on the floor so that the lenses were facing out, and then slid them out into the hallway.

Queen gave a little gasp of delight when she saw the result. It was like being able to see through the wall. Two figures, both tagged with a red icon, were creeping along the passage, just a few yards from the door. She raised two fingers to signal Rook, then inspiration dawned. She took a step back, aimed her pistol at the wall, and fired twice.

The bullets punched through the thin plaster and then kept right on going through the heads of the two mercenaries. Queen saw both men go down, the one closest to the door pitching forward, and then his image, along with everything else that was being transmitted in the virtual display, abruptly vanished. Just visible on the hall floor was the outstretched hand of the dead would-be attacker. The Skorpion pistol in his grip had landed squarely atop Rook's glasses, smashing them to bits.

"O-kay," Rook said slowly. "That wasn't quite what I had in mind."

"It was a good idea," Queen said. "I just wish we had a spare pair."

Deep Blue's voice sounded in her head. "You do. Use your glasses, Queen. You can use the q-phones to view the feed. I'll configure them remotely."

Queen relayed the message to Rook, and then took her q-phone out and placed her thumb on the dark screen to unlock it. It immediately glowed to life, and showed a picture of what Queen was looking at, which at that moment happened to be the phone in her hand, creating an infinity mirror effect. She took the glasses off and extended them around the door frame so that the phone screen showed the now empty hallway.

Rook was looking at the display of his phone as well, which also showed the feed from Queen's glasses. "Where'd they go?"

Queen knew there were at least three more gunmen, and possibly as many as six more, but evidently the loss of their vanguard had caused them to reconsider their tactics. "Keep watching the hall. I'm going to check the balcony."

Staying low, with the glasses held up over her head like a periscope, she crept through the French doors and scanned the ground below. She immediately spotted two mercenaries, crouched down behind a parked car in the driveway. Their guns were trained on the front of the house. The men were hunkered down. Not going anywhere.

They're covering someone, she realized, and extended the glasses out a little further, tilting them down to reveal the front porch almost directly beneath her. She expected to see a line of men preparing to storm the house, but something much worse waited below.

"Shit," she muttered.

There were more mercenaries near the front of the house, but they weren't getting ready to make a tactical entry. Instead, they had opted for a scorched earth policy—literally. Two men poured the contents of large red metal canisters onto the side of the house and all over the porch. If she had any doubts about what was in those cans, they were swept away when she caught a whiff of gasoline fumes.

There was no time to sort through the options. Queen placed her phone on the floor and raised her SIG. The weapon was equipped with a sensor that linked its holographic sight to the glasses, so now the phone showed not only the scene below but also a highlighted section where her shot would strike. She adjusted the barrel until it was centered on one of the gas-can toting mercenaries, and pulled the trigger.

The mercenary dropped, but before she could line up a second shot, the men by the cars opened fire on the balcony. As bullets hammered into the wooden railing, Queen was forced to retreat inside. She didn't see what happened next, but she could smell it. The odor of gasoline was replaced by something else: the acrid tang of smoke. At first, there were just a few wisps of black vapor, but in a matter of seconds, the smoke became a cloud, roiling with convection waves as the fire spread.

Rook crept out the bedroom door but returned a moment later, shaking his head, accompanied by a trail of smoke. "No good. The first floor is already engulfed. They must have doused it first."

"Looks like we've only got one way out," Queen said, jerking a thumb at the balcony.

Rook didn't challenge the assessment, and she knew he wouldn't. They had worked together—been together—long enough that they didn't need quantum technology to communicate. He stooped down and relieved one of the corpses of a Skorpion. He released the magazine, checked it and slammed it back in. "Out of the fire and into the frying pan."

"Don't be a pessimist," Queen said.

Rook grinned. "I was talking about them."

Queen returned his smile. "Right. Let's get cooking."

Mulamba didn't share their almost psychic bond. "What are you saying?"

"We're going that way." Queen pointed to the balcony.

"But they are out there!"

"Not for much longer," Rook said. He edged outside, using the smoke for concealment, and unleashed a burst from the machine pistol. Rounds sparked off the hood of the car parked below. A hand holding an identical weapon appeared above the front fender, and Rook drew back an instant before another volley raked the wall above the balcony. Rook was already back inside, so he didn't see the man at the other end of the car move out into the open, training his weapon on the doorway, ready to take a well-aimed shot the next time an opportunity presented itself.

Rook didn't see it, but Queen did. She saw everything in her phone's display and with just a slight adjustment, isolated the man in the targeting box and took the shot.

"Got him."

"Good, 'cause we gotta go right now."

Queen knew he wasn't exaggerating. The room was filling up with smoke, stinging her eyes and lungs, and heat was radiating up through the floor. In a few minutes, or perhaps only just a few seconds, the fire would burn through, plunging them into the inferno, but there were still at least two more mercenaries outside, waiting for the flames to drive them out.

She put the glasses on and stowed the phone in a pocket, then turned to Mulamba. "We have to jump. You'll have to go first so we can cover you." She didn't ask if he could do it. He didn't have a choice. "Drop, roll and then run for cover, got it?"

He gave her a terrified look, but then Rook clapped him on the shoulder. "He's got it. Am I right, Joe?"

Mulamba managed a wan grin. "*Hakuna matata.*"

Queen gave a three count, and at the word "Go!" both she and Rook laid down covering fire while Mulamba clambered over the rail and dropped to the ground.

"Your turn!" Rook shouted. He triggered another burst as she rolled over the rail. For a moment, she caught sight of Mulamba, on the ground and looking dazed, and then she hit. The impact jolted through her, sending a throb of pain up from the soles of her feet to her knees, but she remembered her own advice and tucked into a roll to reduce some of the effect. She came up searching for a target, saw movement and fired.

Rook landed beside her and rolled into a crouch, sweeping the barrel of his Skorpion back and forth, looking for someone to shoot. When no return fire came, he pivoted and scooped Mulamba off the ground. Queen turned in the direction of the parked car and ran. Rook stayed right behind her, half-dragging Mulamba.

Smoke billowed from every window of the farmhouse, obscuring everything to either side, but she could hear distant shouts and then the report of machine pistols. The mercenaries that had been covering the rear of the house were coming around to join the fight.

Queen rounded the front end of the vehicle, finger poised on the trigger of her SIG, but found only sprawled bodies. At least that much had gone in their favor. Rook and Mulamba ducked down next to her, and as Rook fired blind into the smoke, Queen tried the door.

Unlocked.

She crawled inside and a quick search revealed a key under the driver's side floor mat. She slotted it into the ignition and gave it a turn. The engine turned over almost right away, but as it settled into an idle, she could hear a rattling noise. Some of Rook's shots had perforated the hood and found their way into the car's mechanical guts. It was running, but there was no telling how long it would continue to do so.

The window above her shattered, spraying her with glass fragments, but she stayed focused on the task of contorting her body into the driver's seat while keeping her head down. Rook fired out the Skorpion, and then tossed Mulamba into the backseat.

"We're in! Punch it!"

Bullets hammered into the car, drilling right through the metal panels. Queen winced as a fragment dug into her right thigh, but she didn't let off on the accelerator. The car fishtailed a little as she wheeled it around, throwing up a spray of gravel, and then she straightened it out, aiming for the driveway.

The rattling noise from the engine intensified to an earsplitting crescendo and the smell of burning metal filled the interior of the vehicle. Indicator lights on the console flashed, telling her what she already knew: this was going to be a short ride.

The noise of the engine tearing itself apart nearly drowned out every other sound, but Queen realized that she no longer heard the distinctive crack of rounds striking the car. She raised her head and saw that they were almost to the end of the drive. A glance back showed the farmhouse, fully wreathed in smoke and fire. She also saw a pick-up truck, loaded with armed mercenaries, rolling out from behind the curtain of flame.

Queen eased off the gas a little to make the turn onto the road, but when she pressed it again, the response was sluggish. She floored the pedal, but the engine continued to clatter.

Their rented sedan was a tiny speck in the distance, perhaps five hundred yards away. "Come on," she said, willing the car to hold together just a little bit longer, but the universe rejected her plea. The engine gave a final sickening *thunk*, and the clattering ceased altogether, plunging them into near total silence.

"Stay with Joe!" Rook shouted, and he was out the door before the car could come to a complete stop. He bolted toward their car, running all-out like an Olympic sprinter.

Queen had no intention of leaving Mulamba behind, but staying with him wasn't the same as staying put. She threw her door open and swung out of the seat, only remembering the wound in her thigh when the first step sent a stab of pain through her entire leg.

Pain she could handle, but the tissue damage was another story. The bullet fragment had gouged into her quadriceps, and now the entire muscle was inflamed. She steadied herself against the car, ignored the agony and begged her muscles to keep going just as she had pleaded with the engine a moment before. Unlike the car, her body listened.

Mulamba, still in a daze, was slow to exit, but as soon as his door was open, Queen grabbed his arm and dragged him along. Her leg throbbed with every step, threatening to collapse beneath her, but through sheer force of will, she stayed on her feet and kept moving, almost faster than Mulamba could manage.

Behind them, perhaps two hundred yards away, the pick-up full of mercenaries burst out of the driveway and skidded onto the road. Queen reached back and fired the SIG, emptying the magazine. The truck was well outside the effective range of the pistol, but Queen wasn't shooting in hopes of hitting someone. She was just trying to buy them a few more seconds.

She saw Rook reach the car and yank the door open...the left door. *Wrong side, Rook.* He threw his head back and shouted, "Friggin' backwards England!" She heard him despite the distance, and for a second, she wondered why his curse hadn't come through on the comm link, but then she remembered that he had sacrificed his glasses during the escape.

Rook didn't let his frustration slow him down. He leaped across the hood and got in on the right side. A moment later, the car's tail lights flashed and its backup lights came on. A cloud of rubber smoke rose up and half a second later, she heard the squeal of tires, time delayed because of the distance the sound had to travel.

This is going to be close, she realized. She and Mulamba were at the mid-point between the sedan and the pick-up full of mercenaries. The latter had the advantage of moving forward and a higher range of acceleration, but as long as they were moving away from it and toward Rook, there was a chance. She considered trying to reload the SIG, but wasn't sure that she could juggle one more task.

Move your ass, Rook!

She started and nearly tripped as a loud report sounded right behind her. It wasn't the mercenaries, but Mulamba, firing the Skorpion Rook had given him. He let off two long bursts and more than a few of his rounds found their target, sparking off the truck's hood, shattering the headlights and windshield. The pick-up swerved and slowed, and Queen thought maybe he had hit the driver as well.

Another shriek of tires and grinding brakes signaled Rook's arrival. He had swerved out into the road at the last second, and now idled beside them. Queen got the rear door open, pushed Mulamba in, and then climbed in after.

"Go!"

Rook was already going, accelerating down the straightaway as fast as the car would go, not exactly street-racer fast, but enough. "And remember to drive on the left!"

Rook muttered a curse, and Queen felt the car swerve into the other lane. Behind them, the pick-up was starting to move forward again, but Mulamba's volley had definitely taken the wind out of their sails, and Rook was able to increase their lead to the point where it was clear that the mercenaries had given up the chase. A few minutes later, they passed a string of emergency vehicles— police cars and fire trucks—responding to the towering column of black smoke, and Rook slowed to a less conspicuous pace.

"Well, that didn't quite go according to plan," he said, "but I think we're clear."

Queen finally allowed herself to breathe normally. She widened the hole in her blood-soaked jeans to fully expose the injury that now throbbed in time with her heartbeat. At the center of the oozing wound was a piece of dark metal that looked almost like a tiny shark tooth. She massaged the surrounding tissue until it was close enough to the surface for her pluck it out with her fingernails. She would need stitches to close it, but that would have to wait a while longer.

She glanced over at Mulamba. "Are you all right? Any injuries?"

The Congolese president stared back at her for a moment as if uncomprehending, but then broke into a broad smile. "I am free! Thank you, thank you so much."

Rook looked over his shoulder. "Introductions all around. Joe, Queen...Queen, Joe."

"Queen? That is your name? And he is Rook? I see now. You are chess pieces. And I must be the king you are meant to protect."

Rook laughed aloud, and Queen found herself chuckling, not so much at Mulamba's mistake as at the idea of King needing protection. "Not quite, Mr. President...Joe. But we are going to make sure you get back home safely. No offense, but things have gone completely to shit since you've been away."

"No offense taken." Mulamba's elated smile slipped a little. "If I am truthful, things there were completely shit before I left. That is what I have been trying to change."

Queen nodded, but she was only half-listening. She held a hand to her ear, as if keying a concealed microphone and spoke aloud. "Blue, we need transport to the Congo."

She was hoping to hear him say that *Crescent II* was already on the way. At Mach two, they could have Mulamba back in his office in Kinshasa by dinnertime, and that would be the end of it. But Deep Blue never got the chance to say it.

"No!" Mulamba cried. "I cannot go back. Not yet."

Queen worked her jaw, trying very hard to stay calm. "Mr. President, maybe you didn't understand what I just said. Your country is on the brink of civil war. If you don't go back, millions of people will die—*your* people."

He shook his head emphatically. "Even I cannot prevent that now. I must go to Belgium."

"Listen, we just put our asses on the line to get you out of that place back there. Our friends are in your country, knee deep in it so that you'll have somewhere to go back to. So don't tell me it's too late."

Deep Blue's voice sounded in her head. "He might not be wrong, Queen. Things have taken a turn for the worse."

Queen clenched her teeth, but before she could reply to either man, Rook spoke up. "What's in Belgium? I mean aside from the world's best waffles."

Mulamba, evidently excited at the prospect of being able to tell his story, leaned forward, sticking his head over the back of the passenger seat. "In Belgium, I hope to find the truth about what happened on the day that Henry Morton Stanley found Dr. David Livingstone."

"And why is that so important?"

Mulamba's voice dropped to a hushed, almost reverent whisper. "Dr. Livingstone found something in his journeys. Something of which the world has no knowledge. Something that will save Africa."

SIXTEEN

Near Lake Kivu, Democratic Republic of the Congo

Bishop's awareness returned in a jumble of disconnected pieces. His perceptions made no sense without the context of memories, which at the moment, were elusive.

Hot, humid air, reeking of rot and smoke...a jungle...*Africa. Why?*

A dark-skinned woman lay a few feet away...*Felice, her name is Felice, but how do I know that?* A man lay motionless just beyond her. *Knight. Why isn't he moving?* A ringing in his ears from the explosion... *Explosion? The mortar shells...* Someone had been dropping mortars on them.

The pieces came together in a rush that was almost painful in its urgency. He scrambled up, then almost collapsed as a wave of dizziness washed over him. The head rush, brought on by the effect of gravity pulling blood away from his brain, passed after a moment, and he saw, thirty yards beyond Knight, an enormous crater, still smoking from the shell that had detonated there just a few seconds earlier.

He didn't know why the attacking force was not still raining hell down on them, but he wasn't going to wait around for them to realize their mistake. He scooped Felice up with one hand, throwing her over his shoulder like a bag full of laundry, then hoisted Knight onto the other shoulder, and took off running toward the green wall of jungle.

Shots sounded behind him. Tree branches and leaves disintegrated as bullets tore through. That at least explained why there hadn't been any more mortars. The rebels, believing that the first volley had accomplished its intended purpose, had stopped firing and sent out a party to investigate. Bishop kept running, pushing through a tangle of vegetation that tore at his arms and legs and threatened to pull the human cargo off his shoulders, but he fought through, and after a moment, he found himself in the relative openness of the forest floor.

The tree branches were spaced widely enough for him to move unimpeded. High above, the foliage grew together to form a ceiling that shut out nearly all sunlight, leaving the jungle floor as dark as dusk. Bishop now understood why Africa, with a sun-scorched desert that was bigger than the entire United States, and endless miles of open grasslands, had earned the nickname 'the dark continent.'

He could no longer hear the report of rebel guns behind him, but he didn't mistake that for safety. They might have stopped shooting so they could chase him down. In the eternal night beneath the jungle canopy, it was difficult to tell whether he was being followed, but he had to assume that he was, so he kept running as if the hounds of Hell were biting at his heels.

He gradually became aware of an insistent pounding against his back. At first, he assumed that it was his M240B machine gun on its thick nylon web sling, swinging back and forth in time with his footsteps, and he tried to ignore it. Finally, when the beating grew more insistent, he stopped to shift his load, and that was when he realized the sensation wasn't coming from his gear.

"Put me down." The words were grunted, breathless and not at all familiar. It wasn't Knight. *Felice?* "I can walk. Put me down."

Bishop peered into the darkness behind them. There was no sign of pursuit. He knelt cautiously until the soles of Felice's shoes brushed the ground, and then he released his hold on her legs. She kicked like a swimmer until her feet found purchase. She wobbled unsteadily and caught herself on his shoulder.

"You okay?" Bishop's voice sounded strange in his own ears, as though his head had been stuffed with sawdust. It occurred to him that the exploding mortar shells might have rung his bell a little harder than he realized.

Felice looked herself over. Her dark skin was painted with a lighter-colored coating of sticky dust, and beneath her torn clothing were too many scrapes and abrasions to count, but the amount of blood staining the fabric suggested the injuries were only minor.

A fresh wave of realization washed over him. In his desperate panic to get away from the besieged camp, he hadn't stopped to assess what damage he had taken. He wasn't feeling much pain—just the ache of the exertion and a mild headache, but he knew that sometimes adrenaline had a way of masking serious injury. A glance up and down his extremities showed numerous small tears and scorch marks on his BDUs, and underneath a lot of bloody scratches, but as with Felice, none of it looked serious. Then he remembered. "Knight!"

Knight had been closer to the blast.

Bishop gently shifted his teammate off his shoulder and laid him on the ground. Knight didn't stir.

A cold knot of fear clenched Bishop's gut. He laid a hand on Knight's chest, felt the faint rise and fall with each shallow breath.

Still alive.

Then he got a look at Knight's face and the dread exploded into a horror like nothing Bishop had ever felt before. The emotion tore from his throat in a howl that startled birds and monkeys in the branches high overhead, and in an instant, the jungle descended into a cacophony of primal rage.

SEVENTEEN

Felice let out a cry of her own and clapped her hands over her ears as the bestial roar reached a fever pitch. The big man that had rescued her from the attack looked like something from a movie—a human transforming into a werewolf before her very eyes.

She knew what that felt like.

Darting forward, she reached out and slapped him.

It was like hitting a skyscraper. Her palm cracked loudly against his skin, and pain shot all the way to her elbow. His howl became a snarl of animal fury as he turned on her, and in that instant, she knew he was going to kill her.

But he didn't. He remained where he was, kneeling, hands raised and fingers curled like claws, teeth bared and chest heaving as he breathed.

"He needs you!" She tried to shout it, but the words clung to her throat like molasses. She searched her memory for something that would get through to him...a name. *Knight. He called him Knight.* "Knight needs you!"

A glimmer of humanity flashed in the man's eyes, and with what seemed like a superhuman effort, he swallowed down his rage. His fingers straightened and then his hands fell to his side. For a few seconds, he remained that way, statue still except for his rapid breathing.

Felice was panting, too, but forced herself to move. She circled around so that the supine Knight lay between the big man and herself. She knelt and assessed the unconscious man's injuries. She quickly saw why the bigger man had reacted the way he had.

The left side of Knight's face was a mess of swollen and scorched flesh, but that wasn't the worst of it. Something ragged and misshapen, a piece of metal, protruded from the place where his eye should have been.

Felice let out a gasp, but quickly got control of herself, lest her reaction push the big man back over the edge. She willed herself into a detached, meditative state, and bent over Knight, checking for other injuries that might be even more critical.

His left side had taken the brunt of the mortar blast. There were more chunks of metal embedded in his upper arm. The entire limb was swollen, but the wounds were only oozing blood. There didn't appear to be any arterial bleeding or damage to his torso.

"I need some water. And a first aid kit if you have it. We have to clean and dress these wounds."

The request seemed to pull the big man back from the precipice. He unslung his gear and weapons, and produced a small satchel. Inside was a collection of combat medical equipment, bandages and other supplies. He took out a plastic bag filled with clear liquid and passed it to her.

In the darkness, she could not read what was written on the bag, but she assumed it was a saline solution or perhaps Ringer's lactate. Either one would work just fine for irrigating Knight's wounds. She bit off a corner, careful not to spill too much of its contents, and then directed a stream of the liquid onto Knight's ravaged face.

"By the way, I'm Felice."

"I remember. I'm Bishop. This is Knight."

Bishop and Knight. They were code names, obviously, like the callsigns that fighter pilots and military units sometimes used, but they were also the names of chess pieces, and that took her to a place in her memory she preferred not to visit. She shook her head and focused on what she was doing.

The simple act of getting out the medical kit seemed to have a calming effect on Bishop. He took out a pair of trauma shears and cut away Knight's right sleeve, exposing the undamaged arm. It took him less than a minute to find and sterilize an injection site, and subsequently to insert a needle catheter into a vein and begin a rapid infusion of fluid into Knight's bloodstream.

"What else do you have in there?" Felice asked. "We're going to need to sew up these wounds."

"Not yet. I don't know if they're still on our six, but we have to keep moving."

"Where do we go? There are villages a few miles from here, but I'm not sure it's safe to show our faces."

"We just have to get to the alternate LZ..." Bishop's voice trailed off for a moment, then an ember of his earlier rage flared to life. "Damnit!"

Felice flinched a little, but quickly laid a steadying hand on his forearm. "What is it?"

"My glasses are gone."

She had no idea what he meant by that, but before she could ask for an explanation, he pulled away and took out what looked to her like a mobile phone from one of his cargo pockets. He stabbed a finger at it, then shook it, and when nothing happened, closed his fist around it. There was an audible crack as the device imploded in his grip.

He let the pieces fall to the ground. "We've got no comms. No way to let anyone know we're alive."

Felice grasped his arm again. "Hey. Let's deal with one thing at a time, okay?"

He clenched his jaw so tightly that Felice could hear his teeth grinding, but then he nodded.

"Good. I'm going to bandage his...his face. I don't think we should try to remove any of the metal from his wounds yet. Not until we have time to put in some sutures."

Bishop nodded and withheld further comment, while she packed Knight's eye with gauze and swathed his head with a long strip of self-adhering Coban wrap. "Should we try to wake him?"

Felice pressed two fingers to Knight's wrist. "His pulse is strong and steady. I don't think he's in shock, but he's going to be in a lot of pain. Ideally, he shouldn't be moved at all, but since that's not an option, getting him walking is going to be better for him than riding on your shoulder." Felice gave a helpless shrug. "Sorry. I can't give you a better answer. He needs a real doctor."

"You've done a pretty good job so far."

The compliment was so unexpected, and so totally unlike anything she thought she'd hear from this man, that she found herself laughing. "Well, I know some basic first aid. You probably know more about battlefield medicine than I do."

"You kept your head when I was about to lose mine."

Something in the way he said it made Felice realize that staying cool under pressure was of paramount importance to the big man. His comment was both high praise for her and harsh self-criticism. "Well, I have my bad days, too."

Bishop passed her a small foil pouch. "This should wake him up. Smelling salts."

Felice shook a small capsule out of the packet and crushed it, releasing a strong odor of ammonia and eucalyptus. She expected a strong reaction, but when she held it under Knight's nose, she was startled at the violence with which the injured man returned to consciousness. He jerked and flailed his arms, as if falling out of a dream, and then let out a scream that echoed back from the jungle ceiling.

Bishop caught Knight's arms before he could tear at the bandage covering his face. Knight's one good eye seemed to fix on Bishop's face and he calmed a little, but he kept struggling to reach the wound.

Felice reached in as well, placing one hand on Knight's forehead and another on his chest, soothing him as a mother might soothe a feverish child. "It's okay." She felt a pang of guilt at the lie. It wasn't okay, not by a long shot. "I know it hurts, but you have to settle down."

Whether it was her words and soft touch, or simply the return of Knight's higher reasoning abilities she could not say, but she felt him relax beneath her hands.

"Shit!" he rasped. "It feels like there's a knife sticking out of my eye." His expression grew even more agonized. "Oh, God. There is, isn't there?"

Before Bishop or Felice could give an answer—the bitter truth or a poisonous lie—a voice shouted from somewhere nearby. It sounded to Felice's ear like the Swahili dialect some of the expedition's bearers had used, and while she didn't understand a word of it, the message was clear. *I've found them.*

The shout was followed immediately by the report of a rifle shot, then another and another. Three shots, not directed at them, but at the sky. A signal.

Bishop launched into motion, spinning on his heel, scooping up the enormous machine gun and holding its stock to his shoulder. He swept the jungle with the muzzle but did not fire.

He turned to Felice. "Take him. Run. I'll find you."

And then he was gone, running at a gallop toward the place from which the shots had come.

Without Bishop to hold him, there was nothing Felice could do to restrain Knight, but when he shook free of her grasp, it was not to tear at his wound. Instead, he tore the intravenous line from his arm, then groped for his rifle and rolled over into a prone firing position, facing in the direction Bishop was moving.

Felice gripped his arm. "You heard what he said. We have to run."

"I don't run," Knight said. His teeth were clenched against the pain, but his voice was unnaturally calm.

"But I have to," she said, matching his tone. "And I can't make it on my own."

Felice saw immediately that she had found the right pressure point. Knight's posture relaxed, and then he sprang to his feet.

"Bring the gear."

She closed the med kit, stuffed it into Bishop's rucksack, and hefted it onto one shoulder. Knight was staring at something on the ground, and she saw that it was the crushed remains of Bishop's cell phone. "Should I bring that, too?"

When Knight didn't answer, she gathered up the pieces and shoved them in a pocket. "Which way?"

He stared at her, his face twisting between inscrutable stoicism and unimaginable pain. Finally, he pointed away from where Bishop had gone and then lurched into motion.

They had only taken a few steps when the forest behind them erupted with the noise of machine gun fire.

EIGHTEEN

Kinshasa, Democratic Republic of the Congo

Asya put her fingers through the metal grating that had been erected to close-off half of the small room, turning it into a makeshift detention cell. The wire mesh barrier, the sort of thing used to block off cashier booths and the back seats of police cars was a poor substitute for iron bars, but a cage was a cage.

One of the soldiers guarding them jabbed the muzzle of his carbine at her and grunted for her to move back. She wasn't sure why. King and her were no threat to anyone now. Nevertheless, she moved back a few steps and looked to her brother, hoping to see the glimmer of an escape plan in his eyes.

If it was there, she didn't see it. King just stood there, as still and silent as the Sphinx, staring through the barrier, looking at nothing.

As the troops had herded them through the palace, following a labyrinthine course that seemed designed to keep them away from curious eyes, she had listened as King reported everything to Deep Blue in a series of rapid-fire reports, which he disguised from their captors by feigning a cough. "We've been arrested." Cough. "Regular army troops." Cough. "Don't know who's behind it..." Cough. "...or if we have any allies."

The soldiers hadn't caught on to what he was doing, but as soon as they were in the cell, they performed a more thorough search, taking the glasses and the phones from King and Asya. Asya could see them sitting atop a folding table on the other side of the mesh. King had fallen quiet after they were shut in, and Asya knew why. Their captors would almost certainly be watching and listening carefully to see what the prisoners would reveal. Silence was absolutely necessary, but as the minutes stretched on, she began to feel truly alone.

She was obliged to change her mind about the merits of solitude when the room door opened and Monique Favreau entered, flanked by the two-steroid monsters. They had changed out of their business formal attire, and now wore BDUs with the same camo pattern as the soldiers. Favreau had a holstered pistol on her belt while her goons carried H&K MP5s.

"Look," Asya remarked. "Is dragon lady, come to visit us. I knew there was reason I did not like you."

Favreau stood on the other side of the mesh barrier and regarded her with a bemused expression for a moment. When she turned her attention to King, her look changed to something like...hunger.

"Who are you?" It wasn't a demand so much as a statement of awe, delivered with all the sultriness and intensity that made most American men weak in the knees.

Asya hoped her brother would answer with something defiant or sarcastic—'No one you want to mess with' or 'Your worst nightmare'— but that was more Rook's way of doing things. King said nothing at all.

"No? Nothing? Perhaps I need to ask the question differently. Or perhaps..." Favreau's lips curled in a predatory smile as she shifted her scrutiny to Asya. "Ah, I see it now. Brother and sister.

Perhaps she will tell me what I want to know. Or, perhaps you will tell me to spare her unnecessary *discomfort.*"

"Go fuck yourself," Asya said.

"Later," Favreau replied without missing a beat. "For the moment, I think I will—"

"You've already lost." King spoke quietly, forcing Favreau to stop and focus her attention on him again.

"Oh, I don't think so."

"Mulamba's proposed African federation would mean the nationalization of the oil and natural gas industry across the entire continent," King continued. "Your Big Oil bosses couldn't stand for that, so they had you arrange his abduction in London. But it wasn't enough to just get him out of the picture. You want chaos. Chaos makes the people who live here desperate, willing to give away their natural resources for the promise of stability and a quick buck."

Favreau rolled her eyes and then moved over to the table where their phones and glasses lay. She tried to activate one of the q-phones but gave up when nothing happened. Asya knew that there was no way for her to overcome the phone's biometric security, but she suspected that the phone actually was on, and transmitting every word that was said back to Deep Blue. King's long accusatory statement had been his way of telling Deep Blue what he thought was actually going on in the Congo.

Asya wasn't sure how that was going to help them get out of this mess, but she trusted that King knew what he was doing.

"Are you going to tell me who you are?" Favreau asked, setting the phone down. "You aren't CIA. Senator Marrs believes you are, but we both know that isn't true."

"Let's talk about Senator Marrs. Are you working for him, or is he working for you?"

Favreau laughed. "Neither. We have coincidental...*sympathies.*" She rolled the word around in her mouth like a sip of wine.

"Give him a message for me. Tell him he's wasting time. President Mulamba is free. He's on his way back here. This little revolution is finished."

She made a brushing gesture with her hand. "Let him come back. It's too late for him to make a difference."

"He'll have a very compelling story to tell his people—to tell the whole world—about how *you* are responsible for all of this, about how you were willing to tear the entire continent apart just so you could take their oil."

"This is Africa," Favreau said. "That's how things are done here. Read a history book."

"Oh, I know history, believe me. And I know that sometimes, things change."

"You're very sure of yourself. I like that in a man." Favreau looked at him again for a long moment, breathing quickly as if aroused. Then she turned to one of her associates. "Take them out into the jungle and shoot them."

NINETEEN

Favreau watched as the two prisoners were herded out of the cell and taken away. She had considered shooting them herself, right then and there, but there was something about the man, something compelling.

She marveled at how quickly he had dissected the particulars of what she was doing on behalf of Consolidated Energy. He hadn't gotten everything quite right, and he'd mistakenly attributed their motives to her. In fact, she didn't care at all whether CE got their oil and natural gas leases, or for that matter, whether the inhabitants of the region got rich or got hacked apart with long knives. Her desires were for nothing so banal as wealth and power.

The wealthy and powerful believed that life was a game where the goal was to achieve an ever increasing amount of wealth and power, not realizing that, in so doing, they were consigning themselves to the same endless hamster wheel existence as everyone else. Favreau believed life was a different sort of game, where the true goal was to test oneself—win or die.

When she was young, joining the DSGE had once seemed like the ultimate challenge, but she had mastered the spy game and eventually grown tired of it. She had been drawn to the private sector, not because of the lucrative promise of material reward, but because it was the same game she had excelled at, but with fewer rules and much higher stakes.

The best games always had high stakes.

Favreau was fascinated with games. She had organized the men in her ESI strike team according to a playing card system: ten men, each designated by a corresponding card value, two through ten, with ace reserved for the unit leader. The suit—spades, hearts, diamonds, and clubs—was used as the unit identifier, though rare was the situation that called for the deployment of all four units at any given time. Presently, Spades and Diamonds were in the UK, where they had carried out—and if the American had not been lying, subsequently botched—Mulamba's abduction, while Hearts and Clubs were deployed throughout the Congo region.

The three positions corresponding to the face cards in each suit, she reserved for special roles—consultants or, when the contract called for it, the clients themselves—and as such, it was rare to have a king, queen or jack 'in hand.' For her own part, Favreau, had chosen the designation 'Red Queen.'

One of the younger 'cards' had once asked if she'd taken her name from the supercomputer in a video game about zombies, and although she had no idea what he had been talking about, she rather liked the idea of both the computer and the fact that it was from a game. Her inspiration had been the character from the Lewis Carroll story *Through the Looking Glass*. Unlike the mercurial Queen of Hearts in *Alice's Adventures in Wonderland*, the Red Queen from Carroll's earlier tale was a cold, calculating chess piece that embodied the simple truth that Favreau lived by: to stay alive, you have to keep moving forward. In her case, that meant running toward the fight, not away from it. Retreat was weakness, and weakness was death.

That summarized her philosophy of life.

Her hand dropped to the remote trigger device in her pocket. With less pressure than it would take to pull the trigger on her pistol, she could detonate the RA-115, which lay in a corner of that very room. The explosion would erase the palace and kill hundreds, perhaps thousands in the blink of an eye.

She had no intention of doing so, but the mere fact that she could was as potent a stimulant as any illicit drug. That was true power.

She had learned about the bomb through her personal network of intelligence contacts. A disgruntled Russian official had told her of the sale to Hadir. An informant in the terrorist group, a man who would not have dreamed of selling his information to the West, but owed her a personal favor that he was eager to settle, had told her of the plot to destroy the Suez Canal. Her employers, both her superiors at ESI and the oil barons of Consolidated Energy, had given her carte blanche when it came to carrying out their schemes, so she saw no conflict in stopping Hadir personally or acquiring the bomb for her own, as yet undetermined, purposes. It had already proven quite handy at keeping General Velle in line, but merely using it as a threat—as a tool for extortion—wasn't very satisfying.

There was a line from an American film—*Speed*—which summed up her feelings perfectly. The villain of the movie, a former bomb disposal officer who had himself become a bomb wielding terrorist, told the hero: 'A bomb is made to explode. That's its meaning. Its purpose. Your life is empty because you spend it trying to stop the bomb from becoming.'

That line had stuck in her memory. The tactical nuclear device would one day fulfill its purpose, and she would be the one to make it happen. That was her purpose. The bomb was the instrument—the paintbrush—with which she would create her masterpiece, but like any artist, she needed to find the right inspiration.

She caressed the trigger and thought about the American. There was something about him, something that made her believe he might be a very formidable enemy, the very challenge she so craved.

If her men returned and reported that they had carried out her orders, then she would know that she had read the man wrong, that he was not the man she believed him to be.

But a gut feeling told her that her men would not be coming back with such a report. They might not *ever* return, in fact, and the idea brought the smile back to her face.

TWENTY

King did not share Favreau's rosy optimism with respect to the matter of his own survival, but he was by no means resigned to his fate. As soon as the makeshift cell was unlocked, and he and Asya were escorted out by the steroid twins and a platoon of Congolese soldiers, he began looking for any opportunity to turn the tables on their captors.

"Be ready," he told Asya, as the soldiers entered the cell, brandishing carbines. Two of their number came in to bind the prisoner's hands with zip ties.

There was no time to say more, and really nothing more to be said. King didn't know when their chance would come. If they were lucky, the soldiers would do something very stupid—that wasn't completely beyond the realm of possibility—but it was much more likely that they would have to make their own luck. Unfortunately, without the glasses, there was no way to coordinate with Asya. She would just have to follow his lead.

Nothing that seemed like a good opportunity presented itself as they were hastened to a side exit and into the back of a waiting heavy transport truck, where Favreau's mercenaries were joined by several Congolese army troops. He and Asya were forced to sit on the floor of the truck's cargo bed, in between two rows of soldiers assembled on the inward facing troop seats.

The canvas canopy had been rolled back, exposing the occupants of the truck to the elements, but King's view of the roadside was mostly obscured by the wall of bodies. At first, he caught glimpses of tall buildings, but as the journey progressed, they were replaced by the tops of trees. There were other changes, too. The sudden stops, accompanied by squealing and hissing air brakes, and followed by lurching starts, became less frequent, replaced instead by the back and forth sway of the truck swerving through turns or jouncing over potholes. It was a punishing ride, and King knew from experience that the wooden benches where their captors sat were only marginally more comfortable.

Something wet struck his cheek. At first, he thought one of the soldiers had spit on him, and he studied their blank faces to identify the culprit, but then another gob of moisture hit him, and he realized that it was rain.

In the space of just a few seconds, the afternoon sky darkened and the scattering of droplets became a torrent. Water filled the bed of the truck faster than it could drain out through the gaps in the tailgate. The soldiers did their best to lift their boots up out the flood, but King and Asya were obligated to simply slosh about in the deepening puddle.

A blinding flash seared across the sky and King's retinas, followed about two seconds later by a peal of thunder that reverberated through the truck bed.

Damn, that's close.

The basic rule for estimating the distance of a lightning strike was to count the number of seconds between the flash and the thunderclap—five seconds meant the lightning was a mile away. Two seconds meant only about seven hundred yards.

There was another flare—not a quick flash, but a prolonged burst of light that seemed to come from all around, shifting through degrees of intensity. The thunder boom arrived even before the electrical discharge finished.

They were driving right into the heart of the storm.

The African soldiers took the weather in stride, but King noticed the steroid-twins looking around nervously. Lightning was unpredictable, and while the all-steel frame and roll-over cage construction of the truck could afford some protection against electrocution—acting as a sort of impromptu Faraday Cage—the open bed offered no shelter whatsoever from a direct strike.

King realized this was the moment for which he'd been waiting. He doubted there was a psychic bond between siblings, but tried to project his intention into his sister's brain. He closed his eyes, squeezing them shut tight so that the next flash wouldn't blind him. When it came just a few seconds later, it wasn't lightning that struck the back of the truck.

"Now!"

Even as he shouted it, he was moving, twisting around and aiming a kick up at the nearest of the steroid twins. His boot heel caught the unsuspecting man under the chin, snapping his head back with a crunch of vertebrae that King felt but could not hear over the thunderclap that followed.

Still flash-blind from the lightning, the soldiers were slow to react, giving King time to roll over into a kneeling position. The remaining mercenary's eyes widened in alarm, but before he could even twitch a muscle, King threw himself forward, smashing his forehead into the bridge of the man's nose. The injury had the desired effect of stunning the mercenary, but King's primary goal had been to get closer to the man's weapons, and he accomplished that task by spinning around and throwing himself bodily onto the man's lap. As his fingers knotted around the nylon sling of the man's MP5, King saw the soldiers on the opposite side start to raise their carbines.

There were shouts, but the men couldn't shoot King without hitting their fellow soldiers. The men on the bench to either side of King realized this, too, and almost in unison, they threw themselves flat onto the bed, leaving only the stunned mercenaries and King in the line of fire.

Several carbines fired all at once, but none found a target. In the instant before a single trigger was pulled, Asya, who had scrambled to the front of the bed to avoid the tangle of bodies seeking cover, lashed out with a double-footed kick to the line of soldiers on the bench. The shove not only threw off their aim, but sent two of them spilling over the tailgate.

"Jump!" King shouted.

Asya didn't hesitate. She got her feet under her, scrambled onto the bench and leaped over the side.

Before he could follow, King felt the truck braking. The sudden deceleration threw him forward, but he kept his grip on the sling of the machine pistol. The mercenary, who was just starting to recover from King's initial attack, was pulled off the bench, and fell atop King in the midst of the tangled bodies.

With his hands still bound, King had to wriggle like a snake to get free of the squirming mass, but unlike the other men jumbled together, he knew exactly what he was trying to accomplish. He rolled out from under the mercenary, and without releasing his hold on the nylon sling, got to his feet and heaved himself over the side of the truck.

The sling pulled taut against his grip and for a moment, he feared it might rip right through the flesh of his fingers. His arms were suddenly yanked up painfully, and for a moment, he hung from the side of the truck, a few feet above the glistening mud that covered the road. The still rolling dual wheels were close enough to kiss.

Then, as abruptly as his fall had been arrested, it resumed, and he slammed onto the ground. The dazed mercenary slammed down atop him a moment later, driving the wind from his lungs.

King fought to suppress the pain and rising panic of breathlessness. Everything that had occurred had been a result of action he had taken, and that gave him the edge, no matter what happened. He heard the truck's brakes squealing as it slid to a stop perhaps fifty yards away, and he knew he had to keep moving, had to keep acting instead of reacting, if he was going to survive the next few seconds.

Bending his body like a contortionist, King slipped his bound hands down past his hips and then threaded one leg at a time through the hoop formed by his arms. It took only about three seconds, but that was time enough for the soldiers to start piling out of the truck.

He dropped to his knees beside the mercenary, delivering a double-fisted hammer blow that rendered the man unconscious, and then he brought the machine pistol up. He flicked a thumb across the fire selector, and then swept the muzzle toward the line of soldiers as he squeezed the trigger.

The MP5 bucked in his hands and a long yellow tongue of flame erupted from the muzzle, along with a report to rival the thunder. King had fired thousands of rounds from MP5s, but never in all that time had he ever experienced so much recoil. The pistol bucked in his hands like one of Rook's Desert Eagles. Yet that was nothing compared to the effect of the shots.

Two of the soldiers simply burst, like enormous water balloons filled with blood. A third was only grazed. The bullet took his arm completely off below the shoulder in an eruption of gore.

King let go of the trigger and stared, dumbstruck, at the weapon in his hands. Some part of him understood what had just happened, at least in respect to the matter of physics. The MP5 was loaded with some kind of special overpressure ammunition—probably hollow rounds filled with a dense heavy metal like tungsten or depleted uranium. They would be fired by a larger than normal gunpowder charge or even some new experimental powder that yielded more explosive energy. That was the how and what, but it didn't begin to explain the why.

The surviving soldiers bolted for cover, but they didn't flee. Instead, they brought their weapons around and took aim at him. He fired again, just a single shot this time, and at the noise of the bullet punching through the metal bed of the truck, he spun on his heel and ran.

Another flash of lightning revealed Asya, a short distance away, crouching down near the edge of the road and attempting to wriggle her hands around to the front as he had done.

The lightning also illuminated the surrounding environment: undulating hills covered with lush green fields and trees, pools of brown water in the hollows, fed by raging torrents of rainwater runoff, and in the distance, the blocky shapes of tall buildings. A line of headlights was visible on the glistening ribbon that was the graded gravel road leading back to the city.

"Get off the road!"

Asya looked up just as King reached her. She doubled her efforts and slipped her bound wrists over her left foot, freeing her legs for the much more urgent task of running for her life. He grabbed her arm and hoisted her to her feet. He steered her toward the marshy ground to their right, as the tumult of lightning and gunfire filled the air. Mixed in with the bullwhip like crack of the Kalashnikov carbines, King heard the deeper, rhythmic report of a heavy machine gun. The sound echoed weirdly off the hills, but from the corner of his eye, he glimpsed muzzle flashes right above the headlights of the approaching vehicles.

A three foot wide stream of water flowed between the road bed and the field beyond. *A drainage ditch*, King surmised. It was filled to capacity by the tropical downpour and on the verge of overflowing. He leaped across and saw Asya do the same, but when his feet touched down, the ground tried to swallow him whole. He pitched forward and felt vegetation and gritty mud close in around him.

For a moment, the threat of death at the hands of the soldiers was diminished by the much more immediate danger of drowning. He tried to push himself up, but his hands found nothing solid to grasp. Fighting back a primal instinct, he stopped struggling and instead rolled over, curling his body to get his head out of the mud. His lower extremities sank deeper, the earth sucking him down, but he also felt a cascade of rain on his face, and as it sluiced the mud away from his mouth and nose, he risked a shallow breath and felt the damp air enter his lungs.

It was the briefest of reprieves. Silhouetted on the road, less than twenty yards away, King saw three large vehicles that looked like oversized SUVs. The trucks weren't moving, but while their headlights shone straight ahead, swiveling searchlights were probing the field where he and Asya now hid.

Asya!

Frantic, he looked to where he had last seen her. The grass had closed over the spot, but something was moving beneath the green shroud. He thrust his bound hands into the tangle and felt something solid.

Asya thrashed violently, her desperation accomplishing nothing more than digging her grave deeper. King tried to pull her up but the soft earth beneath him confounded his efforts, and instead of freeing her, he found the mud once more closing over his head.

Recalling his earlier success, he tried rolling again, first pulling away from Asya's struggling form, and then rolling toward her. He felt the earth's grip loosen, and then, like Jonah vomited from the belly of the whale, they were both disgorged out of the soft mud bank and into the rushing water in the drainage ditch.

The current wasn't quite strong enough to sweep them away, but every time King tried to plant his feet against the solid ground below, he was promptly bowled over and returned to the water's embrace. He felt Asya's arm slip away, and when he reached out to her, he found only handfuls of water.

As exhaustion closed over him, he felt a strong arm close around him, drawing him out of the flood. He knew that it wasn't Asya. He intuitively recognized that it could only be one of the soldiers, saving him from drowning to carry out Favreau's death sentence later, but there was no fight left in him.

He let himself be dragged up onto the road, where he was surrounded by a knot of men in camouflage fatigues. Another man pulled Asya, coughing and gasping for air, from the ditch and laid her beside him.

A knife flashed, and before King could take any kind of defensive action, the blade moved close and sliced through the zip-tie that bound his wrists together. Surprised, he looked up into the smiling face of General Mabuki.

"I am sorry I wasn't able to stop them from taking you," the general said. He turned to Asya and cut her bonds as well. "We must go. Things are happening very quickly. There isn't much time."

TWENTY-ONE

Kent, England

Rook checked the rearview mirror again as they turned onto the M20 motorway and headed toward London. There had been no sign of pursuit since they'd lost sight of the truck, and while he wasn't about to relax his guard, he reckoned they were safe for the moment.

He turned his gaze to Mulamba. "Okay. One more time. Why Belgium? And this time maybe ease up a little on the messianic proclamations."

"I shall endeavor to restrain my enthusiasm," Mulamba replied. "This story begins with David Livingstone, a Scotsman who spent many years in Africa, exploring and setting up missions throughout the interior, in the hopes of opening commercial routes and ending the slave trade. Unlike many of his contemporaries, Livingstone did not see the African natives as savages to be exploited without mercy, but rather, he believed that they were also God's children. He was fiercely opposed to human trafficking, and he believed that the only way to bring Christianity and civilization to Africa was by establishing trade in natural resources.

"He was correct in recognizing the vast untapped wealth of Africa, but naïve in his belief that this wealth would change the way his fellow Europeans looked at Africa. Instead of recognizing the humanity of Africans, most saw only a new opportunity to increase their wealth."

"Human nature is a bitch," Rook said.

Mulamba gave a sad look. "*Oui*. King Leopold II of Belgium was perhaps the most notorious of these adventurers. In 1885, he established the Congo Free State, in what is now my country. It was not to be a territory of Belgium, but rather an entirely commercial venture dedicated to exploiting the natural resources of the region. Elephants were hunted for ivory, native forests were cleared for rubber plantations, and of course, there were diamonds and other minerals to be taken. And although they were not slaves in name, the people of the Congo—my ancestors—were just one more resource to be exploited. The conditions on the plantations were brutal. Failure to meet a quota was punishable by death, and the mutilated bodies of men, women and children would be publicly displayed as a warning to others. The right hands of the victims were collected as proof of death, and the soldiers who enforced the quotas were rewarded for the number of hands they collected. Those bounty hunters soon realized it was easier to cut hands off without killing, and hundreds of thousands were mutilated, but still forced to keep working."

Queen, who had been calmly stitching the gash in her thigh with a suture needle from her first aid kit, shuddered. "That's someone's idea of *civilized* behavior?"

"Is that what you're looking for in Belgium?" Rook said, regretting the tone of his earlier statement. "Proof of these atrocities?"

"No. The abuses of the Congo Free State were widely reported, even then. Men such as Joseph Conrad and Arthur Conan Doyle wrote books exposing the brutal treatment of the native population. Please, pardon my digression. I will try to explain.

"In the year 1866, Livingstone embarked on an expedition to discover the source of the Nile River. At the time, this was an ambition on the order of...say, going to Mars. For years, no one heard from Livingstone. No one knew if he was alive or dead. In 1869, a New York newspaper sent Henry Morton Stanley to find Livingstone, and his search took nearly three years. Stanley eventually found Livingstone on the shores of Lake Tanganyika, in November of 1871."

Rook remembered that historic nugget. "'Dr. Livingstone, I presume.'"

"Exactly. Though Stanley probably did not actually speak those words. It is more likely that he fabricated the account of the meeting, to add an element of drama to his newspaper dispatches."

"A goddamned sound bite." Rook sighed. "Just goes to show, you can't believe everything you read in the papers."

"We do not know for certain what Stanley said, or what else transpired during that meeting, because Stanley removed several pages from his diary, which were the only records of his meeting with Livingstone."

"Why would he do that?" Queen asked. "That's like erasing the videotapes of the moon landing."

"Some historians have speculated that the actual account in Stanley's diary would have contradicted what he reported, making him look foolish. Stanley himself claimed that he was embarrassed, because he did not embrace Livingstone, fearing that he might contract malaria or sleeping sickness."

"Wouldn't be the first time someone destroyed evidence to cover their ass."

"I believe he might have been trying to cover something else. Recall that Livingstone had been missing for nearly six years. In that time, he explored parts of Africa that had never been seen by Europeans, and perhaps not even by the natives living nearby. Imagine the stories he had to tell, and now, at long last, he had a chance to share what he had learned with another white man."

"Makes sense. So why the cover-up?"

Mulamba pursed his lips, reminding Rook of the look that Bishop sometimes got during their poker games, when he was trying to decide whether to fold or go all in. "Scientists believe that the first humans originated in Africa, probably in the Great Rift Valley. Yet, throughout all of recorded history, Africa has always been the land of the savages. There is no record of any great civilization in sub-Saharan Africa, in ancient times. The oldest known advanced culture in the interior is the Great Zimbabwe society, which dates back no further than the eleventh century. The birthplace of humanity, and yet no significant advancement for thousands of years. Does that seem likely to you?"

He didn't wait for an answer. "When European explorers arrived in Africa, they found marvelous kingdoms possessing great wealth and power in the interior. These civilizations did not appear overnight, but were, like many other great civilizations throughout history, built on the foundation of previous civilizations. Tribal warfare, often driven by the demand for slaves, destroyed those kingdoms, ensuring that Africa would never be anything more than the land of the savages. Nevertheless, there are stories of great forgotten cities in the depths of the jungle."

Rook rolled his eyes. "You're talking about the plot of every Tarzan story ever written."

"Rook," Queen said, the tone of her voice a warning to be polite, then she turned to Mulamba. "Forgive me for being blunt, sir, but he makes a good point. Lost cities? It's like something from an Indiana Jones movie."

"Where do you imagine the ideas for such stories originated?" Mulamba said. "Until the arrival of European missionaries, the native tribes of the interior had no written language. They had only oral traditions, stories handed down from one generation to the next. Stories of fantastic cities and ancient kingdoms reclaimed by the jungle."

"You said it yourself," Queen countered. "There aren't any ruins. Wouldn't someone have found something by now?"

"When the missionaries and explorers arrived, they brought death on a scale that we can scarcely imagine. It is believed that as many as ten million people died in the Congo alone—fifteen percent of the population—during the Belgian occupation. Who can say what was lost?" Mulamba paused, momentarily overcome with emotion. "However, to answer your question, I believe that something *was* found. There is a rumor that Dr. Livingstone himself found the ruins of an ancient civilization, perhaps on the edge of the Congo rain forest or somewhere in the Rift Valley, during his expedition to find the source of the Nile."

Rook saw where Mulamba was headed. "So Livingstone told Stanley about it. Stanley wrote it all down in his diary, but then decided to tear those pages out. Why the change of heart? And why didn't Livingstone ever talk about it?"

"Livingstone was quite ill at the time, possibly delirious. He died less than two years later, without ever recovering. It may be that he never intended to reveal what he had found, believing that such a discovery would lead to further exploitation of the African people. However, Stanley might have had a much different reason for destroying the record of that meeting.

"For several years thereafter, Stanley tried in vain to organize another expedition to Africa. He might very well have intended to search for Livingstone's lost city himself. Maybe he removed the diary pages so that no one would beat him to the prize. What is known with certainty is that Stanley abandoned his plans for another African expedition when he was approached by Leopold, who asked him to personally oversee the creation of the Congo Free State."

"If Stanley was coming back anyway, what would have stopped him from going after the lost city?"

Mulamba pursed his lips again. "When the ruins of Great Zimbabwe were excavated, beginning in the late nineteenth century, the colonial government of Rhodesia insisted that the city had been built by an unknown white civilization, all evidence to the contrary. As late as the 1970s, archaeologists and museums were threatened with censure or worse if they tried to publish the truth. This was not merely a case of willful ignorance. The government believed, correctly as it happens, that the knowledge of a strong historic African civilization would embolden those who sought to break the chains of colonial domination. It is not a coincidence that the country once known as Rhodesia, named for a white man, is now called Zimbabwe."

Queen caught on faster than Rook. "You think that if you can find evidence of an even older African civilization, it will become a symbol for your united Africa."

"This is no small matter," Mulamba said. Rook noticed that he gradually began speaking more rapidly, with greater passion. "For centuries, white Europeans, and the Arabs before them, justified every sort of atrocity—slavery, rape, wholesale slaughter—by simply saying that black Africans are savages, animals, incapable of achieving civilization on their own."

Rook shifted uncomfortably in his seat. "Well, yeah, but things are different now."

"Are they? The developing nations of Africa are locked in an unending cycle of violence, and what does the rest of the world say? They are savages. They cannot rule themselves. The petroleum companies show up and say: 'let us drill for your oil,' and if the leader of the country says, 'No, this belongs to us,' they simply pay that man's enemies to overthrow the government. And why not? The Africans are savages."

Queen held up a hand. "Look, I get it. We both do. And I agree with you. It sucks. But do you really think finding an old ruined city is going to change things overnight?"

"I don't expect you to understand. You are white. You are American."

"Hey—"

"Until the people of Africa believe that they are capable of greatness, they will never rise above the savagery that prevents them from achieving it. And there are powerful forces working to ensure that the status quo does not change. Why do you think I was taken? They fear the day when Africa says, 'No more. You will not take our wealth and feed us your table scraps anymore.'"

Rook sighed. *De Oppresso Liber*—that was what he'd signed up for when he'd joined the Army, earned his Green Beret, and gone on to be a part of Chess Team.

Freeing the oppressed was a hell of a lot easier when it involved nothing more complicated than shooting some maniac terrorist bent on mass extermination.

He tilted the rearview mirror until he found Queen's face. She was wearing her glasses, which meant that Deep Blue was also listening in, but even with the lenses in place, Rook could still read the uncertainty in her eyes.

He nodded to her, a gesture that said both 'I trust you' and 'let's do this.' She nodded back, then turned to Mulamba. "I don't know if this crazy idea of yours has a chance in hell of succeeding, but that's your problem. Ours is keeping you safe."

"I always wanted to go to Belgium," Rook said, grinning. "Actually, that's a lie. I don't have a clue where Belgium is."

TWENTY-TWO

Near Lake Kivu, Democratic Republic of the Congo

The forest seemed to fold over Bishop. He knew he had traveled only a short distance from where he had left Knight and Felice, and yet when he looked back, he saw no trace of them.

Good, he thought. *If I can't see them, the rebels can't either.*

He slowed his pace, treading so softly that he could no longer hear his own footfalls, and he began paying closer attention to his surroundings. The humid air hummed with activity. Insects swarmed around his head, while birds and monkeys chattered and squealed, as they capered in the tangle of branches overhead. The jungle was a living thing, indifferent to his presence, but just as capable of destroying him as the men who hunted him.

A distant metallic sound reached his ears, and he oriented toward it, keeping the heavy M240B at the ready. Although the machine gun weighed more than forty pounds and was meant to be fired from the ground, or preferably from a stable tripod or turret mount, Bishop's prodigious size and strength enabled him to wield the machine gun as effectively as an ordinary infantryman might shoot a rifle. Even so, it was a cumbersome weapon for moving through the labyrinth of tree boughs, and when he heard the noise again, off to his left and much closer, it took him a moment to swing his body around toward the source. That moment almost cost him dearly.

A man stood there, forty yards away, a surprised look on his face, as if Bishop had caught him with his pants down, relieving his bladder. But the man had his Kalashnikov to his shoulder, and in the instant that Bishop's finger tightened on the trigger of the 240, a jet of yellow flame erupted from the rifle.

Bishop felt hot metal rake his arm, but the sensation was forgotten the moment his machine gun bucked in his hands. The gunmen slumped lifeless, a dozen 7.62 mm rounds perforating his chest, before he could get off a second shot.

Bishop immediately swept the area, just in case the man wasn't alone. There was no sign of any other rebels nearby, but the sound of the brief firefight would bring them running. Bishop considered setting up a hasty fighting position and waiting for them, but he discarded the idea. His goal was to draw the attackers away from Knight and Felice, not take them all on single-handedly. He moved off at an angle from the direction the gunman had been facing, listening intently for any hint of enemy presence.

After about a hundred yards, he recalled that he'd been shot, but there was no pain now and an inspection of the area revealed a hole in his sleeve, but no injury, not even a graze. Bishop didn't believe in luck. Sometimes things just happened, but hoping for miracles to save the day was a dangerous way for a soldier to live.

His path brought him to the edge of the forest, and from the cover of the trees, he could see Lake Kivu stretched out across the eastern horizon. His mental GPS told him that the camp where he and Knight had found Felice was to the north, and he assumed that was where the rebel forces would be found as well. He aimed the machine gun in that general direction and squeezed off two short bursts, and then waited.

He didn't have to wait long.

A dark green shape appeared in the distance, moving slowly along the lakeshore. It was low and flat, barely visible above the tall grass, but Bishop had no difficulty identifying it as an armored personnel carrier, similar to the US Army's Bradley fighting vehicle. The APC rode on parallel tracks like a tank, but it was smaller and equipped with an open gun turret instead of a heavy cannon. A lone soldier sat behind the machine gun, slowly sweeping the barrel of his weapon back and forth in the forest's direction.

Armored troop carriers were not usually found in the arsenal of a rag tag guerilla force and for a fleeting moment, he wondered if these were DRC Army troops, arriving to drive off the rebel attackers. That illusion evaporated when he saw a cluster of riflemen moving behind the tracked vehicle. They wore civilian attire—jeans, canvas trousers, T-shirts—not like the battle dress uniform worn by the gunner in the tracked vehicle.

Another APC appeared right behind it. Then another.

The army was here all right, but not to rescue them from the rebels. The two groups had joined forces to hunt down the last survivor of the scientific expedition.

This was why Bishop didn't believe in luck.

He slung the M240 across his back and melted into the forest.

TWENTY-THREE

To Felice's surprise, they didn't run far. Just a few minutes after their flight began, Knight stopped in his tracks and hissed for her to join him. He pointed to the base of a tree that looked no different than any of the hundreds of others they had passed.

"There."

She didn't immediately understand what he meant, but assumed he had some kind of plan. He knelt at the base of the tree and thrust his hands into the accumulation of decaying leaf litter. She heard him give a little grunt of pain as he drew up a double armful of debris and soil, but he kept at it until he had scooped out a hollow large enough for both of them to lie in.

"Bishop said to keep moving."

"I know what he said." Knight spoke through clenched teeth, but Felice could not tell if he was in pain or merely irritated with her. Given his wounds, she thought it must be the former, but he wasn't letting it slow him down. "Trust me. This is what I do."

She acceded to his wishes and lowered herself into the hole he had dug. He knelt beside her and went to work filling the hollow with the material he had removed. Felice could not fathom what it was about this particular place that had prompted him to choose it as a hiding place, but she took comfort in his assurance. She knew better than to question his expertise—her survival depended on it.

As he piled the leaves on top of her, Felice experienced an instinctive panic at the thought of being buried alive, but the debris was no heavier than a blanket, and when he was done, there were large gaps—albeit artfully concealed—through which to breathe and see.

"We need to stay perfectly still," Knight said softly, almost breathing in her ear.

"How long?"

"Hard to say. Hours. Maybe days. Is that going to be a problem?"

"What if I need to pee?"

She had meant it as a joke to lighten the mood, but Knight took the question seriously. "You'll have to hold it. The smell of urine might give us away."

Felice sniffed. The odor of rotting vegetation was so overpowering, she couldn't imagine anyone being able to make the distinction, but once more she deferred to his judgment. "Wonderful."

"What happened to my eye?"

The whispered question stung her like a slap. She didn't know how to answer him.

"It's gone, isn't it?"

"No. I mean, I don't know. Sometimes injuries like that look a lot worse than they are. Doctors can do amazing things..." Her voice trailed off. She meant what she said, but it sounded like a lie in her ears. Maybe a skilled ocular surgeon could repair the kind of damage he'd sustained, but they were a long way from anywhere with that level of medical care. She wasn't sure how they were going to make it to Kisangani, much less whether they would ever see America again.

Knight didn't say anything for a long while after that, and at first Felice was grateful for the silence, but the complete lack of movement or conversation made the minutes pass with interminable slowness. Finally, she could stand it no more.

"By the way," she whispered, "I'm Felice. It's Knight, right?"

Knight grunted an affirmative, which she took as a good sign. At least he hadn't told her to shut up.

"And your friend is Bishop. I'm guessing those aren't your real names."

"No. My real name is Shin Dae-jung."

"Should I call you Shin?"

"If you want. In Korea, the surname comes first, then the given name."

"Maybe I'll just stick to Knight."

He laughed softly, which Felice took to be an encouraging sign. "That's probably a good idea. Honestly, I've been Knight for so long, I hardly even remember my real name."

"You took those names from chess pieces, right? You're some kind of special military unit, and those are your callsigns?"

"Well, I could tell you, but...you know."

"I know—well, knew—a guy who calls himself King. Friend of yours?"

"Seriously? Wait...shhhh."

The change was so abrupt that she thought he might be joking, but given the circumstances, it was better to err on the side of caution. She immediately clammed up, sucking in a breath and holding it, lest the sound of her inhalations give their position away. Felice strained to catch some hint of noise, but the only sound she heard was the *lub-dub* of her own heartbeat. Eventually, the burn of carbon dioxide in her lungs forced her to resume normal breathing, but during all that time, Knight was as still as a corpse. Then, without any sort of warning, he sat up like Lazarus risen from the dead.

"Bish!" Knight hissed the word, barely louder than a whisper. "Over here."

Felice sat up as well. She didn't see the big man at first, and when she finally did, he was so far away that she wondered how Knight, with only one good eye, had seen him.

Bishop trotted toward them, smiling. "Pick up," he said. "They're coming. We have to move."

"And go where?" Knight asked. "We're better off digging in and letting them pass by. Then we can get back to the LZ."

Bishop shook his head. "There is no LZ. A mechanized infantry company is between us and the lake, and they're sweeping this way. Then there are the rebels."

Up to this point, Felice had been content to stay quiet, but she found this news too unsettling. "You're saying the Army is after us?"

Bishop nodded. "It looks like they're trying to form a cordon around this section of the jungle. They'll surround us and then close the noose. We need to get moving, break through before they can complete the circle."

Knight hauled himself to his feet, wincing and favoring his left arm. Felice got up as well, and realized that both men were staring at her. "What?"

"Somebody's going to a lot of trouble to make sure that no one from your expedition makes it back," Bishop said. "I'm wondering what a geneticist in the backwater of Africa could do to piss off so many people."

"Geneticist?" Knight said with a frown. He looked at Bishop, who just shook his head as if to say *later*.

Felice sensed there was something important about their aversion toward her profession, but without further explanation, she let it go. Instead, she simply said, "The explanation is a little technical."

"Then it will have to wait. We need to move."

TWENTY-FOUR

They trekked for nearly four hours, moving deeper into the forest in what Bishop hoped was a straight line. When they came upon the occasional clearing, he was able to verify that they were still moving west by the location of the sun, but under the jungle canopy, there was no way to be sure that they weren't wandering in circles. There had been no sign of pursuit, but in the dense jungle, Bishop knew that the rebels could be anywhere.

Knight had kept up with Bishop's relentless pace, managing better than Felice, but he grew more listless as the day wore on. Bishop felt concerned, but there was nothing more he could do for his friend.

As night approached, the scant light penetrating the tangled canopy vanished completely, plunging them into darkness, and leaving them with little choice but to stop for the night. They huddled together under a hasty shelter made from Bishop's parachute—still damp from the plunge into Lake Kivu—and in the glow of a chemical lightstick, he handed out an MRE. Knight had no appetite, but Bishop hassled him into eating a piece of bread and drinking some water, along with a hefty dose of penicillin to combat infection from his injuries. He also passed out some mefloquine as an anti-malarial. Knight soon fell into a restless slumber.

After a while, Bishop turned to Felice. "Tell me about your project."

She tore her gaze away from Knight and stared at the green chemlight as if composing her thoughts. "The Congo region sits on enormous reserves of fossil fuel. Despite that, it is one of the poorest nations on Earth, energy-wise. Except for the cities, most people don't have electricity or automobiles, but live the way they've lived for thousands of years. Most of the petroleum that is recovered gets exported to foreign markets, so while there is some revenue from energy production, most Congolese don't see any benefit.

"President Mulamba commissioned my team to find a new source of energy—renewable energy—that would address the needs of the people living here, as well as providing a long term source of revenue."

"You're American. How did you get involved in this?"

"For the last couple years, I've been working with a non-profit agency that's trying to use cutting edge technologies to help developing nations stand on their own. Most of Africa is stuck in the 1950s. Not much has changed in the Congo since the Belgians left. The economy is driven by natural resources, but that's not sustainable in the long term. If the Congo follows the pattern of other developing nations, they'll keep exploiting those resources, with most of the money leaving the country, and they'll deplete everything long before they make any kind of progress. Our goal is to find a way to leapfrog straight into the twenty-first century. Energy production is critical to such a plan. You can't put computers in every school if there's no electricity to run them."

"That doesn't exactly sound like a job for a geneticist," Bishop said.

"We're a multi-disciplinary team..." She paused abruptly and Bishop saw that she was blinking back tears. "I'm sorry," she said, her voice thick with emotion. "It just hit me that they're all..."

Bishop laid a hand on her shoulder. He felt awkward trying to comfort her. He kept such a tight lid on his own emotions that he didn't really have much experience reading or reacting to the emotions of other people. "It's okay."

He didn't know what else to say, but he left his hand where it was until he sensed that she was ready to continue. "I guess I got involved by accident. I was working with a group in Kenya, trying to develop new gene therapies to stop the spread of AIDS, when I heard about some research going on at Lake Kivu, involving extremophiles."

"Like the organisms that live around deep-sea volcanic vents?"

"Exactly. Extremophiles are life-forms—usually unicellular organisms—that can survive and thrive in conditions where nothing should be able to. Many are autotrophs—they produce their own food, like plants—but instead of using sunlight, they can transform heat and energy from chemical reactions into food. Lake Kivu is situated in an area of extreme volcanic activity, which makes it a perfect environment for extremophile organisms to thrive.

"These microbes interact with escaping volcanic gasses, to produce hydrocarbons in huge quantities. There's an enormous bubble of natural gas at the bottom of Lake Kivu—about sixteen cubic miles"

"That sounds like a lot."

"Enough to supply about a hundred large electrical plants, and it's constantly replenishing. Unfortunately, it's also very dangerous where it is. The methane breaks down into carbon dioxide, and there's an even larger bubble of that trapped at the bottom of the lake. If the methane spontaneously ignites—which can happen without any warning—the resulting explosion would release the CO_2 to the surface and suffocate everyone living in the lake basin."

Bishop stiffened in surprise. "You're kidding, right?"

"In 1986, a carbon dioxide cloud released by Lake Nyos, in Cameroon, killed 1,700 people. The cloud was believed to have contained about 300,000 tons of CO_2 and affected people more than fifteen miles from the lake. Lake Nyos is fairly remote, with just a few rural villages. The bubble at the bottom of Lake Kivu is believed to contain 500 million tons, and there are more than two million people living along its shores."

"Why would anyone choose to live near something like that?"

Felice shrugged. "The same reason people live on the San Andreas fault, or in Tornado Alley. You've got to live somewhere. Most of the people in the Kivu region probably don't even know about the danger, and spontaneous eruptions happen on geological time scales—thousands, even millions of years in between.

"Several agencies have been working to come up with a way to mitigate the threat, as well as to harvest the natural gas for energy production, but those solutions carry a lot of risk. Disturbing the gas deposits might very well trigger the catastrophe they're trying to prevent.

"Our research isn't—wasn't—concerned with that, though. We were looking at the cause, the microbes that produce the methane in the first place. If we can find a way to adapt them to a different environment, we would be able to produce an endless supply of renewable energy."

"You want to use bacteria to make natural gas?"

"It's a natural process," she explained. "Scientists in South Korea have found a way to use E. coli to produce gasoline. We just need to find a way to make it efficient and cost effective, and we were very close. Our research would revolutionize energy production everywhere. There would be no more need to drill for petroleum, no more tearing up wilderness areas to sink wells, no more fracking or pipelines. And since the process would be carbon neutral, it would pretty much solve the problem of greenhouse gas emissions and global warming."

"So why would anyone want to stop you?"

"A lot of people have invested heavily in the status quo. This process would be available to anyone, and that would mean the end of the fossil fuel industry."

"So the rebels who attacked us, and the Army...they're all working for oil companies?"

"Possibly. Or they might just want to keep things the way they are. People fear change, even when that change means a better life for everyone."

Bishop had no response to that, so he switched gears. "You said you had to find a way to adapt these extremophiles. You're a geneticist, so I'm going to assume that your plan is to re-engineer their DNA. Isn't that kind of risky?"

She frowned at him. "What have you got against genetic research?"

"Oh, let's see...tinkering with the blueprint of life, creating organisms that aren't supposed to exist and that can't be controlled, only figuring out when the shit hits the fan that there might be unintended consequences... I could go on."

"Humanity has been modifying the genetic code for thousands of years, long before anyone ever knew that such a thing as DNA even existed. Most of our food supply derives from plant and animal strains that were produced through selective breeding. This isn't Frankenstein science. Sure, there are abuses, but that doesn't mean we should go back to living in caves."

He wanted to argue with her, to tell her how he knew firsthand just how much damage one misguided person could cause by playing God, but there was no point. Genetic engineering was a genie that was already out of the bottle. There was no turning back the clock. "Better get some sleep," he said, finally. "Tomorrow could be a long day."

He could tell that she wasn't happy about the way the conversation had concluded, but she nodded and curled up on the ground next to Knight. Bishop continued to watch her until she was snoring softly.

The glowstick eventually faded to a dim green stripe, barely visible in the darkness, but Bishop did not sleep.

TWENTY-FIVE

Kinshasa, Democratic Republic of the Congo

When King and Asya had first arrived in Kinshasa a few hours earlier, they had seen a city poised on the brink of chaos. At some point during their captivity, someone gave it a push.

Mabuki brought him up to speed as their convoy rolled back toward the city. "Shortly after you left the assembly, Army troops loyal to General Velle launched a coup from within the Palais de la Nation itself. They waited until I was away from the palace, looking for you, to make their move. They have taken several hostages, including President Okoa, your Senator Marrs and that woman, Favreau."

Asya let out what sounded like a strangled laugh. She had recovered from her near drowning, but still looked like a drenched rat. Both of them were soaked through, and coated in a thin film of mud.

King accepted a canteen from one of the soldiers and drank a mouthful of lukewarm water. He swished it through his teeth to dislodge the muck, then let it dribble out unswallowed. A little more water spilled on his clothes wasn't going to make much of a difference, but drinking water from an unreliable source was a good way to get the runs, and that was something he definitely didn't need right now. Too late, he saw Asya guzzling from another bottle.

Oh well, he decided. *Can't be any worse than what we were just swimming in.*

The thunderstorm had moved on, but it was still raining heavily. The streets were ankle-deep in water, and it was still accumulating faster than it could drain away. The rain kept most people inside, which was good, because there were soldiers everywhere—their red berets marked them as members of the Republican Guard, loyal to Mulamba's government and under Mabuki's direct command. This part of the city was controlled by pro-Mulamba forces, but if Mabuki's report was correct, several divisions of the army had openly declared their support for General Velle, and now occupied more than a third of the city, including the important Gombe commune, where the Palais de la Nation and numerous other government buildings and foreign embassies were located.

King explained Asya's reaction. "Favreau organized this. She's the one giving them their orders."

Mabuki's brow furrowed. "This is a very serious accusation. She is here as a guest of the government, helping negotiate an end to this crisis."

"Yeah, well I think she's been negotiating a lot more than that. She's a mercenary, working for an outfit called Executive Solutions."

"*Oui*," said Mabuki. "I have heard of them. They were in Angola. Very brutal men."

"And women. She's only interested in what's best for her employers—which in this case is probably Consolidated Energy."

The general considered this for a moment. "You told the assembly that President Mulamba is still alive. Is this true?"

"Last I heard. Favreau took my phone, so I haven't been in contact with my team." King thought Mabuki looked like he needed more convincing, so he added. "I would assume he's on his way."

"His return might not be enough to turn the tide," Mabuki said. "Now that General Velle has made his move, there might be no way to prevent civil war."

For the first time since he'd been given them, King found himself wishing for the instantaneous connectivity of the q-phones. The situation had moved beyond the point where he could advise the government forces on the best way to maintain stability. Now, every choice he might make was fraught with the potential for blowback. That however, was only *one* of the troubling thoughts occupying his mind. There was something else bothering him, a detail that seemed at first glance like a jigsaw piece mixed up with the wrong puzzle.

His mind kept turning over the moment where he had fired on the soldiers with the MP5 taken from one of the steroid twins. The mercenary, along with everyone else in the truck, was now dead. Mabuki's Republican Guard forces had opened up on the army truck, strafing it with rounds from the turret-mounted

DShK 12.7 mm machine gun, and setting the truck on fire in the process. King had lost the MP5 during the plunge into the drainage ditch, but he still recalled how it had felt in his hands, especially when he'd pulled the trigger. It had been heavier, with a lot more recoil than it should have had. He also remembered how it had devastated the bodies of the soldiers.

Bullets killed; that was their job, and they did so in a way that usually wasn't pretty. Even so, some types of ammunition seemed designed to accomplish that grim purpose in a way that was almost sadistic. Overpressure rounds, like those he suspected had been in the magazine of the MP5, contained particles of heavy metal, loosely packed in the hollow core of the bullet. When the bullet was fired, the acceleration would compress the powdered metal against the rear of the hollow core, and then on impact with the target, the powder would be catapulted forward, creating a catastrophic shock wave that caused massive destruction at the cellular level.

Aside from their perceived inhumane effects, overpressure rounds were usually disdained by military forces for purely practical reasons. To accelerate the heavier payload to lethal velocity, the bullets needed more explosive force in the firing chamber. The added recoil not only made the weapon harder to use, but reduced its effective lifespan, and this was particularly true of semi-automatic weapons like the MP5. Firing overpressure rounds in a machine pistol was analogous to putting nitrous oxide in the carburetor of a sports car. You went faster, but at the cost of burning up your engine.

King wasn't surprised that the mercenaries were packing overpowered ammunition. It was entirely consistent with their testosterone-fueled lifestyle. What bothered him was the sense that he had seen something like this before.

Still pondering the significance of this troubling detail, King turned back to the general. "Can you get me to a telephone?"

Mabuki smiled and produced a slim mobile unit that looked about ten years old. "Will this suit your needs?"

King took it and thumbed the power button. The backlit monochrome LCD display showed a strong signal. "I apologize in advance for the long distance charges."

Mabuki waved a hand dismissively. "Let the government pay for it. That way, even if General Velle succeeds, we will still be able to stick it to him."

King laughed and dialed a number.

There was a brief pause between the click of the connection being established and the mumbled greeting. The voice was groggy and irritable, not surprising since it was the middle of the night at the other end of the call, but the voice was still instantly recognizable.

"It's King."

The bleariness—an act, Deep Blue wouldn't be sleeping much with the team in the field and under fire—was completely gone when the response finally arrived. "King. Thank God. What's your situation?"

"For starters, I don't have secure communication."

Silence. The transmission lag was maddening. *Carrier pigeons would be faster*, King thought.

"I kind of figured that," Deep Blue said. "Go on."

"Pawn and I are fine, but things here have gone sideways."

"I've been monitoring the news reports."

King waited for Deep Blue to elaborate, but several seconds passed and he realized that there wasn't anything more to be said. "How are the others?"

"Queen and Rook..." Another pause occurred, presumably Deep Blue trying to come up with a way to share his news in ambiguous terms. "...were successful. They're checking something else out right now, but I expect them to be on their way very soon. I've booked their flight."

That meant *Crescent II* was already en route to pick them up. Mulamba might conceivably be back in Kinshasa in time for breakfast. "Bishop and Knight?"

"No word. Doesn't look good."

Damn.

King closed his eyes, took a breath and went on. "What's the best play here?"

"Remember what you're there for. Advise and support. I know that's not very helpful, but it's all I've got. I trust your judgment on this. You've got a lot more experience than I'll ever have."

King parsed the comment quickly. The 'experience' to which Deep Blue was referring was the sum of several lifetimes spent roaming the planet, championing the defenseless, knowing full well that the outcome had already been written in the annals of the history King knew. His choices hadn't been guided by knowledge of what the inevitable outcome would be, but rather by a more fundamental determination to protect the innocent, help the helpless, to do what he believed was right and the certain knowledge that he would have to live with his choices for hundreds of years thereafter. He wasn't immortal anymore, but that didn't mean he could just wash his hands of the situation. Walking away, or even simply staying on the sidelines as a spectator was unthinkable, especially knowing that Bishop and Knight might have already made the ultimate sacrifice. If he didn't do something, their deaths would be meaningless.

He knew what he had to do.

He glanced at Asya, who was watching and listening expectantly, and he felt his certitude start to crumble.

"I understand," he said. Without hanging up, he turned to Mabuki. "I need to find a way back into the Palais."

The general looked at him expectantly. "To rescue the hostages?"

King shook his head. "No. I left my sunglasses in there. I'd like to get them back."

TWENTY-SIX

Monique Favreau took the news of the Americans' rescue and the death of her men in stride. It confirmed her instincts about the man and filled her with an almost sexual anticipation for the battle she knew would follow.

She was not quite so optimistic about the report that had preceded it.

As the American had hinted, President Mulamba had escaped, or rather he'd been liberated by a commando team working in conjunction with her new nemesis. The failure of her men—two teams, twenty men, against just two people, if reports were correct— was unforgivable, and the very few who had survived the debacle could count themselves lucky that the Red Queen was in a different hemisphere. The news that Mulamba was free and on his way back had forced her to accelerate her original plan. Instead of waiting for General Velle to show up and lead the charge, she'd had to settle for one of his subordinate officers, a colonel in the 1st Brigade, who had happily assassinated his immediate commander, the man between him and Velle, and taken charge, deploying his 2,000 troops throughout the Gombe commune, and personally seizing control of the Palais de la Nation.

The colonel was more ambitious than intelligent, but at least he knew how to carry out his assignments, which was more than could be said for her men in London, who had not only let Mulamba escape but had subsequently lost track of him. She had given them an hour to fix their mistake. Fifty-eight minutes later, her phone rang.

"Ace Diamonds," the caller said.

"I hope you have something good to tell me," she replied.

"Um, I'm not sure exactly." Ace Diamonds had, up until about fourteen hundred hours, Universal Coordinated Time, been Four

Diamonds, and was still getting used to his new position of responsibility. "We're spread kind of thin here, but we've got the international terminals covered...at Heathrow, I mean..."

"Stop!" Favreau closed her eyes and took several breaths to control her rising ire. Despite his ultimate failure, the previous Ace Diamonds had at least been self-motivated and marginally intelligent. "What exactly do you plan to do if he happens to wander past you?"

"Well..."

"He won't be traveling in the open. *He's* not that stupid. The only way to regain a strategic advantage is to think one step ahead of him. What other ways are there for him to leave the country?"

"Ah, military transport?"

"If he had the support of the British Government, we would know about it." Favreau considered her own question. "He was there to get that support. Would he leave without it?"

"Uh..."

"It was a rhetorical question. He has unfinished business. Where exactly was he when you took him the first time?"

There was a long pause, as if the man was asking someone else for the answer. "He was at the Royal Geographic Society."

That was a surprise. Mulamba had been in the United Kingdom to build support for his African federation. Why would he visit a historical institution? She caught herself before asking Ace for more information—that way lay madness.

"Stand by," she said, and ended the call. She immediately placed another, calling a directory assistance number for London. A few minutes later, she was talking to a receptionist at the RGS.

She introduced herself as a French journalist, covering the situation in the Congo. "I am trying to get some background information about the abduction of President Mulamba. I understand that he had just left your offices when he was taken?"

The receptionist passed her off to one of the directors who came on the line armed with a carefully worded legal statement, which could be distilled down to two basic words: no comment.

At the other end of the line, Favreau just smiled. She liked a challenge, and as a seasoned intelligence operative, she knew a thing or two about interrogations. In a voice that was seductive in its helplessness, she said, "I have no wish to scandalize your institution. It's only that the citizens are wondering why President Mulamba would have left at such a critical time. If you could only help me to understand what he was trying to accomplish..." She let the request hang, allowing the man to fill in the blanks.

She could hear the inner conflict in his voice. "Yes, of course. I understand. It's just that I can't comment on the matter. You see, there's to be an inquest, and...well..."

"*Oui*, of course. But if you could only just tell me why President Mulamba came to see you, how could that little thing matter? It could be our little secret. You could be my 'unnamed source,' no?"

"Ah...I...well... He was very interested in the diaries of Sir Henry Morton Stanley. Some foolishness about missing pages."

"Missing pages?"

As Favreau expected, that minor concession broke the dam of his resistance. "Yes, it seems that Stanley removed several pages from his diary, relating to his meeting with Livingstone. No one quite knows why, but I'm sure there's a reasonable and quite mundane explanation.

"We didn't have what he was looking for. I'm not sure the pages even exist. If Stanley tore them out, he would surely have gone the added step of tossing them in the fireplace. I suggested he try the Royal Museum for Central Africa near Brussels. They have the largest collection of documents relating to Stanley, so if the pages exist, they would be there."

Favreau rang off without another word and immediately called Ace Diamonds.

TWENTY-SEVEN

Tervuren, Belgium

Queen got out of the taxi and did a quick 360 degree visual sweep, before stepping aside to allow Mulamba to climb out. Rook, who had been up front with the driver, got out as well, passing over a handful of Euro notes that generously exceeded the amount shown on the meter.

"It is as I told you," the driver said in French. "The museum is closed. Are you certain you wish to be dropped off here?"

"Yes," Mulamba insisted. "This is where we need to be. Thank you."

Queen frowned, wondering if they would not have been better off taking the driver up on his offer and going to a nearby hotel instead. They were too noticeable as it was, and the taxi driver wasn't likely to forget them or their destination. But there was no reasoning with Mulamba, and it probably wouldn't make much difference anyway. They would be done and out of the country long before anyone realized that the missing Congolese president was skulking around a museum in Belgium.

The Royal Museum for Central Africa was housed in a stately palatial structure in the municipality of Tervuren, just a short drive from the capital city of Brussels. The museum grounds appeared completely deserted. The small parking area opposite the museum entrance was empty, except for an enormous statue of a trumpeting elephant that guarded the path into the beautifully cultivated, but uninhabited, forest park surrounding the edifice. The utter lack of activity was due, in part, to the lateness of the hour, but was also because the museum was closed to the public for renovations, which were expected to last several years.

They had only learned of the renovation during the two-hour train ride from London to Brussels. While this development had thwarted Mulamba's goal of finding a scholar or curator to walk him through the Stanley archives, Queen had seen it as a blessing in disguise.

"We'll sneak in, find what you're looking for, and get out before anyone knows we were there," she told him. "Zero footprint."

The African president had not been particularly happy about the idea of breaking and entering, but his eagerness to find the missing pages of the Stanley diary far outweighed his moral restraint.

Which left only the question of how they would actually accomplish the break-in.

"Leave that to me," Lewis Aleman had told her.

Aleman was the team's tech guru. Someone—probably Rook—had once jokingly referred to him as R2-D2, because of his uncanny ability to solve any problem related to computers or electronic systems. The resemblance to the mech-droid from the Star Wars movies stopped there however. Aleman was a tall, lean, endurance athlete and former Special Forces sniper. A combat injury had taken him permanently out of the field, but over the years, he had done more to ensure the success of Chess Team missions from his computer console than he ever could have with a long-range rifle. Although the original design was not his, Aleman's technical savvy had made the quantum computer network a reality, leapfrogging developments in the private sector by decades. If anyone could get them past the security in the museum, it was Aleman.

What was unusual was that Aleman was now communicating with them directly. "Deep Blue is wrapped up with the situation in the Congo," he had told Queen, "so you'll be dealing with me directly."

That wasn't a problem for Queen, but she was concerned about the matter that now occupied Deep Blue's attention. She knew that King and Asya had escaped custody in Kinshasa, and that they were now launching a raid on the national palace, but there had been no word from Bishop and Knight, and it was clear that Deep Blue feared the worst.

Queen couldn't quite bring herself to believe that her teammates were dead. Bishop had always seemed indestructible to her, even before he had been given the regen serum. The fact that he had survived the dire side-effects of that serum, which transformed ordinary people into unstoppable rage monsters, had only deepened her sense of his invincibility. Even though he—like King—was now one hundred percent mortal again, she still couldn't imagine him dead, especially not at the hands of a few rebel fighters.

It was difficult to believe that Knight was gone, too, though for much different reasons. She had known Knight longer than anyone on the team. They had worked together in her first field assignment. He was always calm and coolly professional, essential to the success of any mission, and yet at the same time, almost invisible, which for a sniper was a critical skill. Even though she often forgot he was there, she couldn't imagine a world without him.

It had been Bishop's quiet invocation of the Special Forces motto that had prompted her decision to help Mulamba in his crazy quest. Like him, she felt a keen desire to defend the defenseless. If Bishop and Knight had made the ultimate sacrifice on behalf of the innocents living in the Congo region, then she was going to make damn sure that it wasn't for nothing.

As eager as she was for news—good or bad—she understood the importance of staying focused. King and Asya needed Deep Blue's full attention, and as it happened, she and Rook needed Aleman's expertise.

They strolled along the fringe of the park until the taillights of the departing taxi disappeared from view, then they reversed directions and headed back down the brick sidewalk that ran the length of the museum's north wall. Just beyond the building's corner, illuminated only by streetlights, a wrought iron fence blocked access to the museum campus. The gate to the staff parking lot just beyond—also empty—was secured with a heavy padlock.

"Stealth mode activated," Aleman said. "I've looped the security camera feed, so you're invisible for the moment, and I've bypassed the alarm. Not much I can do about that padlock though."

"We've got that," she replied, and turned to Rook. "Got the picks?"

He took a slim wallet from his back pocket. They'd left their weapons in the trunk of the sedan at a car park in London, but had managed to slip a few other items through the train station security checkpoint, including a set of carbon composite lock-picks.

"I got this," he announced.

"You know I'm better with the..." she licked her lips seductively, "delicate stuff."

"Nice try, babe," he replied in the same tone. "But I'm the key master."

"I'll flip you for it." She made a show of checking her pockets, then said, "Got a quarter?"

Rook rolled his eyes, and jammed his free hand into the front pocket of his jeans. Queen casually took the pick case from him so that he could check the right side, and as he did, she spun around and went to work on the lock.

"Call it in the—hey!"

The lock released with an audible click and Queen handed the picks back to him. "Told you. You'd still be fumbling around trying to get it in."

Mulamba laughed, and Rook shot him a venomous look before turning back to Queen. "You have the glasses. That's cheating."

"That must be it." She patted him on the shoulder, then pushed the gate open just enough to permit access. Rook entered first. As Mulamba passed through the opening, she followed and pulled the gate shut again.

Queen's research indicated that they would find what they were looking for in the Stanley Pavilion, a three-story satellite structure a short walk from the museum palace. They moved quickly to the elegant pillared porch and found the main entrance door, locked.

Rook stepped forward and went to work with the lock-picks, trying several before finding one that he thought would do the job. After a full minute of teasing the tumblers, he said, "These institutional locks are a lot trickier than a big ass padlock."

"Uh, huh."

Finally, the door yielded, and he pushed it open with a flourish.

Queen led the way, her glasses revealing details about the darkened interior of the pavilion that were hidden from unaided eyes. She saw that several of the display cases were empty, while others contained what looked like nothing more than a collection of dusty old knick-knacks without any sense of continuity. In an age of high-tech interactive displays and immersive environment, the Royal Museum was itself a relic from another age.

"I can see why they thought it was time to renovate."

"Well, it's good that one of us can see something," Rook said.

"Don't get all pissy just because I take better care of my things."

"Oh, is that how you remember it? Because I—"

"Are you guys always like this on a mission?" Aleman cut in.

Queen smiled but didn't reply. Banter was standard operating procedure for Rook, but as a rule she didn't engage in it with him during a mission. Right now though, the good humor was a welcome distraction from the uncertainty surrounding the rest of the team's fate, a situation which left her feeling helpless.

They made their way to the reading room, where to their disappointment, they found rows of empty shelves. A computer terminal sat idle on a desk near the entrance, and at Aleman's direction, she booted it up. A password prompt appeared on the screen.

"Hang on," Aleman said. "The good news is, I'm already in the museum's WiFi network... Okay, try this." He rattled off a string of letters, numbers and characters, which she entered on the keyboard, and when the desktop appeared a moment later, Aleman began remotely searching the directory. Queen watched as file folders and spreadsheets began opening on the screen.

"Okay," he said, after several minutes of silence. "The Stanley archive is still in the building, but has been moved to conservation storage, just down the hall." He gave her directions to the nearby room, along with the number of the container with the relevant documents.

The storage room was crowded with plastic totes, each labeled with an inventory sticker. The room had no windows to the outside, and with Aleman's permission, Queen told Rook to turn on the lights.

Still squinting from the change in illumination, Mulamba began scanning the stickers. He seemed to have a sense for the way the collection had been organized, and he found the correct case without consulting the catalogue number Queen had provided.

"Here," he said, his voice bubbling over with enthusiasm. "This is the one."

He loosed the clasp and opened the lid to reveal a nest of packing paper, and several bound books, each vacuum sealed in heavy cellophane and marked with another sticker. He held up one of them. "This is the diary in which Stanley recorded his meeting with Livingstone."

"I thought he tore out those pages," Rook said.

Mulamba nodded. "That is what has been reported. Still, it is a place to start." He pinched the plastic between his fingers and tried, without success, to tear apart the protective overwrap.

Rook rummaged in the desk and found a pair of scissors. "Try these, Joe."

"And be careful," Queen added. "Let's not add anything else to the list of crimes we're committing."

Mulamba seemed not hear her as he sliced open the packet and took out the journal. He thumbed through it quickly, scanning the dates at the top of each page until he found the entries from November of 1871. His expression fell just a little.

"It is true. The pages have indeed been removed." He looked uncertainly at the container but made no move to take anything else from it.

Queen spoke to Aleman in a low voice. "Any suggestions?"

"Wait one. Okay, there is a collection called 'miscellany.' Loose papers, looks like scientific notes, personal letters and so forth. Should be in the same container."

She relayed the message to Mulamba who commenced rooting in the packing material like a kid tearing into a Christmas present. His enthusiasm outpaced Rook's valiant effort at keeping the discarded items in some semblance of order, but after a minute or so, the African president held up another sealed package containing a dark brown manila folder. Mulamba cut it open and shook out several yellowed envelopes. He thumbed through them quickly, glancing at the delicately scripted name on each, before shuffling it to the bottom of the stack.

Rook chuckled and muttered, "Bills, bills, junk mail, bills."

Mulamba let out an excited cry and held up an envelope. "This is addressed to John Rowlands, esquire."

"And that's good?"

"John Rowlands and Henry Morton Stanley are one and the same. Stanley was born as Rowlands...forgive me, that's not quite correct. There is uncertainty as to his parentage. His mother abandoned him as an infant and Rowlands, the man he believed to be his father, died shortly after he was born. In any event, he took the name Stanley when he was eighteen."

"So what is that?" Rook asked. "Letters to my former self?"

"It is unopened," Mulamba said, breathlessly. He broke the wax seal and teased out the folded paper inside.

Queen saw his eyes moving back and forth as he read the contents, growing wider as he digested the information contained therein. Right up to that moment, she had been expecting the search to end in disappointment, a wild-goose chase, which she had agreed to only to placate the African leader. Now, she knew better.

"Aleman, it looks like we got what we came for. Tell *Crescent II* to come get us, ASAP."

A loud noise, like the sound of a very heavy book slamming down on a tabletop, startled the night watchman seated in the security office, in the main building. He laid his Sudoku puzzle on the desk and peered at the monitor, which showed the feeds from the security cameras distributed throughout the museum. Every few seconds, the display would change as the system cycled through the cameras, but nothing he saw accounted for the unusual noise in what was otherwise, at least as far as the guard was concerned, the deadest place on Earth.

He glanced at his wristwatch, then shrugged and stood up. He was just reaching for the antiquated security watch-clock when he glimpsed a figure standing on the other side of the security desk. He stared in disbelief for a moment, as if not quite believing his eyes.

He started to say something, but his voice was drowned out by the bark of a pistol. He was permanently silenced by the bullet that tore into his chest.

The man who now called himself Ace Diamonds looked down at the dead watchman to make sure that he wouldn't be getting back up. Then he took aim with the handgun just in case he did. If Ace had been using overpressure rounds, like his counterparts in the Congo, there would have been no need to verify, but it was hard enough getting guns in the more security conscious European countries. The experimental depleted-uranium rounds were simply out of the question. *Too bad though*, he thought. He kind of liked the way those super-bullets made a weasel go pop.

He rounded the security desk to get a look at the monitor and watched the feed for a few seconds. Finally, he unclipped the walkie-talkie from his belt and keyed the transmit button. "This is Ace D. Looks like we got here first. Diamonds, set up an outside perimeter so we'll know if anyone's coming. Spades, start a full sweep of the museum, just in case."

There was a flurry of responses, though not as many as there would have been just a few hours earlier. The unknown duo that had hit the farm outside Dartford had practically driven a lawn mower through their ranks. When the dust had finally settled, the force of ESI mercenaries had been reduced nearly by half. Just eleven men remained, four from the Spades team, and seven from the Diamonds. Ace, who had previously been the fourth man on the Diamonds team, suddenly found himself the most senior operator still standing.

A search of the desk yielded a map of the complex, and he used it to find the archives, where the Red Queen had told him Mulamba would be going next. He pushed the talk button again. "Ace Spades, this is Ace Diamonds, send a two-man element to secure the structure on the east side. That's the primary target. We'll finish here and then move over to set up our welcoming committee."

"Affirmative. Ace Spades, out."

As he lowered the walkie-talkie, it occurred to Ace Diamonds that he might have been a little hasty in storming the museum. What if Mulamba didn't show until morning? They couldn't hold the museum all night long. It was only a matter of time before...

He let the thought trail off as he stared at the unchanging images on the video monitors. He had thought it particularly lucky that he had been able to blow the door with a small breaching charge, and then make his way to the security office without attracting the watchman's notice. The cameras clearly showed the exterior. Ace would have been visible for several seconds during the time he set the charge. Stranger still, all the door indicator lights were green.

A malfunction?

He kept watching the cameras, certain that he was missing something, but the rotating shots of exhibition halls, labs and corridors showed no change. None whatsoever.

The cameras are on a loop, he realized with a start. *Somebody disabled the security system before we got here.*

With equal parts dread and anticipation, Ace Diamonds raised the walkie-talkie once more. "All units, converge on the Stanley Pavilion—the east building. They're already here."

TWENTY-EIGHT

The shot was barely audible. In fact, Queen didn't even realize she had heard anything until Aleman said, "What was that? It sounded like a gun."

Before she could reply, he answered his own question. "Nine mil. Single round."

Aleman was a walking encyclopedia of firearms trivia, but she knew the only way he could have made that identification was by running the audio transmission through some kind of gun noise database.

"I'm dropping the video loop... Queen, get out of there! You're not alone."

Queen jolted into action. "Rook, lights!"

He knew without asking that something was wrong. He swept a hand across the light switch and then moved to Mulamba's side, pulling the man down into a crouch. Although the room was plunged into instant darkness, Queen clearly saw Rook pluck the letter from Mulamba's grasp and tuck it into the man's inside jacket pocket. "We'll read it later," he whispered.

"I'll recon," Queen said. She turned and jogged out of the room. Her leg throbbed with each step, but she compartmentalized the pain and moved without even a limp. She'd experienced far, far worse, and she was reminded of it every time she saw the bright red brand on her forehead in a mirror.

Ghost images began appearing in her field of view. Aleman was integrating the security camera feed into the virtual environment.

She saw, as if looking through the walls, two figures crowned with red dots, entering the building through the front door. "Two coming in," she whispered to Rook. "Make your way to the fire exit, if you can. I'll go meet the neighbors."

"Be care... Ah, I mean, go get 'em, tiger!"

She smiled in the darkness, then spun away running silently through the dark halls. The two men were creeping along, and as she neared the lobby, she could see the beams of flashlights bobbing. She also saw more red dots outside the Stanley Pavilion, closing in from all directions, moving to cut off all the exits.

Damn it.

"Aleman," she whispered. "Can you call Rook's phone? Let him know that the exit is a no go?"

"I'll try. No guarantee he'll pick up. They aren't really 'telephones' in the literal sense, you know."

"Busy now." She waited until the flashlights were pointing into the corners of the big room, then dashed forward and ducked behind the nearest display case. She watched the lights a few seconds longer, fixing their pattern and dodging between displays until she was behind the two men. The nearest gunman, able to see only what was illuminated in the cone of his flashlight, looked right past her and kept going.

There was no time for subtlety. She sprang forward and punched the man in the throat. It sent him reeling back, gagging softly. As he staggered away, she wrestled the pistol from his grasp and turned it on the second man. The gun erupted in a flash of light and noise, and the man pitched backward into a display case. Whether it was the sudden weight of a human body or the bullet passing through, she could not say, but the glass shattered. The man's bulk snapped the shelf apart, smashing and scattering the contents.

The ghost images of the men outside showed an immediate reaction to the noise of gunfire from inside the Stanley Pavilion. They continued their advance, but now they were in a defensive posture, ready to engage the unseen enemies within. Queen heard a crackle of static and then a voice.

"Three Spades, report."

There was no answer and she realized the sound had come from a radio clipped to the belt of the first man she had taken out. She grabbed the radio and twisted its volume knob down so she could monitor their communications without giving her own position away. Then, she fell back toward the hallway that led deeper into the pavilion.

Another voice sounded, this time as if inside her head. "Queen, we're cut off here. No way out except up. Déjà vu all over again."

She turned, finding Rook's icon in the virtual display. He was only about twenty-five yards away, on the other side of a wall, standing near the rear stairwell. "Go for it," she said. "I'll meet you on the roof."

"The roof?"

There was another inquiry from the walkie-talkie, more urgent this time. She ignored it and addressed Rook's question. "Aleman, what's the ETA for *Crescent*?"

"ETA?" The tech genius sounded confused. "You mean to the rally point?"

The original plan had called for them to make their way into the Belgian countryside, where the stealth plane could land and take them on without attracting attention. The plane was invisible to radar and much quieter than a commercial jet, but when the thrust from its turbofans was directed earthward during a vertical landing, it sounded and felt like a gale force wind.

"Change of plans. We need a pick-up from the roof of this building. How long for that?"

It was an almost unthinkable request. Stealth plane or not, people would notice the angular black aircraft hovering above a building in the middle of the city. Aleman made a choking sound, but thankfully did not point out the obvious. "They're over the channel. Thirteen minutes."

Queen reached the open staircase opposite the entry doors and started up. "Tell them to kick in the afterburners. They need to be here in three."

That too, was an extraordinary thing to request. *Crescent's* sonic boom would advertise its presence to every military listening post in northern Europe, and without the protection of the US government, the only real question was which government would scramble its interceptors first.

In a small voice, Aleman answered. "I'll tell them."

She rounded the banister at the top of the stairs and looked back at the entry. One of the mercenaries eased through the doorway. She fired twice in his direction, missing but driving him back. She considered staying put, holding off their advance to buy a little more time, but it would make little difference. More men were congregating at the main entrance, and on the north side of the building, two more were forcing open the basement level door. She headed into a corridor, following Rook's icon.

She caught up to Rook and Mulamba on the stairs leading up to the rooftop. "Our ride is on the way," she said.

"I heard. Three minutes, huh? You think we can last that long?"

"I guess we'd better."

There was a sloped trapdoor, secured with another padlock blocking the way, but a decisive kick from Rook splintered the hasp and removed that impediment. Queen ushered Mulamba through and ventured out onto the roof of the Stanley Pavilion.

The night was deceptively quiet and peaceful. Queen knew that wasn't going to last long. "Find some cover."

Rook guided Mulamba toward a blocky protrusion that looked like an old disused chimney, one of several that sprouted from the irregular roof. There was no shortage of places to hide, at least temporarily. Unfortunately, as Queen turned to face the trapdoor, she realized that the virtual environment was no longer updating.

"Aleman. Where did they go?"

"Sorry, Queen. There aren't enough cameras inside that building to track their movements."

"Wonderful." She crouched and took aim at the black opening, waiting for the surprise moment when someone would pop out like a jack-in-the-box.

She didn't have to wait long.

A head broke the plane and she pulled the trigger, but in the nanosecond it took for thought to become action, the mercenary ducked back down. Her bullet ricocheted harmlessly off the sloping roof above the opening. A moment later, a hand holding a pistol appeared and fired off several shots in a blind spread. Most of the rounds sailed harmlessly out into the night, but a few smacked into the chimney behind which she was concealed, spraying her with dust and stone chips. Knowing that this was just cover fire to allow another shooter onto the roof, she braved the barrage and lined up another shot.

A figure erupted through the doorway, rolling to the side and scrambling for cover as the bullets continued to fly. Queen squeezed off another shot, but couldn't tell if she scored a hit. The man crabbed away from her and sought the refuge of another chimney.

Queen breathed a curse and drew back. The gun she'd taken was a beat-up looking Browning Hi-Power 9 mm. It was a military surplus gun, old school and not as sexy as a Glock or FN, but reliable and easy to find with the right connections. It had a thirteen round magazine, and she'd fired five times, which left eight shots, or possibly nine if the mercenary had kept one round in the chamber. She had to make every one of them count.

The volley from the doorway ceased, but the man behind the chimney took up the slack, providing cover fire for the other man to emerge. Queen didn't allow herself to be distracted by the noise and fury, and when the mercenary made his move, she fired once and saw the man topple back through the opening.

That one counted, she thought. But there was no telling how many more shooters were lined up and waiting their turn.

"Queen," Aleman said. "Crescent is thirty seconds out. You should see them coming in—"

The roar of a jet turbine drowned out the rest of his comment, and Queen saw the black shape of the stealth transport plane sliding across the sky above the museum grounds.

"Yes!"

The aircraft moved like something from a science-fiction movie, changing speed and direction without banking, in defiance of gravity. She knew that VTOL maneuvering was just about the most stressful activity in aviation, requiring constant and precise control of a dozen different systems, but the pilots made it look easy. The plane spun around and descended toward the rooftop, practically right on top of Rook and Mulamba, and as it did, a section of its belly lowered to form an access ramp.

The turbofans stirred up a tempest of grit, and amid the din, Queen thought she heard the sound of windows breaking.

In the corner of her eye, she saw the open ramp, its edge wavering slightly a few feet above the rooftop. Rook hoisted Mulamba up onto the ramp, who then turned and offered his hand. Rook frantically waved him back.

More shots rang out. Queen returned fire: a shot at the chimney where the gunman was hiding, another round into the open doorway and then she repeated the process to keep the mercenaries at bay until the others were aboard.

"Queen! Move!"

She did. Firing out the last of the magazine, she broke cover and sprinted for the ramp, diving up and onto it like an Olympic high jumper. She felt the hard metal beneath her and kept rolling deeper into the interior of the plane.

"I'm in!" she shouted. "Go!"

She could feel the aircraft moving beneath her, and she spread-eagled to avoid being tossed around the cabin by the acceleration.

There was a loud whine of hydraulic motors as the ramp drew back into the fuselage, and then abruptly, the noise diminished to a low roar.

Queen lay panting on the deck for several seconds, letting the adrenaline drain away. She knew there would be hell to pay for bringing the stealth plane into a populated area, but that was a worry for another day. It was also the beauty of being an off-the-books operation. There would be an uproar about it, but it wouldn't be directed at Chess Team or the Endgame organization, since they didn't technically exist.

She rolled over to look for the others. "What's our next—?"

What she saw hit her like a physical blow. Rook had his back to her and was hunched over an unmoving form, his arms bowed and trembling. She looked around for Mulamba, her brain not quite processing that she had already seen him.

Rook had both hands pressed against Mulamba's chest, as if by so doing he might keep the man's life from escaping through the hole there, but too much of it had already poured out. The deck was awash in blood, most of it oozing from the ragged exit wound.

"Stupid son of..." Rook was almost incoherent. "Damn it, Joe. Why the fuck didn't you...? Damnit!"

Mulamba's eyes were wide with pain or panic, but somehow his gaze found Queen. His lips moved, trying to form words even though there wasn't enough breath left in him to make a sound.

He managed two words.

"Find it."

Then he was gone.

TWENTY-NINE

Kinshasa, Democratic Republic of the Congo

King lifted his head out of the dark water and surveyed the shoreline. It was nearly midnight. Behind him, on the northern shore of the Congo, the city lights of Brazzaville glittered like jewels, but Brazzaville was in another country. Few lights were visible in Kinshasa.

At King's direction, General Mabuki's forces had shut down the power grid, plunging whole sections of Kinshasa into darkness. The army and many of the government buildings had gasoline powered generators, so the blackout was only a minor inconvenience, but King was counting on the darkness to conceal his approach to the Palais de la Nation.

He crept forward, feeling the marshy river bottom beneath this hands and knees, and crawled up onto the grassy bank, immediately seeking cover in the trees that overlooked the river. He gently shook the water from his borrowed AKS-74, and waited for Asya and the rest of the strike team to join him.

The six Republican Guardsmen had been hand-picked by General Mabuki, and all boasted that they had received special commando training. King was suspicious of the claim, but he didn't have the luxury of being choosy. For their sake, he hoped they weren't exaggerating their prowess.

"Stay close to me," he whispered to his sister, reiterating what he had already told her several times.

A low fence ringed the palace property. Beyond it was a lot of open ground. Although the palace was dark, a few tiny pinpoints of light marked the location of soldiers patrolling the expansive courtyard. A lone helicopter—a Russian-made Mil Mi-8 transport helicopter, painted in a military camouflage pattern—sat idle in front of the pillared exterior of the palace. When the nearest patrol started moving away, King whispered the 'go' order, and then slipped over the fence.

The palace grounds were partitioned with hedge walls laid out in a geometric pattern around a large reflecting pool. King darted to the nearest of these and then ducked down, waiting for the others to catch up.

As they huddled there, waiting, King checked his watch. The stainless-steel Omega chronograph—a gift from American astronaut Buzz Aldrin—had been on his wrist more or less constantly for nearly forty years. Winding the mechanism and verifying that it was still keeping accurate time had become something of a daily ritual for him, a habit that had taken root as he had ticked down the days and hours remaining in his long journey through the centuries.

"Two minutes, forty-five seconds to go time," he whispered, then added, "If they're on time."

He did not hold out a lot of hope that Mabuki would be punctual. In Africa, and indeed in most areas of the developing world, people took a rather philosophical approach to scheduling. Things got done when they got done...or sometimes they didn't.

Go time came and went, but King was pleasantly surprised when, not quite two minutes later, he heard the noise of distant explosions and gunfire. The bobbing lights of the foot patrols immediately swung around in the direction of the disturbance and several of the patrols moved off to investigate.

King slipped over the hedge and stole forward, moving from one place of concealment to the next. The noise of the distant battle continued to grow, but King knew that it would be some time before the large force of Republican Guard soldiers got anywhere near the Palais. Mabuki's attack on the forces at the edge of the Gombe commune was a diversion, designed to draw attention away from the vulnerable river approach and mask the insertion of King's team.

For several long minutes, King and his team moved in short spurts across the open area, ducking behind hedges, or sometimes simply lying prone in the open, trusting that their camouflage would blend in with the lawn. King's objective was the smaller annex building, connected to the east wing of the palace, the place where he and Asya had been held captive, though he hadn't been aware of it at the time. He only knew it now because Deep Blue had continued to monitor the q-phones, which were right where Favreau had left them.

The door to the small building was just twenty yards away, but two soldiers stood between that door and King. The men were in the open, easy targets, but without suppressed weapons, King didn't dare shoot them. Doing so would give them away and bring the full might of the Congolese army down on them.

There was only one way to get past the men, and it wasn't going to be pretty.

King leaned back and whispered his plan to the leader of the Republican Guard team. Asya shot him an annoyed look, but he pretended not to notice. He didn't doubt that she was capable of doing what he was about to do, but she was his sister, and if he could spare her a few sleepless nights by outsourcing the dirty work to the locals, then he would.

He gave the signal. Both he and the Congolese guardsman sprinted forward. The soldiers never noticed them. King buried the blade of his AKM Type II bayonet in the nearest man's throat and clapped a hand over his mouth to stifle any cry of alarm. A second later, the guardsman did the same to the second soldier.

King held his hand in place until his target stopped struggling, then dragged the body around the side of the building where, hopefully, it would go unnoticed for a while. He did what he could to wipe away the hot sticky blood that covered his hands, and then moved toward the entrance door, where Asya had the rest of the team assembled.

They went in fast but silent. The dark anteroom was completely empty, along with the rest of the first floor. King soon found his way to the stairs leading down to the sub-basement, where he and Asya had been kept prisoner. He descended, the barrel of his carbine leading the way, and entered the room with the makeshift detention cell.

Their glasses, q-phones and the rucksacks containing weapons and other gear lay on a desktop, left there like car keys and junk mail on an entryway sideboard.

King donned one pair of glasses and handed the second to Asya. As soon as they were on his head, the night-vision feature activated and the room seemed to brighten around him.

"Blue, it's King. Do you copy?"

The relief in Deep Blue's voice came through loud and clear. "Good to have you back on the air."

"Any news for me?"

"Nothing that can't wait until you're finished there."

"That's what I was hoping you'd say." He dug into his rucksack and took out the Uzi he'd brought from Cairo. The weapon was still equipped with the integrated holographic virtual aiming sight, as well as a sound suppressor. "Give me a route to the assembly chamber."

A faint blue arrow hovered in the air before him, pointing the way out, along with a top-down map of the entire building that showed King and Asya as tiny chess pieces, and showed the destination as a red dot. Although Deep Blue didn't have access to the floor plan, he had been able to extrapolate a rough approximation of the layout from their earlier journey through the Palais. There were a lot of blank spaces, but every room and corridor that King and Asya had glimpsed while in custody was now flawlessly rendered as part of the digital model. With Deep Blue guiding him, King could have walked through the maze blindfolded.

In his eagerness, he almost forgot that the guardsman didn't share his enhanced visual abilities. They stared blankly at him, their pupils fully dilated and visible as white dots in the night-vision display.

"Stay close," he told them in French. "But don't shoot anything unless I give the signal."

He moved through the structure more quickly now, his confidence bolstered by the technology that he had earlier found so excessive and even a bit intrusive. The glasses were far superior to any night vision goggles he had ever used, not only providing a much sharper perspective on the unlit environment, but doing so without a disorienting change in depth perception. He knew Asya, similarly equipped, was right behind him. The guardsmen, fumbling along in the dark, were having trouble keeping up, but he didn't slow down.

The glasses registered a change in the ambient light level and King slowed, easing forward to investigate. As he neared a turn in the corridor, he heard voices from just ahead, an odd mix of Swahili and French that, despite being fluent in both languages, taxed his linguistic abilities. He also caught a whiff of fragrant smoke. The glasses weren't equipped with chemical sensors, but King had no trouble recognizing the aroma of nicotine, mixed with the much more distinctive smell of burning cannabis.

He moved closer, his glasses changing from full-dark to low-light mode as the light from the room beyond increased. He eased around the corner, barely long enough for his gaze to be drawn, moth-like, to the old-fashioned oil burning lamp on a tabletop in the center of the room. The glasses instantly registered what he did not have time to make out: the presence of at least six men, all wearing army uniforms. The soldiers were sprawled out around the table, smoking and joking, presumably off-duty, certainly not in a state of heightened defensive alertness.

Although he had drawn back into concealment, King could still see the men clearly in his display, ghostly figures, seemingly visible through the solid wall.

"Pawn, on my signal move in fast." He knew that Asya's glasses showed her the same image. "I'll go left, you go right."

"Ready."

"Go on three... One...two...three." He slipped around the corner, leading with the Uzi.

He shot the first target before anyone in the room was aware of the intrusion. He swung the gun toward the next closest target. The crosshairs moved with him, and when they settled on the head of another soldier, his finger tightened on trigger. The gun coughed and bucked slightly in his two-handed grip. The man fell dead, but King had already moved on.

Asya eliminated her designated targets with equal efficiency. Two were down, the third, who had been facing away when the attack had begun, was just starting to turn when a bullet caught him in the throat. He dropped, a torrent of blood pouring from his mouth, as he fought to get his rifle up.

King killed the last target and swung his Uzi around to engage any survivors. Asya had already lined up a second shot on the wounded soldier and finished the job her first bullet had started...but not before the soldier got his finger into the trigger guard of his Kalashnikov. As he slumped forward, the weapon discharged.

It was just a single shot, and the bullet embedded itself harmlessly in a wall, injuring no one, but it was enough. A gun had been fired inside the palace.

There was a possibility that the report would raise no alarm. Accidental discharges happened in even the most disciplined armies—and the Congolese military certainly was not that—but King resisted the seductive desire to hope for the best.

Asya muttered a curse under her breath, but King silenced her self-recriminations. "It's done. The first rule of war is that no plan survives contact. Shit happens. Stay alert and keep moving."

He quickly turned down the wick of the lamp, plunging the room into darkness, and then he called the rest of the team forward. The guardsmen might have benefited from the light in the short term, but their eyes were already adjusted to the dark. Exposure to even a dim light source would have left them night blind.

He continued through the room, steeling himself for the likelihood that the next encounter would not be so one-sided.

The bobbing yellow glow of a flashlight heralded the approach of a squad of soldiers running to investigate the shooting. Although they no longer had the element of surprise in their favor, King and Asya still had technology on their side. The soldiers went down in a hail of whisper quiet 9 mm, but they didn't go quietly. As their comrades dropped, the soldiers began firing blindly into the darkness where King and Asya were concealed. None of King's team were hit, but it was now almost a certainty that their enemies would be ready for them.

The assembly room, where he hoped to find the hostages, lay just ahead, but to get there, they would have to cross a wide atrium—an area where the enemy forces would almost certainly be waiting.

King consulted the map, looking for a better answer.

He found it.

He called the senior guardsman forward and quickly outlined his strategy. The man nodded enthusiastically, eager for a chance to do more than just trail along in King's shadow, and then he urged his men forward. King took Asya back the other way.

Moving quickly, unencumbered by the guardsmen, they found a stairwell and ascended. They hadn't visited the second floor, so the virtual map was mostly blank, but the landing opened into a hallway that ran in the same direction as the corridor they had just scouted on the first floor. The atrium lay ahead to their left. As King and Asya moved at a jog, the noise of gunfire filled the air. The guardsmen had, right on schedule, engaged the enemy forces assembled on the ground floor of the open hall.

Light spilled through the open passage leading to the balcony, which overlooked the atrium, where the battle was now raging. The army troops had set up mobile generator-powered lights in the big hall. King could see a dozen soldiers on the balcony, firing down at the guardsmen, oblivious to the threat approaching from their flank. He and Asya picked them off from the shelter of the entryway, and with the way clear, they raced out onto the balcony.

None of the soldiers on the lower floor took note of what was happening above, but seizing the high vantage point was not King's ultimate goal. Instead, he moved to the far side of the atrium and plunged into the dark passage opposite the one from which they had emerged. Further down the hall, he found a matching stairwell. The map showed an entrance to the assembly hall just ten yards from the first floor landing.

The stairwell muted the sound of the gun battle, but when they reached the ground floor, King and Asya found themselves in the thick of the fight. The guardsmen, clustered at the eastern entrance to the atrium were firing at a group of soldiers who had taken up a position in the western entrance, a stone's throw from the stairwell. The soldiers, focused on the threat in front of them, paid no heed to the stealthy pair at their rear, but stray rounds were sizzling past them and into the corridor.

"Stay low," King whispered, and then ducked out into the corridor, his sister right behind him.

King felt a rising anxiety as he reached for the door handle. Everything had been leading up to this moment. He didn't know what he would find on the other side of that barrier, but their survival and indeed the success of their entire mission in Africa, hinged on what would happen in the next few seconds.

He turned the knob and pushed the door open.

Electric lanterns illuminated the assembly room, and revealed more than two dozen figures huddled in the far corner of the room, doing their best to avoid being hit by bullets penetrating the wall that abutted the atrium. Several heads turned in their direction and the facial recognition software went completely nuts. Red, yellow and green icons started popping up as the computer instantaneously began separating friend, foe and unknown. There were, unfortunately, plenty of the latter two categories, and many of them were clustered tightly in the midst of the captive dignitaries.

A soldier, marked with a yellow dot, started to bring his rifle around. Asya dropped him with a precise headshot. King however, sprinted forward, desperate to reach his primary objective in the center of the group. He didn't need the red dot to find her. Monique Favreau's white face stood out clearly.

She was looking right at him with an eager, hungry expression.

Another Caucasian man—presumably one of her mercenaries—got his machine pistol up and fired in King's direction. King somersaulted forward and the burst hit the wall behind him, each overpressure round blasting a cantaloupe-sized hole in the wood paneling.

King came out of his roll in a crouch just three yards from where Favreau and the mercenary stood. He fired point-blank without bothering to check the virtual crosshairs and drilled the man between the eyes. In the same fluid motion, he stood up and thrust the Uzi in Favreau's direction. The smoking suppressor floated a hand's breadth from her face.

But he didn't fire.

As satisfying as killing Favreau would have been, his goal from the start had been to take her alive and use her as a human shield, so he could move the hostages to the river shore, where a gunboat would get them clear of the fighting. He did not doubt for a moment that she was the puppet-master pulling the strings of the revolution. The only troubling question was whether the rebellious army forces would lay down their arms to save her life.

Time to find out.

"Drop your weapons," he shouted in clear French, "or she dies."

The noise of the battle in the atrium continued, but there was total silence in the assembly hall.

Favreau just stared at King like a hyena savoring a carcass. Her smile never wavered, but after a few seconds, she spoke in an equally forceful tone. "Do as he says."

For a fleeting moment, King believed he had won. Then Favreau raised her hand.

"Don't," he warned.

She froze, but the thing in her hand was now plainly visibly, and he recognized it immediately. "You know what this is, don't you? It is a remote trigger with a dead-man switch. Kill me and..." She made a little *poof* gesture with her free hand.

"Your way we both die. My way, we both live. Your choice." Without breaking his stare, he went on. "Pawn, get the hostages clear."

"Pawn?" Favreau asked with an air of delight. "How marvelous. Do you play chess? I am called the Red Queen. Did you know that?"

"How nice for you." King maintained his best poker face, but her confidence was eroding his own.

"I love chess. Victory can be achieved only through sacrifice. What, I wonder, are you willing to sacrifice to win?"

"You, for starters."

She laughed. "Look behind me. Do you see it, there in the corner?"

He couldn't help but look, just the briefest flick of his gaze, and when he saw the large green duffel bag, all the pieces fell into place. He had a mental image of Hadir, blown apart by a single bullet—an overpressure round, just like the ones Favreau's mercenaries used. Now at last, he had the answer to the question of who had taken the RA-115 in Egypt.

"It is a nuclear device," she explained. "A small one, just a kiloton, but more than enough to wipe this palace off the face of the Earth."

From behind her, Senator Marrs erupted with an indignant curse. "Good God, she's got a nuke."

"It doesn't change anything." He lowered his voice so she wouldn't hear what he said next. "Pawn, get those hostages out of here. Blue, call Mabuki and tell him to send the gunboat now."

Asya did as instructed, moving forward with a boldness that King knew was all for show.

"It changes *everything*," Favreau said, seeming to ignore what was going on behind her. "You see, I have already won. If I let go of this trigger, we all die, and I win. Checkmate!"

"No. All that happens is that we'll die. And regardless of whether or not that happens, tomorrow morning, every news agency in the world will be reporting the truth about what's happening here. How mercenaries working for Consolidated Energy kidnapped President Mulamba and tried to overthrow the country. It's over, and you've lost."

"Do you think so?" Favreau brought her hands together, moving with exaggerated slowness as if daring him to shoot, and transferred the remote detonator to her left hand. "Let me show you how I win this game."

She knelt down and pried the MP5 from the hands of the mercenary King had killed.

King felt a cold panic surge through his extremities. "Don't!" He jabbed the Uzi at her again, but even he could hear the desperate quaver in his voice.

Favreau was visibly trembling with excitement as she held up the detonator in one hand, the gun in the other. King felt impotent as he waited for her to pull one trigger or the other, but instead she pivoted away.

"What are you willing to sacrifice to win?" she asked, almost breathlessly. "A pawn perhaps?"

Then Favreau thrust the gun toward Asya, and pulled the trigger.

BEAST

THIRTY

Somewhere over Europe

Feeling a little like the universe had just kicked him in the face, Rook slumped against a bulkhead. He noted a rivulet of blood creeping out from under the motionless body of Joseph Mulamba, and realized that if he didn't move, it would eventually pool around his feet.

He didn't move. There was already a lot of the man's blood on him, symbolically and literally. What difference would a little more make?

Queen gazed in silent disbelief at the man they had so badly failed. She squeezed her eyes together for almost a full minute, but then she opened them and sat a little straighter.

"Okay. Let's talk about what happens next."

"Next? We blew it. Game over."

"Knock it off," she said, her tone sharper than usual. "You can have a pity party on your own time. We've still got a mission."

"What mission?" he said slowly, through clenched teeth.

"Helping him..." She pointed to Mulamba's still form, "...save his country. That's what we agreed to do, remember?"

Rook took a deep breath. "How do we do that now?"

Queen leaned over the body and searched it, producing the envelope from the Stanley archive. A corner of the yellowed paper was stained dark red. She slipped the folded papers from inside and began reading.

Rook shook his head. He didn't see the point of chasing after Mulamba's mythical lost city now. It had been a long shot to begin with, and now that Mulamba was gone, the impact of any discovery they made might be negligible. But as Queen finished reading the first page and handed it to him, he straightened up and began reading aloud.

July 19, Friday, 1878

Tonight I revealed the secret I have borne these past eight years, the story that Livingstone told me on the occasion of our first meeting, and which has burned in me like a fire in my belly. Yet I feel no sense of relief, but only deep dismay.

It occurs to me now that I have never put to paper my reasons for keeping secret the true account of what happened that day, and now that His Majesty, Leopold II of Belgium, has demanded that I destroy the record of that meeting and the story I have never told, I feel I must defend the decisions I have made, if only that future generations may judge my behavior.

As the years have passed by, I have variously tried to rationalize my decision to keep Livingstone's tale to myself. I told myself that he was ill, feverish when he spoke and surely not altogether in his right mind. To reveal what he said would only tarnish his well-deserved reputation. The truth, though, is that I kept the story to myself purely as a matter of selfishness. Livingstone told no one else of the Cave of the Ancients. I am certain of that now, and I foolishly believed that if I could find their city without acknowledging that he found it first, my own fame would exceed even his.

Alas, if I had revealed the truth, perhaps I would have found the funds necessary to locate the Cave.

Were these good reasons to keep the story of that fateful day a secret? I do not know. The Ancients may have been nothing more than a fever dream. Livingstone never spoke of them again, after that night. Had I published the account exactly as it occurred, I have no doubt that I would have found investors willing to fund an expedition to search for the Blood Lake and the Cave of the Ancients, but that does not mean I would have found it.

I do not regret that I have chosen to exchange this uncertain reward for the more profitable adventure of taming the Congo. Nevertheless, I cannot help but wonder what sights I might have seen.

Rook took the rest of the pages from Queen, who had already finished reading them. These were on different paper. The handwriting was slightly different, though clearly written by the same person.

November 10, Friday, 1871

Success. I have found Livingstone.

It is a bittersweet victory, for he is not the man I had hoped to find. When Selim espied him, I did not want to believe that this weary old man was indeed the Great Livingstone. He was sickly and pale, with grey whiskers and moustache that did not completely hide weeping ulcers on the skin of his face. He wore a blue cloth cap, and had on a red-sleeved waistcoat and a pair of grey tweed trousers, but all were worn and shabby, and hung on his frail body like a beggar's rags.

In that moment, what I would not have given to have this meeting take place somewhere in the wilderness, and not here with so many to bear witness. He came close, and my courage deserted me. My heart beat faster as I contemplated the horror of embracing him as I knew I ought, and it was only through great effort that I did not let my face betray my emotions in front of the Arabs. Rather, I advanced slowly toward him, feigning a dignity that I did not possess.

Coward that I was, I stood at a distance and called out, "Is it you, Livingstone?"

I cannot recount accurately what he said to me then, for he was mumbling and I understood little of it. He seemed oblivious to the others, but he led me away, into the mud-walled house where he was convalescing. There was a sort of platform that served as a veranda, looking out over the square, where many natives had gathered to watch this historic meeting of two white men. Livingstone sat on a straw mat, with only a goatskin between himself and the cold mud wall. Little wonder his health was in such a state.

I told him of my journey to find him, but his attention wandered. Finally, I asked him directly, "Where have you been all this long time? The world has believed you to be dead."

"I am trying to find the Nile," he informed me, sounding very irritated. "Did you not know this?"

I told him that I did. "I would hear of your travels."

At this, his face became pinched. "I did not find it," he confessed. "But what I did find—" At this, he seemed to regain a measure of strength, for he sat up straighter and addressed the Arabs. "I would speak privately, if you please."

I could see that they were displeased, though whether it was the request or the Doctor's manner,

I cannot say. I have heard that he is greatly opposed to the Arab merchants for their trade in black slaves, but this has not stopped him from accepting their hospitality. Nevertheless, I sent them away so I might hear what he had to say.

"I have dared tell no one of what I discovered," he began, speaking in the low voice of a conspirator. "Of those who found that place with me, none still live."

I imagined that he was speaking in a general way about the interior, where he had been wandering these many years, but this was not the case.

"Many days to the east, about four hundred miles, if I reckoned correctly, there is a volcanic mountain, which the natives call 'the Mountain of God,' but in its shadow is a lake straight from Hell itself. The water boils and is red as blood. Any living thing that touches the water turns to stone."

This declaration struck me as the ravings of a feverish mind, but I continued listening.

"The lake is not deep, and the water rises and falls as the tide. While taking the measure of the western shore, I chanced upon a stone footpath, exposed by the water's retreat. The path led into the lake, which I thought strange, until I realized that it continued to the mouth of a cavern, which was almost completely inundated by the bloody water.

"I became obsessed with the riddle of that path. Who had laid it? What was in the cavern? I concluded that the path must surely have been laid before the lake formed, or perhaps when its shoreline did not reach so far, which surely meant that it was many centuries old, but the cave and the answers I sought, lay beneath the surface of the poisonous water, beyond reach.

"Though it pains me greatly to admit this, one morning, without my permission, several of my bearers took it upon themselves to swim into the cave. Only one of them returned, a good lad named Mgwana, and he was nearly dead when I found him. 'Baba,' he told me—it is the word for Father, and a title of great honor and affection—'I have seen the place of Watu Wa Kale.' That is their word that means Old People, but I took it as meaning the Ancients. He told me many things he had seen before he died, turning to stone in my arms."

The recollection greatly taxed Livingstone, and he asked to take his leave. I prevailed upon him to take a portion of quinine from our stores. After he retired, I recorded this account to the best of my ability, but I think it almost certainly an invention of his fevered mind. He is a devout man and his story seems like something from Scripture; I am reminded of the wife of Lot, who was turned into a pillar of salt, and of Moses turning the Nile into blood.

I shall ask him again when the fever has passed.

November 11, Saturday, 1871

The quinine proved efficacious for Livingstone. His strength returned, and he was much more alert on the occasion of our next meeting. We spoke for many hours, and I recounted the stories of my travels, which having already recorded herein, I will not repeat. Livingstone related more of his travels, a great many things, which I will endeavor to record at greater length.

The matter of the Blood Lake and the Cave of the Ancients weighed on me heavily. I asked the Doctor if he remembered telling me the story. He replied that he did not and that I should dismiss anything he might have said as a feverish delusion. Yet, there was something in his eyes and the way he urged me to forget and destroy all mention of the Cave, that now makes me wonder if there is not something more to this story, after all. Does the Cave of the Ancients exist? And if it does, what sort of wonders might it contain?

I shall have to learn more about this, but I do not think Livingstone will speak of it again.

Rook lowered the papers and looked at Queen with a shrug. "That's it? A crazy story about a cave and a lake that can turn people to stone? I don't think that's what Joe was looking for."

"You're right," Queen said. She stared at Mulamba for several seconds, then reverently crossed his arms over his chest. "He was very brave. I wish this could have been something we could..."

She trailed off and Rook realized she was listening to something that he couldn't hear. "Aleman? What's he saying?"

Queen took out her phone and tapped a few commands on the backlit screen. "Okay, you're on."

Aleman's voice was soft, nearly drowned out by the persistent hum of *Crescent*'s powerful turbofans. "First, I'm really sorry about what happened. It was just bad luck. There's nothing you guys could have done differently. That probably doesn't help much right now..." He took a deep breath. "Second, I don't know anything about this Cave of the Ancients, but I might be able to help you out with the lake."

"The lake is real?" Rook asked. "A lake of blood that turns people into stone? No way."

"Way. I read about it in *New Scientist*. There's a lake in Tanzania—Lake Natron—where the waters are almost pure alkaline.

There's a bacteria that turns the water red, like blood, but the really creepy thing is what happens to birds that fall into the water. The lake is full of dissolved lime, the same stuff that you use to make cement. The lime destroys organic tissue almost instantly, but in the process, it reacts, to form limestone. There are pictures of these birds that have literally turned to stone. I don't think Livingstone— no pun there—was making that part up. And it's about four hundred and sixty miles east of Ujiji, where Stanley met Livingstone."

Queen's eyebrows came together, accentuating the angry red Death Volunteers brand imprinted between them. "And if the lake is real, then the Cave of the Ancients might be real, too?"

"It's worth checking out," Aleman suggested. "And...it might not be such a bad idea to get off the radar, as it were."

Rook sighed and tucked the diary pages back into Mulamba's pocket.

"*Hakuna matata.*"

THIRTY-ONE

Kinshasa, Democratic Republic of the Congo

Asya tried to dodge away from the shot, but succeeded only in getting partly behind one of the Congolese soldiers, who had been guarding the hostages. Favreau's gun barked, and the unlucky soldier burst apart in an eruption of blood that rained down on the horrified onlookers. Asya stumbled back, as if slapped by an unseen hand, and collapsed clutching her side.

King's world closed in like tunnel vision. In that instant, he was completely defenseless. Favreau could have turned her gun on him and he would have died without taking a single defensive measure. He saw only Asya, his sister, awash in blood, unmoving.

He reached her side like a man wandering in a fog and knelt down. His hand hovered above her, but he was afraid to touch her, to confirm that this was reality and not a bad dream. But she was breathing and moving. She was still alive, and that was more than he had dared to hope.

Most of the blood was not hers, but some of it was. After devastating the Congolese soldier, the overpressure bullet had kept right on going, punching into Asya's lower abdomen, just above her left hip. The wound was ugly, a ragged bloody hole as big around as the base of King's thumb.

Some disconnected analytical part of King's brain recognized that Asya was alive because most of the bullet's kinetic energy had been expended in the initial impact with the soldier. There still had been plenty of velocity left in the round, but it had already used up the deadly one-two punch of the powdered heavy metal core. That was of little comfort to King. Asya was not dead, but she was badly wounded, and if she didn't get immediate medical attention, which he was in no position to provide, then her death would be slow and agonizing.

But the realization that she *was* alive helped clear away some of the fog. He found Asya's pouch containing emergency medical supplies—a basic rule of giving aid was to always use the injured person's med-kit first. The pouch was soaked with blood, but the foil and plastic packaging had kept the inner contents relatively sterile. He tore open a field dressing and pressed it to the wound. It wouldn't be enough, he knew, but it was a start.

As his tunnel vision diminished, his awareness of the situation in the assembly hall returned. Favreau was still holding both the gun and the detonator, her eyes dancing with excitement.

"What will you do now?" she asked. She wasn't gloating; the question was sincere. She had made her move, and was now desperate to see what his counter would be.

King was wondering about that, too. If Asya had been dead, he might have just killed the Red Queen and thought to hell with the consequences. A few hundred dead in the palace seemed like a small price to pay to permanently end Favreau's psychotic game. But Asya was alive, and that changed everything.

He knew what he had to do.

"Asya, can you hear me?"

Her eyes found his. "Yes. Son of a bitch, that hurts."

"I need you to hold pressure on the dressing. Can you do that?"

She nodded, winced and then put her hand over the blood-soaked gauze pad.

He slid one arm under her legs, the other around her back and sprang to his feet. Without another glance at Favreau or anyone else, he turned and ran for the exit. There were shouts behind him, but loudest of all was the Red Queen herself, telling her men to let him go. He didn't count this as a lucky break, and certainly not an instance of mercy on her part. This was a game to her, and she had let him go only because she wanted to play with him more.

He burst through the doors and ran toward the atrium. The battle between his small force of Republican Guardsmen and the army troops loyal to General Velle and Favreau had ended, or perhaps moved elsewhere. He had told the Guardsmen to engage just long enough to provide cover for him to reach the assembly hall, and then to fall back, but there were only six of them and dozens of soldiers. Maybe they were all dead.

There were two ways out of the Palais: the front door, which led out onto the streets of the Gombe commune—territory held by the rebels—or out the back door, where a short jog across the palace grounds would bring him to the river.

"Blue, is that gunboat on its way?"

"Affirmative. Mabuki says they're a few minutes out."

"Back door, then..." He fell silent as he saw a group of people emerging from a door halfway between where he stood and the rear entrance. It was Favreau, the enormous bomb slung across her back, leading a small procession that included several of her steroid-infused mercenaries and two hostages—acting President Gerard Okoa and United States Senator Lance Marrs. Favreau guided the group toward the doors. She met King's stare for a fleeting second, then turned to join the rest of the group.

"Forget the boat. I'm leaving through the front door."

"King you ca—" Deep Blue caught himself. "Not the front door. Go back into the west wing. There's another exit at the far end. Stay in the shadows. I'll guide you through."

King turned back into the corridor, following the prompts that flashed in the display of the glasses. As he passed through the west exit, he heard the sound of the helicopter, its rotors spinning up for take-off.

The front of the palace crawled with soldiers, many of whom were busy setting up fighting positions for the coming confrontation with General Mabuki's Republican Guard forces. Favreau might have fled the scene, but the revolution was just getting started.

As the helicopter lifted her into the sky, Monique Favreau flipped a wire-safety clamp over the dead-man remote for the RA-115, closed her eyes and allowed the tension and exhilaration of her confrontation with the relentless American to drain away. He was proving to be every bit the adversary she desired, and she was very much looking forward to their next encounter.

"Where are you taking us?" The demanding voice belonged to Marrs, the politician from the United States. She opened her eyes and fixed him with a withering stare. He recoiled a little, but after a lifetime of getting his way, Marrs didn't have the good sense to know when to shut up. "Was he right? Is Consolidated Energy behind all this?"

When she saw that her Medusa gaze was not going to silence him, she turned away and tried to ignore him, but he pressed on.

"God damn, it is true, isn't it? Listen, it's not too late to fix this."

"There is nothing to fix," she said . "Everything is proceeding according to my plan."

"Bullshit. You're smarter than that. This little revolution of yours is circling the drain. When the truth about CE's involvement gets out, and believe me it will, not only will you lose everything you thought you were going to gain, but CE will be finished. You will be finished."

"How fortunate for you."

"Are you kidding?" Marrs seemed to be on the verge of an epileptic fit. "Do you know who I am?"

"Aside from a pompous, know-nothing who prostitutes his political influence and licks the boots of wealthy oil billionaires?"

His lips curled in a disdainful sneer. "I'm the next goddamned President of the United States. That's who I am. Now, let me talk to someone at CE... I've worked with Dorian Harrold, though I'm sure he'll be surprised to hear—"

Favreau hit him. Her open hand struck his jaw, hard enough to shut it and raise a blush on his sallow skin, but it was really just a slap to remind him that, no matter who he thought he was or was going to be, she was in charge. His mouth hung open for a moment in disbelief, then he wisely closed it. She leaned in close. "Nothing you think you know matters anymore. There's just one thing I want from you. Silence." She relaxed a little and smiled. "It would be better if you gave me that voluntarily, but one way or another, I will get it."

Marrs swallowed and fell back in his seat.

She looked away from him and tried to recapture some of the emotional high she had felt earlier, but it was gone, replaced instead by the depressing realization that Marrs was right. She had been outplayed, and now everything was in ruins. Somehow, the American had discovered the connection to Consolidated Energy, a fact that threatened everything and connected her to Mulamba's abduction. Consolidated Energy and Executive Solutions would survive this by finding a way to disavow everything that she had done, labeling her a rogue agent and making themselves out to be as much the victims as the Congolese. They would cut her loose, maybe even put a price on her head.

Strangely, the idea excited her. She might be on her own now, but she wasn't alone. She had General Velle and his army, and she had the bomb.

This was, she realized, not a defeat at all. It was a perfect opportunity.

THIRTY-TWO

King set Asya down in a shadowy recess near the west exit from the Palais and scanned the perimeter. The army forces holding the seat of the Congolese government were mostly clustered near the front entrance, but there were still a lot of troops spread out around the grounds. About fifty yards from where King hid, there was a GAZ Tigr armored vehicle, similar in design to a Humvee, with a gunner manning a DShK heavy machine gun in the top turret and four more soldiers milling about nearby. More vehicles and soldiers were dispersed along the fence line, close enough that slipping between them unnoticed would be impossible. Not that walking out was really an option. Asya needed immediate medical attention.

He checked her wound. The field dressing was soaked through, but Asya continued pressing it against the injury. He took out a fresh dressing and laid it over the top of the first, tying both around her waist to hold them in place. Only then did he look her in the eye. "How are you doing, kiddo?"

"Kiddo? I may be kid sister, but don't treat me like child." Her attempt at playful mock-outrage was confounded by a tremor of pain that turned her smile into a grimace.

"I'm going to get you out of here. Stay put."

"I can walk," she protested.

"Don't," he said, with all the forcefulness his whisper would allow. He turned away before she could argue, and scanned the area once more, tagging targets in the virtual environment.

With grim determination, he settled the cross-hairs on the gunner in the Tigr's turret and fired a single silenced round. The weapon made a soft huffing noise that went unnoticed by the soldiers at the perimeter. The man behind the machine gun slumped away without making a sound. King moved the Uzi to another target, one of two men on the right side of the vehicle, and took another shot. The soldier went down, and as the other man looked on in surprise, King shifted the muzzle of his weapon and fired again.

As he switched his aim to the pair on the left side, he heard a cry of alarm and saw both men abruptly take a defensive stance. Another target suddenly popped up in King's display. A previously unnoticed sixth man was climbing out of the Tigr, warning the others of the silent attack.

King took out one of the soldiers, but the other two raised their Kalashnikov rifles and started firing. They clearly didn't know where he was. They were shooting into the shadows and none of their rounds came anywhere close to him, but the damage was done. Now, everyone was alerted to his presence. The mechanical coughing sound of a suppressed burst startled King, and both of the soldiers he was trying to target went down.

"Got them," Asya announced through gritted teeth. She struggled to her feet. "Let's go!"

"Damn it, Asya. Stay down." He knew she was not going to heed him, and also recognized that he wasn't going to be able to carry her to the Tigr, especially not with the rest of the Congolese army now looking their way. "Just stay here. Cover me."

He bolted out into the open, making a bee-line for the vehicle. The movement caught the attention of soldiers on either side, and before he had crossed half the distance, bullets started sizzling though the air all around him. He kept going, and when he got within a few paces of the vehicle, he dove forward onto his belly as if sliding into home plate. Above him, rounds began pelting the armored exterior of the Tigr, but a hasty high crawl got him the rest of the way, affording some cover from the incoming fire on his right. He let loose a burst from the Uzi, pointing in the general direction of the troops to his left, then scrambled through the open door of the Tigr and pulled it shut.

A bullet cracked loudly against the side window, the impact hard enough to gouge out a divot and start a spider web fracture pattern. The armor would stop all small arms fire, but unlike the composite plates that protected the Tigr's flanks, the bullet resistant coating on the glass was a perishable product. It would lose its effectiveness after prolonged exposure to adverse weather conditions—or a crap ton of bullets. It might slow down a few more rounds, but King wasn't going to trust it with his life. Keeping his head down, he located the starter switch—like most military vehicles, there was no keyed ignition—and brought the 205 horsepower diesel engine roaring to life.

Without raising his head, King shifted the transmission into reverse. The Tigr started rolling backward. He goosed the throttle a little, holding the wheel steady until the vehicle jolted to a stop with a loud crash that reverberated through the metal frame and nearly shook him out of his seat. Head still down, he moved his foot onto the brake pedal and shifted into forward drive.

The door behind him opened and Asya tumbled inside. "Why don't you watch where you're going?" she said, the pain once more robbing her voice of the intended humor. "You just hit national palace. That's going to cause an international incident."

"Why don't you stop being such a backseat driver?" King punched the accelerator, and the Tigr rocketed forward.

There was another shuddering impact as they crashed through the fence, but the Tigr was made of tougher stuff than the barrier, and its momentum carried it through without slowing. As the hailstorm of bullets started to slacken, King finally risked sitting up.

A stand of trees loomed into view. He cranked the steering wheel hard to the right and felt the heavy military vehicle skid closer to the wood line. Resisting the urge to brake, he instead pushed the accelerator harder. The tires threw up a shower of turf but the Tigr responded and veered onto a new course. He could see a paved road ahead, but between them and it was a gauntlet of troops and trucks, all of whom were now targeting the renegade Tigr.

The interior of the vehicle was suddenly filled with the roar of a heavy machine gun. King glanced back and saw Asya, standing upright in the turret, firing the DShK into the mass of troops.

He bit back a curse and focused on the near objective. "Blue, how's that escape route coming?"

"Sending it to you now." There was palpable helplessness in the disembodied voice. Deep Blue sounded as frustrated and haggard as King felt. "My satellite imagery for Kinshasa is two hours old, but assuming that the army is redeploying to repel General Mabuki's attack, the weakest place in their lines will be to the southwest—"

Asya let loose another burst. The thunderous report drowned out the rest. King felt the tires grip pavement and the Tigr picked up speed. He risked a quick glance back and saw his sister's feet moving back and forth as she swiveled the gun. A haphazard pattern of bloody footprints surrounded her.

"Negative," King said, turned his eyes back to the road. "I need to get to Mabuki by the most direct route possible."

He hooked a left turn, onto the broad avenue that paralleled the front of the Palais and the crowd of soldiers assembled there. Several vehicles were already starting to move, their guns flashing. Red tracer rounds were zipping across his path like laser bolts from a science fiction movie.

"King, that will take you right into the lion's den."

"Yeah, kinda figured that."

There was a whooshing sound in his head as Deep Blue gave a resigned sigh, then: "Hard right, now!"

There wasn't a road, but King saw a vast open plaza with an enormous brick courtyard and a central structure that looked like a UFO trying to break free from the grasp of several enormous concrete hands. King hauled the steering wheel to the right and angled onto the sidewalk between the courtyard and the weird monument. The Tigr jounced over low barriers and other pedestrian obstacles. King swerved to avoid a large bronze statue of a lion. Asya let loose a torrent of Russian profanity that was almost as lethal as the 12.7 mm rounds from the DShk, and sank down out of the turret. She finished with a sharp, "Who taught you how to drive?"

"Watch your language. She's your mother, too," King said. She frequently forgot he was fluent in Russian since his passage through the ages. "Now, stay down."

He was relieved that she was back in the relative safety of the Tigr's interior, but he knew the chaotic ride was almost certainly aggravating her injuries. If this kept up, he was likely to kill her before he could save her.

"Keep going straight," Deep Blue said. "There's a road directly in front of you. Straight shot to Mabuki's location."

"Do me a favor and let him know we're coming in hot."

"Already done."

The vehicle suddenly rocked under the impact of a barrage of machine gun fire. A small convoy of Tigrs and tracked APCs tore across the plaza in pursuit. The high caliber rounds punched through the armor with a shriek of tortured metal and continued right through the windshield, scant inches from King's head. He ducked, but knew that if the next burst hit a little lower, the seat back wouldn't do much to slow the bullets down, and if the rounds hit something critical, like a fuel tank or the tires, they were equally screwed.

"Straight shot is a no-go!" He lifted up just enough to scan the road ahead, spied a cross street and took the turn, slipping into an urban canyon between two modern looking buildings. The assault stopped, but King knew the reprieve would be short.

"You're still in the neighborhood," Deep Blue advised. "There's a right turn coming up in a hundred yards. Take it."

A network of glowing lines appeared in King's glasses, guiding him to the next approaching cross street, which was at an angle slightly sharper than ninety degrees and already a lot closer than a hundred yards. King hauled the Tigr into the turn, clipped the corner and bounced over the curb.

Asya howled another curse as the vehicle slammed down on the road surface, but quickly added, "I'm all right. Keep going."

King doubted that she was all right, but he also knew that moving forward was the only option. This road was also a straight shot, and before long he saw the headlights of the pursuit rounding the corner. King's Tigr was probably a good two hundred yards ahead of the soldiers, which wasn't nearly far enough. The effective range of a DShK was over a mile.

"Right turn, coming up."

Tracers streaked past, and King decided they wouldn't make it to the turn. He turned sharply to the right, blasting through a low concrete barrier. Beyond was a bare dirt field that might have been a parking lot for the nearby building. The Tigr's wheels threw up enormous clots of mud as it fishtailed across the open area, but for the moment they were once more out of the line of fire.

"There's an exit at your two o'clock. A left will put you back on the straightaway."

King saw it, and a metal gate blocking it.

What's one more dent?

The Tigr hit the gate, tearing it off its hinges. In the instant of impact, and too late to do anything about it, King saw something else looming out of the darkness. A seven-ton truck drove into view, blocking his path. He tried to brake and turn away from it, but he was already beyond the event horizon. The left front tire of the heavy truck crashed into the front end of the Tigr and annihilated it.

King was thrown out of his seat and across the interior of the vehicle. He slammed hard against the passenger side door, which crumpled like an empty beer can beneath the truck's big tires. Locked together in a death embrace, the two vehicles continued forward, shuddering and smoking as momentum fought friction. Friction ultimately won.

Disoriented, King fumbled for his Uzi then remembered that he was not the Tigr's only occupant. "Asya!"

She lay pressed against the right side, unmoving. He squirmed around, crawled between the seats and into the rear compartment. There was blood everywhere, too much blood...

A burst from a heavy gun startled him, and he twisted around, raising the Uzi. More reports followed—a chaotic orchestra of several automatic rifles and more than one machine gun. A few rounds struck the exterior, but nothing penetrated. He could see movement outside, soldiers swarming out of the transport, surrounding the wrecked Tigr, shooting...

The shooting stopped. A silhouette appeared, framed in the viewport hole. The door handle rattled as someone worked the latch from the outside, and King took aim with the Uzi, ready to fire the moment the door opened.

"Ceasefire!" Deep Blue shouted, and then he repeated the phrase again and again until King safed the weapon and lowered it.

The door swung open and King saw the smiling face of General Mabuki. "That is twice I have arrived in the nick of time to save you. I think I must be your guardian angel."

King didn't acknowledge the comment, but instead turned to Asya, pulling her toward him as gently as his urgency would permit. "Help me. She's hurt."

The general snapped into action, calling to his men for a medic. "Help is on the way," he said. "We will save her."

King checked Asya. Her dressing was still in place, but saturated. One trouser leg was soaked with blood that had run down from the wound. Her skin was unnaturally pale, but she was still taking shallow breaths.

Two soldiers ran up with an old school litter—canvass stretched between two poles—and King gently laid her in the tattered olive drab fabric while another soldier with a red cross armband began assessing her injuries. King watched the medic work for several minutes to make sure he knew what he was doing. Once satisfied, he took a step back to let the man work.

As his focus gradually pulled back, it occurred to him to ask Mabuki what had happened.

"The rebellion has been quashed," the general said. "When they realized that their leaders had fled aboard a helicopter, the soldiers lost the will to keep fighting."

King didn't quite share Mabuki's excitement. The rebellion in Kinshasa might have been put down, but General Velle still held the eastern part of the country, and Monique Favreau still had a tactical nuclear weapon, not to mention two hostages—one of whom was a US lawmaker. Still, a victory was a victory. He clapped Mabuki on the shoulder. "There's still a lot of work to do, but at least we got President Mulamba his house back."

Then King heard Deep Blue's voice again. "King, I'm afraid I've got some bad news."

THIRTY-THREE

Near Lake Kivu, Democratic Republic of the Congo

Felice awoke to the sound of screaming.

It was her second rude awakening in less than twenty-four hours. The nightmare reality that greeted her on this occasion was not the frantic chaos of an attack, but instead something far more terrifying: the ominous darkness of the primeval jungle, filled with an inhuman howl of pain.

She sat bolt upright and looked around, trying to find the source of the cry, so she could run the other way. There was movement in the darkness, something moving toward the scream, and for a moment the beast in her belly began to stir again...but no, she was wrong.

Wrong about the absolute darkness... There was a faint green glow, almost close enough to touch.

Wrong about the lumbering shape crashing toward her... It wasn't a shape at all, but her protector, the man who called himself Bishop.

Wrong about the scream... It was not inhuman at all, but was erupting from the compact form of the man she knew as Knight.

Knight sat hunched over a chemlight. He had removed his bandages and his exposed, raw, oozing flesh glistened in the green light. He had one hand held up to his injured eye, tugging at the metal protruding from it. His scream reached a climax as the shrapnel came free, releasing a gush of ocular fluid, thick with clotted blood. Then his howl changed to something that was almost like laughter.

Bishop reached Knight a moment later, kneeling in front of him and gripping his shoulders. "Damn, Knight. What the hell did you do that for?"

Knight bared his teeth in a fierce grin, but Felice saw that he was shivering. "Damn thing was trying to work its way into my brain. I had to get it out. Felt like my head was going to explode."

Felice quickly found the med kit and knelt beside Knight. "What's done is done," she said, holding the glow stick close to survey the wound. She couldn't tell if he'd made the injury worse by pulling the splinter out or if it had actually relieved some of the pressure, but one thing was evident: his eye was ruined beyond hope of repair. She tried to act clinically detached as she rinsed the area with saline solution. "But from now on, keep your grubby hands away from it."

"Yes, ma'am."

"Is he okay?" Bishop asked, speaking to Felice as if Knight wasn't even there.

She placed the back of her hand against Knight's forehead. "He might be feverish. I can't tell. It's so damn hot here all the time."

"I'm good," Knight said, sounding almost manic. "Fully mission capable. Drink water, and get back in the fight, am I right?"

Felice turned so that only Bishop could hear her. "Is he always like that?"

Bishop's head shake was almost imperceptible in the darkness.

Before either of them could say more, an eerie hum reverberated through the woods. It reminded Felice of crowd noise—hundreds, even thousands of people all talking at the same time, their voices blending together into a strange hum. It lasted a couple seconds, stopped, and then was repeated, growing louder and more intense, until it seemed to be coming from everywhere.

"What is that?" Felice asked. "Is that a tank?"

Bishop shook his head as he searched the darkness for the noise's source. "I don't know what that is. Get him bandaged up. We might—"

He abruptly brought the M240 to his shoulder, ready to fire. Felice had seen it, too, a hint of movement in the night, the kind of thing that triggered primal fears.

Something lurked in the darkness, just out of sight.

She didn't see it so much as sense it, disturbing the air with its presence. With a focused effort, she turned her back on the jungle and resumed tending to Knight's wounds.

The machine gun let loose with a roar that made Felice yelp. The burst lasted only a second or two. The muzzle flash, almost blinding in its intensity, somehow failed to give any illumination. Bishop continued to scan the darkness, jerking the gun back and forth, but did not fire again. For several seconds, all she could hear was a faint ringing in her ears, the lingering auditory assault of the weapon's rapid-fire report, but then the humming sound returned.

"Hurry," he urged. "We can't stay here."

Felice wrapped a length of Coban around Knight's head to hold a large gauze pad in place over his eye, and then hastily packed the med-kit and everything else into the rucksack.

"I'll get that," Bishop said, but she hefted it onto her shoulder, and then helped Knight to his feet.

"You're going to have your hands full keeping us alive," she replied.

He just nodded.

"What's out there?" she continued. "The rebels?"

"Might be an animal. Or a pack of them. I don't know."

She mentally ran down the list of animals that she knew roamed the Congo. "Lions, tigers and bears, oh my," she whispered to herself. That wasn't quite right. More like lions, leopards, gorillas and warthogs. *Oh my.* Yet, none of those, nor any of the other dozens of dangerous animals she could name, felt like a good fit for the thing—or things—moving in the darkness.

Felice kept a hand on Knight's uninjured right arm. She wasn't sure if she was doing this in case he stumbled and needed help staying on his feet, or because she felt safer being in constant contact with another person. It was probably a little of both. She would have put her other hand on Bishop's arm, but he had already moved ahead, and she struggled just to keep up with him. At times, it was so dark that she couldn't see him—or anything else—at all, and had to simply follow the sound of his footsteps.

The strange droning noise came back from time to time, but if it was the call of a predatory animal, it did not announce an impending attack. After a while, Felice realized that she could see a little better. Dawn was breaking.

What little sleep she had gotten did nothing to refresh her and as they trudged on, fatigue affixed itself to her muscles like barnacles on a ship's hull. The terror she had awakened to had become a fog of misery, and when Bishop called a sudden halt, it was all she could do to not simply drop to the ground in a fetal curl.

"What is it?" Knight asked. He sounded breathless, as if just asking the question had exhausted him.

"There's a road here," Bishop said. "Dirt track. Overgrown and probably not used very often, but it's there."

Felice peered ahead, but couldn't distinguish any difference in the forest's density. Nevertheless, she felt the fog of hopelessness lift a little.

"Risky," Knight observed.

"Why?" she asked. A road was something definite, something they could follow without fear of wandering in circles. A road would lead, eventually, to some kind of human habitation, perhaps to a village, where they could make contact with the outside world and get some help.

"They've got vehicles," Bishop explained. "They'll be using the roads to look for us. But I don't think we have a choice. We can't just wander aimlessly around in the woods. We'll skirt along the edge of the road and see where it takes us."

The trek—Felice was starting to think of it as a 'death march'—resumed, and she soon saw a thin ribbon of twilight overhead and off to the left. Before long, it brightened enough to reveal the trunks of the trees through which they were passing. Further off to the left, a clearing with parallel strips of dirt was packed by the repeated passage of four-wheel drive vehicles.

Bishop stopped abruptly, raising one closed fist. Knight froze in place, and Felice followed his example, even though her curiosity was burning. After more than a minute during which Bishop remained statue still, he turned slowly and whispered. "Do you smell that?"

Felice sniffed the air. There was a hint of wood smoke wafting through the jungle.

"Stay here. I'll check it out." Without waiting for their assent, Bishop moved off, following his nose.

Knight relaxed from his frozen posture and eased himself to the ground, using his rifle like a walking stick and keeping his left arm tight against his torso. Felice squatted down next to him.

"How are you doing?"

He returned a wan smile. "Believe it or not, I've been better."

She nodded. Humor, even dark humor, was a good sign. "Any fever? Chills?"

"Yeah. But I think the antibiotics are keeping it at bay."

She laid the back of her hand against his forehead and then drew her hand back in alarm. He was burning up. "How is the pain?"

He made a strangled sound that might have been laughter. "Hurts like a mother—ah, well you know." He reached up and touched the bandage as if trying to figure out how it had come to be on his face. "The jarheads always say, 'pain is just weakness leaving the body.' I guess my weakness must have been twenty-fifteen vision."

She touched his forearm and gently moved his hand away. Humor was good, but self-pity under these circumstances might be deadly.

"It's okay," he said after a moment. "I'll get an eye patch and talk like a pirate. Girls dig that, right?"

"Depends on the girl, I suppose. Now, if you get yourself a parrot..." Even though his teeth were chattering, his smile broadened and seemed more genuine, so she pressed on. "So, is there a particular scurvy wench you've got your eye on?"

"Ha. Yes. And I think she'd actually get a chuckle out of being referred to that way."

"What's her name?"

"Anna. Anna Beck." Knight's good eye seemed to lose focus for a moment. "We've been together...I guess, a couple years now."

"It must be tough...a relationship, I mean, doing what you do."

He nodded guiltily, and then started rooting around in his rucksack. Felice took that as a sign that he didn't want to discuss the topic any longer, but to her surprise, he kept talking. "Actually, before Anna, I don't think I had been in anything that you could call a relationship. And since I met her on the job, so to speak, I guess we both knew what would be involved."

Felice wasn't sure if he was referring to the long periods of separation or the inherent danger of his profession. She knew that military wives had to reconcile themselves to the possibility of losing their loved ones in battle, but she wondered how Anna Beck would react when she got her first look at Knight's maimed face. Then it occurred to her that Knight was probably wondering that as well.

"Does Bishop have someone at home?"

"Not Bishop. I don't think he's ever even been on a date. He's way too intense."

"I kind of picked up on that. Just figured it was a Rambo-thing."

"Bishop makes Rambo look like Ronald McDonald." Knight took out a cell phone, identical to the one Bishop had crushed earlier in every way but one, namely that it was still intact. He probed it with a finger, held it near his ear and shook it, and then turned it over and began picking at an almost imperceptible seam along its edge. After a few seconds, he succeeded in popping loose the back cover of the phone, exposing its electronic innards.

Felice let the subject go, allowing Knight to focus on what he was doing, but she found her thoughts occupied by the enigma that was

Bishop. She had caught a glimpse of the man that lay just under the rigidly held mask of self-control. There was a beast inside him, a monster of rage that he fought with every minute of his life, a monster that, if loosed, would destroy him and anyone close to him.

That was something Felice understood very well. She had her own beast with which to contend.

THIRTY-FOUR

Bishop moved further away from the road but kept it within sight as he tracked the smell of burning wood. Soon, he detected other odors: strange smells that he couldn't quite pin down, until his stomach rumbled and he realized it was the smell of cooking food.

Further down the road, he heard voices, women talking in a strange unfamiliar language, and small children shouting and laughing. He took that as a good sign. The cook fires might have belonged to a camp of rebels, but he doubted very much that the men pursuing them had brought along their kids.

He slowed his pace and stopped completely when he caught sight of the village. It was little more than a collection of ramshackle huts with concrete walls and thatched roofs, lining the sides of the road. There was a large fuel tank at one end, but there was not a single vehicle anywhere to be seen. Nor was there any sign of modern conveniences: no electric lights, radio antennas or satellite dishes. Bishop was willing to bet that there was no running water either. The smoke rose from makeshift open-air cooking pits outside the huts. The women tending them wore brightly colored dresses and kerchiefs tied around their hair, while the children wore T-shirts and soccer jerseys. The village was primitive, he decided, but not completely cut off from the rest of the world.

He remained there, watching the villagers' day begin, weighing the choices this discovery presented. He had already decided that he wouldn't attempt contact with them. There was no way to determine their loyalties, and it would take only one informant to alert the rebels to the presence of outsiders. The question he now pondered was whether to sneak into the village for food, medical supplies and perhaps even a map, or to simply give it a wide berth and keep going.

He had just settled on the latter option when something changed. The children reacted first, leaving their play and running into the huts to tell the adults. A few seconds later, Bishop heard what they had: the rumble of a diesel engine and the creak of a vehicle chassis rocking back and forth on its suspension. A truck creaked into view a few seconds later. It was a mongrel construct of indeterminable make and model, but there was one feature that was easy to recognize. Affixed to a metal post that had been welded to the floor of the rear cargo area, was a beat-up but serviceable PKM machine gun. A man wearing a soccer team logo T-shirt and camouflage trousers stood behind the gun, mostly using it as a handhold to avoid being thrown when the *technical*—a military term for a civilian vehicle that had been repurposed to serve as a war machine—bounced over ruts in the road. Two more rebel fighters rode in the front. The truck rolled to the center of the village, where it stopped. The man on the machine gun turned the weapon in slow circles, none too subtly letting the villagers know that he could kill any one of them with indifference. The two men in the front got out, their Kalashnikov rifles held at a low ready that was, if not quite menacing, then certainly not friendly.

An older man wearing tattered trousers and a short-sleeved shirt emerged from one of the huts and headed toward the truck. He moved assertively, stamping his bare feet on the ground, but he stopped a respectful distance from the armed men. They spoke what Bishop assumed was Swahili, and while he couldn't understand a word of it, he got the sense that the old man was reprimanding the young guerillas, but was careful to do so in a way that would not end with his own execution.

One of the rebels laughed, then lifted his head and shouted something meant for the whole populace. The old man took a step forward, raising both hands. The gesture looked to Bishop more like a protest than a surrender. The rebel stepped forward, too, reversing his grip on the rifle and jabbing the stock into the old man's midriff.

The women of the village let out a wail of protest, but no one moved to assist the old man. The man at the machine gun made a show of racking the bolt on the weapon, while the two dismounted rebels hurried into the hut from which the old man had come.

There was no hesitation in what Bishop did next. On some level, his decision was the product of a strategic calculation, but that was not what drove him. He was ruled by instinct, and his inner voice did not argue.

He chose a path that brought him into the village behind the technical and opposite the crowd of wailing women and frightened children. A few disbelieving eyes turned toward Bishop as he broke from cover, but the gunner did not recognize the importance of their behavior. He was still glowering at the assembled group when Bishop sprang up into the bed of the technical and broke his neck with a savage twist.

Bishop didn't stop, but instead hopped over the side of the truck and ducked low, keeping it between him and the hut, where the other two rebels had gone. With the coolness of a stalking lion, he padded around the rear of the truck and approached the hut at an angle that kept him out of line of sight of anyone looking out the door.

The old man struggled to rise, his face twisted in pain. When his eyes met Bishop's gaze, there was something else there, too. Apprehension? Pleading? Bishop couldn't fathom why the man would be looking at him that way. He was already helping the villagers. There was no time to ask for an explanation. Bishop pressed his back against the side of the hut and waited.

The rebels emerged a moment later. The first man passed by Bishop without even looking in his direction. When the second man emerged, Bishop stepped in front of him and delivered a close in blow that instantly knocked the man unconscious, and then spun on his heel and delivered a roundhouse punch that landed squarely at the base of the other rebel's skull.

As the second man collapsed in a heap at his feet, Bishop saw the old man moving toward him, shaking his head and repeating a phrase over and over. It didn't sound like a 'thank you.'

"English?" Bishop asked.

The man frowned. "*Non.*" He then said something in what sounded to Bishop like French, but was just as incomprehensible. He gestured at the rebels and then pointed an accusing finger at Bishop.

Bishop fought a powerful urge to simply turn and walk back into the jungle. A little gratitude would have been appreciated, but he understood why the villagers were afraid. It was easy for him to show up and crack a couple of heads, but he would leave, and they would still have to deal with the rebels. There might even be violent reprisals.

The old man turned away from Bishop and addressed the villagers in a loud clear voice. Almost as one, the people began dispersing to their huts. It had sounded like a call to arms, but as Bishop studied the faces, he saw women and children, mostly girls, and a few elderly couples.

"Where are all the men?"

The old man looked at him, as if waiting for the question to be uttered in a language he understood, then pushed past him and entered the hut.

Bishop felt another pang of guilt and helplessness. There weren't any able-bodied men in the village. Maybe they had all gone off to the city to work, been conscripted by the army or shanghaied by the rebels, who were notorious for kidnapping young boys—anyone big enough to hold a rifle—and forcing them to serve as foot soldiers. They would be indoctrinated and set on a lifelong path of violence.

A few moments later, villagers began to emerge from their huts. Some of the women had large cloth-wrapped bundles on their heads, while others carried baskets and herded small flocks of goats. Bishop spied the old man, likewise carrying a sack full of supplies. "What's going on? Where are you going?"

The old man gave him an appraising stare for several seconds. Then, as if his actions were answer enough, he turned and joined the procession heading down the road.

"Was it something you said?" a voice called from across the road.

Bishop turned and saw Knight and Felice emerge from the trees. "More like something I did, but I'm not really sure."

Knight shuffled toward him, but Felice started after the old man. "*Hujambo, bwana!*"

The man glanced at her, but just as quickly turned away and kept going. Felice shrugged and walked back to join Bishop and Knight.

"Where are they going?" she asked

"To hide in the jungle, I think," Bishop replied. "Probably afraid of getting caught up in this. I don't blame them. When we're gone, they still have to live here." He pointed at the men on the ground. "And what I did."

He stopped and cocked his head to the side. He had heard something in the distance, the faint but unmistakable roar of an engine. In a matter of just a few seconds, the noise grew steadily louder. He became certain that there was not just one vehicle, but several. "Time to go."

"Can't we take their ride?" Felice asked.

It was a tempting suggestion, but using the technical would mean staying on the roads, and the roads were dominated by the rebel forces. Their only hope of eluding the men who hunted them was to follow the example of the villagers and flee into the jungle. There wasn't time to explain all that to Felice, so he grabbed her arm above the elbow and hastened her into the trees.

As they passed once more into the forest, the first vehicle in a long convoy rolled into the village.

"They're going to know we were here," Knight said.

Bishop thought it sounded like an accusation. For Knight, a trained sniper, remaining concealed and leaving no footprints—literal or figurative—was of paramount importance. If Bishop had not intervened during the search of the village, the rebels would have moved on and been none the wiser. Now, whatever lead they had gained on their pursuers was gone. The hunters would know that they were nearby and the search would intensify. He didn't regret what he'd done. Sneaking around was Knight's way, not his. If he wasn't going to take risks to help the helpless, then what was the point of being a soldier? Unfortunately, he knew the risk was not his alone. His impulsive action had put Knight and Felice in danger as well.

"Take her and keep going," he told Knight. "I'll try to draw them off."

The tumult behind them intensified as more vehicles entered the village, and then changed in pitch with the addition of shouted voices. The rebels had found their fallen comrades.

"There's no time for that. We have to—"

"Look!" Felice's shout was so loud that Bishop winced, but when he turned to silence her, he saw that she was pointing off to their left. There, standing about fifty yards away was the old man from the village. He waved for them to join him.

Bishop looked to Knight. "Well?"

"I don't have a better idea."

They started toward the old man, and as they drew near, he turned and headed deeper into the forest. Despite his advanced years, the man moved with a spry surefootedness that revealed a lifelong familiarity with the savage wilderness. He set an urgent pace, almost faster than Bishop could move while remaining stealthy. Knight also struggled to keep up. He was drenched in sweat, and the heat and rising humidity sapped his strength by degrees.

He quickened his pace just enough to get close to their guide, and hissed, "We have to slow down."

The old man glanced back and said something in his native language.

He looked at Felice. "What did he say?"

"No idea. I only know a few phrases of Swahili." She was already winded, but sprinted ahead to the old man's side. *"Parlez vous Francais?"*

The old man didn't look at her, but uttered something in French, which was equally incomprehensible to Bishop.

Felice translated. "He says we will be able to rest soon, but right now they are too close."

The engine noise faded into the distance, but the shouts of the men spreading out into the forest remained constant. Bishop knew they were leaving a trail a blind man could follow. He wondered if the old man was leading them somewhere specific. Clearly the rest of the villagers had gone somewhere else, and it occurred to him that the old man might not be leading them to a place of safety after all. Perhaps he was simply trying to make sure that they didn't follow his neighbors, thereby leading the hunters to the villagers' refuge. Or maybe he was going to lead them back to the rebels and turn them in, to ensure the villagers' safety.

No good deed goes unpunished, he thought, but that was the kind of thing Rook might say. It wasn't how Bishop had lived his life. It wasn't how he wanted to live.

Trust the old man, he decided. *But be ready to deal with whatever happens.*

They were moving in a straight line. Bishop confirmed it by using tree trunks and other terrain features as visual waypoints, though doing so underscored just how vast and unchanging the forest was. The old man showed no sign of weariness, but Felice seemed to be flagging. Knight just shambled forward like an automaton, his forehead beading with perspiration. Bishop started counting his steps and was able to get a rough idea of how fast they were traveling and how far they had gone—nearly two miles in the half hour since they'd left the village and the road behind.

Another twenty minutes passed before their guide altered course, making an abrupt ninety degree turn to the right. Soon, they arrived at the edge of a narrow creek that cut across their path. The shallow water looked nearly stagnant, more a series of connected puddles than a proper stream. The fetid water reeked of decay and the hum of swarming mosquitoes was maddening in its intensity. However, the creek seemed to be a reference point for their guide. He immediately changed course again and led them parallel to the water.

Bishop sensed a change in the surrounding jungle. It was subtle, so much so that it took him several minutes to identify the difference. The sparse foliage near the stream showed evidence of being trampled. The forest was a place where animal life existed primarily in the canopy of interlaced tree branches—it was the domain of flora, not fauna. But here, at the stream's edge, the tree dwelling animals, and the few creatures that roamed the forest floor, came together to drink. It was also a place where predators were sure to find easy prey, evidenced by the occasional stripped carcass.

The old man stopped and held a hand out to signal them to do the same. Bishop turned to Felice, who was soaked in sweat and grimacing from the sustained exertion. "Ask him what's happening," he whispered.

She rocked unsteadily on her feet, panting to catch her breath, but nodded. In a whisper, she posed the question in French. The man answered in a low murmur without looking back.

"He says we're close, and that we need to be very quiet now."

"Close to what?"

She shrugged and passed along the inquiry, but got no answer. Instead, the man gestured for them to resume the journey, but set a glacial pace. Bishop snugged the butt of the M240 into his shoulder and elevated the muzzle, just in case they were being led into a trap.

A few more steps brought them to a marshy lake that seemed to be the source of the stream. It was nestled at the base of a dark cliff and a thin trickle of water fell down its surface to replenish the lake. The man pointed to the dribbling waterfall and then touched his finger to his lips, reminding them of the need for absolute silence.

Bishop now saw that the cliff wasn't a solid slab of rock, but was instead a hanging wall, jutting out to form a shadowy hollow behind the waterfall.

"Does he want us to hide in there?" Bishop asked, pointing. During heavy rains, the waterfall would probably transform into a raging torrent, completely obscuring the recess, but under the present conditions, it was completely exposed.

The old man shushed him again and continued along the edge of the lake. There seemed little doubt that the cave was his ultimate destination. As they got closer, he struck out across the marsh, but moved slowly to avoid splashing. Bishop silently consulted Knight with a meaningful glance, but the only answer Knight could give was a helpless shrug.

At the mouth of the cave, the old man paused again, and for the first time since encountering him, Bishop saw real apprehension in his face. He'd barely blinked in the face of the assault by the rebels, but now he seemed on the verge of bolting in panic. The emotion was contagious. Felice drew closer to Bishop, and Knight moved up so that they formed a small defensive cluster, ready to face whatever unknown terror lay beyond that trickle of water. But then their guide gathered up his courage, indicated again to the others that they stay silent and crossed the threshold.

Although the woods were shrouded in darkness, even at high noon, the first few tentative steps were like a plunge into the void. The old man advanced, and it took Bishop a moment to realize that the cave went much deeper than he first realized. The circle of light filtering in from outside shrank to nothing, and still they moved forward into the subterranean night.

Unable to see much of anything, Bishop closed his eyes for a moment and tried to focus on the rest of the sensory picture. The cave floor, which had been at first irregular and ankle deep underwater, had given way to bare rock, but now he felt the surface compress under his weight, like grass or moss on hard ground. There was an odd smell, too, similar to the earthy organic aroma of peat, but also a tang of ammonia.

Bats, he thought. *We must be right under them.*

Despite their best efforts to be quiet, he could hear the faint squish of sodden boots on the cave floor, the creak and rustle of clothes and rucksacks and weapons on their slings.

Then he heard something else. A weird hum echoed from the unseen walls of the cave, rising to a fever pitch in a matter of just a few seconds. It was the same noise they had heard in the pre-dawn darkness.

"Enough of this shit," Knight rasped.

Suddenly a light flared in the darkness. It wasn't very bright, but because his pupils had dilated in the darkness, it felt for a moment like someone had stabbed a toothpick in Bishop's eyes. It was, he realized, just a pale green chemlight, held aloft in Knight's right hand.

The hum stopped instantly, but then resumed again, this time with an intensity that Bishop could feel vibrating through his bones. The old man let out a yelp of alarm and deftly plucked the glowstick from Knight's fingers, hurling it away into the darkness.

As the luminescent tube sailed end over end, it revealed the cavern in a series of flashed images that were imprinted like snapshots on Bishop's retinas. He struggled to make sense of what he was seeing. All of his preconceived ideas about the cavern were wrong.

The cavern was enormous, far too vast to take its measure in the scant light of the glowstick. He realized they had barely left the front porch. There might have been bats overhead—the light didn't reach that high—but the soft material on the floor was not guano. It resembled Old Man's Beard, or some other kind of lichen, but it grew in astonishing quantities. It was just a fringe near the wall where they were walking, but further out, where the chemlight had been thrown, it was growing as thick as corn in Iowa.

Yet, that was not the strangest thing he saw.

There were animals moving about in the midst of the lichen, at least a couple dozen of them. They were about the size of farm turkeys, maybe thirty pounds, and looked bird-like, with what appeared to be feathers, or perhaps colorful scales covering their skin. They had heads with flat broad mouths, like ducks or geese. Unlike birds, though, they had long tails—longer than even their bodies—which were standing straight up in the air like antennae. The creatures might have been grazing on the frilly growth or perhaps pecking for insects, but the disturbance had cause them all to lift their heads in alarm and begin their strange ululating cry.

They were not birds.

Bishop had no doubts about that. In fact, even though he was having a hard time believing it, he knew exactly what they were.

In the preceding three years, to prepare for battle with the renegade geneticist Richard Ridley, the individual Chess Team members had participated in an accelerated educational program that included introductory courses in several scientific disciplines. Bishop recognized the animal species, even though most people, thanks to more than a century of erroneous conclusions reinforced by Hollywood movies, would not have.

The creatures he saw, in that momentary flash of the glowstick, were velociraptors.

The cave was full of dinosaurs.

THIRTY-FIVE

Lake Natron, Tanzania

Rook gazed in disbelief at the lake and the surrounding area. Although he had read Livingstone's account and heard Aleman's confirmation of the surreal phenomena associated with the alkali lake, the reality surpassed his wildest expectations. The lake wasn't blood red, exactly. In the burning light of the morning sun, it was brighter, with a variety of hues ranging from orange to pink. The opaque surface had the appearance of a terrazzo mosaic, or perhaps a stained glass window in a cathedral, shot through with whitish cracks. At the shore, the natural brown of rock and soil was coated a sulfur yellow in both directions, as far as he could see, and at the cusp where water and earth met, there was a darker band that phased between yellow, green and black. Scattered throughout were shapes that were easily recognizable as birds and other small animals, dead and perfectly fossilized.

"This is like something from a Star Wars movie," he told Queen. "The prequel trilogy, I mean, with all the CGI effects. I didn't think I'd ever see anything like this on Earth."

Queen shrugged. "Didn't watch them. Looks a little like New Jersey, to me."

As strange as the immediate landscape was, the real surprise was that Lake Natron was not the lifeless hell pit Rook had imagined it to be. Although there was no evidence of animal life nearby—unless, of course, one counted the petrified remains, just a short distance away, the lake transitioned to a less shocking hue of muddy green and reflected blue sky. Flocks of flamingos stood in the shallows, bobbing their heads down to scoop up mouthfuls of algae rich water.

"Didn't watch Star Wars?" Rook shook his head in mock-despair. "Well that might explain why you don't seem to appreciate my witty pop-culture references."

Humor was his defense mechanism. He had cleaned up and changed clothes on the long flight half-way across the world, but he still felt the memory of blood on his hands. Mulamba's remains now rested in a sealed body bag aboard *Crescent II*, which was parked a short distance away. The plane was perfectly camouflaged, as its digital skin projected an exact image of the terrain beneath it, or the jungle behind it. Billions of tiny color cells shrank and expanded to create the image—a technology based on the chromatophores of the common squid. From a distance, or from above, it was invisible. The area surrounding the lake was uninhabited, so there was little chance of someone stumbling across the aircraft.

"Could be that they aren't as witty as you think." Queen's tone was sharp enough that he knew she wasn't merely being playful. Queen, he knew, had her own way of dealing with loss.

"Touché. So, here we are. What do we do now?"

"Visual recon. We walk the shore until we find the footpath Livingstone described."

"Livingstone said the path was exposed when the lake water receded. It might be underwater now."

"Might be," she replied. Rook got the sense that she wasn't interested in enumerating all the factors that weighed against them in the search. She cocked her head sideways, listening to a voice inside her head, then added. "Aleman says he can set up a program to discriminate manmade artifacts that might not be visible to the naked eye."

A second pair of glasses would have doubled the effectiveness of the search, but Rook refrained from making the irrelevant observation. They didn't have a second pair, so what was the point of saying it? Instead, he fell into step beside her and respected her evident desire for quiet.

They headed south along the western shore. The squat misshapen cone of Ol Doinyo Lengai—the mountain Livingstone's Masai bearers had named the *Mountain of God*—smoldered in the distance, churning up natrocarbonatite lava, which reacted with water to give the lake its unique properties. There was no danger from the ongoing eruption, but from time to time, they could feel the ground beneath their feet vibrate with pent up seismic energy.

Without the glasses, Rook knew his contribution to the search would be minimal at best, so he spent most of the trek studying the terrain, looking for clues that might not be visible to Aleman's software. He tried to see this bizarre landscape as Livingstone might have, or even as the Ancients who laid the path would have. He decided they would not have gone about their choice randomly. A path suggested permanence, a well-traveled connection between the surface world and the cave entrance. Time might have obscured the path itself, but the builders would have chosen the path of least resistance. The hills and mountains they would have chosen to circumvent would not have changed nearly as much, even with the passage of many centuries. That was what he told himself at least. It was something to keep him occupied while Queen brooded.

As they traversed a salt flat with the texture of partially melted ice cream, something caught his eye. There, amid the irregular pattern of mineral mud turned to stone by the passage of time, were a series of depressions, spaced out a couple of feet apart. Each was slightly longer than his hand and looked remarkably like...

"Footprints!"

Queen came over for a closer look. "You're right. Someone walked through this mud when it was wet." She paused, listening to Aleman again, and her eyebrows went up in surprise. "These footprints could be over a hundred thousand years old," she said in an awed voice.

"Get out. Seriously?"

She nodded. "Fossilized human footprints have been found here that date to 120,000 years ago. I don't know if these are the same ones, but they could be."

"So these could be the footprints of the Ancients? Maybe this is the footpath Livingstone was talking about."

"It's worth checking out." She stood beside the prints and then began walking toward the lake's edge, sweeping her gaze back and forth slowly for the benefit of Aleman's computer program. She stopped with the toes of her boots almost touching the water.

"Careful," Rook advised. "One touch will turn you to stone."

"It doesn't work like that," she replied without looking back.

"Maybe not, but why take the chance?" He winced even as he said it. Queen wasn't the kind of person to back down from a dare. "I just mean, touching it probably isn't a good idea."

"Aleman says this might be the place."

"Uh, oh."

She turned, smiling at him. "Ready to get wet?"

They did not actually have to touch the corrosive and poisonous water. Their drysuits and full-face diving masks formed an impermeable barrier between their skin and the deadly lake, but how quickly the vulcanized rubber would degrade on contact with the highly alkaline water was anyone's guess. She decided it was best not to trouble Rook with that little detail.

Because there was no predicting what sort of specialized equipment the Chess Team might need while in the field, *Crescent*'s cargo hold was filled with gear and weapons to meet a broad spectrum of operational challenges in conditions ranging from arctic to undersea.

After suiting up and cross-checking to ensure all seals were intact and that their Daeger LAR VII rebreathers were functioning correctly, Rook and Queen ventured out into the murky red water. It was slow going at first, with the surface creeping slowly up their bodies as they waded through the shallows. The lake bottom was relatively smooth and regular, but because they could not see it, they had to test each step before committing to it. The process was further complicated by their long swim fins, which were perfect for swimming but worked about as well as clown shoes for walking. It was only when the water line was almost to her shoulders that Queen ducked her head down under the water to get a look at what lay beneath the surface of Lake Natron.

Beneath, the water was clear but the opaque red skin that floated at the top shut out nearly all light. Queen, who still wore her glasses under the diving mask was able to see everything clearly, but Rook's way was lit by a high-intensity LED hands-free dive light clipped to the top of his mask. In its brilliant glow, they quickly found traces of the footpath Livingstone had observed—a series of large flat stones that were laid too precisely to be a random occurrence of nature. They followed it further into the lake until they reached a sheer drop off. The path however, did not end there. Someone had carved out a ramp in the porous lava.

Queen swam out over the edge and lowered herself slowly down the face of the submerged cliff, following the course of the ramp with her eyes. The path curled around in a switchback and continued at a gentle slope across the face of the cliff for about twenty yards, and then seemed to fade out of existence.

"End of the road?" Rook asked.

Even though he no longer had his glasses, Queen heard Rook's voice just fine despite the fact that they were both underwater. The face masks they wore came equipped with ultrasound communicators, which allowed divers to speak to each other over short distances.

"It should be right here." She swam closer and probed the cliff face.

What looked like solid stone turned out to be only an accumulation of silt that billowed up at her touch. She continued scooping away handfuls of the fine particles until her fingers grazed the harder lava that formed the cliff face. The beam of Rook's lamp looked like a solid shaft of light, as it stabbed through the cloud of disturbed sediment. Curiously, when he pointed it into the place where she was digging, the shaft seemed to keep right on going.

Without waiting for the silt to settle out, Queen pushed forward into the space she had scooped out and found herself enveloped in a darkness that even the glasses could not penetrate. The effect was only momentary. The suspended particles were like a blanket thrown over her head, but she kept moving forward until she was clear of the cloud. The night vision function of the glasses kicked in again, and even though she was expecting to find herself in the cave Livingston's bearer had described, the sight of it nearly took her breath away.

"Rook, you have to see this."

A beam of light shot past her and then she saw him emerge from the swirling cloud. She knew that he couldn't see as much as she did, but as he reoriented himself, he played the light in every direction, as if he couldn't quite decide what he wanted to look at.

There was a lot to see.

The mouth of the cave was set high up along a wall that dropped away beneath them, descending at least fifty yards. The ramp continued diagonally along the wall to the halfway point, then curled around in a switchback that brought it to the cavern floor directly below the opening. The cave itself looked like the inside of an enormous egg, but with several ramps crisscrossing the gently curving walls and connecting the floor of the cave to dozens of passages that perforated the solid lava.

The honeycomb of passages out of the main cavern could have been attributed to naturally occurring fissures in the lava but the ramps were clearly evidence of human artifice. But they were not the only indications of such. Carved into the walls in the spaces between the openings were enormous bas relief sculptures, images of animals—elephants, rhinoceroses, lions and many that looked like creatures from mythology—as well as human figures in elaborate costumes. Queen studied the latter carefully. The facial features were unmistakably Sub-Saharan African.

"I've seen something like this before," Aleman said. Since the q-phone did not rely on line-of-sight radio wave transmissions, his voice was as clear as it had been on the surface. "Hang on a second."

Queen could almost visualize him furiously entering keywords into an Internet search.

"Those look kind of like the huge stone heads in Mexico," Rook said, playing his light over the sculptures. He hadn't heard Aleman's comment, but Queen saw the same similarity. The carvings bore a striking resemblance to the mysterious Olmec heads, which were believed to be artifacts of the oldest civilization in America. There were conflicting opinions about the heads, but few could deny that the faces—which dated to 900 BC—looked decidedly African.

"There's a definite similarity to those," Aleman agreed. "But that's not what I was thinking of. Okay, here it is. They aren't an exact match, but the style is very similar to sculptures done by the Edo people, specifically in the Benin Empire of West Africa, from about the thirteenth to the nineteenth century."

Queen relayed the information to Rook, then added. "Benin makes more sense than Mexico, but we're a long way from either place."

"People like to decorate," Rook suggested. "Regardless, this looks like the proof Joe was looking for: an ancient African civilization."

"It is interesting," she admitted. "But this isn't exactly a sprawling metropolis. I don't think it's the slam dunk he was hoping for. Even if this place rewrites the history books, I doubt very much that it will trigger some kind of cultural awakening, and I definitely don't think it will be enough to stop the civil war in the Congo."

Rook gave a grunt of grudging agreement. "Still, we're here. Might as well check it out."

He stroked through the water and shone his light into one of the passages. Queen swam over to join him and peered inside the opening. There was a short tunnel that opened into a large chamber, considerably smaller than the main vault, but still quite spacious. The floor was uniformly flat, probably smoothed out by ancient workmen, but littered with shapeless lumps of debris.

Queen paddled closer and fanned away some of the sediment to reveal a carved stone figurine of a lion.

After uncovering several more just like it, Rook said, "Do you suppose this place was their version of a shopping mall?"

"A trading post?"

"Well, I like 'mall' better, but yeah. This was probably their gift shop. I bet if we poked around long enough, we'd find their food court. Maybe we'll find the ancient African Hot Dog on a Stick?"

"Yeah," she said, with just a hint of sarcasm. "It might not be a good idea to put anything you find here in your mouth."

"Okay, think about this. You don't build a mall, or if you insist, a trading post, in the middle of nowhere. Maybe there was a city here, or up on the surface."

"We aren't archaeologists," Queen said. "The best thing to do is to turn this over to someone who knows what they're doing. *But*," she continued before he could protest, "it can't hurt to check out some of the other shops."

Further exploration seemed to support Rook's shopping center hypothesis, though most of the enclosures contained nothing recognizable. Centuries of submersion in the corrosive lake would surely have dissolved anything organic, and probably most metals, too. If the various chambers had once contained consumer products like clothing, sandals or whatever the ancient people needed for the business of daily life, there was no way to prove it. There was, however, one passage that looked very different from all the others. It was a large opening, much broader than any of the others, situated at the end of the large cavern, opposite the passage back to the lake. Queen had been saving it for last, and after half an hour of poking around in the shops, she decided it was time for one last search.

The passage was nothing like the others. Instead of opening immediately into a closed off chamber, the tunnel continued deeper into the surrounding rock, gently turning and descending in places as it went.

"It looks like you're in a lava tube," Aleman told her after a few minutes of travel.

"Does that mean we're headed toward the volcano?"

"Volcano?" Rook echoed. "Wait, what?"

"It's unlikely. Not Lengai, anyway. This tube was probably created by a much older, extinct volcano. The whole cave system had to have been formed before Lake Natron. You're probably safe."

"We're safe," she told Rook. "Probably."

"Just another ordinary day then," he muttered.

As the lava tube continued deeper into unknown territory, Queen began to reconsider the appraisal. It was not the threat of volcanic activity that concerned her. The water temperature remained constant, and was perhaps even a little cooler than at the surface. Rather, it was the sense of being on a journey with no end. There was no evidence of human activity in the tunnel, and the further they went from 'the mall' the less likely it was that they would discover anything more. At some point they would have to turn back, and the further out they went, the longer the return trip would be.

"I'm calling it," she said. "Time to head back."

"No arguments from me," Rook replied.

He placed a hand against the side of the tunnel and pivoted around. Queen did the same and started kicking back the way they'd come.

Rook hesitated. "Ah, Queen, I think we've got a problem."

She glanced back over her shoulder and saw him still poised along the side of the tunnel, not swimming. He was, however, still moving, sliding further down the passage. She felt a surge of panic even as he stated the obvious. "There's a current here."

The flow of the water was gentle enough that, when swimming with it, she had not even felt herself being drawn deeper into the passage. Now, however, there was no mistaking the inexorable pull of the current. In the brief instant that she had stopped to look, it had erased what little progress she had made and pulled her past where Rook was dragging along the wall.

"Damn it." She resumed kicking, adding powerful overhand strokes, but it was like running in place.

"Grab the wall," urged Rook.

She did, placing her gloved palms against the curving side of the lava tube and pressing her body against it to create a sort of friction brake. She could still feel the current softly tugging at her, and saw immediately that this would only be a stopgap measure. She couldn't swim and hug the wall at the same time.

"Okay," she said, not quite able to entirely mask her rising trepidation. "I'm open to other crazy ideas now."

"Only one way out of here," he replied, sounding uncharacteristically grim. "We swim like hell, and hang onto the wall when we—"

Queen didn't hear the rest. Her grip on the wall failed and the current caught her. She careened along the wall for a few seconds, then the abrasive lava snagged the drysuit and scratched at the casing of her rebreather.

"Queen!" Rook's light stabbed through the water, searching for her.

He can't see me.

She fought to get reoriented, but the rush of water and the buffeting impacts with the wall had exponentially increased the difficulty of maneuvering. She tried reaching for the wall again, but in the short distance she'd been swept, the current had gotten stronger. She glimpsed a junction in the passage overhead, another lava tube joining the tunnel like an arterial branch, and as she was drawn under it, she felt a much stronger current take hold of her. She was swept away like a leaf in a hurricane.

THIRTY-SIX

Congo River, Democratic Republic of the Congo

In 1877, Henry Morton Stanley set out from the junction of the Luabala and Congo Rivers, just below the series of waterfalls that would bear his name for a time. He traveled by boat on a four-week-long, thousand mile journey that brought him to another waterfall, which he named Livingstone Falls, in honor of his other great achievement. The beginning and end of this journey, the longest navigable section of the Congo River, would become Leopoldville in the west, a name later changed to Kinshasa, and Stanleyville—renamed Kisangani—in the east. No road connected the two, and driving between them required a circuitous detour through the country's southern region. Nearly a century and a half later, the river remained the most direct route of travel between the two cities. The length of time required to make the journey by boat had improved somewhat. Now, a cargo barge, the most common vessel to be found plying the river route, could make the downriver trip in about two weeks. It took slightly longer going upriver, against the current, from Kinshasa to Kisangani.

"I need to be there before dawn," King had told Mabuki, just eight hours earlier.

He had no doubt that Favreau would head for Kisangani, the seat of General Velle's rebellion. Although the Red Queen had been forced to flee Kinshasa, King did not believe for a moment that the civil war had been averted, especially now that Joseph Mulamba was dead. If he was to prevent bloodshed on a colossal scale, it was imperative to separate Favreau from her backpack nuke. Rescuing the hostages, which included the man who was now legally the President of the DRC, placed a close second on the list of urgent priorities. Both objectives would require a covert trip into the enemy headquarters in Kisangani, and there wasn't a minute to waste. As far as Favreau knew, Mulamba was on his way back to reclaim control of the government. When the truth about his death was finally revealed, General Velle would realize just how valuable his hostages were.

The urgency of the situation was not the only factor compelling King to move quickly. He was by nature a patient man. He could not have survived 2,800 years without learning how to be long-suffering. But there had been a few times in his life where he had felt the need to do something—anything—to keep from going completely insane. He felt that way now.

Asya had nearly died, and while the doctor at the university hospital had said the outlook was promising, she wasn't out of the woods yet. As her brother, King knew he should have been at her side. In fact, he *wanted* to be at her side, and that was exactly why he knew he had to get moving, to get away from Kinshasa and his stricken sister as fast as possible. If he didn't—if he didn't get moving, didn't stay busy—then the rest of the world would go to hell and he would have to live with the knowledge that he could have done something to make a difference but chose not to.

He could have waited for *Crescent II*. Queen and Rook were on their way back, and although they were headed for Tanzania, it would have been a simple thing for the supersonic stealth transport to pick him up and take him where he needed to go. But that would mean staying the night in Kinshasa, staying at Asya's bedside and letting his worry and guilt erode his resolve. He needed to be in motion.

But what he needed and what was possible were two very different things.

The Republican Guard general had laughed at his demand. "It cannot be done. This is not New York City, my friend."

Flying—on any aircraft other than *Crescent II*—wasn't a viable option. General Velle had closed the airspace around Kisangani, and had the ability to shoot down any civilian aircraft that got too close to the remote city. The rebel leader also controlled the entire air armada of the DRC, which really consisted of a pair of Mil Mi-8 helicopters—one of which was currently carrying Favreau across the country.

That left only river travel. Fortunately, the navy had not defected to the side of the rebels. Unfortunately, the navy consisted of eight Chinese made Type 062 Shanghai II patrol craft, only one of which was presently operational.

"At maximum speed, the patrol boat could get you there in two days' time," Mabuki went on. "Maybe more. It is a long trip, and the boat is..." He let the sentence fall away, allowing King to reach his own conclusions.

"Two days?"

"Relax." Mabuki clapped him on the arm. "We have a saying, 'A bald headed man will not grow hair by getting excited.'"

"What the hell does that even mean?" King replied, exasperated. He knew what it meant. He needed to cross a distance that was just slightly less than that which separated Los Angeles and Dallas, in a country with virtually no infrastructure, where the average person earned about a dollar a day. He could shout and stamp his feet until he was blue in the face, but it wouldn't change the fact that he was looking at a two day journey to his next objective...if he was lucky.

The journey had begun promptly, at least insofar as the Congolese sailors were capable of promptness. King was joined by a small contingent of guardsmen, which included the members of the strike team that had accompanied him during the raid on the Palais de la Nation. Miraculously, all of them had survived the battle, escaping with just a couple of minor injuries. "The regular Army soldiers," explained their leader, "do not know how to fight." King hoped that would be true of the forces under Velle's direct command as well.

Viewed from a distance, the Shanghai had the profile of a battleship, bristling with gun barrels, and rising to a raked bow in the front. Up close, it was less imposing. 130 feet long, its guns were a pair of 37mm cannons, one fore, one aft, and a 25 mm twin barrel machine gun mounted behind the radar mast. There were no creature comforts. The low slung boat was intended for short patrol missions lasting only a few hours. King and the soldiers would be riding on the open deck, eating only what they could bring along, sheltered from weather and insects by whatever means they could contrive, with no privacy and no concessions to hygiene.

It was nearly dawn before the Shanghai pulled away from the dock in Kinshasa and started upriver. A low white fog covered the water, giving the appearance that the gunboat was motoring through the clouds. King watched their progress for a while, then found an unclaimed section of deck near the bow, draped a thin mosquito net over the rail and down to the deck, careful not to leave any opening, and as the sun rose over the emerald expanse of the rain forest, he drifted off to sleep.

At about the same time that King embarked on his journey to Kisangani, the Red Queen completed hers. The helicopter, which had less than a day earlier carried her from General Velle's headquarters to the capital city, had brought her full circle. Her intended mission, to negotiate an end to the revolution—an end which would have installed General Velle as the military dictator of the country and pave the way for an exclusive resource partnership with Consolidated Energy—had been thwarted by the news of Joseph Mulamba's escape. Her subsequent gambit to seize control of the country had ended disastrously. Yet she did not feel, what a famous sportscaster had once called 'the agony of defeat.'

In fact, she felt energized.

During the long helicopter ride, she had analyzed her situation like the pieces on a chessboard. Although there seemed to be only a few moves left to her—defend, retreat, surrender—she knew that now was the time for a bold, dynamic strategy. The question that had occupied her thoughts for most of the trip was not actually what she would do, but why she would do it.

Her satellite phone had rung just once during the night, a single call from ESI headquarters. She had not answered, nor had she listened to the voice mail message that had been left. She knew that she had been disavowed, cut loose to face the consequences of failure on her own. Consolidated Energy would deny any involvement, and would bide their time for a while, before making another play for the riches hidden beneath the Congo at the bottom of Lake Kivu. The fact that the phone had been silent thereafter was proof enough that she was on her own. She could still win this game, though. She fully intended to, but what would she do with the spoils of her victory?

As she contemplated that question, the answer came to her like an epiphany.

What are you willing to sacrifice to win? Everything.

General Velle was waiting for her when the Mi-8 touched down at the army base. "This is a disaster," he said by way of a greeting. "You have ruined everything."

He was trembling with rage, and she knew that the only thing that kept him from lashing out her with anything other than words was his certain knowledge that her death would result in the detonation of the backpack nuke.

"It is a setback," she countered, coolly. "Nothing more."

"A setback? My loyal forces in Kinshasa have been defeated. We cannot take the capital without them."

"Kinshasa is irrelevant." She turned to the flight crew. "Do not disembark. We will be leaving again as soon as we have refueled."

"Leaving?" Velle asked, still storming. "And where do you intend to go?"

She returned her gaze to him. "General, you should study your history. You do not rule Africa by capturing cities. You rule by possessing that which everybody else wants. I am going to Lake Kivu, and if you wish to win, then I suggest you begin moving your forces there."

"Kivu? What is at Kivu?"

The Red Queen allowed herself a wry smile. "Everything."

THIRTY-SEVEN

Near Lake Kivu, Democratic Republic of the Congo

One of the raptors darted its head forward and snapped the chemlight up in its jaws. The thin plastic tube burst apart in a spray of glowing phosphorescence that splashed the creature's plumage. The dispersed liquid gave little illumination, returning the cave to near total darkness but the splash revealed the raptor's location. And its movements. The greenish glob began bobbing up and down as it shot through the inky blackness, straight toward the human intruders.

Bishop hesitated for a moment. The existence of these dinosaurs, while theorized by fringe science for years, was something of a miracle. Killing them would be a shame. But they were also predators, and given the path of the glowing specimen, hungry predators.

Seeing no alternative, Bishop swept his M240 in an arc, spraying lead in the path of the charging raptor. In the muzzle flash, he saw that it wasn't alone. The glow-stained raptor went down in a flurry of scrabbling limbs and flying bits of lichen, but the rest continued, swarming. Bishop held the trigger down. The creatures moved faster than he could target, and for every one that went down, three more slipped under his barrage. Knight opened fire beside him, but with even less effectiveness. The heavy caliber rounds from his Intervention sniper rifle gouged up chunks of the lichen covered cave floor, but the rate of fire was so slow that he couldn't track targets with his muzzle flashes. Worse still, the raptors seemed to have no sense of the relationship between the guns' thunderous reports and the deadly consequences that might follow. If anything, the noise seemed to drive them into a killing frenzy.

We can't stop them, Bishop thought. With a sweep of his arm, he thrust Felice and Knight behind him, and started swinging the hot barrel of his machine gun like a scythe.

There was a satisfying crunch as his impromptu club swatted one of the raptors out of the darkness. He felt and heard another impact on the backswing, but then something struck his legs and burning claws raked his chest.

He let go of the M240 and swiped his bare hands at the unseen attackers. His fingers closed on coarse plumage and he flung one of the beasts away, even as its sharp talons slashed at his skin. Another one rushed in to take its place.

Bishop matched their primal fury with his own, clawing and biting at anything that came within reach. There was a sound, like cracking ice, inside his mind. He could smell more vividly. He felt faster, or the world was slower. Pain faded, and he became destruction. A life-taking force. When the attacks ceased, he groped blindly for any raptors that might have gone for Felice and Knight. It was only when he heard their voices—not crying in pain or alarm, but urging him to stop—that the animal instinct driving him began to relent.

As the cloud of rage dissipated, he realized that he could see them. Knight had thrown out half-a-dozen glowsticks, surrounding them in a ring of faint illumination. Several raptors lay scattered beyond the circle, broken and torn, some still twitching, but the attack was over. Knight and Felice were unscathed.

Bishop turned slowly until he found their guide, huddled against the wall with his arms covering his head. Bishop's bloodied fingers curled into claws, as he started toward the old man.

Suddenly Felice was standing in his way, hands outstretched, palms facing Bishop. "Stop."

"Move." Bishop's voice was the low growl of a stalking lion.

"No. Leave him alone."

He continued forward until her hands were pressing against his chest. He could feel her touch against his bare skin, where his shirt had been torn away by raptor claws. Her skin felt cool on his, and to his complete surprise, he found his rage cooling as well.

"That son of a bitch set us up," Knight said. His fever made his outrage seem even more intense than Bishop's. "He knew those things would be here. This was a trap."

Felice refused to yield. "Why would he do that? He could have just left us back in the woods, but he didn't."

"No. He ran us through the jungle until we were exhausted, then brought us here to feed his pets."

"Ask him," she persisted. Then, without breaking contact with Bishop, she turned her head to the old man and rattled off a question in French.

It was only then that the old man seemed to grasp that he was the focus of attention. He answered in a deluge of words, strung together in short little outbursts that came out too fast for Felice to translate. When he finally took a breath, he slowed, and she began to explain.

"Yes, he knew about the beasts, but he didn't bring us here to be killed. They don't attack unless they are threatened. He thought we would be safe here. If we had stayed silent and not shown a light, we would have been fine."

"How does he know that?"

She asked him, then interpreted his answer. "He found this cave when he was just a boy. He says his name is David, and he's been coming here for many years. He says he knows how to move among them without being attacked." She swung her gaze to Bishop. "What are those things, anyway?"

"Velociraptors."

"You're kidding."

"No."

"Dinosaurs?"

"Yes."

"That's impossible, you know. They didn't look like raptors."

"You've seen other raptors?"

"I've seen Jurassic Park," she said, her face revealing that she knew how foolish the answer sounded.

"Jurassic Park got it all wrong. Velociraptors were small, not much bigger than turkeys. Actually, most dinosaurs were more closely related to birds than to reptiles."

"Uh, huh. Wouldn't have guessed you were a dino nut." When he didn't respond, she went on. "I'm no expert on dinosaurs, but I do know a thing or two about evolution. Dinosaurs have been extinct for sixty-five million years."

"That's what I thought, too. I guess we were both wrong."

Felice let it drop. "Whatever they were, they did a number on you." She gently parted the tattered remnants of his shirt. "Are you hurt?"

"What? No. Just a few scratches."

"You don't have to impress me. I already know how tough you are."

"I'm fine." And indeed, he seemed to be. Although his clothing was in tatters, the only sign of injury was a crust of drying blood that she brushed away. There were long red stripes on his swarthy skin, which looked no worse than scratches from a frisky house cat. He'd been lucky.

"What I'd really like," Bishop said, trying to redirect her attention, "is some answers from our friend here. Maybe start with how he found this place."

David nodded at the translated request and sank down on his haunches. He told them the story of how he, as a young and naïve child soldier fighting with the Simba rebels, had fled into the jungle and discovered the cave behind the waterfall. Though his companions had been killed by the creatures inside, David had never forgotten the amazing discovery, and had eventually returned to explore the cave.

Knight, who had been huddled on the floor in silence, looked up. "And he never thought to tell anyone that he'd found living dinosaurs?"

David returned a blank look, even when Felice had translated the question. "Maybe he doesn't know the word *dinosaure*." She tried again, but this time used the word *monstre*—monster—but again, the question seemed to perplex the old man.

"I do not understand," he finally admitted to her. "Why are you asking me about these creatures? Do you not already know of them?"

"We call them dinosaurs," she explained in French. "But they have been extinct—completely gone—for many thousands of years." If he didn't know dinosaurs, he might have trouble grasping the idea of millions.

David shook his head. "No. They are not dead. They have always been here, though few ever see them. They only leave the cave at night, and never come near to the village."

"It sounds like something from a movie," Bishop said. "A lost world. It's incredible."

"Impossible is more like it. Genetically speaking, it's just not feasible. Even if some dinosaurs survived the extinction event, they would have undergone evolutionary changes over the course of time."

"Aren't there some animals today that are the same as they were back then? I remember reading somewhere that certain shark species have been around for over a hundred million years."

Felice inclined her head, ceding the point. "Some species seem to show less genetic drift than others. But the odds of something like this happening on land—I don't just mean surviving, but surviving undetected—are really, really...well, impossible."

Bishop glanced at Knight, who said, in a weary voice, "We're kind of used to dealing with the impossible."

Felice seemed to weigh that, as if she also had some experience with things that couldn't be easily explained. "Here's the problem. For a species to survive, it needs habitat and it needs food, and those things are always in flux. When there's a lot of food, the population will grow until it starts to put a strain on the resources. When that occurs, the population will either migrate or experience a die off. The point is that populations don't remain stable. If dinosaurs have been around for sixty-five million years, someone would know about them by now."

"If what David just said is true," Bishop said, "then a lot of people do know about them. Frankly, the Congo seems like the kind of place where a lot of things might go unnoticed for a long time."

She shook her head. "I just don't know if I can reconcile the existence of modern dinosaurs with what I know about evolutionary biology. There's got to be something we're missing here."

"Hang on a second," Knight said, abruptly. "If the people here already knew about the raptors, then what exactly was it that brought him back to the cave? What was this big discovery that was so important?"

Before Felice could translate the question, a shout echoed through the cavern. Bishop swung his gaze around, seeking out the source. There were more voices, issuing from the direction of the cave entrance, and then the sound of gunfire echoed again in the vast chamber.

The hunters had found them.

THIRTY-EIGHT

"**Follow me,**" David urged.

Felice did not have time to translate, but there was little need for it. Knight gathered up the chemlights and jammed them into a pocket, plunging the group into darkness once more.

Felice grabbed Bishop's hand. He seemed to shy away at her touch, but she squeezed harder, insistent that they not be separated. He relented, drawing her along as they followed the old man deeper into the cavern.

More sporadic shots were fired, though it was impossible to tell whether the rebels were shooting at anything in particular—perhaps fending off another pack of the strange bird-like animals—or simply trying to flush their prey out of hiding. David moved quickly but at a walking pace. In the eternal night, there were greater dangers than being hit by a bullet, especially since they were already so deep into the cavern that they could no longer even see the entrance.

Walking hand in hand with Bishop was awkward at first. He was clearly unaccustomed to any kind of intimate physical contact, but she refused his subtle efforts to pull away, and soon his reluctance melted away, just as his anger had. She remembered his rage and knew how close he had been to giving in to it completely, murderously, but she had also felt that rage shrink away at her touch.

"Is there another way out?" Knight whispered after several minutes.

She passed the question to David, then gave his answer. "He doesn't know, but there is a place ahead, where we will be safe."

"Safely bottled up," Knight growled.

Felice felt Bishop tensing up again, and gave his hand a reassuring squeeze. A few moments later however, she was forced to release her hold, as David led them into a slot passage too narrow for them to continue to walk side-by-side. As the rock walls brushed against her shoulders, Felice felt the beginnings of a claustrophobia-induced panic, which was only partly alleviated when Bishop laid a gentle hand on her shoulder.

Her fear evaporated quickly, however, when she realized that she could see again.

Though faint at first, she could now make out the passage walls, and when she reached out to touch them, she could see her own fingertips limned in a bluish glow. As the group advanced, the light grew brighter.

"Do you—?"

"I do," Bishop whispered. "Keep going."

The passage undulated through the rock in a series of turns. The ambient light grew brighter with each one they rounded, until the passage opened up again, revealing the light source.

For a few seconds, Felice wasn't sure what she was looking at. At first, she saw only a broad expanse of black, dotted with yellow and blue lights, like stars in the night sky. It appeared the passage had led them back outside, and that they were looking at the Milky Way at midnight, but it was daytime outside, and the 'stars' were below her.

"Fires," Bishop observed.

Thousands of small fires were spread out on the cave floor in every direction, as far as she could see. As she stared at them, she gradually began to distinguish the landscape's shape—rocky out-croppings, stalagmites, rising and falling hills—as dark silhouettes against the glow of the flames.

Some of the silhouettes were moving.

At first, she thought it might be shadows dancing in the flickering firelight, but the longer she looked, the less likely that explanation seemed.

And when a low hum filled the air, joined by another and another and another, growing in intensity until it sounded like jet engines, she knew that her eyes weren't playing tricks on her.

This place belonged to the dinosaurs.

ANCIENTS

THIRTY-NINE

Underground

Queen fumbled in the darkness. Her thoughts were muddled by too many sensory inputs that didn't seem to connect...

The last thing she remembered was getting caught in a fast-moving cross-current.

She jolted, as the physical memory of being tumbled by the subterranean river returned, but then she realized that she was no longer in the water. Instead, she was lying on a hard, flat surface. As the pieces quickly came together, Queen's heart began racing.

"Aleman, still with me?" Her voice was loud, echoing strangely in the total darkness. There was no answer, and after a few seconds, she realized that this was because she was no longer wearing the glasses. Her face mask and rebreather were missing, too. The air on her face was hot and humid. She sat up slowly, reaching out in every direction to explore her new environment. "Rook?"

A faint scuffing sound echoed out of the darkness. She whirled, rolling onto hands and knees, coming up in a defensive crouch, hands raised to meet the unseen threat.

Damn it. I can't even tell what direction it's coming from.

"Right here, babe."

The wave of relief at hearing Rook's voice left her almost giddy. "I can't see. I lost the glasses."

"No you didn't." She felt his reassuring hand on hers. "Better close your eyes."

She did, though there was no perceptible difference. A moment later, there was a blinding flare of red that seemed to burn right through her eyelids. She scrunched her eyes closed even tighter and covered them with a cupped palm. It took several minutes for her eyes to adjust to the painful brilliance enough to lower her hands and even attempt opening her eyes. The light felt like grains of sand on her corneas. She squinted through watery eyes and found Rook's smiling face.

"Here," he said, holding something out to her. "Try these."

Her glasses. "So that's where they went." She slipped them on. The photosensitive lenses were clear, but as soon as they covered her eyes, the virtual retinal display went active in night vision mode, automatically adjusting for the intensity of Rook's dive light.

"Why didn't you just give me these in the first place?"

"The glasses work by projecting light directly into your eyes. If you'd put them on, it would have felt like sticking a hot poker in your eyes."

Rook switched off his light, and in the resulting darkness, she discovered that she was finally able to see. Rook squatted calmly on the floor, eyes looking forward but seeing nothing. His mask and rebreather were also gone, discarded somewhere along the way, and his drysuit looked like it had been dragged behind a truck. Hers did, too. She rose to her feet and took a look at her surroundings.

They were in a cavern, not as large as the original cave they had first entered, but still very spacious. The walls were damp, with rivulets of water running down from above and dribbling from mineral formations that she probably could have named, if she'd spent a few minutes thinking about it. Her attention was drawn to a dark pool that occupied the center of the chamber. It was not the pool that she found so interesting, but rather a pile of stones jutting out from its shore like a dock or jetty.

Curious, she started toward it, realizing only after a few steps that Rook couldn't see her. She hiked back and took his hand. "Why don't you use your light?"

"I already saw everything there was to see here. Might as well save the batteries. It sounds like we might be down here a while."

The comment reminded her that she still didn't know where she was or how she'd gotten here. "What happened?"

"You got caught in a wicked current. Not sure, but I think your rebreather might have gotten banged up, or maybe you were breathing too fast. You blacked out."

"Then how did I—why am I not dead?"

"I caught up to you and buddy breathed with you for a while."

She gazed into his confident but completely unaware eyes. "You weren't caught in the current, were you? You came after me on purpose?"

"I wasn't going to leave you. You're—" he shrugged, and looked a little embarrassed, "you know, kind of important to me."

Because she couldn't think of any other way to deal with the overwhelming surge of emotion rising from her chest, she pulled him close, stood on her tiptoes and kissed him.

She might have gone on kissing him, but the sound of someone politely coughing reminded her that they weren't exactly alone. She turned toward the dock again, and led the still somewhat euphoric Rook along by the hand. "So where are we exactly?"

"I'm not sure where you are—exactly," the familiar voice of Deep Blue said, "but I think you are somewhere below Lake Victoria, and roughly two hundred and fifty miles from Lake Natron."

Queen stopped abruptly. "What?"

"It's hard to be more precise. Even though the q-phone signals aren't affected by...well, anything...you're in a three-dimensional environment that we've never really had to take into account.

That's the relative distance you would have traveled if you were on the surface."

She heard Rook laughing and guessed this wasn't the first time Deep Blue had given this explanation. "How long were we in that river?"

"A while," Rook said with a shrug. He didn't hear Deep Blue clarify, "Eight hours and twenty-two minutes."

"Shit." That explained why they were talking to Blue instead of Aleman. Evidently, whatever crisis had occupied their remote handler had passed. Now *they* were the number one priority. "We couldn't have lasted that long on one rebreather."

"This place is like the mother of all waterpark rides," Rook said. "That current shot us out like a cannon. We ended up in a fast moving river. There were air pockets along the way, so we didn't have to use the rebreather the whole time. Eventually, the river dumped into the lake over there."

"So this is the end of the road?"

"Not even close," Deep Blue said, a little too quickly. She could tell he was trying to stay upbeat. "You're in a massive uncharted cave formation. Something that big is bound to have more than one outlet."

"If it did, wouldn't someone have found it by now?"

Even though Rook could only hear Queen's side of the conversation, he seemed to sense her despair. "Queen, this isn't a bottomless pit. Think about what we've already seen. That cave back there at Lake Natron...the mall? Somebody built that, centuries ago. And I think they were using that lava tube as a sort of superhighway."

Her pessimistic retort gave way to raw curiosity. "What do you mean?"

"We were trying to figure out why they would build their marketplace there, remember? I think it was there because that was the end of the road...this road. An underground trading route." He gestured in the approximate direction of the lake. "See that dock? I think this was sort of a transfer station. That lava tube might have been a shallow river before the lake flooded. Or maybe it was a dry road that connected with a river. The point is, if the mall was the end of the road, then there's a beginning. We just have to find it."

"He's right," Deep Blue said. "A couple of years ago, King found evidence of a vast underground network connecting America and Europe. It's possible that these caves are everywhere, and that the ancients knew about them and knew how to use them. Maybe this is why there are underworld legends in nearly every culture on Earth."

Queen relayed this news to Rook.

"Isn't the underworld the same thing as Hell?" he remarked. She reached out and gripped his hand. "Whatever, right? If anyone can walk out of Hell, it's us."

It felt like a lie.

The dock might have been the end of one section of the Ancients' underground trade route, but it wasn't the dead end Queen feared. Instead, it seemed to be a sort of crossroads, with not one but five separate passages leading away. Three of them were narrow and seemed like unlikely candidates for Rook's superhighway, but the other two were wide openings that showed visible evidence of human use—centuries of foot travel, or perhaps pack animals and carts, had worn a ribbon-like groove down the center of each tunnel.

Rook shone his light down each of the tunnels. "Which way?"

"Flip a coin?"

He gave her a reproving look. "Not falling for that again."

"What?"

Rook shone his light down the passage that led out of the cavern on the wall opposite the lake. "I say we go this way."

"There'll be no living with you if you get lucky on the first try." She leaned close and gave him another kiss, this time just a peck on the cheek. "But I hope you're right."

They walked for a while in silence, and in Rook's case, darkness. The tunnel continued to slope down, deeper into the Earth's interior.

"What do you think happened to them?" Rook asked after a while.

"The Ancients? Judging by the fact that the mall was underwater, I'd say the answer is obvious."

Rook made an unconvinced grunt.

"Look at it this way," she went on. "There are cities today that rely almost completely on imports for survival. When the lake expanded, maybe after a volcanic eruption, and their trade route was flooded, what reason would they have had to stay? They probably were assimilated into other cultures. It's happened before."

"So the Ancients might not have been such a big deal after all?"

Queen gazed at him sidelong. In the darkness, he made no effort to hide his naked emotions. He might not even have realized how much his face revealed, but she could read him like a book. Mulamba's death was weighing heavily on him. He had been desperate to find some evidence that would support Mulamba's theory and justify the excursion to the Belgian museum, which had ended so tragically.

She thought about telling him to shake it off and soldier on, but decided that maybe it was better for him to wallow in guilt than face the much more immediate and desperate reality. They were trapped underground, hundreds of miles from the only known entrance, with no food and no way of knowing whether the path they were traveling would lead to escape or take them deeper into the unknown.

Twenty minutes later, they found further evidence of human activity: two broken pieces of carved stone that fit together to form a thick disk, with a square hole through the middle like a Chinese coin.

"It's a wheel," Rook said, inspecting it with his light. "Someone's Flintstone-mobile had a blowout."

Deep Blue was perplexed by the discovery. "Stone wheels would indicate a very primitive level of technology."

"Do you think people were using this during the Stone Age?"

"Cavemen lived in caves," Rook replied, unaware of the long distance conversation with Deep Blue.

"It's a possibility," Deep Blue said. "But metal working wasn't a universal discovery. Metal tools were almost unknown in the Americas until the European discovery of the New World. Regardless, this is a significant discovery."

"Blue says we've made a significant discovery," she told Rook.

"Cool. Does that mean we'll be famous?"

"More importantly," the disembodied voice continued, "A wheel means that Rook is right. You're on a road that leads somewhere. Don't give up."

Queen didn't pass that along. She got the impression it was meant for her ears alone.

The silence settled back over them. Queen wrapped herself in it like a blanket. Conversation would have been an anchor to a reality that she preferred not to think about. This wasn't like combat, where letting one's mind wander might prove instantly fatal. This was more like a prison sentence, where the only way to deal with the fatigue and drudgery, and as she soon discovered, the gnawing hunger, was to set the autopilot and mentally unplug.

She knew it had to be even worse for Rook, who was making the same journey in total darkness. From time to time, she had to guide him around unexpected bends in the tunnel. She missed the first one, and he smacked face first into the wall, before it occurred to her that he was walking blind.

The passage rose and fell according to the whim of whatever natural processes had formed it, but the grooved pathway remained a constant. At one point, the road intersected a wide crevasse, and Queen saw more evidence of deliberate human activity. The Ancients had bridged the gap with loose stones, packed together to form an arch nearly thirty feet thick. Queen realized that it was little more than a pile of rocks suspended above the chasm and held together with little more than friction and Stone Age optimism. She balked momentarily, but Rook just walked across it, blissfully unaware of the potential danger. Feeling a little foolish, she raced to catch up with him. The bridge felt solid beneath her feet.

Shortly after crossing, the passage opened up into another large chamber. The well-worn path continued on, but then ended abruptly. The way ahead was blocked by a massive round stone. High stone walls rose on either side—loose pieces of rock that had been fitted together in a manner similar to that used at the bridge. There was a ramp of piled stone rising to the top of the wall, and at its base were openings to what she could only assume were rooms built into the wall. Queen stared at it in awe. The structure reminded her of something from the Lord of the Rings movies—the subterranean Dwarven kingdom of Moria, perhaps—but she kept that to herself to avoid a harangue from Rook. Instead, she just said, "Rook, you need to see this."

"I already can." He was squinting as if to sharpen his night vision. "There's light coming from up there."

Deep Blue confirmed Rook's observation. "There's definitely a light source on the other side of the wall. Your glasses automatically adjust to the ambient light conditions, so you won't notice it."

Rook advanced toward the wall, slowing as he reached its base, and then cautiously made his way onto the ramp. Queen stayed close, ready to intervene if necessary, but he became increasingly surefooted with each step. When he reached the top, he came to an abrupt stop, and as she slipped around him, Queen saw why.

Beyond the wall was another world.

Queen had no other words for it.

FORTY

The cavern stretched away to the vanishing point in every direction. The high ceiling was irregular, with glistening mineral deposits reaching to the floor, creating the impression of massive support columns, but this was the least interesting feature of the cave. On its floor, at the base of the wall, was an alien landscape that made even the otherworldly surface of Lake Natron look about as strange as a duck pond.

Her first impression was that it was a forest, but she saw almost immediately that wasn't right at all. The things that looked at a glance like trees were... She couldn't really tell what they were, but they definitely weren't trees. She didn't even think they were plants. They seemed more like weird multi-colored fungal growths, crawling up stalagmites, throwing out vine-like tendrils that ended in fan-shaped crests.

It was the lights, however, that really got her attention. "What are those?"

The landscape was dotted with little fires. Blue and yellow flames erupted randomly from the midst of the weird forest. Queen lifted her glasses for a moment to look upon the sight unaided. The individual flames weren't bright but their sum total was enough to cast the entire scene in a perpetual twilight. *It's almost bright enough to read by*, she thought.

From their perch atop the wall, they could see that the road continued beyond the gate, but it did not go far. Less than a hundred yards away, the road ended at the remains of a jetty. It was almost identical to the one in the lake, only this time the stone pier extended out into a pool, at the base of a waterfall. It poured straight down out of the cavern ceiling and drained away in a slow moving river that ran parallel to the wall. The river followed the wall for a short distance before turning away into the cavern.

"If you were right about the Ancients using the river as part of their trade route," Queen said, "then I think our chances of getting out of this alive just got a whole lot better. You up for another swim?"

"Maybe there's a boat."

Queen didn't think that was very likely, but then the underground world was nothing, if not full of surprises. She peered over the edge of the exterior wall. The strange vegetation had grown right up to its base, sixty feet below. "We're going to need to get down there somehow."

"Check this out." Rook knelt down for a moment and came up holding a long wooden rod, tipped with a flat sliver of stone as long as his forearm. "This is an *assegai*, a traditional African throwing spear."

He drew it back, striking a javelin thrower's pose, but the wood crumbled in his grip and the stone head fell at his feet.

Queen laughed. "This is why we can't have nice things."

Rook retrieved the spear head and inspected its sharp edges. "This might come in handy," he said, tucking it in his belt.

Queen realized it was the only tool or weapon they possessed.

They headed back down the ramp and approached the massive stone that barricaded the road. The round stone sat in a long trench. It was apparent that the Ancient engineers had designed it so it could be rolled out of the way, providing access to travelers on the subterranean highway. Wooden rods protruded from the enormous wheel, presumably to give the gatekeepers leverage, but like the spear shaft, these disintegrated when touched. Rook braced a shoulder against one edge of the stone but it refused to budge.

"I don't think we're getting through this way," Queen remarked. "We'll have to climb down the outside of the wall."

Rook gave the stone another futile push then admitted defeat. "Why do you suppose they put this here?"

"Why does anyone build a fence? Maybe this place was some kind of border checkpoint."

"Pretty sophisticated for a forgotten civilization. I think Joe was right about them. I bet we've barely scratched the surface."

"All the more reason for us to get back to the surface," Queen said. She was a little surprised to discover that she actually meant it. Rook's optimism was starting to rub off on her. Every discovery they made reinforced the idea that the subterranean world was not merely a hopeless maze of branching caverns created by random acts of nature. It was something that had been charted, developed and utilized by people from a forgotten age.

They returned to the top of the wall and scouted a route down into the wild forest. Because it had been constructed using pieces of stone, rather than large cut blocks, there were ample hand and foot holds, which Queen, an accomplished rock climber, negotiated with the ease of a spider. The larger Rook was less graceful. When he was about halfway down, a rock shifted under his foot and broke loose, unleashing a small avalanche. As he slid down the nearly vertical face, he rolled away from the cascade of falling stones.

Queen dodged away from the rock fall, but quickly moved to Rook's side. He sat up, spitting dust, and she helped him to his feet. "You keep trashing this place and they're going to eighty-six you."

"I should be so lucky." His hands were scraped and raw, and there was a ragged tear in the right leg of his drysuit. He shifted his weight onto his right foot and grimaced a little.

"You okay?"

"I'll walk it off. Not like I've got a choice."

As the dust cloud from the avalanche settled, they got their first close look at the strange underground forest. The cavern floor had a thick layer of fine soil, an accumulation of centuries, or perhaps millennia, of decayed organic material, on which grew a dizzying variety of plant-like organisms. Queen examined the nearest of these, first touching it with a gloved finger, probing its texture and pliability. Then she tried tearing off a piece. It was spongy, like the texture of a mushroom, but as tough as leather. As she pulled on it, something moved in the soil nearby. Startled, she hopped back a step.

Beneath the carpet of vegetation, the soil was alive. Worms, as big around as her thumb, wriggled through the dirt, and insects that looked a little like enormous beetles scurried away from the disturbance.

"Shit," she said. "I hate bugs."

Long before she had become the deadly Chess Team operator known as Queen, Zelda Baker had been plagued by a veritable encyclopedia of phobias. She had conquered each and every one of these through her own relentless will power and a program of sensory immersion that had pushed those irrational fears to the point where they simply evaporated. But here in this utterly alien environment, fatigue and privation were stirring up some of the old fears. She took several deep breaths, trying to remember the discipline that had enabled her to overcome her perceived weaknesses...but now everywhere she looked, she saw them, thousands of them, millions, a squirming nightmare that lay between her and the river's edge.

She stripped off her glasses and handed them to Rook. "Take these."

He did and for a moment, just stared through them in disbelief. "Okay," he said finally. "Better watch where we step."

Without the glasses, Queen could make out only large details of the landscape. The strange flames, which reminded her a little of the Bunsen burners she'd used in high school chemistry classes, appeared to be erupting out of the ground randomly, like little geysers of fire. Some jetted ten feet into the air, while others were flickering, as if their fuel source was nearly exhausted. She recalled that one of Mulamba's goals had been to create a source of energy independence for the African states, by securing underground deposits of natural gas. She also remembered that Bishop and Knight had gone missing while trying to rescue a science team that was doing research into some kind of renewable energy source.

Don't think about it, she told herself.

The flame jets were an interesting phenomenon, but not unprecedented. An underground coal seam in Centralia, Pennsylvania, had been burning ever since it was ignited in 1962, and that was just one of thousands like it. In the Karakum Desert of Turkmenistan, a massive natural gas deposit had been intentionally set on fire by Soviet geologists in 1971 to prevent the uncontrolled release of methane, after a sinkhole opened up destroying the drilling equipment that had been intended to harvest the gas. More than forty years later, that fire was still burning, earning the site the ominous but very appropriate nickname The Door to Hell.

If that place is the door, then this road must be the Highway to Hell. She almost verbalized the thought to Rook, but the more she thought about it, the less funny it seemed.

They reached the stone pier, and Rook searched the surrounding shore. "No boats."

"After the way that spear shaft turned to dust in your hands, I'm not sure I'd trust anything the Ancients might have left lying around anyway."

Rook considered that for a moment, then took the spear head from his belt. "Got an idea."

He ventured out into the forest and hacked down a plant that looked a little like a yucca, with a long stem that ended in a broad fan-shaped growth. Carrying his prize over his shoulder, he returned to the pier and deposited it in the river. The current caught hold of it and whisked it away. It was still floating on the surface when Queen lost sight of it.

"We can make our own boat." Rook was grinning. "Lash a few of those together and we'll have a raft."

"A raft?" Queen was doubtful. "It sounds like something from a Jules Verne novel. But then so does everything else down here."

FORTY-ONE

Congo River, Democratic Republic of the Congo

King stood in the bow of the Shanghai, as it plowed up the Congo River. Mile after mile of the river vanished under its hull, but little else seemed to change. A liquid treadmill. The Congo was the ninth longest river in the world. It was only about two-thirds the length of the Nile or the Amazon, shorter even than the continuous watercourse of the Missouri-Mississippi river system, but its claustrophobic jungle setting, with only a scattering of settlements on its banks, made the journey seem like an endless Herculean labor. Because of the northward bend in its course, King knew that they were now even further from Kisangani—from Favreau, her hostages and the bomb—than when they had set out from Kinshasa.

The patrol craft had been forced to reduce its speed as the river fractured into braided channels that wove between islands of sediment, which had accumulated over the course of countless millennia. The boat's pilot had to negotiate a maze of marked channels to ensure that they did not run aground or wander into a dead end.

At midday, King spied movement in the tall reeds on the river bank. He zoomed in on the area and saw something that looked like an enormous black barrel, moving through the bushes. When one end of the barrel opened up to reveal a pink mouth with long white tusks, he realized it was a hippopotamus. He pointed it out to one of the soldiers.

Instead of the indifferent reaction he had expected, the young Congolese seemed agitated. He called out to his comrades, sharing the news of the discovery with them before turning back to King.

"This is a very dangerous animal," he explained, shouldering his Kalashnikov rifle as if expecting to do battle with the hippo.

King was familiar with the reputation of hippopotamuses. Despite their almost comical appearance and often cartoonish depictions in popular culture, they were considered the most dangerous animal in Africa. Hippos were responsible for more deaths than predatory lions and crocodiles. They were fearless, often attacking small boats, and slashing at helpless swimmers with their razor sharp teeth.

"I don't think they'll mess with us," he told the soldier. "We're the biggest thing on this river."

The young man looked unconvinced and muttered a phrase that King didn't recognize.

"Mokèlé-mbèmbé," the soldier repeated. "He is 'the one who stops the flow of rivers.' There are creatures in the river that would not be afraid of this boat."

"My father knew a man who was killed by Mokèlé-mbèmbé," another soldier said.

Deep Blue's voice sounded in King's head. "*Mokèlé-mbèmbé* is the local Loch Ness Monster. For over two hundred years, there have been reports of a river monster in the Congo. Some of the crazier theories suggest that it might be a dinosaur."

King considered this. It sounded ludicrous, but so did a lot of the things he had experienced firsthand.

"I wouldn't worry about it too much," Deep Blue continued. "People have been looking for it for over a hundred years with no success. There are plenty of things that can kill you in the jungle, but dinosaurs aren't one of them."

Deep Blue's assurance notwithstanding, talk of the legendary river creature spread like a plague, with the soldiers relating more second hand accounts of Mokèlé-mbèmbé's deadly rampages and discussing other monsters King had never heard of. What struck him most was that the soldiers, who seemed unfamiliar with the term 'dinosaur,' were describing animals that almost perfectly resembled creatures that had been extinct for more than sixty-five million years.

There was *Kongamato,* which translated to 'breaker of boats,' a flying creature that sounded suspiciously like a pterodactyl. One man's uncle had been killed by Kongamato. Another soldier claimed to have actually seen *Mbielu-Mbielu-Mbielu,* an enormous beast that, if his description was to be believed, might have been a stegosaurus, but his story was challenged by another man who said the creature sounded more like *Emela-ntouka,* a horned animal larger than an elephant, with a beaked mouth and a bony frill around its head—a ceratops.

Deep Blue refrained from further commentary, but soon interrupted with news that was even more disturbing. "King, there's been a development. Senator Lance Marrs just arrived at the Mombasa airport."

King excused himself from the storytellers and found a corner of the boat that was marginally more private. "Marrs is free? What about Okoa?"

"No word on Okoa. Marrs was released unconditionally and put on a plane earlier this morning."

"It sounds like you think that's a bad thing."

"As soon as he got off the plane, he started making calls to his colleagues in the Senate. I'm accessing the NSA call logs now. Stand by." Despite ongoing concerns about invasions of privacy, King knew that the National Security Agency had continued to monitor international telephone calls using its sophisticated SIGINT monitoring network. While the sheer volume of traffic made it impossible to listen to every single call, the transmissions were nevertheless recorded and scanned by the NSA's supercomputer for keywords that might indicate terrorist plots or other threats. "Okay, this is a call he just made to Roger Hayes, Chair of the Senate Subcommittee on Energy."

King heard the scratchy sound of background static and then Marrs' oily voice filled his head. *"Roger? It's Lance."*

"Lance? Damn it, it's—what time is it? It's the middle of the night here. I don't care what it is you need—"

Marrs tried to cut in, but lag time caused the two voices to overlap for a few seconds. *"Roger, just shut up and listen. This can't wait. I need you to draft a resolution demanding the President formally recognize the government of President Patrice Velle of the Democratic Republic of the Congo."*

"Formally...what?" Senator Hayes still sounded bleary. *"Ah, crap. I heard you were involved in that Congo mess. I was hoping you were smarter than that."*

"I've been here for the last two days trying to negotiate a solution that will guarantee access to their natural gas reserves. But the situation has changed, and if we don't act quickly, it will all go to hell. Velle controls the Congo's natural gas reserves. If we don't make a deal with him now, he'll find someone else who's willing to pay. Frankly, I don't intend to let that happen."

"Lance, simmer down. You know these two-bit African dictators never last. If he's still around in a couple months, maybe then we can talk about formal recognition. No matter what he says right now, eventually he's going to want what only we can give him."

"It's not going to work that way this time. Velle is threatening to destroy the Kivu natural gas reserves if we don't recognize his government. He can and will make good on that threat."

King stopped listening. "Shit."

Deep Blue halted the replay. "Satellite imagery shows Velle's troops leaving Kisangani. He's heading for the Lake Kivu region."

"Velle doesn't matter. It's Favreau we need to be worried about. She doesn't give a rat's ass about whether the US formally recognizes Velle's government. She's got the bomb, and she's itching to use it."

"I'm sending *Crescent* to pick you up."

"What about Queen and Rook?"

"They're...occupied."

King did not like the evasive tone of the comment, but he let it go. Right now, the only thing that mattered was stopping the Red Queen before she could initiate her deadly endgame.

FORTY-TWO

Below

David tugged at Felice's arm. "Come. There is a place where we will be safe."

The passage through the cave had brought them to a ledge overlooking a vast subterranean plain that was teeming with...

"Dinosaurs," she muttered, shaking her head. No matter what Bishop and Knight said, no matter what crazy things she herself had experienced, what she was seeing was simply impossible.

David led them along the ledge, which was nothing more than an irregular horizontal fracture in the wall of the cavern, one of many that formed a staircase leading down to the floor. There were a few raptors roaming about on the jagged protrusions below, and when they spied the group, they lifted their heads and stood motionless, watching, probably attempting to gauge whether the moving shapes were dangerous or edible.

The ledge ended abruptly at a steeply sloped debris field, the aftermath of a slide that had occurred at some point in the distant past. There were a few raptors near the lower reaches of the slide, watching them and humming their weird warning. David moved out onto the slide and then started climbing up. Bishop peered into the shadows above, then urged Felice to follow their guide. A short scramble brought them up to a recessed scallop in the cavern wall.

"Can they climb up here?" Bishop asked.

David stared at him blankly, then looked to Felice for a translation.

"What? Oh, sorry. He says he's hidden here before. It's safe."

Her mind was racing.

Dinosaurs!

Dinosaurs were extinct. They had been completely wiped out by an asteroid impact sixty-five million years ago. The disaster had killed off seventy-five percent of all life on Earth, in what scientists referred to as the Cretaceous-Paleogene extinction. The asteroid had thrown up a cloud of iridium rich-dust that had settled to form a distinctive black band in sedimentary rock around the planet. Below that band there were dinosaur fossils, but above it, there were not. If even a few dinosaurs had survived that extinction event, their population would have recovered and spread out to new habitats, and the story of that migration would have been recorded in the fossil record. It was not. Dinosaurs were extinct.

Nevertheless, she could not argue with what she was seeing. She lingered at the edge of the recess, staring down at the plain below.

What she saw still boggled her mind. There was a herd of enormous, thick-bodied creatures, as big as elephants, but with twenty-foot long necks and tails that were even longer, calmly grazing on the strange vegetation sprouting from the cavern floor. They were unbothered by the flame jets. Creatures with ridged backs that reminded her of stegosauruses, though she knew they were something different, roamed across the landscape. Every few seconds, dark shapes leapt from the ground in a flutter of outstretched wings, gliding up toward the high ceiling, and dropping back down. The raptors seemed to be everywhere, darting their heads at the ground, as if pecking for insects and worms, and mostly leaving the larger dinosaurs alone. But given their earlier ferocity, she had no trouble imagining a pack of them taking down a juvenile. And out at the limit of her vision, something very large moved, swift and low to the ground, like a lion stalking its prey.

"Okay," she said. "If the impossible is possible, the question is 'how?'"

"Is it a question that you have to answer right now?" Bishop said, pulling her back into the shadows.

She hushed him, not for fear of alerting the raptors, but so she could think.

"Habitat and food. They have both down here. Maybe this cave was here sixty-five million years ago. Maybe that's how they survived." She shook her head. It was an oversimplified explanation. The Cretaceous-Paleogene extinction had been a lot more than just a huge explosion. The dust cloud from the asteroid impact had shut out the sun for nearly a decade, interrupting photosynthesis and demolishing the foundation of the food web.

"The food web!" She turned to Bishop, eager to share her revelation. "Don't you see? This place is a self-contained ecosystem. The dinosaurs that survived adapted to conditions here. That's why they never migrated away."

She stopped, realizing that even that was a little too simplistic. "An ecosystem begins with producers—plants. But plants need sunlight to grow...unless..." She stepped back out onto the ledge and peered down at the weird vegetation growing in the vast flame-lit plain. "Where did those fires come from?"

"I don't know. Maybe the dinosaurs are rubbing sticks together." Bishop pulled her back again.

"Blue and yellow flames," she continued, still thinking aloud. "Pure ethane burns blue, and methane burns yellow. Those are gas fires, natural gas fires. And they've probably been burning for..." She turned to face him as yet another realization dawned.

"Oh, my God. That's it." She removed the backpack she'd brought from the expedition camp and unzipped it for the first time since fleeing. As she opened her MacBook Pro laptop computer and booted it up, she could almost feel the irritated stares of the others, but there was no way to explain it simply. The screen lit up, glowing just slightly brighter than Knight's bundle of chemlights. When the boot sequence was complete, she opened the file containing all the data the expedition had gathered.

She turned the screen so they could follow along. It showed a picture of what looked like pink donut sprinkles over a white background. "This is the bacteria we recovered from the bottom of Lake Kivu. It's a variant of Escherichia coli that has adapted to the extreme conditions at the bottom of Lake Kivu..." She could see that she was already losing them. "All life forms need energy to live. Normal E. coli, like the kind we have in our intestines, relies on our body temperature to stay alive. The organisms at the bottom of Lake Kivu get their energy from the chemical reactions of volcanic gases filtering up through the lake bottom. They produce their own food supply through the process of fermentation."

"Fermentation. You're saying they produce alcohol?"

She smiled, pleased that Bishop understood. He was much more than a grunt, as was Knight. "Exactly. All cellular organisms ingest carbon compounds and convert them into a fuel called ATP, either through respiration or fermentation. Fermentation isn't as efficient as respiration, but when there's an abundant food supply, that doesn't matter as much. A by-product of fermentation is hydrocarbons, like ethanol—alcohol—or sometimes methanol compounds. That's why decaying organic matter produces methane. It's what's been happening at the bottom of Lake Kivu, only the microbes aren't subsisting on organic carbon. They're getting it from volcanic outgassing."

"Okay. What's that got to do with dinosaurs?"

"For dinosaurs to live down here, to actually thrive down here, requires a complex eco-system."

"I get that," he replied. "They have a food chain. Plant-eaters and meat-eaters."

"It's more complicated than that. In an ecosystem, energy is lost as it moves from one trophic level to the next, roughly speaking by a factor of ten. It's like a pyramid where each level is only a tenth as big as the one below it. One meat-eater needs ten times its mass in plant-eaters, and each plant-eater needs ten times its mass in plants. And the amount of available energy in those plants—in terms of calories—is about a tenth of what the plant needs just to survive. On the surface, the plants get that energy from sunlight. If any part of the pyramid is disrupted, the whole system collapses.

"The dinosaurs went extinct because of widespread climate change, probably the result of the Chicxulub asteroid impact, which prevented plants from growing. The food web collapsed."

Bishop nodded slowly. "So for there to be that many raptors down here, there have to be even more prey animals for them to eat."

"Right, but the plants are the important thing. They're the base of the food pyramid." She crawled back to the edge of the recess and pointed out at the landscape below. "Ordinary plants require sunlight for photosynthesis. Whatever those things are, they're getting their energy from some other source."

"The light from the fires?"

"Maybe. They might not be photosynthesizing plants at all, or if they are, they've evolved over the last sixty-five million years to be able to use that energy more efficiently. The animals would have had to undergo adaptive changes as well. That's why they never migrated back to the surface. They might wander out once in a while, but this is their primary habitat. They've got everything they need down here."

She watched the raptors roaming the plain. Those closest to the cavern wall were still motionless, alert to the presence of intruders, but most of the others were busy dipping their heads and scratching at the vegetation, searching for prey. "But it's the base of the pyramid that matters most. For those fires to be burning like that...the amount of microbial metabolic activity must be off the scale. That's what we were looking for at Lake Kivu: a bacterial organism that could produce hydrocarbons on a commercially viable scale."

"What do you mean by that?" Bishop asked.

"We already know how to use microbes to make fuel. They do it naturally. The problem with biofuel production is the same as with the food web. You have to put more energy into a system than you get back from it, not to mention that the land used for growing your fuel crop isn't available for food production."

"You think the bacteria in this cave have figured out a way to make fuel more efficiently? Like a closed system?"

"I do. And I'd bet money that the microbes in the soil of this cave are identical to the extremophiles we found in Lake Kivu."

Bishop pondered the idea for a moment, then shook his head. "As much as I hate to stand in the way of scientific progress, right now our only priority is getting out of here."

Felice started to protest, but then realized that she had gotten carried away by the euphoria of discovery. She closed the computer and slid it back into her pack.

Bishop nodded and turned to Knight. "I'm going to head back up and see what our friends are up to. Stay here and keep out of sight, no matter what happens."

That sounded ominous to Felice. "What are you going to do?"

"We need to make them believe that we're raptor food. I'm going to make sure that they do."

FORTY-THREE

Bishop climbed down to the ledge and made his way through the narrow passage back to the first cavern. As the glow from the gas fires diminished, he cracked a chemlight and kept going. The phosphorescent tube provided enough illumination to negotiate the winding tunnel, but it wasn't much use in the open darkness of the cavern. He left the glow stick to mark the mouth of the passage, and continued on without any light at all, feeling his way along the wall.

After a few minutes, he spied an irregular circle of daylight, made small by the distance. The entrance. He paused, listening for signs of men creeping through the darkness or raptors lurking nearby. Unlike the movie monster version, these velociraptors did not seem to be hyper-intelligent pack hunters. Their earlier attack had probably been defensive rather than a predatory action. He didn't doubt that they were deadly, though. Their long talons and sharp teeth were certainly capable of tearing a man to shreds, but he suspected that they would shy away from anything larger than themselves, unless they felt threatened.

Hearing nothing, he kept moving along the wall, until he could see silhouetted figures. There were four of them, and as he got a little closer, he could see that they were sweeping their rifles back and forth, ready to fire at the slightest sign of activity.

Time to stir things up, he thought. He took aim with his M240.

He let off a three-second long burst that felled one of the rebels and sent the others diving for cover. The survivors quickly returned fire, concentrating their shots on the area where they'd seen the muzzle flash. Bishop was already moving from that spot, but the incoming fusillade forced him to go prone and low crawl away from the wall.

More rebels joined the firing line at the cavern mouth, adding to the storm of lead. Bishop let fly with another volley, then rolled to the side and started squirming back toward the wall. There were at least ten shooters now, firing off sporadic shots and shouting back and forth to each other.

A pall of smoke hung in the air above the entrance. Bishop thought he could hear the hum of agitated raptors, but it was almost completely drowned out by the nearly constant sound of rifle fire echoing through the cavern. Rounds smacked into the nearby wall, spraying chips of stone down on him, but Bishop didn't think the shooters knew where he was. When he reached the base of the wall, he began crawling back the way he'd come.

After about a minute, the incoming fire slacked off. Bishop looked back to see flashlight beams roaming the darkness. The rebels were coming in after him.

So far, so good.

He got up and skirted along the wall until he spied the chemlight marking the passage. Before going in, he looked back to check on the rebels' progress. He couldn't see the cave entrance or any of the men, but shafts of light were crisscrossing the darkness.

There was another burst of rifle fire, which told Bishop that the rebels had encountered the pack of stray velociraptors. The battle unfolded in an eruption of noise and light. Bishop heard shouts and screams over the tumult, then he heard something else. A rustling sound, like something crashing through tall grass.

Bishop felt a chilling premonition as the noise grew louder. His plan to lure the rebels into a battle with the velociraptors worked exactly as he'd planned, but he had made a serious miscalculation. The frightened dinosaurs were intent on escaping the mayhem, but they weren't fleeing out into the jungle. Instead they were going to a place of familiar safety, what Felice had called their primary habitat. The stampede would take the raptors right through him.

This wasn't the smartest thing I could've done, Felice thought as she stood motionless, just a few steps away from a lone velociraptor. The dinosaur seemed to be shivering, puffing up its plumage, as it vocalized with its weird hum.

In the recess at the top of the rock slide, David urged her to come back up, while Knight drew a bead on the raptor with his big rifle.

Why did I do this again?

As soon as Bishop had left, intent on scouting their route back to the surface, Felice had realized that she might not get another chance to acquire a sample of the soil from the cavern ecosystem. Without a word to the others, who would almost certainly have insisted she stay put, just as Bishop had instructed, she had hefted the pack over one shoulder and started down the natural staircase of fallen rocks. No sooner had she reached the cavern floor when a lone raptor darted over to determine whether she'd make a tasty morsel.

Maybe because they looked so much like birds, or perhaps because they had mostly kept their distance instead of relentlessly hunting them down, like the dinosaurs in movies, Felice had assumed that, as long as she didn't surprise them, the creatures would leave her alone. She had been mostly right.

The raptor began thrusting its head at her, mouth open, displaying the long, sharp teeth that she'd only ever seen in the mouths of fossilized skeletons and computer-generated movie monsters—Spielberg had gotten that much right. The creature didn't advance, but kept bobbing its head at her, making a soft hissing sound, as if scolding her.

No, she realized. *He's testing me. Trying to see if I'll put up a fight, or turn and run. I wonder which one will get me eaten.*

Before coming to Africa, Felice had read about how to deal with the local wildlife. Some animals would flee from displays of aggression, while others would attack. "Which kind are you, bird brain?"

Size, she recalled, was often a deciding factor.

Felice raised her hands over her head, trying to look as big and menacing as possible, and took a step forward. "Shoo!"

The raptor ran off squawking.

Felice stood there with her arms raised for a few seconds longer, afraid that if she moved, her bladder might let go. Finally, when her legs felt a little less rubbery, she started moving again.

"Felice," Knight hissed. "Get back up here!"

She ignored him. The hardest part was already behind her. She wasn't going to turn back now.

It was uncomfortably hot and humid on the floor of the cavern, and in a matter of just a few seconds, she was drenched in perspiration. Some analytical part of her brain connected the humidity to the ecosystem question. Water was a part of the organic metabolic process. The cave was like a gigantic greenhouse, constantly recycling water, air, nutrients and energy.

She headed for a spot where blue flames rose up from the cavern floor. There was a scorched circle about eight inches wide around the fire, but beyond that the vegetation appeared to be thriving. She pushed into the strange growth, vaguely aware of things slithering and crawling away from her footfalls. The air smelled of ozone, the invisible smoke from the burning alcohol, and it occurred to her that the atmosphere might not be safe to breathe.

Close enough.

Felice unslung the pack and took out a specimen tube. With one foot, she gently pushed away the overgrowth to reveal the soil beneath, loose and loamy, and wriggling with insects and fat worms. She would have liked to take a few live samples—compare the DNA of the creatures that had evolved in this environment with their modern counterparts. But she felt like she had already pushed the envelope a little too far. One test tube full of soil from this place would probably be enough to keep her busy for the rest of her natural life. She stuffed the sample into a Ziploc bag, and the bag into her backpack, then hurried back to the base of the slide. She did a quick check to make sure that there weren't any raptors sneaking up on her, then scrambled up the slide to rejoin Knight and David.

Both men looked like they were having trouble choosing irritation or admiration, but before either could say a word, the sound of gunfire issued from the passage below. The noise was barely audible, muffled by the turns in the narrow passage through to the neighboring cavern.

"Get back," Knight said. "Away from the edge. Stay out of sight."

Felice was about to comply, but saw that Knight had laid down at the edge of the recess, aiming his rifle at the mouth of the passageway below. She sprawled out next to him.

"Do you listen to anyone?" Knight said, not looking at her.

She ignored him.

There were more shots, and even Felice's untrained ear could distinguish the subtle differences in the sounds made by Bishop's machine gun and the rebel fighter's assault rifles. After the initial exchange, she heard only the latter, and then silence.

She waited, listening, the seconds stretching out to an agonizing infinity, but there were no more shots.

Suddenly, a raptor exploded out of the passage, and over the edge, tumbling down the slope in a flurry of talons and feathers. Something else emerged onto the ledge right behind it—not a single velociraptor, but three of them, tangled up with another figure.

Bishop.

Felice watched incredulous as Bishop, standing poised on the precipice, stripped the clinging, clawing dinosaurs off his body one by one. He caught one by the throat and with a whip-cracking motion, snapped its neck. A second raptor had its teeth clamped onto his shoulder and was raking his back with the spur-like claws on its hind legs, but with his hands now free, Bishop reached back, closed his fingers around the duck-shaped head, and squeezed until the creature's eyes burst out of their sockets. A third, which had somehow gotten its legs twisted around the sling of Bishop's machine gun, tried to bite Bishop's face, but instead Bishop got his own teeth around the thing's neck and he bit down hard.

His victory had not come cheap. Raptor talons had flayed skin and torn deeply into muscles. Blood streamed from a dozen gash wounds. Yet that was not the worst of it. As he was fighting, Felice felt as if she was watching him transform before her eyes—Dr. Jekyll becoming Mr. Hyde, Bruce Banner metamorphosing into the Hulk. It was not a physical change precisely, but his human essence being consumed by a darker, bestial entity.

Bishop seemed to sense that she was watching. He turned slowly, letting the dead raptor fall from his jaws. His face was a mask of blood and feathers. He looked like some kind of savage tribal warrior, but his eyes...

His eyes were the same.

Felice breathed a sigh of relief...

That turned into a gasp of horror as a swarm of velociraptors broke from the passage and swept Bishop over the edge.

FORTY-FOUR

Underground

Definitely Jules Verne, Queen thought as the raft slid along the subterranean river.

Rook knelt at the front of the makeshift craft, using a semi-rigid length of plant stalk like the punt of a Venetian gondolier, nudging the raft back to center stream whenever the unpredictable current brought them too close to the bank. Queen sat at the rear, using a broad, fan-shaped leaf like a rudder. Rook had selected two more stalks with their fans still attached to be used as oars, but thus far there had been no need to use them. The current was swift, carrying them faster than they could have walked through the dense vegetation that flourished on the valley floor. Walking wasn't really an option. The local flora was not the only obstacle they would have faced on foot.

They spied the first creature only a few minutes after their river journey began. Based on its size, Queen had assumed it was an enormous elephant, but then it had raised its small head, which was situated at the end of a neck that was nearly as long its massive body, and she knew that what she was seeing could only be a dinosaur.

She pointed it out to Rook, who in characteristic fashion, tried to conceal his astonishment with a quip. "Whoa. That's a lot of Bronto burgers. Better keep an eye out for Sleestaks. Those things always gave me the creeps."

"It's a Paralititan," Deep Blue had informed her a few seconds later, the disbelief audible in voice. "An herbivore sauropod from the Cretaceous period."

"You should go on Jeopardy," Queen told him.

"As it happens, I was just doing some research on the subject. There have been rumors of giant monsters in the Congo region for years, which has led a lot of folks to believe that dinosaurs might have survived to the present day, hidden in the jungle."

"Or under it."

"Those monster legends might indicate that dinosaurs living down here have been able to migrate to the surface from time to time. There's got to be an exit to the surface somewhere in the Congo Basin."

"So this is a good thing," she replied, not completely sincere. "If they've been coming and going all this time, why aren't there more recent fossils?"

"Most dinosaur skeletons are found in deserts," Deep Blue said, "where the conditions are favorable for preserving and fossilizing the remains. There's not much of a fossil record at all in the tropics, so we have no idea what kind of creatures might have once lived in Central Africa. The Congo Basin itself is only about a million years old. Most African dinosaur fossils date to more than ninety million years ago, well before the rest of the dinosaurs went extinct."

"Now we know where they went," Rook said, "and why the Ancients built that wall. Maybe why they stopped using the underground route, too."

"An actual lost world." Deep Blue's voice held a tinge of wonder. "It might not be what Mulamba was looking for, but a discovery like this will change everything we think we know about the world. And it will change the way the world views Africa."

Queen wasn't so sure about that. From a scientific standpoint, the importance of the African continent was already well-established, if not completely understood. It was almost certainly the birthplace of the earliest humans. For most people however, Africa was just a primitive land, inhabited by strange wild animals. What they had found here might just reinforce that belief.

The mind-boggling novelty of the sighting quickly wore off as they spied more dinosaurs, not just Paralititan, but a dizzying variety of the evidently not-quite-extinct creatures. Deep Blue attempted to identify them based on what little was known of dinosaurs living in Africa. The conversation ceased when both she and Rook realized that, if this lost world supported populations of plant-eating dinosaurs, then it almost certainly would contain predators—not the humanoid insect-lizard hybrids that had plagued Rook's Saturday morning cartoon-fueled nightmares perhaps, but animals much bigger and much more dangerous.

They soon discovered that even the river was not entirely safe. Large reptilian and amphibious creatures swam across their path. For the most part, the animals ignored them or scurried away, but a few were curious enough that Rook laid aside his punting pole and drew his spear head, ready for combat. A massive snake, easily larger than an Amazonian anaconda, trailed in their wake for several minutes, its serpentine body undulating along the surface at an astonishing speed. Queen had no doubt that, if it had chosen to attack, the snake could have crushed the little raft in its massive coils, and then gulped them down whole, but after a while it got distracted by something on the shore and lost interest.

Much sooner than Queen expected, the river brought them once more into territory claimed by the Ancients. The unique topography of the cavern and the wild vegetation hid the structure from view until they were practically on top of it, or more precisely, right under it.

The Ancients had built another enormous wall, but unlike the first, this one intersected the river, spanning its breadth with an arch of carefully fitted rocks. As the raft slid beneath the bridge, Queen saw that the wall was the beginning of something far more impressive than anything they had previously encountered.

The landscape inside the walls was not much different than what lay outside. The dense vegetation had not been stopped by the barrier; if anything, it actually seemed more prolific, possibly because the wall kept out the large grazing dinosaurs. But even the tallest 'trees' were dwarfed by what the Ancients had built.

Three-story and four-story structures sprouted up on both sides of the river bank, and behind them were even taller buildings—towers that seemed intent on reaching the very ceiling of the cavern. More bridges spanned the river, along with piled stone piers, where vessels much larger than the little raft could have been moored. As they moved deeper, with no end in sight, Queen realized that this place was not simply another outpost on the Ancients' trade route.

"This is their city," she said, breathless. "We found it."

"If Joe could have seen this..." Rook didn't finish the thought. The discovery made the Congolese president's death seem all the more tragic.

"Let's make sure the world knows about it. About everything."

She steered the raft toward a nearby pier and hopped off, splashing in the shallows. Rook pulled the little craft further along the pier and toward shore, and then joined her. Together, they clambered up onto the stone dock and made their way into the Ancients' city.

The ground was thick with the strange plants, and little blue fires burned at random intervals throughout, but the Ancients had laid out their city in a methodical fashion similar to a modern urban grid. Instead of wandering into the city depths, they backtracked, skirting the river until they reached the wall, where they ascended a ramp to walk atop it. Higher up, level with the tops of many of the stone structures, the view was even more impressive. What they could not see however, was a way out.

"This couldn't have been the end of the road," Rook said. "They wouldn't have built this city here, in the middle of nowhere. There's got to be a way to the surface."

Queen thought it sounded like he was trying to convince himself as much as her. There could have been any number of reasons to found the city in such a remote location. Most likely some unique natural resource, like gold or diamonds. She decided not to share those ideas with Rook. Unfounded optimism might not help their situation, but at least it kept the mood light. "We'll walk the wall. If the road continues, there's got to be another gate. If not, we'll get back on the river."

"Better remember where we parked," Rook said.

The wall curved around the city like the rim of an enormous wheel, most of it hidden by the towering structures in the middle. They soon lost sight of the river, but their attention was drawn to a large hump that sat beside the wall. As they got closer, it became apparent that the hump was a fortress guarding the main entrance to the city. The city gate was broader than the one they had encountered earlier, but with a similar design—a massive rolling stone barrier that could allow or block access. One thing however was very different.

"Uh, oh," said Rook. "Looks like someone left the door open."

"They must have abandoned the city when the lake cut off access to the other end of the highway. No sense in closing the gate if you don't ever plan to come back."

"Guess not." He scanned the area outside the walls. "If there's a road, it's been completely covered over."

Queen peered further out, magnifying the distant landscape in her glasses, which she'd taken back from Rook. She saw what he could not. "There's a wall. Maybe a couple klicks out, but it's there. I think we're close to the cavern's end. I just hope that when we get there, we'll find the route they took back to the surface."

"We'll find it," he replied, confidently. "We're good at finding stuff."

She laughed, but then wrinkled her nose. "God, what's that smell?"

In the hours that they had spent traversing the subterranean world, they had gotten accustomed to the unfamiliar and unusual smells that filled the hot, humid environment. This odor was very different, and not at all unfamiliar. Rook bobbed his head back and forth, sniffing experimentally, then his face twisted in disgust. "Gross. Smells like a mixture of rotting meat and chicken shit."

"I guess you would know, farm boy." Rook had grown up on a farm in rural New England, so Queen didn't doubt that his olfactory senses were more discriminating than hers. "But I doubt there's a chicken coop down here."

She shook her head. "Whatever that is, it's fresh...well, you know what I mean."

The smell got worse as they approached the fortress, and when they reached the ramp leading down to the gate, they saw its source. The broad courtyard just inside the city entrance was strewn with decaying carcasses. The remains clearly belonged to very large animals, perhaps even as large as the Paralititan, but the bodies had been torn apart like Thanksgiving turkeys, so that nothing recognizable remained. There were dozens of them, some just bones nearly picked clean, but several looked like recent roadkill, torn open to reveal red meat and pink entrails. There was no vegetation, just an unsightly mass of bone fragments and a gray-white substance that, based on Rook's identification of the odor, was almost certainly manure.

"Uh, I don't think I want to meet the guy that lives here now," Rook whispered.

"Blue, did T. Rex live in Africa?"

"No." Before Queen could breathe a sigh of relief, Deep Blue continued. "Africa's version of the Tyrannosaur was the Carcharodontosaurus."

"Car-car...what?"

"It means 'shark tooth lizard.' Slightly bigger than T. Rex. If that's what we're dealing with, you'd better give it a very wide berth."

"Nice."

"What did he say?" Rook said.

"That we're probably in deep dino shit." She sighed. "But it looks like shark-tooth is out for the moment, so let's move while we can."

They snuck down the wall, Rook gripping the stone spear head, which would have seemed a comical thing to do if it hadn't been their only means of self-defense. They skirted the base of the wall, but their route could not completely avoid the killing ground. There was still no sign of the beast that called the place home. The only things moving were the carcasses themselves, which squirmed with insect larvae. The stench was overpowering. Queen's empty stomach roiled with nausea. She fought back a fit of dry heaves with each breath.

They paused beside the gateway, searching for signs of activity. Queen looked to Rook with an inquiring glance, and got a shrug in return. Then, still brandishing his spear head, he moved out. Queen stayed right behind him.

They had gone only a few steps when an oddly familiar sound reached Queen's ears. It was a deep pop, not much different or louder than the noise made by a book hitting a table top. Isolated as they were, deep underground, any noise was cause for alarm, but this sounded suspiciously like...

"Did you hear that?" Rook whispered, glancing back. He recognized it, too.

Before Queen could answer, the ground seemed to rise up right in front of them. Almost faster than she could comprehend, the creature, which had blended in perfectly with the surrounding vegetation, rose to its full height, towering over them. The creature might not have been a Tyrannosaur, but it looked to Queen exactly like every representation of a T. Rex she'd ever seen in pictures, movies and plastic figurines—thick torso, massive muscular hind legs and tiny forearms that looked almost useless. As it stood, its body tilted forward until its back was almost parallel with the ground, its long tail sticking out straight behind it for balance. Its head, which was larger than Rook was tall, swung in their direction, orienting on the sound of Rook's voice.

"Yogi's hairy sphincter!" Rook spun on his heel and grasped Queen's arm with his free hand. He bolted for the open gate, Queen at his side, nearly outpacing him.

The ground vibrated beneath their feet as the massive Carcharodontosaurus started after them, pounding the earth with its immense bulk. Queen felt its hot breath on the back of her neck. She told herself it was just her imagination, but then she heard the click of its jaws snapping shut and felt something brush against her hair. *It's right there!* Even a moments delay would seal her fate.

Rook pivoted hard to the right as they reached the gateway, pulling Queen out of the way of another chomp. The dinosaur's momentum carried it forward, skidding through mounds of its own refuse, but it recovered far more quickly than Queen would have believed possible, whipping its tail around for balance as it turned toward them and charged again.

While Queen looked over her shoulder at the rampaging beast, Rook searched for a place to hide. He angled toward the open doorway of a small structure that, like everything else they'd seen, was constructed of rocks stacked and slotted together—a three-dimensional puzzle. They slipped through the portal and headed for the deepest corner of the stone hut.

The hut had no roof, or if there had been a roof, it had long since collapsed, but this was something Queen discovered only once they were inside. The Carcharodontosaurus probably could have easily reached over the top of the low wall and snatched them up in his powerful jaws, but it evidently had little experience hunting prey in its own lair. It tried to follow them through the door.

The beast got most of its massive head through the opening, but Queen and Rook were just out of reach. It reared back, then thrust forward like a striking viper. When its bulky torso slammed into the surrounding door frame, the entire wall collapsed inward.

Queen pressed back even harder into the far wall, as a shower of loose stone fell at her feet. With the resistance of the barrier suddenly gone, the dinosaur shot forward into the middle of structure, crashing to the floor, half buried by the aftermath of its intrusion.

Rook pointed to the huge gap where the wall had been and shouted, "Go!"

Without waiting for Queen, he charged to the predator's left side, leaping across the uneven pile of stones, while the beast struggled to recover. Its monstrous head started to move, tracking Rook, and Queen saw her opening. She sprinted off the wall and slipped past on the creature's right.

"Ideas?" she shouted as she chased after Rook. Behind her, the Carcharodontosaurus thrashed free of the hut, tearing down the rest of the structure in the process.

"You mean other than *run?*" Rook shot back. "Sorry, that's all I've got."

But as Rook headed for the open gate again, she saw that there was a method to his madness. Out in the open, they might be able to outmaneuver the gigantic beast. *Operative word, might,* she thought, but given the circumstances, an imperfect plan was better than no plan at all.

Rook slipped around the corner, through the opening, and because Queen was just a couple of steps behind him, she didn't have time to react when he came to an abrupt stop. She collided with him and bounced back like she'd hit a brick wall. Rook did not appear to have noticed. He was just staring straight ahead in complete disbelief.

"Damn it, Rook." She sprang back to her feet, poised to resume running. "What the f—"

The curse died on her lips. Until that moment, she would have thought herself incapable of astonishment. She had witnessed dinosaurs walking the Earth. What could compare to that?

A figure was charging toward them. He was drenched in blood, teeth bared in a rictus of pain or fury, perhaps both, howling like some kind of Viking berserker.

But that was not what stunned her into paralysis.

It was the fact that she recognized him.

FORTY-FIVE

Near Lake Kivu, Democratic Republic of the Congo

The Red Queen stepped down from her chariot and into the wreckage of what had been, just two days earlier, the camp of the science expedition. The scientists had been looking for a way to transform Lake Kivu's natural gas reserves into a bounty of cheap energy for the Congo region, empowering the developing nation to rise to an equal footing on the great global game field. Joseph Mulamba was not wrong in believing that the thirteen cubic miles of methane at the lake's bottom would play a pivotal role in how the game played out. His mistake was in thinking that it was the prize that would go to the victor. Favreau knew differently. The lake was not the prize. It was the pawn that she would maneuver to checkmate her enemies.

General Velle stepped out of the helicopter right behind her and looked with disdain at the burned out husk of a truck that sat in the middle of the camp. The ruined tents had been cleared away to create a landing zone for the helicopter, but the canvas skins along with all the other detritus had been heaped up in a pile at the edge of the clearing. The bodies of the science team were probably there as well, mixed in with the rest of the refuse. A few had escaped into the forest, but a relentless search had run them to ground. The latest report was that the survivors were holed up in a nearby cave. Favreau did not think they would be of any consequence, but she knew better than to leave anything to chance. She had directed General Velle to send more rebel fighters to reinforce the pursuit.

The perimeter of the camp was ringed by a dozen Type 63 armored infantry vehicles, representing most of the fighting force Velle had sent into the Kivu region at her earlier behest. Along with the regular DRC Army troops loyal to Velle, there were fighters representing a plethora of loosely organized rebel groups, some of whom had been operating in the area since the Simba Rebellion of 1964. Most had been rebels in name only, fighting to protect their criminal enterprises—poaching mostly. More often than not, they were paid by corrupt government and military officials, like Velle, to maintain order in the region. The alliance with the rebels had been a critical factor emboldening Velle to make his bid for control of the country. Although he could only count on a small portion of the legitimate military in distant Kinshasa to support him, he fielded a combined army of fighters in the east. Nevertheless, he made no secret of his displeasure at having to move his base of operations to the edge of the country.

"I cannot rule from a tent," he complained.

Favreau kept a cool expression, though inwardly she was weary of having to explain herself to the pompous officer. "This is where the power is," she told him, gesturing out to the lake. "If you had stayed in Kisangani, you would have been vulnerable."

"To whom?"

She patted him on the arm. "General, you must think that I underestimate your importance in all of this. I want you to be the ruler of this country as much as you do. But victory will not be achieved by open war. To win, you must force the Western nations to make your new government legitimate."

"And why would they not do so? I am offering them exactly what they want, full access to the natural gas reserves."

Favreau shook her head in a mockery of long-suffering. "General, you do not understand the Western mind. They see you as a thug. Useful to them for clearing away the old regime, but not someone with whom to conduct respectable business. The United States has paid a heavy price for supporting ruthless dictators in the past. The eyes of the world are on them now, and they do not wish to be perceived as fomenting bloody civil wars as a means to securing natural resources and building their empire—especially if it's true. They will recognize your government only if you give them no choice. They would prefer to cast you as the villain, ride in as the benevolent savior and install their own puppet regime. That is why you must be here. They will not attack here for fear that you will make good on your threat to destroy Lake Kivu."

Velle grunted, then turned away, joining a group of his toadies. Favreau assumed they would be more sympathetic to his complaints. That suited her purposes as well. There was a lot to do.

She watched as the rest of the passengers debarked from the Mil Mi-8. The Russian-made helicopter could carry up to twenty-four people, and on this trip, every available seat had been filled. In addition to a handful of Velle's senior officers, she'd brought what was left of her ESI contingent. She had lost some in Kinshasa—killed by the resourceful American operative. She had sent two more to escort Senator Marrs to Mombasa, where he would deliver her demands to his colleagues in the US government. Those men would almost certainly learn that Favreau had been disavowed. The mercenaries still with her—a random draw of Hearts and Clubs—had no idea that they had been declared a rogue element. They probably wouldn't have cared.

The next to last man out held no allegiance to her or to Velle. Gerard Okoa stepped down from the open hatch and looked at the wrecked camp in dismay. He had said very little during his captivity, which pleased Favreau. Between Velle and Marrs, she'd had her fill of impotent men blustering about not getting the respect they deserved.

She looked past the interim president to the last man off the helicopter, the leader of the Hearts team. "Find a nice safe corner to hide Mr. Okoa. He still has an important part to play."

As Ace Hearts moved off, she instructed the rest of her men to procure a boat, then went back aboard the Mil to finish her own preparations.

She knelt beside the olive-drab canvas pack that covered the RA-115 and opened its flap, revealing the smooth metal housing of the bomb. It was connected to the helicopter's electrical system to maintain the quality of its fission core, but its battery backup was fully charged. If it became necessary to deploy the bomb in the lake, it would be fully operational. In its present configuration, however, it would not operate as needed. For the one-kiloton-yield device to ignite the submerged gas deposits, it would have to be at the bottom of the lake. The problem was the signal from the dead-man switch, which had served her so well, would not reach through the four hundred odd yards of water in between.

As she delved into the device's electronic guts, her satellite phone rang. She glanced over at the caller ID display and saw that it was the phone she'd given to Lance Marrs. She picked up.

"*Bon jour*, Senator."

Marrs did not bother with salutations. "Let me talk to General Velle."

"Whatever you have to say, you may say it to me. We both know that the General is not the one you need to be negotiating with."

A growl came over the line. "All right, damn it. Look, you've got us up against a wall here. We can't just give in. Our position has always been that we don't negotiate with terrorists—"

"Please, Senator. We both know that is not true."

"Yes, *we* both know, but Joe Public doesn't, and we have to keep it that way. People are going to ask why we decided to support an illegal military dictatorship over the legitimate democratically elected president, and we can't very well tell them that it's because you are threatening to nuke the natural gas reserves, can we?"

Favreau sighed, though in truth, she had anticipated this. "What if President Okoa signed an order, granting General Velle emergency powers?"

"It's shaky. When Mulamba shows up, that emergency order won't be worth spit."

"Senator, I don't think you fully appreciate the situation. I have given you an ultimatum. Convince your colleagues to do what must be done. I assure you, any political embarrassment will be minor compared to what you will suffer if you fail."

Favreau ended the call, and stared at the phone for a moment, wondering whether Marrs believed that she would follow through on her threat. It was doubtful that he did. His experience in politics had probably convinced him that no one ever kept their promises, and that threats and ultimatums were almost always a bluff.

Marrs struck her as the sort of man who was foolish enough to think that she was bluffing. As she went back to work on the bomb, she found herself hoping that she would get the chance to show him just how wrong he was.

King studied the military camp, tagging targets and assessing the weaknesses in the perimeter. The enemy forces were clearly not expecting an attack, but what they lacked in discipline, they made up for in sheer numbers. There were more than a hundred of them, and he had just six Republican Guard soldiers.

He recalled something Queen had said. *We're a team. That's how we win.*

She had known as well as he that situations like this sometimes required them to operate independent of each other, but even separated by vast distances, they were still a team, still working together like the pieces on a chessboard to execute the winning strategy. Right now, though, the team—his team, the Chess Team—was exactly what he needed. When the five of them were together, they were unstoppable.

He willed his thoughts back into the moment.

Crescent II had rendezvoused with the patrol boat on the river, much to the astonishment of the soldiers and crew who wondered aloud if the dark boomerang-shaped craft was Kongamato come to destroy them. In a way, he supposed it was true. The stealth plane had shuttled them to a battlefield where the odds of survival were extremely low. If they did survive, they would certainly have one hell of a story to tell.

Crescent had delivered them to a jungle clearing about twelve miles from Lake Kivu, as close as they could get without being detected. A thermal sweep of the area had revealed the location of several rebel patrols. The stealth plane had stayed on station, conducting high-altitude reconnaissance to guide King's team around enemy forces, until they were within sight of the camp, but it had since been forced to break off for refueling. King had debated waiting for the plane to return to provide surveillance, and if necessary close-air support and a quick exfil, but he had ultimately decided there was nothing to be gained by waiting.

He studied the camp a few moments longer, then outlined his plan to the rest of the team. It was a quick, brutal plan, and if it worked, he would find himself face-to-face with Favreau and her backpack nuke.

She had asked what he was willing to sacrifice to win, and now he had his answer.

He was about to give the order to move out when Deep Blue's voice filled his head.

And gave him hope.

FORTY-SIX

Below

With a bone-shaking jolt, Bishop slammed into the cavern floor amid a flurry of claws and jaws. He felt a flash of something that might have been pain, but his nearly overloaded neurons could no longer distinguish one sensation from another. The strange vegetation that grew right up to the base of the cliff had cushioned his fall, but something hard and heavy had slammed into him. It was his M240; its sling, frayed by the onslaught, had come apart during the fall, and turned his best weapon into a gravity powered projectile. More raptors tumbled down from the ledge. A few actually appeared to be running down the nearly vertical cliff face in defiance of gravity. They landed all around and atop him, and scurried away.

A part of his brain knew the creatures weren't interested in attacking him, but only in fleeing from the noise and death in the adjoining cavern. That voice of reason however was very hard to hear over the roar of the primal rage beast that Bishop had fought to control every moment of his life. The raptors' talons had done more than tear his flesh. They had almost completely severed the part of him that was human.

Almost.

He rose to his feet with a howl and started swinging. His fists encountered only empty air. The surviving raptors had all fled out across the cavern floor. He turned, gazing up at the ledge to see if more were coming. There weren't any more raptors, but something else was coming out of the tunnel, or more precisely, someone. The searching rebels had followed the stampede into the passage. The leader of the small band spotted him and raised his Kalashnikov.

The beast inside urged him to scale the cliff, brave a storm of lead and tear the attackers apart. The human told him to run, not out of fear, but to protect his friends. If he ran, the rebels wouldn't be looking for the others.

He ran.

As he turned away, he glimpsed Knight and Felice, two prone figures barely visible in the recess high above. He shook his head, hoping that Knight would understand. *Don't fire at them, you'll give away your position. Stay hidden; I'll be fine.*

A thud somewhere off to his left, and a rifle report a millisecond later. The shot went wide, missing Bishop, but if the gunman knew anything about how to use his rifle, he'd be able to correct his aim. Or he might just get off a lucky shot.

Bishop zigged left for a few steps then right, then left again. Bullets chased him across the plain, but as he increased the distance, the shots became less frequent and less accurate. A few raptors ran along with him, as if hunting him, and perhaps that was exactly what they were trying to do, but he made no attempt to discourage them. If the rebels believed that the dinosaurs had finished him off, maybe it would clear the way for the others to escape. He didn't dare stop, not yet.

As he ran, putting one foot in front of the other in an almost mechanical rhythm, he felt the rage finally begin to subside. There was still a lot of pain. His anger had anaesthetized him to much of it, and now it was returning with a vengeance. His entire body throbbed with each step. But he didn't stop.

The velociraptors had finally scattered, and he thought he had seen the last of them. He wasn't overly concerned about the creatures. They were dangerous, but didn't exhibit the hyper-intelligent pack hunter behavior that had mischaracterized their appearance in dinosaur movies. Without a mass attack, they would never be able to take him down. Right now, dinosaurs were the least of his—

"What the hell?"

There was something on the horizon, something that didn't belong in a cave deep beneath the Earth's surface, especially not when that cave was a time capsule sealed up for more than sixty-five million years. But there it was: a wall of some kind. As he got closer, he saw that the wall was only the beginning. Beyond it lay an entire city.

A noise like an avalanche rumbled out of the ruins. Before he could even begin to process this latest sensory input, Rook ran out of the city gates.

Rook?

Queen came out behind Rook, bumped into him and nearly fell. They saw Bishop and froze in their tracks.

Queen?

I'm hallucinating, he thought. *It's the only explanation.*

Then a dinosaur the size of a city bus appeared behind them both.

Please let me be hallucinating.

The Carcharodontosaurus charged. So did Bishop.

Queen felt one of his hands close on her shoulder, then she was hurtling through the air. Rook was swept away in the opposite direction, leaving nothing between the enormous predator and the last person Queen expected to find in the underworld.

The dinosaur snapped its head forward, jaws agape, but Bishop was faster. He broke to the right, avoiding the bite, and as he slipped past, he lowered his shoulder and bulldozed into the monster's left rear leg.

It should have been about as effective as tackling an oak tree, but Bishop's timing was uncannily perfect. He slammed into the dinosaur's foot just as it was rising, and his momentum swept the mighty limb back just enough to trip it up. With its head still lowered, the Carcharodontosaurus did an ungainly face-plant, which twisted into an uncontrollable sideways roll that shook the cavern floor.

"Bishop?" Rook was crouched, the spearhead gripped in his right hand. He grinned like a maniac. "Didn't anyone ever tell you it's not polite to drop in without calling first? What if we'd been—"

The dinosaur's roar cut him off, and suddenly it was back on its feet and coming around for another attack. Bishop was also poised for action. His face was drawn into a bestial snarl, and despite the fact that the monster towered above him, there wasn't a hint of fear in his eyes.

Even Bishop could not hope to defeat such a beast, but his resolve was inspirational. Bishop wasn't alone, after all. Queen scrambled back to her feet and began waving her arms. "Hey, asshole. Over here."

The dinosaur paused, swiveling its gigantic head so that one of its fist-sized black eyes stared at her.

"Shit!" Rook yelled, also waving his arms to distract it. He began jumping up and down. "That was a really dumb idea, babe. No, you stupid gecko, this way! Tasty treat, right here!"

The head tilted in the other direction, and for the first time, the monster seemed to realize that it had found prey that behaved very differently than its usual fare. For just an instant, Queen wondered if they might be able to frustrate it into simply giving up.

Bishop, however, opted for the less subtle approach. He charged again.

With its side-facing eyes, the dinosaur didn't see his approach. Not that it mattered. Bishop launched himself at its snout, gripping one of its nostril ridges in his hand, and swung himself up onto its head. The Carcharodontosaurus barely seemed to notice. With a flick of its head, it flung Bishop away. Amazingly, Bishop landed cat-like on his feet, and whirled around for another charge.

"Great plan!" Rook shouted, still waving his arms. "We'll piss it off until it drops dead from terminal irritation."

Bishop ignored the comment. He ran at the creature again, and once more, the dinosaur with its attention divided between the two shouting figures to either side, did not appear to notice his approach. Bishop got in close and ducked past its stubby forearms, crouching beneath it.

Rook understood immediately and flung the spearhead in Bishop's direction. Bishop caught the stone flake out of the air, and in a single smooth motion, oriented its sharp tip upward and drove it into the monster's exposed belly.

The dinosaur let out a deafening shriek and leaped back, thrusting down with its tail for added propulsion. Its entire ponderous mass lifted so high into the air that Queen wondered if it was going to take flight. Instead, it landed with an earth-shaking thump, several yards behind where it had been, its full attention now fixed on the annoying little creature that had just bitten it. Queen saw that Bishop's hands were coated in fresh blood, but empty. The spearhead remained buried in the dinosaur's soft tissue.

This is hopeless, Queen thought. "Back to the city," she called. "We can lose it in there."

It was the only plan that had a chance of working. They could lose themselves in the streets or hide in buildings made of sterner stuff than the little stone shed where they had first sought refuge. They might even be able to find more weapons. But she didn't move and neither did Rook. It was all for one and one for all. If Bishop refused to flee, then they weren't going anywhere, and Bishop, unfortunately, seemed to have lost the ability to understand English.

The Carcharodontosaurus gave another screech and leaped again, this time to the side, thrashing its tail violently, as if to swat at an annoying insect. Huge drops of blood splattered the ground where it had been, but as it landed, Queen saw that it was bleeding from two wounds: the gash in its belly, and some kind of puncture on its torso, just behind its foreleg.

It yelped again, and there was an eruption of blood from its snout. Then, a series of red blossoms sprang up on its right flank and the monster went into a frenzy. Even Bishop yielded ground as the dinosaur started rolling, flinging gobs of blood, as it scratched the air and whipped its tail to drive off whatever was attacking it. Over its agonized shrieks, Queen heard a loud, mechanical sound, similar to the noise she and Rook had heard just before encountering the creature.

The sound of gunfire.

The dinosaur abruptly leapt up and ran for the city gates.

Queen dropped flat when she'd recognized the noise for what it was, but when no further shots came, she got back to her feet. Rook was already up and heading toward Bishop, who hadn't really moved much at all. The big man just stood there, his chest heaving from exertion, his arms trembling as though he thought the fight might resume at any instant, his eyes...

His eyes were blood red with primal fury.

"Bish?"

He blinked, and as if by magic, his eyes were normal again. The red had simply been blood trickling down from a gash in his forehead.

There was movement in the periphery of Queen's vision, just beyond Bishop, and when she turned her head to look, her glasses immediately tagged three figures—one with green, and two more in yellow. A name and several lines of information appeared in one corner of the display. The facial recognition software had recognized Felice Carter, an American scientist, formerly with a now defunct bio-tech firm called Nexus, which was itself a division of Manifold...

Queen felt a slight chill at the name and stopped reading, peering instead at the other two figures. One of them was a small wizened-looking African man, lugging, almost dragging, an enormous M240B machine gun that Queen knew belonged to Bishop. The other man wasn't African, but looked Asian, though it was difficult to tell, since most of his face was obscured by a veritable mummy-wrap of bandages that completely covered one eye. He wore camouflage BDUs and carried a long rifle—

"Knight!" Rook exclaimed, running toward the approaching trio. "Man, you look like I feel."

Queen gasped. Of course it was Knight. *The bandages must have fooled the facial recognition software,* she thought. *Oh God, what happened to him?*

She ran after Rook. It was only when she reached the little group and threw her arms around Knight in a hug that made him wince, that she realized Bishop still hadn't moved.

FORTY-SEVEN

Felice stared at the display on her computer, amazed at the story it told. At first, it had all seemed unbelievable. These four relentless soldiers finding each other in a cave deep beneath the Congo rain forest seemed unlikely, but now that she studied the map of Queen's and Rook's journey, from the shores of distant Lake Natron, everything made sense. Joseph Mulamba had, without realizing it, set them all on the path to this reunion.

Fearing that the wounded Carcharodontosaurus might recover his courage and come after them once more, the group had postponed all discussion until they reached the relative safety of the recess atop the landslide, the vantage point from which Felice, Knight and David had watched Bishop's mad dash across the cavern floor. The rebel fighters had taken a few potshots from the shelter of the passage, before losing interest and heading back to the surface, leaving the others free to follow Bishop, which had turned out to be a fortuitous decision.

Introductions had been made—Felice had not failed to notice that the two new arrivals were also named for chess pieces—and then Queen and Rook began telling their story. Someone had suggested they link Queen's q-phone—a functional version of the broken devices that Knight and Bishop had possessed—to Felice's laptop, and the entire journey had been revealed, with several hours of video and a map of the superhighway used by a forgotten civilization.

The Ancients had established their trade route right through the middle of the subterranean lost world where dinosaurs still roamed. That isolated ecosystem, which skirted the edge of Lake Natron, had been created in the vast spaces left by earlier volcanic activity, and was sustained by unseen extremophile microbes, which turned carbon and carbon dioxide into natural gas compounds that had been burning for millions of years. They provided the necessary energy for the food web. Felice suspected that the archaeologists who would one day study the site would discover that the Ancients had done a lot more than simply pass through the lost world. Had they perhaps learned how to utilize the naturally occurring fuel for cooking and other uses?

When the story was finished, Felice took advantage of the uplink to check the last results from the data she and the science team had collected at Lake Kivu. Most of her suppositions were confirmed. She skimmed over the gene sequence of the extremophile, which was indeed a variant of E. Coli. She would need a laboratory to fully make sense of the information, but it was clear that the organism had adapted to live and thrive in conditions where other microbes would have died. She was eager to compare it with the soil sample from the cavern, and begin experimenting with it under controlled conditions. If her hypothesis was correct, they might very well be able to produce enormous amounts of ethanol using a very small amount of carbon, along with water and carbon dioxide.

Indulging her scientific curiosity took her mind off the horror and misery of everything that happened in the last few days. The respite was brief, though.

"Felice," Queen said. "Pack up. Time to go."

While she had been poring over the data, the four soldiers had busied themselves with more immediate concerns, tending to injuries and discussing what would happen next. The joy of their unexpected reunion had quickly given way to a grim solemnity. Felice thought she understood it. They had been through hell. Queen and Rook had suffered the one-two punch of witnessing Mulamba's death, followed by a nightmare journey without food, water, sleep or hope. Knight had been maimed, and although he refused to stop pushing himself—or perhaps because he had pushed himself this far—he was feverish, probably suffering from an infection that, if not treated, would kill him. And Bishop...

Felice wasn't sure how Bishop was even able to stand. The raptors had almost torn him apart, but his physical injuries—which didn't seem to have slowed him down much—were only scratches on the surface, hiding a much deeper wound to his psyche. He had barely spoken since the reunion, and while his teammates seemed to take that in stride, Felice was worried that something had broken inside him.

She slid the computer into her pack and rose as the others began moving down toward the ledge, with Queen in the lead. "What about the rebels?"

"They aren't going to be a problem," Queen answered.

The journey back to the surface seemed to take forever. In the glow of chemlights, Felice got her first good look at the upper cave, and saw it as David had first seen it fifty years before. She saw more of the strange vegetation, but she also saw ruins—stone huts constructed in the same fashion as the city of the Ancients. This had once been an outpost, a gateway to their forgotten civilization.

She let out a yelp of surprise when she saw human figures silhouetted at the mouth of the cavern, but the others seemed unconcerned and just kept moving forward. When she got a little closer, Felice realized why. The men standing at the entrance were not rebel fighters but soldiers, wearing the red berets that marked them as members of the Congolese Republican Guard. Except for one man, a Caucasian. Felice recognized him immediately.

It was the man who had once stopped her from destroying the world.

FORTY-EIGHT

Near Lake Kivu, Democratic Republic of the Congo

If King's reaction to seeing Felice Carter fell short of astonishment, it was only because he had not thought about her in a very long time. The incident which had begun with her discovery of an elephant graveyard in Ethiopia, and unfolded into a series of deadly encounters with a madman who called himself Brainstorm, seemed like ancient history to him now.

King did remember, of course, and he remembered that, at the time, she had been a uniquely dangerous person. If that was still true, it was a complication he didn't need right now.

Felice's presence was not the only thing that put a damper on what should have been a joyful reunion with his teammates, two of whom he had thought dead, and two lost somewhere in the bowels of the Earth.

It wasn't just that he felt a pang of guilt when he looked at them, though he couldn't ignore what he saw. Knight's eye was beyond saving, and while such a permanent and disfiguring injury was a horrible thing to happen to anyone, for Knight, a sniper of unparalleled ability, it verged on catastrophic. Bishop looked like he'd been through a meat grinder. Queen and Rook were relatively sound by comparison, but clearly approaching the limits of their endurance.

He thought of Asya, his own flesh and blood, who had escaped being literally blown apart by a mere quirk of fate.

I was supposed to protect them. Instead, I nearly lost them all.

What weighed on him most heavily though was the knowledge that it wasn't over yet. He was going to have to ask them to keep going, to reach down into the depths of their souls and soldier on.

"Here's the situation," he began. "The enemy is setting up at the science expedition camp—where Knight and Bishop found Miss Carter—about ten klicks from here."

Knight looked up. *"Ten?"*

"Geez, what were you guys doing?" Rook said. "Wandering in circles?"

King had also been surprised when Deep Blue had revealed the coordinates of the entrance to the cavern where Queen's q-phone signal had been pinpointed. If it had been much further away, he would not have risked leaving his forward position to come look for them. As it was, his assault team had endured an hour long run through the jungle, followed by a quick, but decisive firefight with the small group of rebels holding the cavern, leaving them a little more tired and little lighter on ammunition. On the other side of the equation, the team was back together, but he still was undecided about whether or not that was a good thing.

"The enemy numbers approximately one hundred fifty," King said. "Mostly rebel irregulars, but some lightly armored DRC regular army forces. There's also a small group of contractors brought in by Executive Solutions..."

Queen made a face and Rook made a noise to go with it.

"...led by a particularly nasty she-devil named Monique Favreau. It's General Velle's revolution, but Favreau is the brains of the operation. They've got a hostage: President Gerard Okoa. Keeping Okoa alive is a high priority, but not number one. You should know that the ESI mercs are packing an experimental over-pressure ammunition. It's nasty stuff. One-shot lethal. We've seen it before." He paused a beat. "In Suez."

Rook was not the first to understand, but he was the first to offer comment. "Fuck. My. Donkey. Ass."

"Where is it?" Queen asked, referring to the bomb they had lost in Egypt.

"It's with Favreau, at Lake Kivu. There's a huge natural gas deposit underneath the lake. This whole situation is a bid to win control of it. Favreau has taken it a step further. She's threatening to use the nuke to destroy it."

Felice sat up. "Wait, a nuke? An atomic bomb?"

"A small one, but yes."

"You can't let her do that."

"Obviously."

"No, you don't understand—"

Bishop spoke up, and his low quiet voice commanded everyone's attention. "There's an enormous bubble of carbon dioxide at the bottom of the lake. If it erupts and comes to the surface, it will suffocate everyone in the surrounding valley. Two million people." He glanced at Felice as if looking for her approval. She gave it with a grateful nod.

"Right," King continued. "Favreau probably knows that, and I doubt she cares. But that's one more reason why we absolutely cannot let that happen.

"She has the bomb wired to a dead-man switch. If we kill her, she lets go and... Well, you're all smart kids, figure it out." He stopped as something occurred to him, then he turned to Felice. "If the bomb went off on the surface, would it still pop that bubble?"

Felice shrugged. "I don't know. Probably not. The region is very volcanically active, but lake eruptions are rare. Evidently it takes a pretty big disruption to trigger a CO_2 release."

King nodded. "That's what I'm counting on. Favreau's been using that damn nuke like an umbrella. Last night, I was as close to her as I am to you now, and I couldn't kill her because she had her hand on that switch. If she'd let go, a lot of innocent people would have died. But out here, it's just her and us." King turned his attention back to the team. "If there's no other way to stop her, we kill her, and the hell with the consequences. Got it?"

He let that grim possibility hang over their heads for a moment before continuing. "I don't know about you, but I'd just as soon not get blown all to hell, so let's talk about how we're going to take this bitch down."

As King began outlining his assault plan, Felice booted up her laptop. She still had a wireless Internet connection via the q-phone, and she used it to run a simulation of the possible outcomes of an atomic blast at the bottom of Lake Kivu. Once again, there were no surprises. The computer model confirmed her hypothesis. She planned to tell King about it as soon as he concluded his briefing, but to her surprise, he sought her out.

"I'm a little surprised to see you here," he said, walking up behind her.

"Likewise," she replied. "But you know how it is. If you want to save the world, you can't do it from Seattle."

He didn't smile. "It seems to me like someone with your..." He paused, searching for the right word, "condition...would want to avoid high-risk situations. Unless something has changed?"

"As far as I know, I'm still a ticking time-bomb," she admitted. Like many people with chronic illnesses and disabilities, Felice did not dwell on her life-altering situation and refused to let it define her existence, but she was always aware of it.

Three and a half years earlier, as part of a different—but similarly ill-fated—expedition in Ethiopia, Felice had discovered the fossilized remains of an early hominid life form secreted away among an elephant graveyard, and subsequently been infected with...something. She wasn't clear on exactly what it was. Her field was genetics, but what had happened to her was better explained by either a theoretical physicist or a spirit medium. The short version was that she had somehow become the host for the living memory of an ancient human ancestor, a consciousness that was linked—psychically or through quantum entanglement, Felice didn't know which, or if there was even a difference—like a hard-wired connection, to every human being on the planet. If that circuit was overloaded, say by the triggering of Felice's fight-or-flight instinct in a life-threatening crisis, the result would be the mental equivalent of a power surge in an electrical grid.

King's concerns were not unwarranted. He had been present when a group of bandits, intent on assaulting Felice had been at the receiving end of such a surge and were transformed into mindless zombies. And that had been triggered merely by the threat of violence.

"I spent two years learning meditation and biofeedback techniques to control my emotions," Felice continued. "I can enter a trance state at will, completely shut myself off to all external stimuli. Is it enough? Who knows? But I'm not going to let fear of what might happen control me, or keep me from doing something that I feel is important."

King nodded slowly. "I can't argue with that." He took a breath, let it out slowly. "You know what we're about to do. And you know how it might end. I want you to stay here."

The request did not come as a surprise. "I get it," she said. "And you're right. I'm no soldier. I wouldn't be of much help."

"I'll ask David to stay with you."

"There's something you need to know," she blurted. "Maybe it doesn't even matter, but I've been running simulations on the possible effects of a nuclear explosion at the lake bottom. The research we were doing identified an extremophile as the source of most of the natural gas. If the gas bubble were to erupt violently, it would almost certainly bring some of those microbes to the surface.

"This is an extremely durable and robust organism. It has adapted to survive...no, make that *thrive*, in extreme environments. Imagine what would happen if it started colonizing on the surface? This rain forest is an all-you-can-eat buffet of carbon. Add to that the boost of CO_2 released from the lake and the fact that atmospheric carbon dioxide has doubled since the last time the lake erupted, and you've got a recipe for disaster."

"Worse than two million dead?"

"The microbe turns vegetation into natural gas with a very low flashpoint. It would transform the entire Congo Basin into a flammable swamp. In the short term, that would be disastrous for the people who live here. In the long term, it would spike greenhouse gases even higher, creating a positive-feedback loop. I don't even want to think about what might happen if the organism escapes Africa, and ends up somewhere like the Amazon."

"Okay, I get it. It doesn't change what we have to do." He turned away, and Felice was left to wonder if she'd made the right decision in burdening him with the additional responsibility. It was a hard thing to have the fate of the world in your hands, but she was starting to realize that it was even harder to accept that sometimes it was out of your hands.

She watched the team make their final preparations. She hadn't felt this helpless since Ethiopia. There was nothing she could do now to help them succeed.

Her gaze fell on Bishop.

Maybe there was something she could do after all.

She found herself moving toward him, and as she approached, he straightened and turned toward her, awkwardly expectant. She didn't meet his eyes right away. Instead, she stared at the ragged slashes that crisscrossed his broad, muscular chest. He had thrown away the tattered remnant of his shirt, and now looked like some kind of mighty barbarian warrior. She could not help but be impressed.

Attractive? Hell, yes. The scientist in her recognized him as a prime alpha male specimen, and who was she to argue with biology? But there was more to it than that.

She placed her palms flat against his chest, just as she had done after the first raptor attack. Once more, she felt him recoil ever so slightly, as if her touch might make him vulnerable. Vulnerability, she supposed, was the only thing that truly frightened him.

She lightly touched one of the scabbed over gashes. "Are you all right?"

"I'm a fast healer. And it's not as bad as it looks."

At last she was ready to meet his eyes. As close as she now stood to him, he towered above her, and she had to crane her neck to look up at him. She opened her mouth to speak, then closed it as the words deserted her. She tried again. "So, listen, I..."

"Yes."

"What, yes?" she said with a laugh.

"Whatever it is you were going to ask me, the answer is yes."

"Good."

His lips curled into something that she recognized as a valiant attempt to smile, then he started to turn away.

"No, wait," she said, and circled around to face him again. "You need to listen to me. I..."

Damn it, what am I trying to say?

She took a deep breath and looked him in the eyes again. "You are, without a doubt, the strongest, toughest, most bad-ass person I've ever met. But there's something inside you that's..." The words eluded her once more.

"You're right," he said in a quiet, almost embarrassed voice.

"It's eating at you. You think you can control it, but..."

"I know."

"I can help you." When he didn't respond, she continued. "Believe it or not, I've actually got a little experience with this kind of thing."

He nodded. "King told me."

"Did he?"

That son of a bitch, she thought. But at least he had saved her the trouble of explaining it to Bishop.

"Okay. Well, the point is, I can help. I want to."

His eyes stayed locked with hers for several seconds, then something caught his attention and his gaze flicked away. The rest of the team was lining up to begin the mission.

"I have to go." He knelt and picked up his machine gun.

Felice felt the moment slipping away. "Will you let me help?"

"I already have," he said in a quiet voice, and then he turned to join the others.

FORTY-NINE

As dusk settled over Lake Kivu, Monique Favreau decided she had waited long enough. It would be mid-morning in Washington by now, plenty of time for Marrs's colleagues to digest her ultimatum and reach some kind of consensus.

She was giddy with excitement. Some would probably want to buy her off, while others would demand military action. Unable to agree, they would choose instead to stall for time by offering to negotiate, but she would give them nothing. They would bow to her will or she would destroy their prize.

The simple act of disconnecting the bomb from the helicopter's stand-by electrical system felt like a pivotal moment. The battery back-up would keep the bomb primed and operational for a few hours. That was plenty of time to get it in position, but just barely enough to bring it back and plug it in again. That time constraint would set the tone for the negotiations with the Americans. There would be no room for equivocation or stalling.

She carried the device on her back through the camp, to the tent where General Velle had established his command. Okoa was there, seated at a folding table, not bound but under constant supervision from two of her men and a handful of Velle's soldiers. Favreau ignored the general—the man who would be president—and went instead to the man who, legally speaking at least, had the actual job.

"Mr. Okoa. Your country stands on the brink of civil war. Your leader, President Mulamba, has not returned, and there are rumors that he might be dead." She had heard no such rumors, and had not heard from the team dispatched to intercept Mulamba in Belgium, but reasoned that if Mulamba were alive, she would have heard about it. "This is a crisis," she went on, "and demands swift decisive action. You must sign an executive order, granting General Velle special emergency powers to restore order, until a new government can be created."

Okoa slowly raised his head. He wore an expression of incredulity. "General Velle *is* the crisis."

"Let us put aside pretenses. How we came to be here is irrelevant. What matters is how it ends."

"Why do you need me to sign a piece of paper giving you what you have already taken?"

"For the sake of your people, Mr. Okoa. A formal decree is necessary for reconciliation to begin. General Velle has practical authority, but you must give him legitimate authority to restore the peace."

Okoa stared at her for a moment through narrowed eyes. His blunt face seemed to tremble with barely restrained anger. He turned to Velle. "It will take more than a piece of paper to make your government legitimate."

"Not in the eyes of the world," said Favreau. "The African Union and the United Nations will recognize such a decree as legally binding. They will honor General Velle's request for monetary assistance and peace-keeping troops, and of course, facilitate the development of the natural gas reserves, for the good of all."

"Ah, so now we come to the heart of the matter." Okoa kept his gaze fixed on Velle. "You don't care what our people want. You desire only to please your foreign *masters*." He filled the last words with such contempt that Velle's face darkened, as if he had just been slapped.

Favreau smiled patiently to hide her annoyance. This was taking much longer than it should have. "Mr. Okoa, all of this posturing is irrelevant. You see this device that I am carrying? You know what it is, do you not? A one kiloton tactical nuclear device. If General Velle's government is not formally recognized, here and abroad, then I will use this device to blow up the Kivu natural gas deposits. Tonight."

Okoa's gaped at her. "Why would you do such a thing?"

"Isn't it obvious? To win, of course."

"But you would be destroying the very thing you are trying to possess."

"The fear of losing something is a weakness. The nations of the West fear losing control of the natural resources of Africa more than they fear having to support the government of a military strongman. You, Mr. President, fear the pain and suffering that will come to your people, even more than you fear losing your own life. To protect them, I think you will sign this paper."

Okoa's eyes began moving rapidly, as if searching for some alternative to the awful choice Favreau had set before him. Then, he sagged in defeat. "I will sign. General Velle, you have a formidable ally. I wonder, does she also control you by threatening the thing you most fear to lose?"

Velle's nostrils flared, but he did not reply. Instead, he slid a folder across the tabletop toward Okoa. Inside, on a sheet of paper, emblazoned with the presidential seal depicting an ivory tusk, a spear and the head of a leopard, was the executive order that would turn the Democratic Republic of the Congo into a dictatorship.

Favreau did not wait to see him sign the paper. This small victory had been relatively easy. Okoa had been able to look her in the eyes and see what she was willing to do. Marrs and the American government might not be so easily swayed.

She turned and left the tent, heading for the lakeshore.

FIFTY

Near Lake Kivu, Democratic Republic of the Congo

Ten figures swam silently through the dark waters of Lake Kivu, stealthily approaching the military camp.

The water felt cool, refreshingly so for Queen, who was still wearing a drysuit. During the long hike through the jungle, the insulated neoprene dive garment had felt a little like wearing a sauna, but with no changes of clothing available, their choice was either that, or as Rook had suggested, fighting naked. It was a tempting thought. The drysuit really was stifling, but the dark color helped her blend with the jungle shadows.

The nearby shore was lit by dim campfires, but in the display of her glasses, she could easily distinguish the Type 63 armored infantry vehicles that formed a semi-circle around the enemy position. The tracked vehicles looked like baby battle tanks, but were designed primarily to shuttle ground forces and provide fire support, courtesy of a 12.7 mm turret-mounted machine gun. Presently, the vehicles were sitting idle, their crews sprawled out on the flat exterior surfaces. Some tents had been erected inside the protective circle and a few soldiers roamed the encampment, but aside from token patrols, there was no security. In the center of the camp, unguarded, sat the Mil Mi-8.

While still thirty yards from shore, the group split into two. King would be leading Rook and four of the guardsmen in search of the bomb and President Okoa. Queen, Bishop and the remaining guardsmen had a different goal.

Knight was somewhere outside the camp, providing over-watch with his sniper rifle. Like the chess piece that was his namesake, he moved and fought indirectly, unconventionally and often decisively. That was what he did best. Or at least it had been. While the rest of the team were nearing the limits of physical and mental endurance, Knight had gone somewhere into the dark territory beyond those limits. His wasn't just a wound to the flesh. Some soldiers lost the will to live after an injury like his. Queen had no doubt that he could hold it together long enough to finish this mission, but she didn't allow herself to think about what would happen after that.

She scanned the shore, verifying that there were no enemy troops present, then motioned for the others to follow her in. They low crawled out of the water and crept forward to the edge of the camp. "We're set," she whispered.

"Roger," came King's voice. "Standby."

She glanced up the shore and saw the blue icon that marked King moving into position. Stealth was critical. If everything went as planned, they would get in and do what needed to be done without alerting the enemy. That was, of course, the optimal outcome. If they were discovered and the incursion turned into a pitched battle, the parameters for success were a lot looser. They included the intentional detonation of the RA-115 device, which would kill all of them, but neutralize the greater threat to the innocent civilians living along the shores of Lake Kivu.

Several new yellow icons began appearing in Queen's virtual display. From their two respective locations, King and Queen could now keep track of most of the enemy soldiers as they moved around the camp.

"Set," King said, after a few seconds. "Let's do this."

Queen kept one hand on Asya's silenced Uzi, which King had given her, and held her other up in a pre-arranged 'get ready' signal. The weapon was now synchronized to her glasses, and she used it to sight in on the Congolese soldier wandering past the helicopter. She fired and a few seconds later, he was gone. Her hand came down and she, Bishop and the two guardsmen picked up and hastened forward. They stopped beside a tent, waited a few seconds, then made the final push to the helicopter.

The Mil Mi-8 looked to Queen like an ordinary military chopper—a Huey or a Blackhawk—that had gotten the stretch limo treatment. Behind the typical bubble window cockpit, the cabin morphed into a long fuselage with a series of round porthole windows. The main rotor, jet turbine intakes and tail rotor boom all sat perched atop the main cabin.

Queen and the others ducked down below the right-side landing gear pod and waited again. To get inside, they would need to reach the sliding door on the left side of the aircraft, which was much more exposed.

She crept to the rear of the craft and ducked under the tail assembly. There were just a few yellow icons moving here and there, but no enemy forces in the immediate vicinity. *Now or never*, she told herself, and stepped out into the open. She moved smoothly down the right side of the cabin and then swung herself up and into the interior.

There were two men inside, big, muscular Caucasians. The facial recognition software identified them as former soldiers and probable ESI mercenaries about a nanosecond before Queen put one silenced round in each man's eye. She kept moving, sweeping through the cabin like an avenging angel. Maybe in a way, that was exactly what she was, exacting retribution for Joseph Mulamba's death at the hands of men who belonged to the same murderous organization that had taken his life.

There was no one else in the helicopter.

Bishop came in a moment later, followed by the two guardsmen. The latter trained their Kalashnikovs on the open doorway. Bishop took a moment to check the bodies to make sure that they were as dead as they looked, then headed forward to the cockpit where Queen was waiting. He settled himself into the flight chair.

Everyone in the team had received some aircraft training, but Bishop was the only one of their number with actual time in the seat of a helicopter. Queen watched him study the controls. "You can fly this thing, right?"

His expression was typically unreadable but after looking around for a few seconds, he said, "I need your glasses."

The request caught Queen off guard, but made perfect sense. Bishop was going to fly an unfamiliar aircraft, in enemy territory, in the dark. He should be the one with both night-vision and high-tech instantaneous computer access. But she had gotten used to the idea of having the glasses on, of being in constant contact with someone who could answer any question, of being able to see what no one else could see. She and Rook never would have survived the journey through the subterranean realm of the Ancients without them.

But I don't want to give them up, she thought, and thinking that made her realize just how dependent she had become on the glasses. She nearly snarled at the small sign of weakness. She stripped the glasses off and handed them over, along with her synchronized q-phone. "I hope you'll take better care of them than you did your last pair."

As she moved back into the cabin to join the guardsman, she heard Bishop say, "We have the helo. Standing by."

FIFTY-ONE

King scanned the open ground that separated him from the command tent. He had identified it as such during his initial survey of the camp, but he had no way of knowing if Favreau and General Velle were inside. If they were not, his plan for a stealthy surgical victory was finished. There would be no alternative but to fight.

He watched the tent for a full minute but no one came or went. When Bishop's voice sounded in his head, reporting that the helicopter was secure, he knew he could wait no longer.

"Let's go," he told Rook.

They moved smoothly from the shadows and strode toward the tent. The guardsmen had removed their berets, and in the darkness, he hoped that anyone who happened to be looking in their direction would assume that they were just four more soldiers carrying out camp business. He and Rook could not blend in quite so easily, but they would be exposed for only a few seconds, and once they reached the command tent, it wouldn't matter anymore.

One of the guardsmen stepped forward and drew back the flap of the tent, allowing King to move inside. As he crossed the threshold, several targets appeared in his virtual display. He brought the Uzi up and trained it on a figure tagged with red. It was General Velle.

It took a moment for the people in the tent to realize what was happening—more than enough time for Rook and the others to move inside. King kept his gun trained on Velle, but behind his glasses, his eyes were scanning the other targets. He identified two of the ESI mercenaries, both marked with red, and Gerard Okoa as well, but there was no sign of Favreau.

Damn it.

Comprehension dawned on Velle's face, quickly transforming into anger, but before he could open his mouth, King moved forward, thrusting the business end of his Uzi into the general's chest. "Tell your men to stand down." King glimpsed movement off to his right, one of the mercenaries going for his weapon. King moved quickly, slipping around Velle's bulk, putting the general between himself and everyone else.

The implied threat wasn't enough to stop what happened next. The mercenary got his gun up, and then the tent erupted in violence, noise and smoke.

The mercenary was blasted off his feet by a burst from Rook's Kalashnikov. The mortally wounded man's finger had been in the trigger well of his MP5. A second thunderous report sounded and ragged holes appeared in the overhead canopy.

The guardsmen opened fire, gunning down the officers who had been standing to either side of Velle. The other mercenary ducked behind the table, seeking cover, and got off a shot that vaporized an unlucky guardsman, but Rook brought his rifle around and unloaded it in a sustained trigger pull. His bullets tore through the tabletop and stitched up the mercenary's chest, dropping him before he could fire again.

The fight was over as quickly as it had begun, but King knew that the plan for a stealthy exit was now as dead as the men strewn about the tent. Over the ringing in his ears, he could hear shouts from outside.

Velle had jerked in surprise when the firing started, but the hard steel muzzle pressed to the base of his neck kept him rooted in place. Nevertheless, he remained defiant. "You are all dead men."

"We'll live or die together," King said. "Your choice."

When Velle did not respond, King gripped his collar and shepherded him through the carnage to the front of the tent.

"Rook, open the door so that our friends outside can hear the General's answer."

Rook waited until King had Velle in position, and then drew back the flap slowly, keeping himself out of the line of fire. King nudged Velle forward until he was framed in the opening.

"Live or die?"

Just outside the tent, a ring of soldiers had gathered, their weapons at the ready. King could feel Velle quivering with rage, but after several tense seconds, he spoke. "Stand down."

King didn't wait to see if the command was heeded. He pulled Velle back inside and nodded to Rook, who let the tent flap fall back into place, hiding them from view.

"Smart decision," King said. "Now, where's Favreau?"

"I don't know who you are," Velle said, ignoring the question, "But if you put your guns down now, I will let you walk away."

King swiped the Uzi's suppressor across the back of Velle's head, just hard enough to elicit a cry of surprise. "Favreau."

"She is gone." It was Okoa. "She left some time ago."

"Left? Where did she go?"

Okoa shook his head. "I do not know. She had that bomb with her. She said she would destroy Lake Kivu."

King felt his blood run cold. They were too late.

"She is bluffing," Velle snarled. "It is a threat to force the United States to recognize my government, nothing more."

"I do not think she was bluffing," Okoa countered. "There is a madness inside her."

"Where is she?" King pressed, giving Velle another meaningful tap with the Uzi.

"She would not do this," the general persisted. "Destroy the very thing she desires, and kill herself at the same time? It is—" He stopped abruptly, as if recognizing the truth in Okoa's words.

"Look who just figured it out," Rook said.

Okoa, who had not moved from his chair during the entire incident, now rose to his feet and circled around to stand in front of Velle. "You know what this woman means to do. She does not care about you or what happens to our people."

Velle stared back, his earlier anger giving way to uncertainty.

Okoa pressed the point home. "You know what will happen if she destroys the lake."

The general swallowed nervously. He knew. "She has a boat. On the lake. She left...perhaps half an hour ago."

On the lake. Half an hour. King's mind turned over the information, calculating the dire possibilities. "Okay, here's what's going to happen. We're going to walk out of this tent like ducks in a row, and get on the helicopter. You're going to tell your men to stand aside and let us pass, and then we're going to find Favreau and stop her. Understood?"

"Wait," Okoa said, holding up a hand. He kept his eyes locked with Velle's. "Patrice, for better or worse, you are now the leader of our nation. I have given you that authority and I will not challenge you. The safety of our people is your responsibility now."

"Why do you say this?"

"Let these people go. Let them save us all if they can. But the country must not lose another leader." He turned to King. "I have signed an executive order granting General Velle emergency powers. He is the legitimate leader of the country, and I ask you, as a representative of the United States, to recognize his authority. Take the helicopter and do what must be done, but allow the General to leave."

The request was as much a surprise to King as it was to Velle. "I don't have time to screw around here. And *I* don't recognize his authority."

"Then recognize mine," Okoa insisted. "Are you here to help us, or to force us to do your bidding?"

King saw the passionate sincerity in Okoa's eyes. He released his hold on Velle's collar and, without lowering the Uzi, stepped around to face the general. The big man's eyes were still blazing with indignation.

"Tick tock," Rook murmured.

King turned back to Okoa. "Mr. President," he enunciated the words, "right now, all I care about it stopping Favreau from blowing up the lake and killing two million innocent people. I can do that with or without any help from the General. The smart play is to bring you both along. I don't have time to learn how to trust him."

Okoa did not relent. "Patrice, let them go. I will remain with you, not as your captive but as your partner."

"I..." Velle's voice caught. He took a deep breath and then tried again. "I will agree to this."

Every fiber of his being told King not to trust the man. Velle was a traitor to his own country, a megalomaniac bent on personal glory, willing—eager even—to sell the wealth of his nation and the future of its people to foreigners.

"We could just shoot him," Rook suggested. "That would clear up this question of who's in charge."

King ignored the remark. Like it or not, Okoa was right. The Chess Team had come here to preserve the peace and protect the innocent, but the ultimate responsibility for both rested with these two men.

"Right this minute, the only thing that matters is stopping Favreau," he said. "General, I'm going to walk out of here and get on that helicopter. If you have dealt in bad faith, whatever happens will be on your head."

He heard Rook suck in an apprehensive breath.

"Although if we fail," he continued, lowering the Uzi. "I doubt any of us will be around to regret it."

Velle stepped away. He was breathing rapidly, almost panting, and still bristling with anger. He looked defiantly at Rook and the guardsmen who still had their weapons trained on him, and then he stalked to the tent flap. He grabbed hold of it with such ferocity that the entire tent shook as he pulled it back.

"Go!" he snarled.

King looked to Okoa once more and saw him nod.

In the long silence that followed, King heard the sound of the helicopter's engines powering up.

FIFTY-TWO

Bishop listened to the standoff that was transpiring just a short distance away. He had completed a hasty pre-flight check, but had held off starting the turbine engines until the confrontation was resolved, to avoid revealing their presence. Escaping in the helicopter had always been the trickiest part of the plan. It would take at least a full minute for the turbines to reach optimal take-off power, a minute in which the entire camp would know that something was amiss. One or two well-placed bullets would spell the end of their bid for freedom. King had been counting on using Favreau and Velle as human shields to discourage anyone attempting to destroy the helicopter, but that plan was now dead.

Favreau was going to use the bomb. Bishop didn't know anything about the woman, but he understood that much about her. If her threat of destruction had been merely that, a threat, a bluff, she would not have gone out on the water. There was only one reason for her to do that.

She had to be stopped.

Two million lives depended on it.

In a moment of absolute clarity, Bishop understood what he had to do.

He slid out of the pilot's chair and poked his head into the main cabin. "King needs you."

Queen didn't hesitate. While she hadn't been able to follow the confrontation in the command tent, she had heard the gunfire and was already poised for action. Bishop slid the door open and gestured for Queen and the guardsmen to move out.

As she hopped down, scanning the surrounding area, Queen seemed to remember that she no longer had her glasses. "Where is he?"

"He'll find you," Bishop said. He slammed the door shut and threw the combat lock.

He half-expected Queen to start pounding on the door, demanding to be let back in, but the only sound he heard was the tense three-way exchange between King, General Velle and President Okoa.

Bishop moved back to the cockpit and started throwing switches in sequence. There was a loud backfire and then the twin Klimov TV3-117 turboshafts started spinning. A low whine filled the aircraft, quickly rising in pitch and intensity as the main rotor began to turn. Bishop felt the airframe shudder with the torque. He tightened his grip on the collective and cyclic controls, and watched the RPMs build.

"Bishop!" King shouted over the din, and Bishop realized he had mentally tuned-out the standoff in the command tent. "We're outside. Open the door."

There was an undercurrent of dread in King's voice. *He knows*, Bishop thought. *Of course he knows. This is exactly what he would do, in my place.*

Bishop said nothing. He slowly twisted the throttle, increasing the RPMs, and then, moving his hands and feet in a complex ballet of synchronized activity, eased back on the collective, tilted the cyclic forward, and held the rudder steady. The Mil rolled forward a few yards, and then Bishop felt that indescribable sensation of the ground reluctantly letting go. The helicopter continued forward, picking up speed without gaining any altitude. The right wheel clipped a tent, which was already flapping like a loose sail in a hurricane, and then he was out over the dark waters of Lake Kivu.

The Mil bore as much resemblance to the helicopters he had trained on as a luxury sedan did to a city bus. The controls were the same, as were the basic principles of operation, but there was a whole lot more aircraft to pay attention to. Fortunately, the flat surface of the lake was the perfect place for him to get familiar with it, provided that he didn't nose into the water. As the helo picked up speed, he increased the collective pitch and started climbing into the night sky.

With each foot of altitude gained, his view of the lake and the surrounding landscape broadened, all of it lit up like daylight in the virtual display of his borrowed glasses. At just a hundred yards, he could make out Ile Idjwi, a long strip of land that bisected the southern half of the lake. He scanned the narrow channel that ran between the island's western shore and the mainland. Nothing. He didn't think Favreau would have gone in that direction. For maximum effect, she would head for open water.

He glimpsed a long streak of white on the lake's surface, diffuse at its western tip, but sharpening to an abrupt point about seven miles east of where he flew. He zoomed in, and the dark object at the head of the wake resolved into the familiar shape of a rigid-hulled Zodiac, similar to the kind used by SEAL teams and professional dive service operators. A lone figure sat at the craft's stern, operating the outboard engine.

"I see her," Bishop said.

"I read you, Bish," King said, and Bishop suddenly realized that it was the first thing King had said to him since he'd taken off. "Now, I don't suppose you'd like to come back and pick us up so we can do this together?"

"I don't think that's a good idea," Bishop replied, wondering if he should elaborate. He wasn't accustomed to explaining himself, but what he was doing was unexplored territory for him. His way of dealing with problems was to tear through them, obliterate them, and if the problem was bigger than expected, all he needed to do was unleash his volcanic rage.

Bishop felt no rage now. In fact, he didn't think he had ever felt quite so calm in his entire life.

FIFTY-THREE

Lake Kivu, Democratic Republic of the Congo

Favreau wasn't watching the sky, nor was she scanning the surface of the lake ahead. Her eyes were fixed on the display of a portable echosounder that showed a depth profile of the lake bottom. One corner of the display showed the actual depth in feet, a number that had been steadily growing larger with each passing second.

1180 feet. *Not quite deep enough.*

Because Lake Kivu was situated on a volcanic rift, two land masses slowly pulling apart like a spreading wound in the Earth's skin, it was very deep. Its maximum depth was 1575 feet along the rift, making it one of the deepest lakes in the world. The methane reserves, which were created by microbial reduction of volcanic gasses rising out of the Earth, would be most concentrated in that deep zone.

1300 feet.

The lake bottom was sloping rapidly now. Soon she would be deep enough.

Deep enough to ignite the vast field of dissolved methane and deep enough for her to survive the aftermath.

Monique Favreau was not afraid to die, a fact which had more than once tipped the balance in her favor to avoid that outcome, but neither did she have a death wish. When she had conceived of this plan, she had run the numbers and decided that it was indeed survivable.

A generous estimate, one in which the bomb sank at the rather astounding rate of three and a half feet per second, gave her about eight minutes from the time she dropped it overboard until detonation. In eight minutes, she would be able to travel nearly two miles away from ground zero. That was well outside the blast radius of the device on dry land, and while underwater explosions behaved very differently, she felt confident that two miles was a safe distance. Similarly, the water would shield her from any thermal or radiologic effects. In short, she had little to fear from the bomb itself.

The effects of igniting the methane reserves were more problematic. For one thing, when the gas bubble came to the surface, it would create a suffocating layer over the lake, extending several miles in every direction. That was easily enough overcome with a self-contained breathing apparatus (SCBA) tank she had appropriated from the Kisangani airport fire brigade, but that was minor concern in comparison to some of the other effects that were likely to occur. For one thing, she had no idea if the outboard would still function in air that was oversaturated with CO_2. Also, there was a very real possibility that the sudden change in the lake's chemistry might alter the specific gravity of the water to the point where the Zodiac would no longer be buoyant.

These possibilities did not concern Favreau so much as excite her. There was one outcome, however, that she considered unlikely enough to almost be dismissed entirely, namely that Marrs would be able to deliver on her demands. The game demanded that she listen to his dissembling, his request for concessions, for more time to gather support, but in the end she would do exactly as she had promised. She would teach him a lesson he would never forget. She would teach the whole world.

She cut power, allowing the Zodiac to coast forward, and took out her satellite phone, preparing to make that final decisive call. That was when she heard the low hum of a distant engine, which had been drowned out by throaty roar of her own outboard motor. She cocked her head, trying to pinpoint the source of the sound.

The running lights of an aircraft were visible in the sky to the west. Favreau picked out the red and green lights, on the left and right sides, which told her the craft was moving toward her.

It could only be the Congolese air force Mil, but what was it doing out here? Her mind raced with possibilities, none of which boded well. She could easily imagine Velle brokering some kind of deal with Marrs, a deal which required him to take possession of the RA-115 and perhaps even eliminate Favreau in the process.

The engine noise grew louder, rising in pitch as the sound waves piled up on top of her. The helicopter would be overhead in just a few seconds.

She set aside the phone and found the remote for the dead-man trigger, which she waved above her head in one outstretched arm. It was no longer wired to the bomb, but Velle would have no way of knowing that.

If that didn't frighten him off, it would take only a second to pitch the bomb over the side, and then there would be nothing he could do to stop her.

"What's he doing?" Queen asked, staring out across the lake at the lights of the retreating helicopter.

King silenced her with a cutting gesture. He knew exactly what Bishop was doing, and it was taking every ounce of his self-restraint to refrain from interfering.

Around them, the soldiers were being roused. Velle had given the order for them to abandon the camp, leave the tents where they were and board the armored infantry vehicles. Busy with the evacuation, the soldiers had ignored the intruders in their midst, allowing King and Rook to move through the camp to where Queen waited. King had warned the others to keep an eye out for Favreau's remaining mercenaries, but the ESI men had disappeared, possibly secreting themselves aboard the tracked vehicles or simply slinking away into the jungle. The rebel fighters had been told to leave the area, but without motorized transport, their chances of surviving the worst case scenario were slim. This was true for Chess Team as well, but King had already decided that they weren't going anywhere.

The virtual display allowed him to see what Bishop saw, and he watched in silence as Bishop scanned the lake's surface, looking for Favreau's boat.

"I see her."

"I read you, Bish," King said, his voice quiet. "Now, I don't suppose you'd like to come back and pick us up so we can do this together?"

"I don't think that's a good idea." There was a pause then Bishop went on. "If the bomb is still wired to the dead-man trigger, all I need to do is take Favreau out from the air. That will detonate the bomb, but if Felice is right, a blast on the surface won't be enough to cause the lake eruption."

"The blast will also knock you out of the sky." King felt Queen grip his arm. She couldn't hear what Bishop was saying, but evidently she grasped his intent.

"That's why it makes more sense for me to do this alone," Bishop said in an unnaturally calm voice. "No sense in all of us getting killed."

King felt numb. He wanted to argue with Bishop, tell him that he had a better idea, a strategy that would let them win without such a sacrifice. He considered ordering Bishop to return so that he could go instead. He didn't have Bishop's familiarity with the helicopter, but maybe Deep Blue could talk him through it.

I didn't fight my way across three millennia so Bishop could die on the next big mission.

Even as denial and helplessness raged within him, King realized that he had been wrong. His obsession with protecting his friends had overshadowed what should have been his real purpose: to help them give their lives meaning.

Bishop was about to risk his life to save two million people, and perhaps—if Felice's estimates were correct—the whole world.

King couldn't think of anything more meaningful than that. He swallowed down the emotion that was thick in his throat, and whispered, "Godspeed, Erik."

FIFTY-FOUR

Bishop saw the woman in the Zodiac waving an object over her head. The warning was clear: *back off or I'll blow us all to hell.* He looked past her and spotted the familiar olive-drab cylinder of the backpack nuke. The sight filled him with a sense of relief. Favreau hadn't deployed it yet. If she blew the bomb now, only she and Bishop would die.

"Do it," he murmured. "Save me the trouble."

Her wave-off became more frantic, and Bishop knew that what he had to do needed to be done quickly. He eased back on the cyclic, allowing the helicopter's forward momentum to take it the rest of the way, and used the rudder to maneuver to a stop directly over the little boat. He spun the Mil around until he could just see her through the transparent bubble window beneath his feet. Then, with the same calm detachment that had gotten him this far, he twisted the collective-pitch control, flattening the rotor blades.

The helicopter dropped like a stone and Bishop closed his eyes, waiting for the brilliant light that would—

There was a cacophony of metal crunching and shearing apart, bulkheads twisting, the rotor blades snapping off their axle. The Mil jolted violently and Bishop felt the flight seat collapse beneath him. A spike of pain shot up his spine as he was driven straight down by the sudden stop. His head snapped forward, glancing off the cyclic control stick, and the taste of blood filled his mouth, as his teeth were slammed together, removing a small piece of tongue. The impact left him momentarily stunned, but as that moment gave way to the next and then another, he knew that he had failed.

The bomb had not detonated.

It seemed impossible that Favreau could have avoided the crash without inadvertently releasing her grip on the trigger.

Was the bomb a dud after all? He couldn't take that chance.

Wracked by pain, Bishop hauled himself up. In that instant, the helicopter started to roll beneath him, and he was thrown sideways into a bulkhead. As he struggled to move again, a wave of cold water blasted him back.

The calm that had guided him through what he had expected to be the last few seconds of his life fell into ruin, as agony and desperation reawakened the beast within.

He pulled himself out of the cockpit and into the half-submerged cabin. Water streamed in through dozens of cracks in the fuselage, but most of it was rising up through the sliding door, which had buckled inward upon impact. The pressure change in his ears told him that the helicopter was already sinking.

Bishop plunged both hands into the water and found the bent metal door. With a heave, he wrenched it out of its track and pitched it aside, then dove down into the water. He kicked away from the submerged aircraft and followed the line of bubbles trailing away from it, clawing his way back to the surface.

The Zodiac floated just a few yards away. The impact of the falling helicopter had evidently caused it to squirt free, like a bean from its husk.

While his kamikaze dive had not quite had the expected effect, it had done significant damage to the rigid-hulled inflatable craft. Though it was still afloat, several of its inner tube-like air cells had collapsed, allowing the lake to pour in.

As Bishop stared at the Zodiac, incredulous, he saw a hand appear on its far side, gripping the air bladder. Another hand fell beside it, and then a bedraggled Monique Favreau hauled herself up and out of the water.

Bishop saw that her hands were empty. She had lost the dead-man trigger in the crash, but the bomb had not detonated.

The bomb.

Bishop's gaze fell on the canvas pack, still nestled inside the boat, held in place by its own weight. Favreau looked at it, too. Then she saw Bishop.

When their eyes met, her dazed expression hardened into a mask of triumph, and then with deliberate glee, she wrapped her arms around the bomb and lifted it onto the inflatable gunwale. It seemed to hang there for a moment, wobbling indecisively, as if trying to find a balancing point. Bishop waited for Favreau to warn him off with some kind of threat, but she had nothing to say. Instead, she gave it a final shove and sent it plunging into the depths.

Bishop, driven more by feral instinct than rational decision, slid beneath the surface and dove after it. With the water blurring the image projected against his retinas, it took him a moment to locate the olive-drab cylinder, sinking steadily toward the lake bottom. He pulled himself deeper, kicking his legs with the desperate ferocity of an animal fleeing a wildfire—only Bishop was chasing the very thing that would bring the flames.

And somehow, he caught it.

The pressure of the water squeezed his head like a vise, but he gritted his teeth through it and wrapped his arms around the sinking object as if, by simply seizing hold of it, he would fix everything.

There has to be a timer. The thought seemed to come from somewhere beyond him, and for a fleeting instant, he thought it was King, guiding him through what he had to do next. *Radio signals don't travel through water. She must have replaced the dead-man switch with a timer. Or some kind of automatic trigger. You have to disable it.*

His head felt like it was going to implode, and his blood was starting to seethe with the buildup of acidic carbon dioxide. Even though he was no longer swimming, the bomb itself was dragging him deeper.

I've got to get it back to the surface, he thought, and he spun his burden around so that he and it were aimed upward.

But even with his tremendous strength augmented by primal rage, Bishop could not overcome the laws of physics. His furious kicking slowed the downward plunge, but he could not reverse it.

The timer, repeated the voice. *That's the only thing that matters.*

He stopped struggling and instead reached for one of the clips that held the canvas flap in place. It fell away to reveal a red LED display—numbers, but inexplicably they were counting up.

101...102...

It wasn't a timer at all. It was a depth-gauge, ticking off the feet as it sought out the bottom of the lake.

He had no idea how to disable it, and no time to figure out.

Think. A depth gauge means it's set to blow when it reaches a certain depth. So don't let it do that.

How? I can't stop it. It's too heavy.

127...128...

Favreau had chosen this place for a reason. It had to be the deepest part of lake. If he could get the bomb to shallower waters, even a few feet might make the difference.

Which way?

Favreau had traveled east. He needed to go west. But which way was that?

150...151...

At the top edge of the virtual display, barely visible through the smear of water pressing against his eyeballs, was a tiny blue icon.

A chess piece.

He turned toward it, and hugging the bomb to his chest, he started kicking as hard as he could.

Something snapped inside his skull—an eardrum rupturing—and a spike of pain shot through his head, but strangely some of the pressure eased.

337...338...

He no longer even knew what the red digits signified. All he knew was that he had to keep swimming, even though his legs burned and his chest was starting to convulse with the irresistible demand to draw a breath.

The numbers on the depth gauge kept changing and Bishop kept swimming toward the glowing blue chess piece, until he just couldn't swim any more.

FIFTY-FIVE

Lake Kivu, Democratic Republic of the Congo

As dawn drew near, the eastern sky above the lake turned a haunting shade of purple, and *Crescent II* glided through it like a Valkyrie, looking for fallen heroes to carry off to Valhalla. In her hold, the Chess Team, minus one, gathered around King, staring at the image displayed on his q-phone. He had patched in the wing cameras so that they could all lend their eyes to the search effort, as the plane flew back and forth across the lake, looking for Bishop.

There had been no flash of light, no explosion and no cloud of invisible death creeping across the lake to suffocate them all. Whatever Bishop had done, he had stopped all of those things from happening.

King had seen it all, at least up to the point where Bishop's glasses had stopped transmitting. It had happened so abruptly that, even after watching the playback several times, he still wasn't sure what he was seeing. One moment, there was frantic movement, the backpack with the bomb framed in the foreground, moving slightly as Bishop swam, the bright red digits flashing as they ticked off the change in depth. Then, with the gauge showing 406 feet, the view swirled violently, focusing on nothing at all, and then just a moment later, went off-line. Bishop's q-phone was still connected to the quantum computer at Endgame headquarters in New Hampshire, but the short-range connection between the glasses and the phone had been severed.

The q-phone showed only a little more movement in the seconds that followed, then stopped altogether. Deep Blue, in a solemn voice, told them that the q-phone was now 1364 feet below the surface.

"What does that mean?" Queen had demanded, even though they all knew exactly what it meant.

"He dropped the phone," Rook said, with an unconvincing shrug. "Probably when he was swimming for the surface."

Bishop had been holding his breath for nearly two minutes when the feed went dark. It would have taken him at least that long to swim back up. But King didn't voice his thoughts.

"He was regenning," Knight said. Despite being told by everyone that he needed to rest, he had risen from the cot in the medical bay to follow the search. His pallor was improving, thanks to a heavy dose of antibiotics and a regimen of fluid replacement, but he was still weak, feverish and, King thought, possibly delirious.

"Are you saying the cure didn't take?" Queen asked, full of hope.

"He was standing right next to me when that mortar round hit, but was back up and walking in just a few minutes."

"Come to think of it," Rook added, "he was pretty torn up when he showed up in the lost city. But by the time we got back topside, he hardly had a scratch."

King knew that wasn't quite true. When he had joined the others at the cave entrance, he had seen Bishop's wounds for himself. Some of them were bone deep. That Bishop had been able to fight on had nothing at all to do with the rapid healing properties of the regenerative serum Richard Ridley had forced on him, and which had been subsequently purged from his body. If he had been 'regenning' as Knight had suggested, those scratches would have healed completely in a matter of seconds. Knight was grasping at straws.

Again, he had not said this aloud, reasoning that, until they found his body, there was no reason not to hope. But after hours of flying back and forth over the location marked by the q–phone, hope was beginning to seem more like self-delusion.

The intercom crackled to life. "We've got a radar contact, bearing 230 degrees."

King walked over to the two-way and depressed the transmit button. "Let's have a look."

The plane banked and started off on the new heading, and just a few seconds later, the target came into view, and the ember of hope that the pilot's announcement had briefly brought glowing to life, fizzled out completely. He keyed the intercom again. "Take us down."

The plane decelerated and came back around until it was directly over the sighting, at which point the pilot engaged the vertical lift thrusters and started a slow descent. After a quick visit to the weapon's locker, King hit the switch to lower the loading ramp, and as soon as it was fully deployed, they all walked out onto it.

A blast of spray, stirred up off the lake by the thrusters, eddied back up to drench them, but no one backed away from the edge. A few seconds later, the bottom of the ramp was almost kissing the surface, right next to a partly-wrecked rigid inflatable boat, in which sat Monique Favreau.

Her eyes went wide when she recognized King. "So he was one of yours." She had to shout to be heard over the roar of the thrusters. "I should have realized. I knew that you would be a worthy adversary."

King's only answer was to level the MP5 he'd taken from the dead ESI mercenaries the night before. The overpressure ammunition made it noticeably heavier in his hands.

Favreau stared at the gun and then nodded slowly. "You know how you were able to beat me, don't you?" She raised her eyes to the others, meeting each gaze in turn. "Sacrifice. You are all pawns that he will sacrifice in order to win."

"They aren't pawns," King said. "They're family. That's why we win."

The roar of the thrusters mostly drowned out the sound of the shot.

The search went on for nearly two weeks. A deep water submersible was flown in, and a magnetometer sweep of the location of the q-phone led them to the unexploded RA-115. Further investigation indicated that the nuke had been set to detonate as soon as it reached 1400 feet depth. Bishop had succeeded in dragging it to shallower waters, preventing it from reaching that critical depth. He had given his life to stop the bomb from detonating and releasing the toxic cloud.

That was the reality that they could no longer deny.

Bishop, that stoic, immovable force they called brother...was dead.

EPILOGUE

Ten Days Later, Crawford County, Illinois

"Ready... Aim... Fire."

Seven rifles thundered together for the third and final time, then the voice of the gunnery sergeant leading the rifle team sounded another loud order. "Present arms!"

The seven marines executed a sharp left-face and brought their rifles forward in a crisp salute. The gunnery sergeant did the same with his saber, and immediately the mournful sound of a bugle filled the void of silence.

King stood motionless. It was still hard to believe.

Bishop. Gone.

It would have been easier to accept if there had been a body, something to make Bishop's death an incontrovertible fact.

The search team leader had explained the challenges of trying to locate the body. The depth where Bishop had been lost would have overcome any natural buoyancy, and the thick sediment on the bottom would have closed over a body, erasing all trace of him. They had only been able to locate the bomb in those conditions because of the close proximity of the q-phone and its metal casing.

"We could drag the bottom for years, and never find him," the search expert had confessed. They didn't have years, and dragging the bottom of a lake that sat atop a bubble of deadly gas was not a workable solution.

Knight had held onto his hope the longest. He was convinced that Bishop was still alive, that the removal of his former regenerative abilities hadn't worked, and that Bishop must have survived. But if that was true, where was he? Regenerating from trauma on that scale might well have put him past the tipping point, completing the unrecoverable transformation into a mindless rage beast. It was a kinder fate to hope the man had simply died.

King let his eyes wander over the small crowd attending the service. There were many faces he did not recognize. Bishop had evidently touched many more lives than King would ever have imagined.

Although Chess Team was no longer part of the military, Bishop was a veteran of both the USMC and the Army, and Deep Blue had made arrangements to ensure that he be accorded full honors, as such. His family deserved that much, but had requested that he be laid to rest, if only symbolically, in a cemetery just outside the eastern Illinois city where he had grown up.

As the last notes of Taps hung in the air, two Army Rangers in dress blues took hold of the flag draped over the empty casket and lifted it, holding it taut, and began folding it into a tight, precise triangle. When they were finished, the flag was passed between them and they saluted it at each exchange. The Marine gunnery sergeant approached and saluted as well, then slipped three shell casings, one for each volley the rifle team had fired, into the folds. He then took it from the Rangers, did an about face, and handed it off once again, this time to King.

King turned, and with the same grave formality as the military honor guard, walked to the front row of the gathering where he knelt before a middle-aged woman in a black dress.

"On behalf of the President of the United States and a grateful nation, please accept this flag as a symbol of our appreciation for your loved one's service to Country."

Ruth Somers squeezed her husband's hand and then took the flag with a nod. There were tears in her eyes, but King saw something else, too.

Derek and Ruth Somers had brought a young Iranian child into their home and into their lives, yet all their love could not purge the inexplicable anger that had burned within him. That anger had taken him to very dark places, and while he had found an outlet for it in military service, he had never been able to overcome it completely, something which they, as his parents, no doubt felt was a failing on their part. Now, at last, he had found the peace that had eluded him in life, and they, too, would be able to start healing.

It pained King that they would never be able to know just how many people had been saved by Bishop's sacrifice, but the events that had transpired in the Congo, along with all other details of his service as part of Chess Team, could never be revealed.

The situation in Central Africa was, slowly but surely, improving. Without intending to, Senator Lance Marrs had ensured a quick return to regional stability by doing what President Chambers could not. He had rallied the President's political rivals to recognize the presidency of General Velle, not realizing that Velle had formed a partnership with Gerard Okoa for a transitional government. Peacekeeping troops from the US military, as well as the United Nations and the African Union, had mobilized to restore order. Civilian contractors were lining up to help build the infrastructure that would create a world class natural gas extraction facility on the shores of Lake Kivu. Consolidated Energy, citing a desire to explore alternative sources of energy for the twenty-first century, had opted out of the bidding.

The scientific world was abuzz with news of a previously unknown subterranean ecosystem, where thousands of plant and animal species long thought extinct continued to thrive. Although, something of a turf war was brewing between conservationists and archeologists. The former wanted the unique biome to remain untouched, and the latter wanted access to the magnificent physical remains of an African society that was believed by many to be the oldest civilization on Earth, predating the emergence of the Sumerian culture by at least a millennium.

Joseph Mulamba would be remembered for his heroic vision that had made these discoveries possible. Bishop's pivotal role, sadly, would never be known.

King spied another woman in the audience, black hair that matched her funeral attire, tears spilling down her face—a face that was eerily familiar. Faiza Abbasi, Bishop's biological mother. King imagined that she, too, felt responsible for Bishop's anger, but unlike his adoptive parents, she would not be able to find comfort in a lifetime of memories. She had been forced to abandon her son to save him from her husband's enemies during the Iranian Revolution. She had been reunited with Bishop only a few years earlier. No doubt, she had looked forward to making up for the lost years, but now the opportunity to get to know her son better had forever passed.

King tore his gaze from Faiza, and looked instead at the woman standing next to him, his fiancée, Sara Fogg, They had been engaged for only a little over a year—though King had been waiting a considerably longer time to consecrate their union—but with their busy lives, there just never seemed to be time to plan a wedding. Fiona, his teenaged foster daughter, stood next to Sara, making no effort to hold back her tears. Perhaps it was the dark formal dress she wore, but she looked older than he remembered.

Further down the row, he saw the rest of the team. Rook and Queen, holding hands in a way that seemed uncharacteristically intimate. It had taken a long time for both of them to realize they belonged together, time in which either one of them might have been subtracted from the equation, just like Bishop now had been.

Knight, who stood with Anna Beck at his side, had come very close to being subtracted as well. His recovery had not gone smoothly. The secondary infection from his wounds, aggravated by the subsequent ordeal and a slew of exotic pathogens, had required a stomach churning regimen of antibiotic therapy that had left him looking gaunt and frail. The patch that hid the place where his left eye had been did not cover the angry scar tissue that ran down his cheek. Yet, through it all, he had resisted the dark gravity of depression, thanks in no small part to Anna Beck's unflagging support.

Pawn's recovery had gone much more swiftly. Her wounds had not been serious, and after just a few days in the hospital, she had demanded to join in the search for Bishop. The doctors had protested, but King had bowed to her wishes. He and she were both made of sterner stuff than anyone knew. Nevertheless, her close call was just one more reminder of how quickly things could change.

Life happens, no matter how hard you try to stop it, King thought. *And maybe that's how it's supposed to be.*

He realized now that his procrastination had just been another way of trying to protect his loved ones, to keep that dream, which had sustained him during his long journey through time, perfectly preserved like an insect in amber.

It was time to let go of that frozen moment. Time to start living. *Tonight*, he promised himself, *we'll set the date.*

The service concluded and the attendees filed past the casket to pay their last respects. Mr. and Mrs. Somers went last, after which King escorted them to a waiting limousine that would take them to the wake. As the car drove off, another limo arrived. Out stepped the former President, Tom Duncan—Deep Blue, joined by Domenick Boucher and Lew Aleman, none of whom could afford to be seen attending the funeral of a soldier with whom they had no public reason for being associated. To do so would raise questions and defeat the point of having a black organization. The three walked with King back to the few remaining at the cemetery: the Chess Team members and the staff of Endgame. Everyone who knew the truth about who Bishop had been and all that he had done.

Duncan—Deep Blue—unexpectedly assumed the position of attention and called out in a low but commanding voice. "King."

King likewise came to attention and took a step forward. "Yes, sir?"

"Assemble for roll call."

King felt a surge of emotion as he grasped what Deep Blue was doing. He pivoted and faced the gathering. "Chess Team, fall in."

Queen, Rook and Knight moved forward, their expressions revealing that they understood as well, and formed a line beside him, intentionally leaving a gap between Queen and Knight.

King wasn't sure what to do next. They had never established a protocol for this eventuality. It occurred to him that Deep Blue was now doing exactly that.

"King?"

King took a deep breath. "Here, sir."

"Queen?"

Queen followed King's lead. "Here, sir."

"Knight?"

"Here, sir."

"Rook?"

"Here, sir."

"Bishop?"

Silence.

Deep Blue allowed a moment to pass. "Bishop? Somers?"

Another pause. "Bishop, Erik Somers?"

King had to struggle to find his voice. "Bishop, Erik Somers, is not here, sir."

In the pause that followed, the only sound was of someone softly crying. Then Deep Blue did something that King did not expect.

"Pawn?" There was a stir of confusion. "Pawn, Machtchenko?"

Asya overcame her surprise and quickly stepped forward. "Here, sir."

Deep Blue studied her with a look that evinced both solemnity and pride. "A piece has left the board, but Pawn, having demonstrated exceptional valor, has advanced. Will you take Bishop's place, Asya Machtchenko?"

Asya stared back at him, stunned.

In a less formal tone, Deep Blue added, "According to the rules of chess, a pawn may be promoted to any of the first rank positions, even if that piece is still in play, but I think one Queen is more than enough."

Asya nodded, dumbly, though whether she was agreeing with Deep Blue or signaling her acceptance was anyone's guess. Deep Blue took it as the latter. He reached out and pressed a carved wooden chess piece into her hands.

"Welcome to the team, Bishop."

CODA

Goma, Democratic Republic of the Congo

With more than a million inhabitants, Goma, on the northern tip of Lake Kivu, had seen more than its share of ethnically fueled violence. The recent political unrest that had gripped the nation had very nearly fanned the smoldering embers of old tribal feuds to life again. For several tense days, only the heavy presence of foreign peacekeepers had kept the situation from devolving once more into chaos. Gradually though, as news of the fantastic discoveries nearby had reached the ears of the populace, the lingering animosity had given way to a unifying sense of hope. Instead of fear, a spirit of anticipation gripped the city.

Felice Carter was only peripherally aware of what was happening in the world outside her laboratory. She found solace in her work, the only thing that kept her from reliving the tragic ordeal of those days spent hiding in the forest and what had happened after. But that was not the only reason she had sequestered herself in the laboratory on the campus of the University of Goma. If her research bore fruit, and she fervently believed it would, it would usher in a new era of energy production. It would mean an end to reliance on fossil fuels and the inherent exploitation of the natural resources of developing nations to fuel the ravenous appetites of the global energy market.

After sequencing the DNA of the E. coli variant she had discovered in Lake Kivu and in the soil of the cavern near the Ancients' city, she had gone to work identifying its weaknesses. The bacteria was well-suited to large scale biofuel production, but if it was unintentionally introduced to the surface world, either through a natural disaster, such as the long-dreaded lake eruption, or through human error, such as a mishandling of the bacteria at one of the biofuel production facilities that were now in the planning stages, the result would be a runaway ecological catastrophe. Her goal was to identify the best ways to shut down the extremophile quickly, and thereby ensure that, even in a worst case scenario, the organism could be tamed.

Thus far, the gram-negative bacteria had shown a vulnerability to the antibiotic ampicillin, but medical history had taught scientists the danger of relying on a single cure. So before she was willing to release her research, Felice wanted to make sure that there were many different ways to kill the organism.

She bent over a line of petri dishes that hosted colonies of the bacteria grown in agar and began adding carefully measured doses of streptomycin to each. The DNA map indicated that the extremophile had the same vulnerability to the broad spectrum antibiotic as more common variants of the bacteria, but this test would reveal whether the organism had other defenses hidden in its genetic code.

"Dr. Carter?"

She frowned but did not look up until her task was finished. Kabika, a nursing student who had volunteered to work as her lab assistant, was standing in the doorway.

"There is a man here to see you."

Felice frowned. In the last two weeks, she had been inundated with phone calls and e-mails from scientists and biotech upstarts in every corner of the globe, all eager to reap the benefits of her work. This was the first time someone had actually bothered to come see her in person, but she knew it probably wouldn't be the last.

"Tell him to make an appointment," Felice said, turning back to her experiment. "Sometime next year, maybe."

Kabika approached the table, her forehead creased with uncertainty. "This man is very insistent. He says that he is a friend."

"A friend?"

"Yes. He said that you promised to help him."

Felice stared back at the young woman, trying to make sense of the request. *Promised to help?* Could it be David?

No. David had been whisked off to Kinshasa to give a full account of his discovery of the cavern. And besides, she certainly hadn't made any promises to him. In fact, she could think of only one man that...

All thoughts of experiments and antibiotic therapies momentarily forgotten, Felice ran for the door.

ABOUT THE AUTHORS

JEREMY ROBINSON is the bestselling author of thirty novels and novellas including *Island 731*, *SecondWorld*, and the Jack Sigler series including *Pulse, Instinct, Threshold* and *Ragnarok*. Robinson is also known as the #1 Amazon.com horror writer, Jeremy Bishop, author of *The Sentinel* and the controversial novel, *Torment*. His novels have been translated into twelve languages. He lives in New Hampshire with his wife and three children.

Visit him online at: www.jeremyrobinsononline.com

SEAN ELLIS is the author of several thriller and adventure novels. He is a veteran of Operation Enduring Freedom, and he has a Bachelor of Science degree in Natural Resources Policy from Oregon State University. Sean is also a member of the International Thriller Writers organization. He currently resides in Arizona, where he divides his time between writing, adventure sports and trying to figure out how to save the world.

Visit him on the web at: seanellisthrillers.webs.com

CPSIA information can be obtained at www.ICGtesting.com
Printed in the USA
BVOW02s0055211114

376071BV00003B/107/P